ACKNOWLEDGEMENTS

This has been a long, long journey, from age nine until seventy – from a boy striding around the bedroom humming a 'Bolero'-type marching tune for the Normans, to trying to make a film about Harold on the family cine camera but having no storyline, to a planned four-part script for television, and finally to telling the story in a book. I would like to pay homage to the many people who have helped me along the way.

First and foremost, I give heartfelt thanks to my wife, Cate, for her constant encouragement and for her inspiring observations, which often helped me see the characters in a more human light and added a crucial dimension to the story. Also, to my family – my daughters, Mim and Soph, and my brothers, Rick and Nige, – as well as to my old friends, Jim Waters and George Stolarski, I extend my love and gratitude for their steadfast support and all their constructive suggestions. Also, to the many people whose names I haven't mentioned, who have read and given me feedback on the various drafts over the years, I offer my deepest thanks. Finally, to all at Aurora House, for their welcoming and much-needed assistance – most especially to Linda Lycett, for steering the ship with such care and expertise across the daunting, mysterious sea of publication; to Brian McMullen, for his gracious and long-suffering guidance through the labyrinth of the production process; to Meredith Anderson, for her patience with my technological ineptitude as well as her incisive and meticulous editing; and to Josie Dietrich, for getting the whole thing started – I send an almighty thank you.

Last, but not least, I owe a huge debt of gratitude to Bulwer (Lord) Lytton, whose monumental novel, *Harold, The Last of the Saxon Kings* (1848), provided the vessel upon which to embark.

MAIN CHARACTERS

Jack Stalwart *(a composer)*
Mary *(his wife)*
Captain Guitaro *(a busker)*
    (Saxons)
King Edward
Earl Godwin
Githa *(his wife)*
    (Their children)
Sweyn
Harold
Queen 'Didi' *(married to King Edward)*
Tostig
Gurth
Leofwine
Wolnoth
Haco *(Sweyn's son)*
Edith *(Harold's de facto wife)*
    (Their children)
Edmund
Magnus
Gunhilds
Vera *(Edith's mother)*
Gladys *(Edith's friend)*
Bernard *(a naval officer)*
Earl Algar *(Harold's rival)*
    (His children)
Morcar

Aldyth
Edwin
Earl Siward *(Commander of the army)*
Bishop Alred *(Head of the Council)*
Archbishop Stigand
Stavros *(an army captain)*
Eric Braithwaite *(a reporter)*
Mr Jenkins *(a shopkeeper)*
Scarf *(a ruffian)*
    (Normans)
Duke William
Matilda *(his wife)*
Judith *(Matilda's sister, Tostig's wife)*
Bishop Odo *(the Duke's half-brother)*
Baron Fitzosborne *(Head of the army)*
Taillefer *(a minstrel knight)*
Iko *(a young knight)*
Charles *(a factory owner)*
    (Others)
Lanfranc *(a lawyer)*
Gryffyth *(a rebel leader)*
Lord Hardrada *(King of the Vikings)*

PROLOGUE

Perhaps, as someone once said, all new ideas were *destined* to start out as heresy? Certainly, no one had ever listened to Mary, I reflected. Even I hadn't listened to her until it was almost too late. For years, I'd watched her opinions provoke argument and amusement, sometimes outright anger and scorn, as they were consigned like the ravings of Cassandra to the green fringes of La La Land. Although Mary never claimed that her ideas were new. In fact, she gave numerous examples of groups throughout history—from pre-colonial Aborigines, to the followers of Pythagoras and the early Christians, to Israeli kibbutzim, hippy communes, and latter-day communities in post-austerity Greece—who, for the most part, had lived in exactly the way she espoused, without using money, sharing not buying and selling.

I had to admit there were times when even I had argued against her. It was her dogged persistence and her inescapable logic that drove people mad, and maybe how she said it, as if it were fact—which I now realised it was. It should have been obvious. The elephant in the room. Even blind Freddy could see it! Thank God she'd hung in there and kept working at me, otherwise we'd have been lost to each other.

Anyway, it was all academic now, I sighed. The invasion had already begun and the time for new ideas was gone. Now, all our so-called leaders, who at every turn had opposed and rejected any possible change of direction, were desperately hammering in the last unblooded human nails to shore up the roof and walls of their collapsing edifice. Soon, all they'd have left to consume would be their own intractable words.

And, out of the dust, what would tomorrow bring? Would we make the same mistakes again? Would there even be a tomorrow?

I shook my head and looked back at where we'd been. The ravine below me and the wide plain beyond it lay in darkness. The battle had been raging on and off for days across this ravaged stretch of country, once all flourishing vinyards and apple orchards. By a miracle, during a lull in the fighting, we'd managed to cross it under the cover of night without being detected.

Just then, there was a sudden flash as a small bomb exploded down on the plain, briefly backlighting the charred, leafless skeletons spiking the ruptured earth. The rattle of small arms fire quickly followed, then shouts, muted and dark. Silence returned. The Blakeston's farm, I thought with grim certainty. I'd come to know old Jim quite well. He told me he used to be an international soccer player and had shown me the cuttings to prove it. I hoped they'd made it out. A moment later, wide sheets of blue flame flared along the length of the hilly horizon, telling instant tales of destruction, conjuring up glowing images of towns destroyed and dwellings razed by bigger, mightier bombs.

'Thank God we're safe!' I exclaimed out loud, the sound of my own voice shattering my reverie, making me aware of where I stood, high up on the ridge, keeping guard while the others slept. The air was still, cold and dry against my face. It was nearly midnight. The ground felt hard and crisp beneath my boots; the barbed wire bit through my woollen gloves into my hands. The acrid stench of sulphur dimly pervaded my nostrils as I stared about me on the edge of the copse.

To my right, a ghostly track sloped away into the gloaming. To my left, it rose and disappeared behind a straining band of trees, while in front of me, the icy bracken dipped down like a buttress and rolled off into the night. Clouds hung low over the plain, almost suffocating, virtually motionless, an unbroken, lead-laden, slowly undulating canopy of deadly mud-brown smoke, shot through and splashed here and there with lurid greens and reds, like some sickly upside-down chessboard advertisement for the disco floor of hell.

I gave a cold laugh. Despite all the horrors, it was hard to take seriously. Although we'd been running for months, it still seemed like only yesterday I'd had my forty-sixth birthday and farewell parties combined. On the day I left. When sanity still clung on by its fingertips and we thought things could yet be saved. Before the dams burst and violence flooded the world.

Another burst of gunfire crackled like fireworks in the distance. Homemade guns, I decided, evaluating the tinny resonance of the sporadic shots. Now even children could print their own weapons. 'This is insanity!' I whispered to myself. 'Why didn't we stop it?'

They say wisdom only comes with hindsight. For me, it began with a train ride. And that crazy dream! How could I have been so blind? Looking back on it now, I could laugh about it, but at the time I was anguished and depressed, locked in a battle both with myself and with Mary.

I stared into the darkness and went over it again in my mind. For the many we'd loved and lost, for the ones who'd wanted the madness to end and had suffered for it, and for all those who had yet to make their choice and might someday read this...I remembered.

PART ONE

1

I gazed out through the scratched, greasy glass at the suburbs of Melbourne passing by in the night. Here and there, the black skyline was lit up by small bonfires and burning car bodies. To the right and left, strings of glowing red tail lights flowed away into the darkness like rivers of molten lava. Half of the streetlamps were out.

It seemed like the whole world was going mad. The goalposts had all been shifted. There were no more verities. God was dead and the prospect of heaven a sullied myth, thanks to the shameful doings of those who purported to offer comfort and hope but had turned salvation into a business, where peace meant a piece of the action, caring was a finite, tax-deductible commodity, and the only sharing that took place was on the stock exchange. Government *for* the people was a long-forgotten ideal, the uniting of nations just a soundbite, an impossible dream, a misnomer for strategic interests and pragmatic alliances.

Everything was out of kilter. Homes and hopes were being torn down to make room for half-empty luxury apartment blocks, while thousands of homeless slept on the street. More and more businesses were closing down. Full-time employment was a thing of the past and many over forty found themselves already on the scrap heap. Addiction and mental illness were at record levels: families were fracturing under the strain and the sense of local community was all but gone.

Fortunes were being made and spent on sport and entertainment, while on the back of a single idea, youths still in school could become instant internet millionaires. Meanwhile, the lifetime labour of many went unnoticed and barely rewarded. Spawned by commercialism and mass consumption, that over-bloated, three-headed monster of excess, waste and greed ruled the day. Yet people seemed content to remain oblivious, safe in their echo chambers of like-minded opinion, happily sipping coffee with their earplugs in, relating to life through a screen.

Now, it was all open slather. The boundaries had all been crossed and the generations blended into one. You could look and act and be however you wanted. In the mirror of our affluent social identity, with the demise of traditional, once dependable support structures, the self-obsessed, superficial face of narcissism had appeared. Me! Me! Me! Bigger houses, bigger cars. Everybody tail-gating each other and blocking out each other's view. Image was paramount. Old or young, everyone seemed to need a following on social media. Precocious children vied to become the latest overnight singing sensation, while septuagenarians drove about in open-top Ferraris, and bearded middle-aged fathers gelled their hair like teenagers and rode down the street on skateboards. And, of course, every city worth its name just had to have its own giant ferris wheel.

Who could blame those disregarded, less fortunate kids for being depressed? There was no way out, no future, neither in this world nor the next. For many of them, life was compressed into a meaningless here-and-now existence of alienation, fear, and frustration. Hung up and strung out, like bats in a cave, it seemed they were only good for how much low-cost guano they could generate. At least virtual reality and drug-induced fantasy offered them some escape, some kind of feedback, some action they could take to get a reaction, out there on the edge, on the tipping point of self-destruction.

In wilful response, armed with cans of spray paint and indelible ink—soon copied by others, emulated by would-be warriors as a tattooed tribal statement or exploited as the latest art form—these invisible legions of the abandoned had defaced every pristine surface of the cities, the heritage of our civilisation, and even their own bodies, with infantile scribbling.

The train I was on was no exception. Comprised of individual compartments leading off a narrow corridor running down the length of each carriage, it was the kind that had been around since the dawn of the railways but was then phased out in the modern era. With the recent unprecedented level of vandalism to rolling stock, it had been recommissioned and was already a mess. Despite my dismay at its condition, once we got going out of Geelong—with the sun setting over the flat countryside, the old familiar rattle, the whoosh and click of the sliding doors, the upholstered bench seats, and the lacquered woodwork—the train brought back comforting memories of my childhood...of a time that was lost forever.

Like the coming of the Ice Age, the climate of war had descended upon the city, bringing down the curtain on our time of play. Although we were too far south to expect any bombs to be dropped on us, and with the American missile shield in the Northern Territory to protect us from any attack, the government had embraced the prospect with relish. Straightaway, whole sections of the grid were snuffed out like candles on a birthday cake, as power was cut off in rotation to conserve energy. While able-bodied men joined up and shipped out in droves, those left behind locked themselves away behind closed doors.

We as a nation had always touted ourselves as being a major player in the arena of world affairs, when really we were out in the back blocks and way behind the times. The Sixties had finished swinging and gone home before we even made it onto the dance floor. Swallowing whatever flattery we were fed hook, line, and sinker, we had been a convenient launch-pad and sidekick in more wars, not of our own making, than one. Our numerous ground-breaking inventions were sold off overseas for lack of local interest, our economy was a pawn to foreign powers, and our manufacturing industry decimated, sucked into the maw of giant conglomerates. We told ourselves we were leaders of the pack, but we were always just a little bit too late. If only we'd realised that, like Crocodile Dundee, we were at our best at home in our own element, following our own star and doing things our way.

But, no, we still needed the approbation of our masters: to prove that we were worthy sons, that we could punch above our weight. In fact, like some latter-day Davy Crockett, one of our more recent Prime Ministers had actually boasted that he would shirtfront the resurgent, fearsome Russian bear! That showed how pathetic we were. Like cast-off children trying to emulate the behaviour of their parents in a desperate need to be loved. And now the call was to unsheathe our rattling sabres. To prepare to get our feet wet. To shoulder arms and rally round the flag boys, around the Union Jack and the Stars and Stripes. I'd read somewhere that now they were even calling up sixty-year-olds. I could well believe it, such was our absolute commitment.

Meanwhile, each night, marauding gangs of unsupervised, disaffected youths—self-styled vigilantes—roamed the streets looking for anyone or anything they deemed un-Australian: terrorising individuals, targeting the shops and restaurants of whichever ethnic minority they had chosen as their latest victims. Sometimes they encountered resistance or were set upon themselves by organised immigrant groups out on their own rampage, often resulting in full-scale battles, particularly in shopping malls and at train stations. With most of the adult males away fighting, they decided to have a war of their own. To play *their* part. Unfortunately, more often than not, that seemed to involve raping some poor defenceless girl or beating someone's head to a pulp, each outrageous assault then posted with orgasmic self-conceit on the internet. At times, in different areas, the police could barely contain the situation. Things were getting out of control and there was talk of martial law being declared.

Just then, as if to emphasise the point, my thoughts were interrupted by a burst of white-hot phosphorescence as a cluster of flares went off like Roman candles, for a brief moment illuminating a brawl between rival school kids on a passing football oval. The gang mentality in action. It went right back to the children's playground, I sighed, where, to hide their fear of the bully, they were forced to become bullies themselves. Then they were gone, drifting out of sight as the train veered away round a bend.

A few seconds later, a neon-lit hoarding, a relic from more optimistic days, sailed past the window. It was going too fast for me to catch more than a glimpse of the no doubt overpriced electric sports car it was advertising, but its bold lettering stood out bright and clear, *'Australia…The Future…Coming Soon!'*

'It's already here,' I murmured to myself bitterly. We'd caught up with it and we hadn't even noticed. Or, rather, *it* had caught up with *me!*

I couldn't believe this was happening! I was actually leaving Mary and the kids to go off to war. It was ludicrous! I didn't want to fight. Certainly not to kill anyone. *'Be a conscientious objector,'* Mary had pleaded with me. *'Or hide! We could always make a run for it! Why won't you stay and protect us?'*

But I *was* protecting them, I'd protested. If no one went to fight, we'd be overrun in seconds. We'd be murdered in our beds.

It was kill or be killed; there was no other choice. Why couldn't she *see* that? I wasn't doing this just for the hell of it, I was doing it because it was *right!*

Since early Settlement, when the time came, every generation of male Stalwarts had been ready to take up arms in defence of the nation. It was a family tradition. It was who we were. It was how we got our name, *Stalwart*, back in the old country in the fourteenth century, for services rendered to the king. Why should *I* be any different?

Whichever way I looked, it seemed fate had me in its sights, signed and sealed from the start. All I had to do was deliver. I knew the litany of my ancestors' accomplishments off by heart, they'd been held up to me as the standard so often. I could still recall my mother extolling it to me one day and my surprise at her unexpected, almost vehement passion: '*Your great-grandfather followed the patriotic drum to the Great War, didn't he? He was promoted and decorated and came back to Melbourne a hero. He went into business and made a fortune!*'

Yes, I thought with a sigh, and my grandfather, too, had gone to fight. Although proudly Australian, he still thought of himself as British. While working for the family firm, he'd seen the next war coming and had enlisted. He rose to the rank of major. Apart from a shrapnel limp picked up in North Africa, he also had returned unscathed. The tales of his exploits caused great merriment around the dinner table and became legendary at his club.

I couldn't help smiling at the old man's bravado, despite my unease at its backdrop of human misery. The exemplary successes of my forebears seemed somehow blithe in the face of such devastation. After all, there were many whose lives hadn't had the same happy outcome.

Next in line was my dad. Luckily for him, the jammy bastard, war passed him by.

I thought it had skipped me, too!

Along with many of his generation, he'd avoided Vietnam, in his case missing the ballot by just one day. Perhaps out of a double sense of guilt, he liked to joke that he led a charmed life because he was born with a silver spoon in his mouth. Turned on by the mini skirts and the freedom and colours and music of the Sixties, he'd sailed over to England to check out the scene. Part of him already felt like a rolling stone, he once told me, and he'd been happy to believe that the times they were a-changing. For a while, he'd even worn beads and a caftan, floating through the summer sunshine in a euphoric haze of peace and love— until reality hit, as he put it, when The Beatles broke up and Kent State finally blew away the dream.

Arriving back home, he'd struck out on his own as a freelance graphic artist before going into advertising. He would often take my brothers and me away with him on his overseas trips. He gave us the broadest education money could buy, instilling in us a sense of ethics, a love of country, and the appreciation of a good bottle of red with a Cuban cigar. He was a tender-hearted wastrel, really, spending freely, quite often more than he earned, but he wanted his boys to have the best and be a success.

My mother had supported his every endeavour and shared his fluctuating political views—veering from open-armed liberalism to die-hard conservatism and back again—especially after they'd had a few sherries and a couple of whiskies. Born in the era of tobacco, they were both heavy smokers. While my mum had finally given up, my dad continued right on puffing, cheerful to the emphysemic end. But they always wore poppies on Remembrance Day.

They were gone now, but I could still feel them watching me. *All* of them. Now it was *my* turn to do my bit. It was my duty.

Duty! The word tormented my brain! What about my duty to my own family? Or did history have claims on them, too? I could imagine their collective answer shouting back at me: *'If we don't defend civilised society, there will be no family life!'* *'You can't have one without the other!'* My head felt like it was bursting!

Now I thought about it, it was no wonder Mary and I were at loggerheads. We were from opposite sides of the planet, in more ways than one. We were poles apart from way back, for generations!

Eager for the thrill of a lifetime, *her* great-grandfather had also answered the clarion call to the First World War. Giving a false name and lying about his age, he was sent straight to the muddy, blood-soaked fields of France. He was a veteran killer of Germans before his fourteenth birthday. Not surprisingly, he went home to foggy England twisted and numb, and became a violent alcoholic. He married a girl, but she left him, leaving behind a son, Mary's grandfather.

Escaping his abusive home as soon as he could, the poor boy had knocked about all over, working at this and that, getting into scrapes, not knowing which way was up. After Dunkirk, he was conscripted into the RAF and came out a sergeant. He opened up his own workshop as a mechanic and saw out his days pottering about in his garden allotment, back a bit from the tracks. Mary described him as a tough but gentle man, with a permanent roll-up dangling from his bottom lip. Apart from blaming his deafness in one ear on a bomb that had gone off too close to him, he never spoke about the war.

I peered down at the rails flashing by in the shadows beneath the window and thought about our families. Though our backgrounds were similar chronologically, the difference in their effects was stark.

Like my own, Mary's dad had grown up to the sounds of the post-war boom. A bit of a rock 'n' roll rebel in his younger days, he'd been a nifty dancer and always carried a comb in his back pocket. He worked in a factory and rode a motorbike. He and his socialist girlfriend from the typing pool became weekend hippies together. Buxom and beautiful, with long flaxen hair, she was the child of refugees from Soviet expansion into Eastern Europe and hated all things authoritarian. They were married on a hilltop, amid garlands of flowers, and soon Mary came along. To provide for his young family, he studied accountancy at night school and got an office job with the Water Board. Just prior to being killed in a car crash, the year before I met her, he was made Senior Clerk. A kindly old man, with a white mop of hair and a ready grin, Mary said he'd always urged her to follow her heart.

I shook my head and sighed. Any way you looked at it, we were destined to clash. Her whole history only emphasised the emotional damage of war, while I had been raised on its valour.

Throughout my sheltered childhood as a young, white, private school Aussie male of English descent, I was steeped in the old-fashioned, upper-middle class values of fair play and a fair go, Donald Bradman, Wimbledon tennis, the Sunday roast, classical music, and Christmas by the beach. Thriving on a mostly Anglo-American diet of black-and-white Hollywood romances, blockbuster war movies, heroic adventures of the British Empire, and daring tales of the bush, my attitudes and aspirations had congealed into a sort of mythical, ideal self-image—an amalgamation of Gregory Peck, Indiana Jones, James Bond, Wolfgang Mozart, and Clancy of the Overflow—one day, in some way, taking the field for Australia and writing my name in the record books.

Even as a boy, galloping around the garden on an imaginary horse, I'd played the hero, on a quest for fortune and fame: more often than not as a rugged cavalry captain, in a dusty but well-cut uniform with a flesh wound of mud to the shoulder, being chased behind enemy lines; or as an intergalactic secret agent working undercover on an alien planet; or a world-renowned archaeologist searching for lost cities in the Amazon.

Well, I wouldn't be galloping around the garden any more. *This was for real!*

I gulped at the horror of it, as if looking over a precipice. I wanted to cry, to go home, to escape into Mary's arms. But then, as the conviction drained out of me like sand through an hourglass, my mind rebelled: *No! Think about the atrocities! The rapes! The beheadings! You have to stay strong!*

I breathed in deeply, expanding my lungs to the full, and my heart began to pump. Like struck flint, my nerve reignited and held fast, my back straightened, and I came back onto the even keel of reason. Sure, I knew all about Western hypocrisy, the ugly face of imperialism and the centuries of exploitation, but I also knew about the insane violence of so-called religious extremist terror groups and that they had to be stopped. Not to mention the inhuman cruelty of those despots enslaving people to our north. All right, *everyone* had blood on their hands, but I still believed in the ultimate nobility of fighting for what was right and good.

Mary and I thought alike on so many issues, I moaned to myself. Why couldn't we agree on *this?* She'd told me that I saw things in black and white. I said there was right and there was wrong, and that was that! There was no way forward for us. We wanted such different things out of life.

But did we, really? I wanted love and a home, too, didn't I? I knew I didn't want to go off and kill, and maybe get killed myself. I couldn't even begin to think about my fear of the pain and the dreadful wounds I might suffer, or worse still, of being captured and tortured. There was no point in going there. It always came back to the same old conundrum: we couldn't have peace without fighting for it. That was the cold, hard fact. I just had to grit my teeth and get on with it.

Then, why my continuing uncertainty?

I searched inside my mind, scouring my motives, confronting myself. Did I truly believe my own rhetoric? *Was* I just trying to be a hero? When it all came down to it, what was I anyway? Sure, at school I had excelled in cricket and tennis, but on arriving at university the lure of girls and the social whirl soon took my mind off the ball. Although I'd managed to get my degree in music history, while my brothers had gone on with their careers I had simply rambled and ambled through life, waiting for the wave that would carry me on...*To what? Glory?...No!* I protested with my whole being. *To achieve my full potential!*

How had it come to this?

As long as I could remember, the dramatic imagery of classical music, especially when combined with the emotional intensity of the theatre, had thrilled me. Eventually, it led to a stint on piano below stage in an orchestra pit and some late-night dabbling at composition but without real conviction or commitment. To supplement my meagre income, I'd played at wedding receptions and formal functions. Early on, I even had a gig in a late-night bar. The first set of after-midnight-Manhattan jazz-blues morphing into Debussy had seemed to go all right, but after the break, when I followed it up with a cool medley of Mozart, Berlioz, and Rachmaninov, it cleared the room. The manager described it as 'morgue music'. When they let me go, the pleasure was mutual. I only worked there once.

Then, out of the blue, came the chance I'd been waiting for. Through my agent, I'd managed to get a couple of TV commercials, for which I'd duly cobbled a few pieces together.

No other work was forthcoming. Just when I'd all but given up hope of ever making a decent living out of music, one of the directors contacted me. He liked what he'd heard and wanted to offer me a commission. He was filming a documentary about the Red Centre and asked if I'd be interested in writing the score. *Would I be interested!* I was packing my bags before I'd even put the phone down. A few days later, with a lucrative contract and a hefty advance in my pocket, I headed north.

Meanwhile, over on the other side of the world, in England, as a little girl Mary had wanted to be a teacher. Seated at her blackboard with a clipboard on her lap, she would arrange her dolls around her and take the morning roll. She loved school, became a Brownie, and got a weekend job at a vet's. Later on, she trained to be a nurse, went on marches for third world justice and social equality, and saved up to buy a car. Then, one day, after breaking off a relationship that was always going to go wrong, she applied through an agency for a job at an outback hospital. Within a week, she was on a plane to Australia.

Our eyes first met across a crowded café in the main street of Alice Springs and my world was changed forever. It was when my real life began. *When the trouble started!* I grinned to myself half-jokingly. We fell in love under the pink glow of Uluru, and by the time we flew to Melbourne a year later, Mary was already pregnant.

At first everything was perfect. We were ideally suited, so our friends all told us. Joyfully, the babies arrived as planned: one, two, and three. We had it all! The commissions were coming regularly, and I had the offer of a part-time job lecturing at a coastal university. We still owned the small, one-bedroom apartment in the city we'd bought when we first arrived, before the prices skyrocketed. And now, having lived in larger, rented places while Matthew, Benjamin, and Naomi grew up and went to school, with my earnings, plus what my parents had left me, we had enough for a deposit on a house of our own. So, we decided to go for the dream: more space, fresh air, and a life near the sea for the kids. We loaded up our eight-seater bus and drove south, moving to a white, Victorian weatherboard on a half-acre block not far outside the bayside city of Geelong.

Yet, underneath it all, I was still restless. The first irritable cracks had started to appear—the stupid comments and frustrated arguments over nothing but about everything. Mary set the bar high for caring, helping whoever she could, there was no disputing that. In one form or another, she'd been doing it for most of her life. It just wasn't my way, that's all. It wasn't enough for me. Of course, I wanted to be of use to society as well, not just to be a success, but to do it by adding my own creative voice to the mix, to express the universal condition and, hopefully, raise people's spirits. Whenever I tried to explain it, in contrast to her hands-on, practical contribution, it always sounded lame. All I knew was that very little touched the human heart as deeply as music.

Over the ensuing years, we'd tried hard to accommodate our differences, but all too often the cogs of our happy life ground out of alignment. Although I was working solidly, I still hadn't found my true artistic direction and the pressures at home didn't help. Meanwhile, Mary's mother came to live with us, which only added to the strain, what with her cigar smoking and her pacifist ideas.

Then, like a rumbling volcano finally erupting, war flashed over the horizon, bringing with it conscription. I'd watched it building up, but the speed of it all took me by surprise. I followed its approach on the news with dread. I'd always said I wanted a life of action and adventure, and now I was going to get it.

The arrival of my call-up papers one morning brought everything to a head. When I told Mary I intended to go, she was furious. She said I was wrong, that the whole world was sick and needed healing, not bloodletting. That they needed me *there!* Torn between my love for her and the kids, the expectation of my parents, my own proud manhood, the opinion of my peers, my natural avoidance, and my abhorrence of the escalating savagery overseas, my emotions got the better of me. In defence of the decision I'd struggled to come to, my voice rose in anger as I let fly at her: *You can't just ignore a cancer! It has to be cut out!*

Throughout the following days, in between periods of icy silence and thunderous sulking, out of earshot of the children as much as possible, in exhausting bouts of fiery passion, we'd argued our reasons and justified our positions over and over again, finally yelling down each other's words until neither of us could hear.

Mary only wanted her family.

I needed a *mission!*

Well, now I had one.

I groaned at the overwhelming inevitability of it all. I felt like shit! My nose was blocked, and I was going hot and cold, definitely running a temperature. The conflicting thoughts were bombarding me from so many directions at once that my mind was in overload. Struggling beneath a landslide of doubt and self-recrimination, I stared vacantly into the night, searching among the scattered fragments of my beliefs for the missing shard that would give me the answer. Slowly, bit by flickering bit, my eyelids began to droop and close, as the sluggish, hypnotic clattering of the wheels on the rails outside lulled me, transporting me back to earlier that day.

In a blur of coal scuttle helmets, sooty leather waistcoats, bare brawny shoulders, tattooed muscular arms, and girls riding pillion, with straining breasts and scornful, seductive laughs, the gang of bikies had roared past on both sides of the bus, hooting and yelling at me, nearly knocking me over as I lifted the beer out of the back. With mounting anger, I slammed down the hatch and strode round to the near side, but they had already gone. I glared after them as they careened along the avenue of parked cars, slumped back on their cowhorned Harleys, and then powered away into the trees at the bottom of the road.

'Damn, bloody barbarians!' I muttered in their wake. 'Should be banned!' As the thought struck me that I sounded just like my father, I gave a rueful grunt, and with a self-righteous shake of my head, turned away.

Juggling the slab with one hand, I unlatched the picket gate and side-stepped through into the front garden. Tapping it closed behind me with my foot, I walked up the gravel path. Ahead of me, Matt and Ben's bicycles were propped up against the porch, with Naomi's red tricycle standing nearby. Through the open front door, I could hear one of my dad's favourite true blue '80s Aussie folk anthems playing. The party was still going strong. He would have enjoyed it.

There were rapturous shouts of greeting as I entered the crowded lounge. More for the beer than for me, I reckoned. Coloured balloons bobbed around the walls, alongside homemade banners, wishing me *Happy Birthday, Dad!* and *Bon Voyage, Jack!*

Everyone seemed happy. I certainly wasn't, though I couldn't show it. *What the hell was I doing?* I thought miserably.

Our family and friends were there. Among them, over by the fireplace, I saw the children sitting with easy affection near Mary's mother. Elsewhere, my three brothers had all come to see me off, somehow having managed to obtain leave at the same time. Even my old mate, Bernard, had been able to get away from his ship.

He and I had known each other since secondary school. As teenagers, he used to call me 'buffoono', which always cracked me up laughing. Slightly older than me, and of Italian descent, he was full bearded now and carrying a bit of a paunch, but otherwise he was still the same, with the broad shoulders, long body, and powerful legs of a rower. He had been the strongest boy in our class and was liked by everyone.

As it has always been, it was *de rigueur* for us teenagers to act and sound tough—in the process establishing a thoughtless pattern of delinquent behaviour that, more often than not, would lead to ongoing male violence, when those same cocky, hardnut kids become real hardnut adults. Sadly, some of us never found a way to outgrow it. The *world* hadn't found a way to outgrow it!

Bernard, though by nature as gentle as a lamb, nevertheless still believed in might for right. Whereas I, although I acted tough, didn't have my heart in it and was only play-acting. I had never had a real fight in my life and always shied away from what I considered the mindless stupidity of it. Many times, we'd sat up late at night drinking coffee, arguing about the world situation. I used to think of him as an alarmist, but most of his predictions had eventually been proved right. And now, here he was, second in command of a destroyer. As with my brothers, who'd all enlisted in the army, forever in two minds I wasn't sure whether to feel happy or sad for him. That morning, for my birthday, as a metaphor he'd given me a pair of binoculars, joking that I should use them sparingly in case, while trying to see the bigger picture, I failed to notice the immediate danger—the immediate danger I would soon be looking at down the barrel of a gun!

Meanwhile, over by the window, ever sartorial in his thin tie and stovepipe trousers, Iko, the 'cool', slim, Japanese local computer genius, and easy-going believer in the fibre-optic future, had found something in common to chat about with the mighty Stavros, our black-bearded, curly-haired next-door neighbour from the Peloponnese.

Mary wasn't in sight.

As I threaded my way across the floor, with a fixed, awkward grin on my face hiding my anxiety, I peered about the room for her. Things were so tense between us. Then there she was, in the kitchen. Fair-haired, forthright, and frightening! She turned in my direction and gave me a bleak, desolate smile. She still didn't want me to go.

All of a sudden, to my horror, I heard the ponderous crunching of tyres as my taxi to the station pulled up out the front. The moment had arrived!

I wasn't ready!

I needed more time!

I had to *think!*

I forced my eyes open in alarm and was shocked to see my own haggard face staring back at me, its square jaw, shadowed eyes, and dark, dishevelled hair reflected in the rain-speckled window of the train carriage. I looked how I felt!

As if there wasn't enough on my plate already, somewhere along the line I'd caught a cold, probably from the quietly sympathetic Indian cab driver—Ranjit something or other, according to the friendly face on his dashboard licence. Choked up and unable to do more than croak directions to him, for the most part we'd made the trip in silence, so it was hard to tell.

Now, when I thought about it, as I'd climbed in behind him I'd noticed he didn't look well. It had hardly registered, my mind being totally numb and my eyes flooding with tears as I watched my whole world receding through the rear window. I hadn't even considered the possible ramifications of his ill health when, as we turned onto the Surf Coast highway, in a sudden fit of sneezing he nearly collected the tail end of a peloton of

Sunday riders. As we swerved into the outside lane, all I could remember thinking was how ridiculously militaristic they were in their plastic helmets, with their little triangular flags bouncing along on aerials behind them.

Because of the petrol shortage, and the fact that our myopic leaders had failed to invest in solar-powered engines until the very last dollar had been extracted from fossil fuel, there were far fewer vehicles on the road and very little danger for cyclists. While the rest of the congested world rode their bicycles as they had always done—for the simple pleasure of it, bare-headed, often with a basket on the front—we, as usual, had to be different, had to be micro-managed and controlled for our own good. As for their fluorescent, skin-tight Lycra outfits, I could only imagine that they had squeezed themselves into them by some form of injection moulding. Then again, perhaps I was just being cynical? After all, my feelings were in turmoil.

Mary's and my final parting had been such agony: no stoic blessing on my leaving, as in the latest novel I'd been reading. I remembered her cold kiss, all the pent-up, desperate emotion, her words searing in my head: *'There are times when I wish I'd never met you, Jack!'* The utter desolation of that cold, matter-of-fact statement had hit me like a fatal blow. *'Don't go, Daddy! Daddy, don't go!'* little Naomi cried out, tearing my heart into shreds as I shut the car door.

I screwed up my eyes in anguish and threw myself back in my seat. This self-mortification was too much! I couldn't go on like it. I had to stop flagellating myself. I ran the back of my hand across my forehead, wiping the cold beads of sweat from my brow. I needed to pull myself together. First, I'd stay the night at the apartment, I resolved, and try to shake off this damn cold!

I opened my eyes again and took in my surroundings. By the dim glow of its few remaining light-globes, I surveyed the depressing interior of the carriage. Some of the seats had been slashed and the grimy, mottled green walls were daubed with graffiti, unintelligible except for the slogans: *Mossies Out, FUN Roolz,* and *NI4NI.*

For a few moments, my gaze lingered on the passenger sitting opposite me. A retired army type, I decided. He had to be ninety if he was a day. With mottled red cheeks and a gin-sodden nose, steel-grey hair, and a clipped moustache, he was wearing a camel overcoat and a regimental tie. He was sitting erect and reading a newspaper, peering through his bi-focals with rheumy eyes. He appeared such a classic stereotype that I thought I must be hallucinating, as if I hadn't slept for a few nights, which I hadn't.

I turned away and listlessly picked up the antique, gold-embossed, linen-bound book lying next to me on top of my canvas overnight bag. Lately, there had been talk of my doing the music for an upcoming movie about the Norman invasion of England in the eleventh century, when the relatively free and easy-going Anglo-Saxon society had been attacked by a neighbouring totalitarian state, and I'd been devouring everything I could find on the subject for background material. This one had been popular nearly two hundred years before. Full of Norse gods and ghostly apparitions, it told the tale of Harold, the Saxon champion, giving up his family to fight for his country—uncannily mirroring my own dilemma: only *his* wife encouraged him to go!

I opened it to the kids' handmade bookmark and gazed down at it with tender affection. I flipped it over. Along with lots of hugs and kisses, the back of the card was signed in the boys' neat, confident scripts, with their sister's decorative, spidery scrawl below. *Good luck, Dad! Come back soon! We love you!* My eyes swam and a hard lump pressed at my throat. With a tormented sigh, I closed the book and put it down again. I leant back and massaged my temples.

Just then, the compartment door slid open to admit a tall, sallow-faced Army Chaplain—a beanpole of a man, like a visiting spider crab, with a bib and collar showing under his military jacket. We both looked up at him as he placed his briefcase on the luggage rack and sat down. I took an instant dislike to him, personifying as he did the very *nux vomica* of my condition, the seed of insanity poisoning my mind—the insoluble contradiction of opposing, absolute faiths: Love and War. Nevertheless, I was prepared to give him the benefit of the doubt. After all, I was wrestling with some of my own. And you shouldn't judge a person by the cover, I thought, even if you could read them like a book.

'Evening, Father!' the passenger opposite me greeted him with gruff familiarity.

'Hello again, Colonel!' the clergyman nodded in recognition, the semblance of a smile hovering around his thin mouth without actually landing upon it.

Colonel! Just as I thought! I congratulated myself with grim amusement as I stared out through the window once more to check where we were. I turned back round and reached for my bag to put the book away.

'What's that you're reading, there, old chap?' the Colonel suddenly asked, pointing to it with a dark nicotined finger.

Startled, I half-held it out to him. 'Er...It's about the Normans and Saxons.'

He leant forward and inspected the title. "*Harold, The Last of the Saxon Kings*'. Know it well!' he chortled with pride. 'Read it when I was a boy! Battle of Hastings. 1066. Last ditch patriotism and all that. Grand stuff!'

'Yes...' I replied distantly, having too much on my mind to want to discuss it. I unzipped the bag and slipped it inside.

'Good reading for these times, I'd say,' the Colonel said, and snapped open his newspaper again.

'Yes, I suppose so,' I murmured in reply. Then, for some misplaced reason, feeling sorry for him because of his age, probably, and not wanting to appear impolite, I gestured towards the harrowing photograph on the front, showing blazing cars and scattered bodies in an Arab street. 'Things look pretty bad over there,' I offered.

'It's a mess all right!' he grunted, nodding his head. Frowning through his glasses and sticking out a moist bottom lip, he began to rattle through the pages, scanning their contents and providing a scathing summary. 'War in the Middle East...Race riots and urban violence across the globe...Virus alarm's over. Another one on the way...Protests and crackdowns everywhere...Nationalist fist-shaking from east to west...Terrorist atrocities, even here... Refugees wandering about all over the place...Ruskies on the move...NATO falling to pieces...The Brits and Frogs at each other's throats...Chain of command in disarray. History repeating itself. Nobody wants to be first to push the button!'

He threw the newspaper down on the seat in disgust. 'Unless the allies can coordinate a response, and damned quickly, it's only a matter of time before we're overrun on all fronts. Too many years of prevarication, not knowing where to draw the line, that's been the trouble. If we don't stand firm soon, it'll be too late!'

'Are you planning to enlist, my son?' the Chaplain inquired in a lofty monotone, joining the conversation.

'Yes...I mean...I've been called up,' I replied. 'I have to report tomorrow morning.' Straightaway, I felt somehow weakened, resenting having to explain myself to these overbearing strangers. Neither of their familiar dogmas offered me anything new.

'Need every man we can get!' the Colonel boomed his approval. 'Can't rely on the Yanks. Tearing apart at the seams. Haven't got the resources, for all their technology. Haven't got the will either, I'll be bound. Too busy protecting their own interests!'

'Oh, I'm not sure that's fair, you know, Colonel,' the Chaplain chided him, tossing back his head in dissent, but with a sly smile of tacit approval. The two obviously knew each other quite well. 'They have been our protectors for a long time, thank the Lord!'

'Well, natural enough I suppose,' the Colonel conceded with an amiable shrug, 'what with the climate going mad and the food and water shortages. Not to mention the economic collapse. Still, Panama, that's their main concern. The oil fields of Mexico. Meanwhile, South America's in turmoil. Africa's a slaughterhouse. Full of disease. India and Asia are the same. China and its friends'll come out from behind the scenes next, you mark my words. Like a damned tidal wave they'll be. Nothing to stop 'em!'

All of a sudden, without warning, a hot tide of effervescence swept up through my sinuses, exploding in a wild sneeze.

'Bless you,' said the Chaplain.

'Excuse me,' I gasped, with a half-apologetic smile, shaking my head. I pulled out a crumpled handkerchief and blew my nose with resounding gusto into the least soggy corner I could find. 'Well, at least no one's gone nuclear, yet,' I said thickly. 'That's something to be thankful for.'

'Absolutely!' the Colonel puffed out his cheeks in vigorous agreement. 'Gives us our chance, don't you see? If we can just get our act together and stop 'em in the north, it'll put the wind up all those other tin-pot dictators. Make 'em think twice before trying their luck over here!'

'But is war really our only option?' I blurted in semi-rhetorical dismay. Even as I spoke, I braced myself for his predictable response.

The Colonel fixed me with a withering glare. "Course it is!' he barked with scathing intensity. 'Only way to damned well deal with tyrants and maniacs! Got no choice in the matter. Can't reason with 'em. They don't speak the same language. No time for scruples. Shoot 'em like the mad dogs they are and be done with it, that's what I say! What d'you think, Father?'

'Much as it grieves me,' the Chaplain intoned with deep solemnity, 'I'm afraid I am forced to agree with you, Colonel.' He laid his cold, distant eyes on me, peering down the long ridge of his nose as if into my very soul. 'My son, this is a just war, have no doubt in your mind about that.'

'Might even be Armageddon! War to end all wars!' trumpeted the Colonel.

'I thought Christians were supposed to love their enemies?' I replied, barely masking my scorn, challenging both the Chaplain's double-sided hypocrisy and his smarmy confidence.

'As we do! As we do!' he answered with infinite patience, as if to a backward child, raising and lowering his leathery blue chin and furrowing his brow in an aspect of superior wisdom, while sending a vexed look to the Colonel out of the corner of his eye. 'The Church commands us to pray for the souls of *all* we are forced to overcome in defence of our families.'

'And our country!' threw in the Colonel.

'To protect the weak from oppression...'

'And preserve our freedom!'

'Exactly,' the Chaplain nodded. 'Just as Our Lord, Himself, prayed for those who were about to kill Him, "Father, forgive them for they know not what they do." No, there is no incongruity here, my son.' He held up a bony, admonishing forefinger, pointing towards heaven. 'And remember one other thing that He said, 'Greater love hath no man than this that a man lay down his life for his friends."'

'And that means on the battlefield, by Jove, not turning the other cheek!' thundered the Colonel. At that very moment, the train lurched and slowed down, as the approach lights of Southern Cross station went by. 'Ah! We're here at last!'

The Chaplain stood up and reached for his briefcase. 'I hope that helps to resolve your doubts, my son?'

As we jolted to a halt, I turned in my seat and looked out at the dark, wet platform. Doors banged, there was a shrill whistle blast, and passengers rushed by.

'I don't know,' I sighed. 'I'm not sure what I think.'

2

Clutching the two wrapped bottles to my chest as though they were liquid gold, I stopped on the threshold of the convenience store and bent down to push them into my bag. Then, straightening up to my full, aching height, I stepped out onto the footpath. There was hardly anybody about. I grimaced up at the black, cloud-laden sky. At least the rain had stopped, that was one good thing. I shivered with gratitude and pressed my shoulders deeper into my coat.

Standing near me, on the corner opposite Southern Cross station, Melbourne's main country rail hub, was a newspaper boy wearing a beanie and hood, calling out in a commanding, sing-song voice to the rapidly dispersing travellers: 'Read all about it! Read all about it! World War latest!'

Part of a resurrected gimmick to boost failing sales of hard copy news in the face of the digital invasion, I was happy to give him my support. I walked up to him, laid down the correct money and took the top copy from a stack beside him. 'Cheers, mate,' he said, very fast out of the side of his mouth, and without breaking rhythm carried on yelling: 'Read all about it! Latest from the front! Get yer papers 'ere!'

Beneath the harsh glare of halogen and the all-seeing eyes of the surveillance cameras, the wide, usually busy junction of Collins Street and Spencer Street was awash under a glistening film of water. One of the storm drains had become clogged and a gurgling torrent was gushing along the curb like a thick stick of twisted liquorice. Not a cab was in sight. To my right and left, the long, straight thoroughfare of Spencer Street stretched away into the darkness, virtually devoid of traffic.

Train services, particularly at night and at weekends, had been drastically cut. All the fast food outlets in the station, bar one, were closed. An armoured car with blackened windows and its lights off stood by the entrance plaza, its occupants either inside the vehicle watching or else grabbing a coffee and a burger. Two or three separate batches of recently disembarked passengers came out onto the concourse and hurried over to the superstop, just as a half-empty, triple-sectioned tram arrived.

For a moment I considered taking it, but I decided it would be easier if I walked. I waited while it picked them up and then sailed away with a *whoosh* towards Docklands, clanging its bell. Rolling up my newspaper and gripping it tightly in my fist, I followed after it as quickly as I could.

The going was hard. I was breathing through my mouth and my throat was bone dry. *Was* Mary right? I kept asking myself as I strode along the pavement. Was this rush towards war driven by nothing but political self-interest and nationalistic propaganda? Was that how it had always been? Had every generation of service men and women been used as pawns? I couldn't believe that. They'd *had* to fight!

Suddenly, out of nowhere, with a deep-throated roar, a trio of motorcycle police zoomed like heavy cavalry up Spencer Street towards me, their red and blue lights flashing and their sirens blaring. A moment later, they raced by me, ploughing through a wide, black puddle, splashing my legs and soaking my paper.

Aghast and dripping wet, I staggered round in time to see them turn at the station and disappear from view. Growling with angry resignation, I stuffed the sodden roll into an overflowing rubbish bin and strode grimly on, the bottoms of my saturated jeans flapping against my calves and my soft leather shoes squelching with every step.

Unsure as to whether the proposed curfew had come into force yet, I decided to take a short cut to our apartment. So, at the first opportunity, with some trepidation, I turned right up the uninviting laneway of Francis Street, its entrance squeezed between a tower of tarpaulin-clad scaffolding and a corner café with its doors and windows all boarded up.

As I entered the gloomy interior, I could see heavy metal grills forbidding rear access to the darkened buildings beyond. Graffiti was sprayed over everything, even in the most impossible places: dynamic, invective calligraphy, bursting with chaotic action and colour. Maybe, one day in the future, somebody would unearth them and look on them as they did Egyptian hieroglyphics or the frescoes of Pompeii? Among the indecipherable tags, the ghouls and vampires, and the usual obscenities, the repeated word FUN stood out. I knew what it meant: the Fundamentalist Ultra-Nationalist Party. I'd seen their slogan and heard them on the news. *Come to the FUN Party!* They were a right wing neo-fascist group, known for their violence towards immigrants and their connections with organised crime. More than one of their members had even made it into the Senate. Fun? There wasn't much of *that* in my life right now, I reflected sourly.

A few steps in from the entrance, the dank, fetid air smelled palpably of fungus and urine. I could almost taste it. Off to one side, in the darkness, a fully-grown, collarless, black doberman had its legs splayed for leverage and its long snout thrust into a rotting garbage heap, ripping and snapping at something putrid with its lethal incisors. I considered turning back but didn't have the energy to take the long way around. Giving the brute a wide berth, I eased my way past it along the wall of an office block and headed off as calmly as I could.

Ahead of me, a limpid layer of oily smoke floated above a circle of bedraggled vagrants, warming themselves around a forty-four-gallon drum beside the road. Other shabby groups huddled in twos and threes nearby, hands in pockets, standing close together, conversing in low tones. They watched with sullen, dangerous looks as I went by, then turned their backs and ignored me.

On the opposite side, an old woman with wild, matted grey hair lay slumped in the gutter, mumbling into her own vomit. At the sound of my passing, she half-lifted her unseeing, scowling face from the ground and, like the broken wing of a fallen bird, without looking at me, lashed out her arm in my direction as if thrusting me away, while railing at her own private demons with a bitter, incoherent snarl.

An ambulance siren began to wail in the distance, answered an instant later by an angry chorus of dogs barking over in the next street. There were far-off shouts, police whistles and a small explosion.

I quickened my pace. Soon, within the murky shadows along the edge of the lane, I made out a young woman standing in the semi-lit recess of a doorway, smoking a cigarette. Above her, a sign offered *Self-Defence Lessons.* Light was showing through an opaque, wire-meshed window beside her, but there was no sound from within. Nearby, a silver Mercedes saloon was parked up on the footpath.

She had one hand thrust in the pocket of her open ornamental fur jacket, holding it against her to keep warm, at the same time shifting from foot to foot on a pair of platform-soled, thigh-length boots that were far too big for her and sagged down around her long, straight legs. Her skinny, full-breasted body was barely hidden by a low-cut blouse and a skimpy red skirt. Glowing in the half-light, her shaven head was crowned with bright green spikes, rigid with gel. She couldn't have been more than eighteen.

Her eyes, lined with kohl, like Nefertiti, though darting from side to side, kept coming back to me, observing my every move. The place had to be a front, I decided. I could just imagine her sensei-pimp-boyfriend inside, kicking the stuffing out of a class of teenage acolytes or, more likely, given the silence, cutting the latest delivery of cocaine with talcum powder.

Why else would she be out there and alone in such a godforsaken spot? Her pretty face, adorned with multiple piercings, had a disturbing hardness to it. In another life she would have been someone's cherished daughter, I thought sadly. I wasn't being judgemental—you couldn't blame a person for doing what it took to survive—but the poor girl must have been freezing. I acknowledged her plight with a raise of my eyebrows and sent her a sympathetic smile.

With a nonchalant shrug, she turned away. Lifting her cigarette to the wide, dark smear of her lips, balancing the filter between the tapered tips of two black nail-glossed fingers with genteel precision, she took a final drag and blew a dismissive stream of vapour towards the sky. Then, tossing the butt onto the ground, she pulled out her mobile phone and began scrolling through her messages. I hurried on. Just to add to my feeling of depression, a bit further along, clinging to a wet, tar-black brick wall, a torn Army recruitment poster commanded me to remember: *Your Mates Need You!*

'I'm coming, I'm coming,' I muttered with annoyance to the stern-faced infantryman pictured on it.

I shivered and sneezed, recoiling from the atmosphere of the place. It was like being underneath a rock, in a damp, hidden netherworld seething with anger and fear. Was *this* what I was going to fight for? Was *this* what I wanted to save? They didn't have birthday parties down here that was for sure.

But that didn't mean they weren't worth defending, my mind argued with itself. This could be anywhere. Throughout history, in every country, under any government, they had always existed—the derelicts life left behind. *All* societies failed them. If we didn't have to keep on defending ourselves against other countries' aggression, maybe we'd have time to really help them. It was too big to answer now. That would have to come later when the war was won.

Although Francis Street was one-way, there were plenty of parking spaces, but none of them was taken. No one with any sense would leave their vehicle here, I thought. Not on a Sunday night; not these days. Melbourne wasn't the safe place it used to be—and hadn't been for years. Now, with the spate of car bombings and the ever-present danger of terrorist attacks, people were becoming maybe not scared exactly, but wary, tending more and more to keep to themselves and stay at home after dark.

Continuing along the narrow, dilapidated lane, carefully avoiding the deep cracks and potholes in the bitumen, I halted for a moment to take in the variety of brightly illuminated hoardings high up on the sides of the distant buildings. Their alluring, semi-erotic imagery, advertising the latest self-warming lingerie, luxury island holiday resorts, and state-of-the-art domestic robots, shone in stark contrast to the dismal scene here below.

Just then, I became aware of an incessant, throbbing noise coming from the sky. I stared up at the dark blanket of cloud, listening intently. Somewhere over the city rooftops, the pounding pulse of a helicopter was coming towards me. Meanwhile, a short way ahead of me, standing in the darkness beneath the purple neon sign of a cat, a couple of bar staff taking a break outside the back of an almost concealed nightclub were doing the same.

Twenty metres beyond them, on the other side of the lane, where an industrial section spanned the road, the whine of a forklift came to a stop and, moments later, a factory worker ducked out from under a half-open roller door to discover the cause of the racket. None of them so much as gave me a second glance as I passed, like a wreck in the night. Tired, hungry, and footsore, I trudged on towards the top of the street.

Soon, above the increasing intensity of the thumping waves of sound, I could hear the melodic tones of an acoustic guitar echoing from the far end, bringing an unexpected, welcome relief from the nightmare world I was in. As I drew closer, I could make out a group of buskers standing together on the pavement, chatting quietly as they packed away their instruments. One of them, a young woman, like a Pre-Raphaelite painting with her long auburn hair and pale, luminescent skin, gave me a friendly smile. I returned it with a heartfelt one of my own. Two of the three men, one clean-shaven, one with a full bushman's beard, exchanged amiable nods with me; while the third, a woolly-bearded Aboriginal, was busy laughing and joking with a small boy who was trying to close the lid over a snare drum. The bright stickers on their cases proclaimed them to be *Captain Guitaro & The Landing Party.*

With his back to them, their leader, Captain Guitaro, dressed in a diamond-patterned, multi-coloured, knee-length coat and a wide-brimmed, grey felt hat with a purple plume, stood strumming out the last few notes of a lilting tune at the edge of the curb, almost drowned out by the noise of the propellers. A guitar-case lay open at his feet. As I approached, the small cluster of cleaners and office staff who had stopped to listen gave up against the din and drifted away. Going past him, I tossed what coins I had in my pocket into the almost empty case. Captain Guitaro gave me a nod and a grin of thanks.

'Sounds good!' I saluted him, with an empathic smile, one weary journeyman to another, my faith in something greater and purer restored, albeit briefly, by the sweet, common balm of music.

I walked on, sneezing, to the end of the lane and turned left into King Street, a tree-lined dual-carriageway running between imposing department stores, banks, and offices.

Being one of the main boulevards that made up the city grid, it was unnervingly deserted and desolate. To my right, standing like blind three-eyed sentinels, the vestige of some dead civilisation on a forgotten planet, a bank of traffic lights blinked out their repetitive, computerised message to the answering *rat-tat-tat-tat* staccato of a little green man. On either side, the high, chiselled faces of the surrounding buildings stared down at me, dark and forbidding, an impenetrable audience of stone. Maybe it was just my overwrought imagination, but for some reason I had a sense of foreboding, an icy prickling of danger on the back of my neck. Of course, it wasn't helped by the squealing rotors and thrashing blades of the machine prowling the sky above. I couldn't see it yet, but I could tell it was circling closer.

It had started to drizzle again. With my bag slung over my shoulder and my hands thrust deep into my pockets, I shelved my problems as far back in my mind as I could and concentrated on getting to the apartment. All of a sudden, in a rapid burst of action, a quartet of generic black SUVs appeared out of the darkness and swept by me in quick succession, their imperious wipers waving at half-speed and their huge wheels sending up fine jets of spray behind them. I watched them sail away into the distance, then crossed over to the island separating the four lanes.

There I waited, while a low, white, stretch limousine approached from the opposite direction. On reaching me, it slowed right down almost to a standstill and crawled past, inspecting me through its darkened windows, the *hiss* of its tyres on the wet tarmac like the bated breath of a cobra. I braced myself. Just when I was sure it was going to stop, all of a sudden the engine gunned into life and it took off, jumping the red lights and coasting away, like a pale ribbon of silk, down towards the river—to club land and the casino, no doubt. I gave a huge sigh of relief, blowing out the lung-full of air I hadn't realised I was still holding, and with a resolute roll of my shoulders physically shook off the sleazy residue of the experience.

If that was how unsettled I was by a simple car, what would I be like on the battlefield? I berated myself. I lumbered over to the far side and continued up the road to the next intersection.

Thankfully, Little Collins Street was a bit brighter and there were some signs of life, although not enough to completely dispel my anxiety, born as it was out of the nagging feeling that I was making a terrible mistake. A few pedestrians were out and about, holding up umbrellas, while small parties of diners hurried, arm in arm, towards the glowing table lamps of the only two open restaurants. A solitary moped was parked at the curb outside the door of a minimart.

The street had a welcoming European flavour to it, with its wider pavements, striped awnings, and hanging baskets, but the low, dark timberwork of the shopfronts was cold and damp, and the bougainvilleas looked wilted and sad. There was room enough for cars to come down the street two-abreast, nevertheless it was unseasonably quiet. The war was taking its toll. I set off on the last leg of my journey *to where I could finally sit down!*

After a while, the road broadened out. On one side, a row of tables and chairs set between large earthenware plant pots outside a café all stood empty. Opposite them, above a low brick wall, a rain-swept beer garden lay closed and deserted.

The lighting in this section was virtually non-existent. Despite there being more space, it felt distinctly claustrophobic and threatening.

Ahead of me, on my left, was Church Street, the one-way cut-through to the parallel thoroughfare of Bourke Street that I wanted to take. With mounting concern, despite the thickening layer of noise up above, I heard strident whistle blasts, raucous shouts, and indistinct chanting echoing down it from that direction. There was an interrupting screech of brakes, followed by a blaring car horn, then loud, angry yelling.

As I drew level and turned into it, I was immediately greeted by an approaching clamour of frenzied shouting, running feet, and shrill police whistles. At the same moment, the darkness about me suddenly evaporated under the piercing white spotlight of a helicopter hovering directly overhead, its deafening roar reverberating off the blank office walls on either side.

Seconds later, a fleeing crowd of what, judging by their clothes, I took to be mostly artists, writers, intellectuals, old and new wave hippies, religious pacifists, and students, surged around the corner at the far end and ran pell-mell along the lane towards me. Anti-war demonstrators left over from some rally and being attacked on their way home, I instantly concluded. I stood riveted to the spot in shocked fascination. Some still clung onto their placards, advocating *Co-operation Not Annihilation!... Peace and Love!...*and *Wake up, Humanity! War is Insanity!* Sure enough, hot on their heels charged a howling, fanatical mob, wearing black berets and tracksuits, with armbands bearing the initials FUN on them. They were wielding baseball bats and chanting ferociously, 'Fun! Fun! Fun!' as they gave chase.

Two of the terrified protesters—a long-haired youth in an anorak and a pretty girl in a baggy, Rastafarian woollen cap— gripped each other's hand and swerved off like rabbits, bolting towards the yawning portcullis entrance of an underground carpark. Immediately, four of the black-garbed thugs split away from the pack and sprinted down the tunnel after them. I shuddered to think what would happen to that young couple once they were cornered.

Lastly, sprinting in close pursuit of all these, rushed a squad of burly riot police in visored helmets and flak jackets, carrying batons and shields.

Once again, I was struck by the absurd predictability of the characters hurtling my way, like actors taking clichéd rôles in some familiar stage play. With my debilitating head cold, I felt detached from them all, as if watching from a distance, inside myself. I couldn't have cast it better if I'd tried. I could already hear the music. *Those whom the gods wish to destroy they first make mad* was right, I thought, and laughed in silent despair. It was *all* mad!

Then all artistic sensibility was obliterated as, right in front of me, the three sides came into contact. There was a blurred confusion of bodies, incoherent yelling, and people screaming, while coloured flares exploded among the battling groups. As they swarmed around me, I was caught up in the mêlée and sent spinning. Before I could raise my arms to protect myself, a heavyset, fist throwing, fleshy faced man in a tight beret and a black leather coat backed violently into me and turned on me in fury. *I'm not one of them!* I tried to shout in my defence, but the words wouldn't come. With a rumbling growl of disgust, and his one good eye, next to a black patch, burning with rage, he shoved me hard with both hands towards the side of the road.

Reeling from the bruising blow and struggling to keep my balance, the irony of his mistake was the last thing I thought of before a policeman suddenly loomed out of a cloud of orange smoke, his snarling face obscured behind the clear plastic spade of his visor, and smacked me on the side of the face with his baton. My head exploded in a flash of brilliant white light and a tsunami of pain engulfed me as I went sprawling onto the road. Soaring in and out of a tide of blackness, the sounds roaring, jumbled and distorted, as if the wires in my brain were all shorting at once, my vision came and went in fractured close-up glimpses of wet grit and grimy asphalt.

Eventually the world stopped whirling and I came to. I lay there unmoving, my head pounding, trying to reconnect my strobing senses. Meanwhile, the anti-war faction had broken free and run off, followed by the rest, taking their running battle back down Little Bourke Street. The noise of the helicopter receded and darkness returned.

When, at last, the smarting agony on my face subsided, I let out a bone-weary groan and pushed myself up onto all fours. I pressed my hand to my cheek, forming a canopy over the wound, absorbing the burning pain. For a while I remained motionless, letting my eyes refocus and collecting my strength. Finally, I lifted my head...and gave a small laugh.

To my fragile amusement, I saw facing me the window of a 'New Age' bookshop glowing with coloured fairy lights. Behind its wire-mesh and reinforced glass lay a collection of occult books and magazines, crystal pendants, tarot cards, runic inscriptions, statuettes of wizards, and plastic pixies sitting on red and white-spotted mushrooms.

At the front, on the left of the display, a large poster for *The Emissary*—the latest book and DVD in a series entitled *Servants of Xzyatan*—showed a wizened, bald-headed alien, with his black eyes staring out from a shiny, featureless face, seated at a large telescope between open velvet theatre drapes tied back on either side. Kneeling before him were a group of citizens, their arms outstretched in supplication. Beyond them, the curve of the earth stretched away to the stark silhouette of a ruined city. Flying saucers with flashing lights hovered in the sky above. In the top corner of the poster, illuminated by licking flames, was a gleaming red, black, and gold symbol of a snake, shaped like a letter 'S', wrapped around a cross-swords 'X'. The caption at the bottom warned ominously: *The Final Invasion...The stage is set!*

At the other end of the window sat a painted plaster statue of a stereotypical Gypsy fortune-teller, gazing down at a crystal ball in her hands. Around her feet was an array of astrological charts, printed pamphlets, china mugs decorated with the signs of the Zodiac, and a scroll saying *Be Prepared! Read Your Future in the Stars!*

'It's got a funny 'abit of doing that, the future,' a cheerful voice suddenly came from behind me. 'Just when you don't expect it... *whack!*...it hits you right in the face!'

Very slowly, gingerly testing my neck muscles to protect them from spasming, I twisted round and looked up. An old, bearded tramp, wrapped in a tattered overcoat tied at the waist with string, was hovering nearby.

'Yeah, great. Thanks for telling me,' I replied with a lopsided attempt at a smile, and groaned again.

'You all right there, mate?' the tramp asked with concern.

I nodded and hung my head for a few moments, breathing hard, gathering myself to move. Then, with all the energy I could muster, I pushed myself up and, grabbing hold of my bag, stumbled over to the shop, slumping down below the fortune-teller with my back against the weather-worn, panelled stallriser. Tentatively, I touched the epicentre of pain next to my right eye and winced. I pulled my hand away and stared at the smear of blood on my fingertips.

''Ere, you wouldn't be able to, you know, cross me palm with silver, would you, mate?' ventured the tramp, shuffling closer.

With a weary, aching laugh, I dragged my bag over to me and unzipped it. Inside, along with my clothes and my book, were the two precious bottles of whisky wrapped in brown paper bags. I pulled one out, unscrewed the top, took a large swig, and held it out to him. 'Here you go.'

The tramp's eyes lit up as he grabbed hold of it. 'Crikey! Just what the doctor ordered!' he exclaimed.

'Keep it,' I said. Two bottles was a bit optimistic, anyway. I laughed to myself, mocking my own over-indulgent self-pity.

'Good on ya, mate!' With a toothless grin, the tramp held the amber liquid up to his gleaming eyes and smacked his lips. 'This'll take care of tomorrow very nicely!'

I threw him a weak smile and leant my head back against the shop front. I could feel a trickle of warm blood mingling with the rain running down my face. I moaned and closed my eyes.

*

Leaving the cold, grey glow of the concrete landing behind me, I stepped into the darkened apartment. Outside, I could hear the muffled wail of an ambulance siren fading into the distance, while the echoing clang of a door slamming a few floors below me rang up the stairwell. Sweeping the wall with my hand to locate the switch, I turned on the hall light and entered. I closed the door and leant back against it. There was silence. Thank God, I'd made it! I felt like I'd been through a war zone and I hadn't even been inducted yet!

Setting my bag down on the carpet, I staggered over to the bathroom and went in. Tugging on the cord of the strip-light above the mirror, I gripped the edge of the sink and leant forward to inspect my injury. Although my eye was bloodshot, the gash beside it wasn't too bad. The rain had washed it clean and the bleeding had stopped. Mercifully, the pain had eased to a dull throb. *I needed a drink!*

Taking a box of tablets from the medicine cabinet behind the mirror, I pressed out two from the foil, filled a glass with water, and swallowed them. Then, wetting a flannel and holding it to my bruised cheekbone, I collected my bag and stumbled the few paces down the hallway, past the galley kitchen, to the bedroom.

On entering, I felt my way along the side of the mattress in the dark, switched on the bedside lamp, and sank down on the edge of the double bed with a sigh. I unzipped my bag and pulled out my book, followed by the second bottle of scotch. Placing the book on the bedside table, I removed the wrapping, unscrewed the cap and took a mouthful, shaking my head as the liquor bit in my throat.

Still clutching the bottle, I pulled back the collar of my coat and reached into the inside pocket. Taking care not to spill a drop, I withdrew the well-worn, official letter. I unfolded it and scanned its contents. With a groan of resignation, I dropped it onto the quilt and stood up. My bladder was bursting and I needed something to eat.

Sipping from the neck, I stumbled over to the small flatscreen TV on the dresser facing the end of the bed, picked up the remote, and pressed the button. To my immediate pleasure, a documentary about 'The Sixties' came on the screen, showing kaleidoscopic images of happenings, love-ins, peace marches, and flower power music and fashion. I watched in fascination for a few moments, thinking fondly of my dad, singing along and swaying on my feet. Then I turned and strode from the room, leaving my instruction to report for military service lying open on the bed in the flickering, psychedelic light.

By ten o'clock I was blind drunk, feverish and feeling decidedly sorry for myself.

Beyond the drawn curtains of the lounge, the rain-swept city was quiet. Cocooned beneath the halo of light from the standard lamp beside my chair, I sat rocking to and fro in front of the computer monitor, a burning cigarette held tightly between my lips. I didn't normally partake, but, hey, the condemned man was allowed a final smoke, wasn't he, on his last night of freedom?

In short, ponderous bursts, I prodded at the keyboard with one finger, trying to compose 'the lament of the reluctant conscript', intermittently humming a tune to go with the lyrics. On the shelf above me, the almost empty bottle of whisky stood next to an overflowing ashtray and the half-eaten cheese roll I'd bought at the station. Semi-comatose and seeing double, I stared at the words floating elliptically around the screen, straining to keep them from moving, to remember what I wanted to say.

I'm just sitting here waiting
I wait for the morning to come
They say then I must start hating
But I don't hate anyone

I was flying on automatic pilot now; in fact, I was beyond it. My brain was numb, the inspiration gone. It was too hard to focus. My head was spinning. I was about to crash. The suffocating air felt like a padded wall around me. Barely realising that I was even doing it, I reached out for my glass, but the effort was too much. Letting out an exhausted groan, I gave up and dropped my arm. Without consciously making the decision to go, like a parachutist leaping from a plane, in sluggish automatic sequence I shut down the computer and lurched unsteadily to my feet. Taking rough aim, I hurriedly jammed my cigarette into the pile of butts, stretched out a shaky arm to switch off the lamp, then spun round and propelled myself towards the door. *I had to lie down!*

As I reeled back into the bedroom, a newscaster was speaking on television: *'...while the leaders of the United States and Great Britain landed in Canberra today for their meeting with the Prime Minister, to discuss the worsening situation.'*

I veered over to the set. With legs like rubber, teetering on the balls of my feet in an erratic figure eight beside it and my arms flailing to stop myself from falling, through half-closed eyelids I watched the footage of their arrival. There were shots of the short-haired, stocky Prime Minister of Great Britain and the lean, balding President of the United States, waving as they stepped down from their planes, followed by ones of them both together, along with our own white-bearded Prime Minister, all smiling and shaking hands on the steps of Parliament House.

'The main items on their agenda will be the further implementation of the tripartite defence agreement, and continuing trade and economic co-operation.'

Somehow, I managed to locate the remote. I snatched it up and changed the channel. A montage of military parades, taking place in front of cheering crowds in different capitals around the world, came on. *Was there no end to it!* With a scornful growl, I stumbled away down the bed, kicking off my shoes as I went, and threw myself full-length on top of it, sinking my face into the soft sanctuary of the pillows.

Soon I couldn't breathe. I rolled over onto my back and lay there, panting in short shallow gasps through my mouth, but it wasn't enough to stop the room from spinning. Flaring my nostrils, I began taking in deep sniffs of air, pumping it out again through my stuffed-up nose like a chugging, overloaded steam train, fighting the mounting urge to throw up. A wave of sorrow and isolation flooded over me. I missed my family so much! I needed to see their faces again, to know that I wasn't alone.

Levering myself onto my elbows, I twisted round and squinted up at the row of framed photographs on top of the bookshelf. There they were: Mary and the kids on our cycling holiday; my mum and dad in their garden, waving happily at me; my three brothers in officer's uniforms, arms folded, grinning like heroes. I gave them all a crooked smile, the tears welling in my eyes. With a sorrowful cry, I collapsed back onto the bed.

Immediately, my thoughts went rolling and tumbling beneath the barrelling dumpers of uncertainty, tossing me about from side to side on the mattress, the crucial memories sweeping by too fast for my whisky-sodden mind to even formulate the questions I needed to answer. After a while, as a voice from the TV finally cut through to me, I lifted my throbbing head and peered at the blurred double-image of a sandy-haired reporter filling the meandering screen. Wearing a light tan safari jacket, he was facing the camera and speaking into a hand-held microphone.

'So, in a climate of social, political, and economic upheaval, we are once again being treated to an awesome display of armed might, as the superpowers and the not-so-super powers flex their military muscles on a grander scale than ever before. This is Eric Braithwaite, for the Late News, at the May Day celebrations.'

Dripping with perspiration, my bruised face cracked into a mordant, stupified grin as I sang out the timeless distress call to him in a helpless, drunken cackle, 'Mayday! Mayday!'

Then, like a drowning swimmer caught in a rip, turning one last time in search of a landmark, I attempted to focus on the digital clock beside me, struggling to bring its swirling numbers into line. Eventually, they settled long enough to make sense: *10:52.* Was *that* all it was? I laughed in forlorn surprise. So early...

but too late! With a final, despairing moan, I slumped back on the pillow and let go into unconsciousness.

In an instant, as swiftly as a dealer shuffling cards, reality was enfolded and swept away on a stream of incongruous images, plummeting me over the edge, down into the depths. The afterglow of the clock's red numerals hovered before me in the blackness, then faded away.

One minute I was falling, the next I had landed in a different dimension, in a zany amalgam of time and place where present day logic existed side by side with the past.

While in most dreams, at best, one gets a fleeting sense of there being a narrative—something intangible and unseen that one can't quite get a grip on, its presence felt rather than known, and within which the memorable fragments bloom like flowers on a stem, with their roots hidden deep underground—maybe it was the fever, maybe it was my emotional state, plus the alcohol, or maybe I just filled in the gaps from all the history books I'd been reading, but this was like no other dream I'd ever had. In it, a story was told in its entirety from start to finish, each scene implanted in my memory, clear as day, right down to the finest detail.

In a last, vivid flash of awareness before succumbing to its unfolding pageant, I suddenly realised where I was. I was in my book! But an absurd, hybrid version of it! A surreal, parallel world. A disturbing black comedy, where bicycles replaced horses and telephones and computers appeared alongside swords and shields. A cautionary allegory dredged up from my subconscious, where the old and the new intertwined to weave a tapestry of my future.

It was like Mad Magazine meets Monty Python meets 'Family at War', or 'Doctor Strangelove' meets 'Henry V' meets 'The Sullivans', all rolled into one, inside something resembling a

Sunday night armchair costume drama. Through back-to-front contortions of context, turning history on its head, it told the tale of the Norman invasion—that celebrated, seminal moment of supreme self-sacrifice and patriotic fervour in which a nation's identity was forged—and challenged the sanctification of *any* such battle by taking issue with its causes and effects.

And in excoriating the sacred cow, laying bare its inner workings with the knife-edge of debunking satire and the dismembering tongs of a subversive alternative truth, the burning issues confronting me and the tortured arguments Mary and I had had about them took centre stage, held up to the light in all their blow-by-blow detail with the same irreverent spirit as those socio-political parodies I'd inherited in my youth, playing out in caustic, comic juxtaposition before my eyes.

Only, it wasn't in Saxon England. It was Saxon Australia!

The ones I loved were all there. The people I knew, and those I'd recently come across who'd stuck in my mind, filled out the roles and became the characters. I, too, was in it, of course. As well as being the observer, in some strange osmotic way I was also Harold—although his face was hard to make out, at one and the same time reminding me of both myself and some well-known actor, someone I felt I knew but whose name I'd forgotten, although it was there on the tip of my tongue.

With irresistible strength, the colliding rivers of tormenting thought gushed and roared through the canyon of my mind, eddying and foaming, then cascading over the falls, crashing down together in a swirling flood of repercussions and frightening inevitability, submerging me in what would become an ever-widening lake of blood.

My dream began.

3

There was a cold, white mist, suffused by the glare of a late morning sun. Gradually, it began to dissipate, like a frosted-glass window being lowered at the top, exposing a clear strip of sky. As the tendrils of vapour wafted away, the barbed-wire top of a cyclone fence appeared. Behind it, attached to a steel pole with a rope tied around it, was a wooden sign, warning: *Keep Out! Government Appropriation. For Military Use Only*. It began to shake.

Moments later, as the intensity of the rattling increased, with triumphant shouts it was hauled away from the fence by two emaciated, middle-aged vagrants pulling on the rope. They dragged it down to the earth and proceeded to break it apart.

Beyond them, on an empty stretch of waste ground littered with rubble and rubbish and overgrown with weeds, groups of shivering, dejected homeless people were milling about as if waiting for something, anything, perhaps even death, to happen. Some were clustered around small campfires, staring vacantly at the low flames, while others stood motionless, like cut-out photographs, weighed down, numb and exhausted, uncertain how to go on.

There were refugees of every colour and every race, the old and the young, all wearing worn, ragged clothes, destitute, frightened, and dispirited. From as far apart as the Horn of Africa and the ravaged Middle East, to the mango groves of Sri Lanka and the golden stupas of Myanmar, they'd come: starving families, the lucky ones who'd escaped, their funds exhausted, fleeing famine, war and persecution, gathered together, shoulder to shoulder, in the only true multicultural society—that of the dispossessed. An air of deep melancholy hung over them like a shroud.

Gaunt, white-bearded old men wrapped in torn blankets and threadbare coats lay huddled on the stony ground, while thin, eager children explored the rock-strewn area around them, tottering about on unsteady legs. Here and there, those with the energy roamed the site collecting more firewood. There were low sobs and the heart-rending sound of babies crying.

A grizzled, once handsome Pashtun tribesman, a battered pakol pushed back on his head like a brown pastry mushroom-cap, sat in the dust, rummaging around in his jacket pockets. Finally, with a flicker of surprise, he came up with a stale piece of almond cake. Giving her a sad smile, he passed it to his young granddaughter kneeling beside him, stroking a mangy dog lying next to her.

Meanwhile, the two men from the fence approached one of the fires and threw the pieces of their broken sign onto it, on top of another declaring: *Private Property*. As the wood ignited, the combined, forbidding, stenciled words blazed out a final injunction to the circle of watchers.

Just then, a guitar started playing in the distance, followed by weak shouts, cheering, and dogs barking. At this sudden commotion, everyone stopped what they were doing, lifted their heads, and sat up. They looked round, craning to see. Some rose stiffly to their feet. People were moving with excitement towards the far end of the compound.

There, the wide wire gate had been forced open to allow a large handcart loaded with provisions and a maypole to rumble through the gap, accompanied by smiling locals from a nearby country town. The homeless people crowded around them, laughing with thankful relief.

Walking along to one side, smiling as he watched the small procession go by, was the busker, Captain Guitaro. Wearing his multi-coloured coat and wide-brimmed, plumed hat, he was strumming a tune as they all streamed past. Behind him came the members of 'The Landing Party', all now dressed in early Colonial costumes—the young woman, with her wild red hair and long linen skirt, on fiddle; the clean-shaven man, in first settler's knee-britches and tricorn hat, blowing a tin whistle; his bearded companion, wearing braces and a collarless shirt, plucking a banjo; the Aboriginal, in loin-cloth and body paint, burring through a didgeridoo; and the boy, in a yellow and black convict's uniform, banging a small drum—joining in with him as he began to sing:

Come gather round, friends
And I'll tell you a story
About a man of whom history books sing
They sing of his greatness
They sing of his glory
But they don't tell everything
About Harold
Harold
Harold
Harold
Last of the Saxon kings

On the crowded waste ground, a bonfire was soon lit and trestle tables set up, while little boys and girls ran about, jumping for joy as the maypole was raised. Wine casks and beer bottles were opened, and *joie de vivre* prevailed. Around a portable barbecue sizzling with sausages, homeless people and townspeople feasted together at the tables, laughing merrily, all talking at once.

People hugged each other in gratitude and, here and there, kisses were shared in outpourings of revived tenderness. As the warmth of the sun broke through, a weather-beaten swaggie sat back against a cartwheel, his eyes closed in contentment, puffing on a fat cigar.

Deeds of the patriot
Courage and conquest
Still hold a familiar ring
But they can't describe
What moves a man deepest
No, they don't even begin
To show Harold
Harold
Harold
Harold
Last of the Saxon Kings

With trepidation, two hungry young boys approached a table laden with sandwiches and cakes. One of them put out his hand, then hesitated, and looked timidly up at the plump woman standing there before them, her cheeks red as apples, with a floral scarf tied around her head. She gave him a cheerful smile.

'Go on, luvvie, 'elp yerself!' she said brightly. 'Everything's free! Take what you want and some for luck!'

The boys' dark-ringed eyes lit up in gratitude. Beaming their thanks to her, they both tucked in.

Further back, in a cleared space in the centre of the compound, two circles of revellers holding onto coloured streamers were skipping around the maypole in opposite directions.

They don't say where his heart was
They don't speak of his dreams
They don't tell of the love of his life
They don't know what that means

All of a sudden, in the midst of the festivities, a squad of Saxon policemen dressed in navy blue uniforms and pudding-basin caps, carrying wooden batons, marched onto the waste ground, led by a moustachioed sergeant. Striding along beside him at the front was the imperious figure of a Norman knight, wearing a high, conical helmet with a long nose guard, and a dark three-piece suit and tie under his half-open, long mailed coat.

Raising his arm, the knight brought the column to a halt. After giving an order to the sergeant, for a few moments he stood arguing toe-to-toe with him, gesticulating angrily at the crowd. A ripple of trepidation ran through the bystanders, which soon turned to outright panic as the sergeant gave a reluctant nod and, putting a whistle to his lips, blew the signal for his men to break up the gathering.

Uproar followed as the police moved in, lashing out to right and left with their batons. Amid yelling and screaming, as the tables and barbecue were overturned, and the fires kicked out, the merry makers scattered.

They say greatness is measured
By physical prowess
And glory by victory's sting
But what makes a hero
And what makes a coward is
His fight for the light within
He was Harold
Harold

Harold
Harold
Last of the Saxon Kings

The dancers at the maypole stopped and fled in fear, leaving their vacant ribbons spinning in the air. All around them, those townspeople and refugees who tried to resist were beaten, while others were dragged off under arrest.

One by one, the band members were forced to leave, until only Captain Guitaro was left playing. Finally, he, too, was shoved away by the police. With a sad smile and a shake of his head, he sauntered after them. Nearing the gate, he looked back once over his shoulder, with regret—across the debris of overturned tables, scattered food, and broken bodies, to the maypole, its tattered streamers dangling and forlorn, like a bride left ravished by her feudal lord. High above, the pitying sky was cobalt blue.

*

The next morning, with the aid of her wooden staff, her woollen poncho thrown back and a wicker basket hanging over one arm, Vera Swanneck, a sturdy, majestic woman in her late fifties, hurried with purposeful strides up the road leading to the front of her white weatherboard house. At the same time, a group of injured men and women, some being helped along by family or friends, one on crutches, others bandaged and limping, came hobbling down the slope towards her. As they went past, Vera nodded to them with a grim smile. One tipped his hat to her.

Meanwhile, inside the house, in a whitewashed back bedroom that had been converted into a makeshift hospital, Vera's daughter, Edith, was busy clearing up after a night treating those injured in the police attack. In her late twenties, she was tall and

52

slender. Her face, with its pale complexion and earthy beauty, wore the healthy outdoor blush of a classic English rose.

Her sleeves were rolled up, and her firm breasts pushed against the stained white apron covering her navy blue shift as she reached down to retrieve the bits of cotton wool, lint, and soiled bandages littering the floor. While depositing them in a waste bin, a strand of her long blonde hair, tied back in a ponytail, fell loose across her warm brown eyes. Pushing it back behind her ear, Edith lifted a white enamel bowl of discoloured water and straightened up.

Looking once more around the room for any forgotten pieces of rubbish and finding none, Edith turned towards her companion.

'I'll just remove this. Can you manage here, Glad?' she asked. Her clear, melodic voice had a soft London accent to it, with a discernible Aussie lilt.

Sitting on the edge of one of the two single beds, Gladys, her older, robust, portly friend, was busy bandaging the arm of Mr Jenkins, a stout, florid, middle-aged local shopkeeper. Perched in rigid attention on a Bentwood chair next to them was his buxom wife, with a pork pie hat on her head, wearing a tight woollen overcoat and clutching a handbag.

Gladys nodded, gripping a safety pin in her mouth. 'Mm...' she murmured. She removed the pin and stuck it into the bandage. 'No worries...Nearly done.'

Edith left the room. As she made her way along the narrow hallway, careful to keep the liquid from slopping up over the sides of the bowl, from somewhere ahead of her came the voice of a disc jockey on a radio.

'Well, we all know who the Harold in this song is, but no one seems to be able to identify the lady. I wonder who she is? Riding high in the charts, here's "Captain Guitaro and The Landing Party".'

With that, a violin struck up, followed by a solo guitar. Then, as the full band came in on their instruments, Captain Guitaro's rich, engaging tones resonated throughout the house, crooning a tender love song.

Oh, Harold's in love with a lady
The lady of the hill
He said that she's the fairest
And he loves her still

Though he's away
So far from home
Across the wide blue sea
Yes, Harold's in love with a lady
And her true love is he

As the song continued, Edith entered the spacious lounge, with its polished boards, thick rug, a brick fireplace faced by twin padded armchairs and a long couch, and an open piano against the wall. She crossed the room and stepped down into a small laundry leading off to the side. Walking over to the large stone sink under the window, she emptied the bowl and ran the tap. On the shelf above her, a transistor radio was playing.

The kiss they shared
At his goodbye
The promise he did make
Means that Harold's in love with a lady
Or else her heart will break

With a heavy sigh, she reached up and switched the music off before the next verse could begin. Drying her hands on a towel, she turned off the tap and for a few moments stood gazing wistfully out through the window. Just then, Gladys leaned in at the open doorway.

'The last of them's just going, Edith.'

'Thanks, Glad.' Edith hung up the towel and removed her apron. 'While I see them out, would you mind looking in on Edmund for me, please? He should still be asleep.'

'Will do,' Gladys nodded and hurried away.

Edith went back into the lounge, over to where Mrs Jenkins was helping her husband towards the front door. He had his arm in a sling.

'Get him straight home to bed now, Mrs Jenkins,' she said with an encouraging smile.

'I will, Miss Swanneck, and thanks for everything.'

'Thanks for all your help, Miss,' echoed Mr Jenkins, as she opened the door for them. Following behind his wife, he stopped on the threshold. 'Those damned Normans'll pay for this when the Godwins get back, you mark my words!'

Edith nodded wearily. 'Goodbye.'

As they shuffled away, she remained standing in the doorway, lost in thought, not noticing her mother's arrival up the garden path until she was almost upon her.

'Edith! Just let me unload these herbs,' Vera exclaimed with excitement, as she swept past her into the house. 'You have to come with me!'

'Where to, Mum?' Edith smiled in surprise, following her into the kitchen.

'The King's procession's coming down the knoll road. There's going to be a demonstration!' Vera replied, emptying her basket onto a benchtop.

'What? After yesterday?'

'*Because* of yesterday!'

'Knock, knock,' Gladys said, entering the room. 'He's sleeping like an angel,' she informed Edith. 'Bless his little cotton socks!'

'Thanks a lot, Glad,' Edith grinned.

'And it isn't any wonder, what with all the to-ing and fro-ing that's been going on all night,' Gladys tutted.

'Oh oh, she's off!' Vera laughed.

Gladys smiled at her. 'Hello, Vera.'

'Gladys, I have to drag Edith away for an hour or so. Will you be all right by yourself?'

'Of course, dear, we'll be fine.'

'Make yourself a cup of tea and put your feet up,' Edith suggested. 'It's been a long night.'

As they turned to leave, Vera paused. 'Gladys, you know I'd double your wages if I could.'

Pulling out a chair and sitting down, Gladys slipped off a shoe and began to massage her stockinged foot. 'That's nice,' she said, looking up at her.

'But I don't have the money.'

'Don't worry, dear, I'll just charge you triple when you've got some!'

With a chuckle, Vera led Edith out of the kitchen.

Exiting the house through the back door, they made their way down the long backyard. On either side of them were low outbuildings and tin sheds. A few chickens, scratching about in the dirt, moved with noisy irritation out of their path as they went by.

Vera strode on ahead, thrusting her staff into the earth beside her, until they reached the far end and went out through a broken section of waist-high, bluestone wall. Beyond them, flanked on either side by dense woodland, rose a steep, grassy knoll. Turning to the right, they walked away around its base.

*

With flags flying in the breeze, spoked wheels turning, pennons waving, gloved fists gripping handlebars, high nose-guarded helmets gleaming, and the buzzing scream of lightweight motorcycle engines shattering the tranquil air, the royal procession came up the dusty, unmade road that ran past the back of the knoll.

At the head of the main body, sitting rugged-up in his motorcycle sidecar, was King Edward, the gaunt, white-bearded, half-Norman Saxon monarch, his goggles down over his eyes, and his straggly, grey hair blowing out around him in the breeze from beneath a leather flying cap.

Following behind him were other sidecars and a column of Norman knights, mounted two-abreast on motorbikes with pennons attached to their panniers. Meanwhile, riding out in front of the procession were two liveried heralds holding up the Norman and Saxon flags.

As they roared along beneath the canopy of trees, the King looked across at the man travelling beside him in a second sidecar. Only half his own age—with his short dark hair shaven up above his ears at the back and sides, his broad shoulders and thrusting chest stretching the material of the burgundy jacket buttoned up over his thick neck, his strong jaw clenched, and his thin lips set in a tight smile—his Norman cousin, William, sat with military bearing, gripping the door of the capsule, enjoying the sensation of speed.

At the edge of the road, a family of locals heading off to market on their push bikes moved out of the way and wobbled up onto the bank as the column raced past. One of them zig-zagged crazily and fell off into the bushes. Brushing the leaves and twigs from his face, he struggled to his feet and angrily shook his fist.

Not even noticing them, King Edward returned to his reverie, thinking about his life. Born the son of Saxon royalty, in order to protect him from the violent power struggles of the time he had spent his youth hidden away in a monastery in Normandy, the land of his mother. While there, he had been befriended by his cousin, the all-powerful Duke of the Normans.

Then, ten years ago, still grieving over the recent unsolved murder of his younger brother, and reluctant to leave his untroubled, other-worldly way of life behind him, he had been persuaded by the now exiled Earl Godwin—the man he was almost certain had been his brother's killer—to fill the vacant Saxon throne. Although he hadn't been able to prove anything, he thought to himself with angry contempt, he'd still managed to damn well throw him out!

So, encouraged and supported by Duke William, he had returned, accompanied by his Norman favourites, to take up the crown and wait for the chance to get rid of the Earl, which he had done at the first opportunity. Celibate and pious in the extreme—to the point where, with some jocularity, he knew, his subjects called him 'the Confessor'—such was his saintly ambition that he had even consented to marry the Earl's daughter.

'That should keep a lid on him!' he muttered aloud with terse satisfaction at the thought of it. He takes my brother, I take her. Revenge is sweet!

The King lifted his head and smiled at the sunshine, breathing in the warm, rushing air. And now, here he was, enjoying the company of his cousin on his State visit, thus demonstrating to his subjects his armed protection, while reassuring him of his continued safety and peace of mind.

'Ah!' he sighed contentedly. 'Peace of mind!'

Just then, lining the road up ahead, a small but vociferous crowd of jeering demonstrators came into view. Brandishing anti-Norman placards, demanding *Out, Normans! Out!*, *Go home William!*, and *Bring back the Godwins!*, they were pushing against a cordon of police who, with arms linked, were straining to hold them back.

At the same time, Vera and Edith came out of the trees at the base of the knoll and, making their way down the slope through the bushes, joined in at the edge of the crowd. Leaving her mother, Edith quickly squeezed her way through the press of bodies to get a better view.

As the procession drew closer to them, the demonstrators grew angrier and noisier. With raucous shouts and curses, they finally broke through the cordon and surged forward onto the road, carrying Edith along with them. Seeing the vanguard revving their engines and roaring towards them, with a flurry of blows from their batons the Saxon police fought to regain control, forcing the men back, leaving a few stragglers behind, including Edith, in the path of the oncoming riders. In the desperate scramble to get out of the way as the heralds approached, she was knocked to the ground.

Seconds later, the vanguard raced by in a cloud of red dust, followed by the rest of the column. As he sailed past the yelling, furious crowd, Duke William, standing erect in his sidecar, stared down at Edith lying in the dirt. For a moment his cold eyes met hers, before he swept on by up the road.

While the last of the riders came through, Vera pointed in desperation at her daughter and was finally allowed through by the police, who continued holding the crowd at bay.

'Edith!' Vera cried, rushing to her side.

'It's all right, Mum, I'm not hurt,' Edith answered, wiping the dust from her face and pushing herself onto her knees.

As Vera struggled to help Edith up, there was the sound of an engine stopping behind them. They both looked round to see a young Japanese knight sitting there on his motorbike.

'Are you injured, Lady?' he asked in a clipped but concerned voice, stretching out a gloved hand, ignoring the aggressive taunts of the nearby protesters.

Edith hesitated for a moment, then took hold of it. 'No, I'm fine, thank you. Just a bit winded, that's all.'

The knight pulled her to her feet. 'I am glad.' He bent forward at the waist. 'My name is Iko. May I know yours?'

She gave him a quizzical look. 'It's Edith,' she replied.

'I am sorry to meet you under such circumstances, Lady Edith.'

'So am I,' she said, dusting herself down.

Iko tilted his head. 'Forgive me, Lady, but your accent sounds Norman?'

'Yeah? Well I come from that part of the world,' she answered, without further explanation.

'Which you bastards have enslaved with your class system and your lust for money, and your damned love of war!' Vera interrupted with a snarl, putting a protective arm around her.

'Because we are born into it, madam, does not mean that we all agree with it,' Iko retorted calmly.

'Well, do something about it, then! Talk's cheap! We live in freedom here and we don't need you or your bloody New World Order!'

'But thank you for your concern, Sir Iko,' Edith interceded, as scornful laughter and applause came from the remaining onlookers.

Iko inclined his head with a warm but guarded smile. 'As they say here, Lady, it is all good!' With that, he bowed to Edith, gave a swift, curt nod to Vera, and sped off up the road.

'Mum, your language!' Edith teased her with a laugh, taking hold of her arm.

'Oh, they're so arrogant!' Vera scowled as Iko rode away, while the crowd yelled after him with howls of derision. 'They think they can ride roughshod over people. Just knock 'em down, and then stick out a hand and expect everyone to thank them!'

'He was only trying to help.'

'The only help we need is for Godwin to come back!' Vera growled. 'He'd make the King get rid of that cousin of his and his Norman thugs!' Giving Edith's arm an affectionate squeeze, she watched with her as the royal procession disappeared into the distance.

*

Coming up a rise further along the road, King Edward raised his hand, bringing the column to a halt. Instantly, Duke William leaped out of his seat and hurried over to him.

'I say, Edward, are you all right?' he exclaimed in a highly pronounced, upper class English voice.

'Completely unharmed, thanks, William. A bit surprised, perhaps.' The King rose to his feet. 'Come on, let's stretch our legs.' Giving the Duke his hand, he stepped down from his sidecar.

'Dash it all, Edward! How can you allow that to happen?' the Duke remonstrated as they walked away across an open stretch of scrubby ground. 'If this was Normandy, those hired louts would've been hanging by their balls from a prison cell ceiling long before they even got *near* this road!'

'I'm sure you mean well, William, but I don't need to be told how to run my own kingdom, thank you.'

'I'm sorry, Edward. It's just that I'm so concerned for you.'

'I know, cousin,' King Edward smiled. 'Look, a certain amount of freedom can be risky, I'll grant you, but in the long run we've always found it to be most beneficial. It allows people to let off steam and helps keep them more easily under the yoke. Why, if we tried to suppress every show of discontent, we'd end up with a police state on our hands. Much too precarious. Far too much work!'

'Still, somebody allowed that to happen. Somebody was bought.'

'Well, this was Godwin territory, y'know. Old allegiances die hard.'

'All the more reason to crush him, then.'

'You can't crush Godwin,' the King laughed.

'Why? Because he's in exile?'

'No. Because he represents an idea. His son, Harold, stands for it even more than he does. The lazy working classes and all those good-for-nothing young layabouts think he's a hero. I'm told they even sing love songs about him! Together they've captured the public imagination. People think they'll bring back some kind of mythical lost freedom, a life of "she'll be right, mate!' and 'no worries!"'

'Bah! Freedom from what? They've got too much of it already, if you ask me!'

King Edward's voice went up a notch, growing heated. 'Freedom from the rule of law, damn it! From moral judgements and sound values decided on by *my* government!'

'Anarchy!'

'Exactly! And that's why we had them banished. No, William, suppression isn't the answer. The only way to kill an idea is to undermine it, to take it apart from within, sap its credibility. Godwin's strength is his sons, of whom only Harold and Tostig count for anything. The rest are merely bit players.' With a chuckle, the King hoisted up his robes and began to urinate into the bushes. 'It's like a game of chess, really.'

As he politely turned his back, understanding dawned on the Duke's face. 'With Harold and Tostig as his knights. And you've already taken his queen by marrying his daughter!' he exclaimed.

'And Godwin thought he was buying power by suggesting it to me, the poor, deluded fool! Meanwhile, Tostig has just married your wife's sister, which makes him family...'

'And so removes him from the board!'

'Now do you see?' King Edward grinned, rearranging his clothes. 'Marrying Matilda was a very smart move, William.'

'I'm beginning to think you're right!'

The King laid a fingertip against the Duke's cheek. 'And then, as I promised you, dear cousin, when I die the kingdom passes to you and so is made safe.'

'I'm extremely grateful for your trust, Edward, and you know I'll take jolly good care of it, but you'll still be king for a long time yet, I'm sure.'

'Sometimes I hope not. My heart's just not in it any more. I've tried my best and I think I've done a reasonable job...'

'People say you're a saint.'

'I know! I know!' King Edward laughed tiredly. 'Well, perhaps I am. Still, I do yearn for freedom myself, from all these worldly cares. To take my rest and hopefully get some small reward for all my efforts,' he sighed. 'Come on, we'd better head back.'

'But, what about Harold? He could still cause us trouble.'

'Don't worry,' the King replied, as they approached the waiting procession. 'What can he do with you firmly on the throne and his own brother in your pocket? Assuming, of course, that he and his father dare show their faces again!'

'Mm,' the Duke murmured. 'Look, if you ever *do* need help, Edward, in dealing with Harold or anybody else, you won't hesitate to ask, will you?' He helped the King back into his sidecar. 'My chaps are always eager for a good scrap, y'know.'

'Thanks, William, but let's hope it doesn't come to that.' King Edward pulled down the lower lid of one eye in shared secret meaning. 'I'm sure we can get the house in order before the new tenant arrives, eh?' he chuckled. 'Now, home for tea!'

4

As their last remaining darts thudded into the outline of the Norman infantryman drawn with chalk on a wooden board propped up against the back of a hot dog stand, the pair of young boys quickly ran up to collect them. Then, laughing with excitement, they continued hurling their missiles at the target.

All around them, on the edge of the small park, crowds were gathering. Rising above the general hubbub, vendors could be heard calling out their wares. Nearby, other stalls faced onto the city thoroughfare, lined on both sides by expectant townspeople held back by police. Suddenly, a great cheer went up as the royal procession came past.

Smiling from his sidecar, King Edward waved a limp hand to the excited throng, many of them taking photographs and selfies or talking animatedly into their phones, and nearly all waving little blue and silver Norman flags.

Among the line of cheering faces, a number of stony-faced Saxons, not waving flags, glared at the King and his guests as they went by, staring after them in anger as they rode on down the street and in through the wrought-iron gates of the palace.

*

Taking the steps two at a time, Duke William bounded up the last flight of wooden stairs to the upper landing. Meanwhile, plodding with laboured breath behind him, came Bishop Odo, his lean, balding American half-brother, loosening the black clerical collar under his loud check suit as he climbed.

Bringing up the rear were Baron Fitzosborne, the Head of the army—a burly Prussian, with close-cropped hair, and a walrus moustache hanging down below his pock-marked, bulbous nose—and Taillefer, a swarthy Afrikaner, with a shaggy oval of blond facial hair around his fleshy mouth, wearing a battered slouch hat with a wide, leopard-skin band.

'Have you seen what they ride here, Fitz?' Taillefer laughed with contempt, the clump of his riding boots echoing up the staircase. 'They're so damn quiet! No noise! No speed!'

'You're right, Taillefer!' the Baron barked back and shook his clenched fist. 'Zese Saxons have no balls! Zey just dawdle around like sheep!'

As the Duke reached the top and strode across to the door of his apartment a pretty, young chambermaid suddenly arrived along the corridor. 'Oh, I'm sorry, sir! I didn't know you were back!' she exclaimed in a timid voice.

'Come in, my dear, come in!' he beckoned, pushing open the door.

'Shall I pull your bath for you now, my Lord?' she asked with uncertainty, as they all entered.

Duke William and Bishop Odo exchanged raised eyebrows and salacious looks.

'You can pull whatever you like, my sweet!' the Duke smiled, showing a broad set of white teeth. Seeing her baffled look, he waved his hand in dismissal. 'Yes, go on then.'

Blushing, the girl escaped into the adjoining bathroom and shut the door. Duke William turned away and began to unbutton his jacket. 'Do the honours would you, Fitz,' he called over his shoulder.

While Baron Fitzosborne walked over to a dark mahogany sideboard, unscrewed a bottle, and poured them all a glass of red wine, Bishop Odo went back to the door and closed it.

He spun round to the Duke. 'Well?' he asked with an eager smile.

'Well what?'

'Well, what did the old fart say?'

Accepting his drink from the Baron, Duke William paused, staring at them both. Suddenly, he laughed out loud. 'It's mine! He reaffirmed it! When he dies, the kingdom comes to me!'

'That's great!' The Bishop smiled. He raised his glass 'So here's to the next king of this virgin land. My brother. Congratulations!'

'Half-brother,' Duke William grinned at him, chinking glasses.

Bishop Odo shook his head and sighed. 'How cruel is fate!'

'And soon ze ruler of ze whole world!' toasted Baron Fitzosborne.

The Duke bowed. 'I thank you!' As they all chuckled, he breathed in deeply through his nose. 'Aah! It smells like Normandy already!'

'I dunno, Billy-boy,' the Bishop gave a sceptical shake of his head. 'I got a feelin' some of these Saxons are still resistin' the Spirit.'

'Don't worry, brother,' Duke William smiled at him. 'The toe of my boot up their arses'll soon remove any blockage! Now, drink up, gentlemen, we'd better get ready for the banquet.'

Bishop Odo yawned and stretched out his arms. 'I guess this means another of cousin Edward's *amazingly* boring affairs!'

'Tiny plates of food, watered-down wine, and sanctimonious songs,' grumbled Baron Fitzosborne. 'Pah! Must he always be so devout?'

'Always!' the Duke laughed.

'Yeah, the King's as gentle as a dove, even with his stomach,' the Bishop added with rueful sarcasm.

'Yes,' Duke William nodded. 'But as wily as a serpent when he wants to be.'

At that moment, the bathroom door opened and the chambermaid reappeared. 'Your bath is ready for you now, sir.'

'Ah, good!' the Duke answered, his eyes lighting up, looking her up and down. 'So, my friends, I'll see you all shortly. And Tai,' he called after him, as they began to file out. 'Bring your instrument with you, will you, there's a good chap?'

'What had you in mind, boss?' Taillefer grinned.

'Something stirring, I think.' Duke William's gaze lingered on the chambermaid. 'Mm...something definitely stirring!' With lascivious chuckles, they all went out, closing the door behind them. 'Now, my sweet,' he smiled, undoing his shirt. 'I'd say it's high time we had a little feel to see if it's ready to plunge in, wouldn't you?'

As he put his arm around her, with a cry of fear she squirmed out of his grasp and fled to the door. The Duke watched her go.

'Ah, well,' he sighed with amusement, 'there's always one fish that escapes the barrel!'

With a shrug, he turned and went into the bathroom, kicking the door shut behind him with his heel.

*

King Edward sat with his eyes closed, stroking his long white beard, listening in rapture to the singing of the choir.

Beside him was his Queen, the dark-haired, only daughter of Earl Godwin. Full-breasted and short-statured from her mother's side, her chiselled, attractive face remained impassive as she watched the musicians with a critical eye.

Younger than the King by a good twenty years, their marriage had been one of convenience, completely devoid of physical passion. Nevertheless, while not sharing his all-consuming religious fervour, she had found solace in the trappings of the Church, especially in their mutual love of sacred music, and over time had become his devoted companion.

Despite having her heart's happiness bartered for political gain, she was still her father's daughter and had accepted her lot as being in the national interest. Like him, she detested everything Norman, in particular Duke William: not only for his autocratic world view and his total lack of social conscience, but also for bringing out the worst in her husband's dichotomous nature.

Masking her feelings, the Queen looked around the dining table, inspecting their guests. Seated beside her was the gruff, humourless Baron Fitzosborne, gritting his teeth and toying with the tiers of medal ribbons on his barrel chest. Not even courteous enough to pay attention, she thought with distaste.

Next to him, to his right, at the end of the table, was that odious and odorous ruffian, Taillefer, slumped back in his chair and gazing fixedly at the ceiling, obviously trying to block out the song. She could smell him from there!

On the other side of the King sat the insidious Duke, pomaded and smoothly shaven, dressed in a royal blue caftan jacket with silver buttons. He seemed distracted, staring hard at the tablecloth, oblivious to everything.

Beyond him, at the far end, reclined the supercilious Bishop Odo, like some supreme pastor in his white suit with red bib and black collar, his hands clasping the gold medallion lying on his spindly midriff, with his eyes shut, apparently savouring the performance. With an inaudible sigh, she turned away and retreated once more into the song.

Meanwhile, below the dais occupied by the royal party, a hundred or so Norman knights and pro-Norman members of the Saxon Court were dining at half a dozen long white-clothed tables. Waiters in uniforms scurried about the room distributing plates of food and replenishing drinks, to be met with scathing looks and sullen frowns at the meagre fare. All the diners wore full evening dress. The Queen was the only woman present.

Within a low enclosure to one side, a small choir of monks, watched by a silent group of musicians, were singing an a cappella chant in the round, their voices overlapping, echoing in rotation throughout the dark, wood-panelled banquet hall.

We praise God with our lamentation
Making solemn each celebration
We don't always feel it
But it's our vocation
And the training is hard

We don't play or take physical pleasure
Through self-denial we can measure
Our own non-attachment
And our spiritual treasure
But the training is hard

We draw strength from our holy relics
The pure example of those saintly clerics
Saves us from a life of
Emotional hysterics
Yet the training is hard

We shall inherit a new tomorrow
Free from this world of sin and sorrow

And the lustful temptations
Of this body we borrow
Still the training is hard

As the song came to an end and the monks filed out, King Edward sighed with deep satisfaction, not noticing the lacklustre applause from the audience.

'Ah! Sheer delight!' he exclaimed. 'One of my very favourites! A little short, perhaps, but immensely uplifting!'

'Twenty minutes of zat garbage and he calls it short!' Baron Fitzosborne muttered under his breath, gripping his knife and fork in his large fists.

Nearby, Taillefer looked aghast at his almost empty plate. 'Is this all we get?' he scowled. 'A single chop, carrots, and two tiny potatoes!'

'A fine aid to the digestion, your Majesty,' Bishop Odo said with a smile from the other end of the table.

'Thank you, Bishop,' the King nodded. 'I must say it always brings tears to my eyes.'

'As I'm sure it has to us all, my Lord.'

'You don't seem to have enjoyed the singing, Duke William?' inquired the Queen, leaning forward to see him.

'I'm sorry, my Lady,' the Duke answered, stifling a yawn. 'I was preoccupied with the trip home.'

'Are you planning on leaving us so early?'

'In the morning, I'm afraid,' he nodded.

'Oh, what a pity,' she lamented, with barely veiled sarcasm.

'Oh dear, that soon?' said King Edward.

'I'm sorry, Edward. Duty calls.'

'Ah well, can't be helped.'

Duke William smiled and put his hand on the King's arm. 'Look, cousin, how about we finish off this wonderful meal with a rousing Norman song? What d'you say I get Taillefer there, my minstrel, to do a turn for us?'

'Well, all right,' King Edward agreed with some trepidation, lowering his voice. 'Just don't forget I have to tread a fine line here, William. I need to keep the locals happy too, you know.'

The Duke drained his glass of white wine. 'Ah, what the hell!' he laughed. 'You can put the blame on me!'

With that, he gave a nod to Taillefer, who rose from his seat and stepped down to the enclosure to speak to the musicians.

There was a roaring cheer from the knights at the lower tables as Taillefer pulled a well-worn bass guitar from its case and, plugging it into a portable amplifier, began to thump out a rhythm with his thumb. A devilish gleam lit up his eyes as he looked at them and laughed. A moment later, with a broad grin, he threw back his head and roared out an up-tempo marching song in a deep, gravelly voice.

Almost at once, the Normans in the hall joined in, cheering and clapping, stamping their feet and banging their cups on the tables in time to the driving beat, and singing along in raucous union with each chorus. Meanwhile, the hapless musicians tried their best to follow the tune, but soon lost track and gave up in confusion.

We're carving out an empire to our name
A new world order borne upon the flame
We are the élite
Our power is complete
Survival of the fittest is our aim
We're capitalistic
Militaristic
Feudalistic
Opportunistic

Masters of the game

We are the Normans!
We are the Normans!
And if you should lose
It'll only be you
Who's to blame!

Hereditary title to the land
Puts us a cut above our fellow man
We're the upper class
Leaders to the last
A pedigree against which none can stand
With kindness cruel
We're born to rule
The fools it's true
Up school! Up school!
All wealth is in our hands

We are the Normans!
We are the Normans!
Taking more than our share
Isn't fair
But we don't give a damn!

Our market-place philosophy's the best
For making sure the weak don't pass the test
Our business-world mentality
Leaves no room for morality
Success is what we seek and nothing less
We're the head of the line
The fruit of the vine

In the Grand Design
Created to shine
Much brighter than the rest

We are the Normans!
We are the Normans!
And our privileges royal
Mean we're free from the toil
And the mess!

We're Normans and to serve us is your fate
We'll overcome your ignorance and hate
Our mighty iron fist
Makes it futile to resist
This vision of the future we dictate
We're the way you need
The truth to heed
The life to lead
Our noble breed
Is greater than the great!

We are the Normans!
We are the Normans!
We're the chosen ones
You'd better run
Before it's too late!

We are the Normans!

At its yelled finale, there was a deafening shout and thunderous applause from the knights. Amid the uproar, King Edward smiled with hesitancy at his Norman guests, then cast an anxious look in the direction of the Queen, who sat, tight-lipped and humourless, staring back at him.

*

Side by side, step by step, King Edward and Duke William slowly descended the wide staircase leading to the entrance hall of the palace. At its foot, two lines of uniformed palace staff stood rigidly to attention, forming an avenue towards the open front door. As they came down, the Duke took the King by the arm to assist him.

'Thank you, William,' King Edward smiled.

'Are you sure you'll be all right on your own with these awful Saxons, Edward?'

'Of course I will. There's life in the old dog yet, y'know. Or, as Bishop Odo would say, I still know how to kick ass!'

'Good!' Duke William laughed. 'But if they do ever get too much for you, just call me and I'll be straight over.'

'Don't worry, cousin, I'll be fine.'

'And you will keep your eye on those Godwins won't you, Edward? Especially Harold.'

'William...'

'Well, you never know.'

'Do you suggest I keep an eye on the Queen as well? She is the Earl's daughter, after all.'

'Oh, you know what I mean. Mind you, it never does any harm to put a woman in her place, if you ask me!' the Duke chuckled with chilling sincerity.

On reaching the bottom of the stairs, they proceeded along the aisle between the ranks and walked out together through the high, porticoed entrance, onto a balcony at the top of a wide flight of stone steps. Behind railings in the distance, the watching crowd cheered. At the foot of the steps, a column of mounted Norman knights waited with their engines running. There was another loud cheer from the crowd as King Edward and Duke William turned to each other and embraced.

'I probably won't see you again, William,' the King smiled. 'Not in this life anyway.'

'Don't be so silly, old boy, of course you will!' the Duke snorted. 'I'm only a stone's throw away. I'll pop over again in a year or two. Meanwhile, make sure you stay in touch, let me know what's going on.'

'I will,' King Edward nodded. 'Have a safe trip.'

Duke William bowed. 'Goodbye, Your Majesty,' he grinned. 'And thank you again for everything. For your hospitality, and your trust...not to mention your magnificent wedding presents!'

'Only the best for you, William.'

'I'd expect nothing less! Cheerio!'

With that, the Duke skipped down the steps towards his sidecar. At the same time, with a sneer, a hefty, unshaven man in the middle of the crowd adjusted his grip on a large tomato, weighing it in his hand; then, drawing back his arm, he hurled it towards the palace.

As Duke William reached the bottom, Baron Fitzosborne approached and saluted. 'We're ready to go, my Lord,' he informed him. All of a sudden, the over-ripe missile splattered onto the ground at their feet. 'What ze...?' he gasped.

The Baron spun round and glared in fury at the crowd. Beyond the railings there was a commotion as the police rushed in to arrest the culprit.

The Duke stared down at the burst fruit and the spray of juice on his trouser leg. 'Once this place is mine, Fitz,' he said with ice cold menace, 'the first thing these Saxons are going to get is a good hard lesson in Norman discipline!'

'I agree, my Lord. Zese scum need kicking into line!'

Duke William strode over to his sidecar and climbed in. 'And no one's going to stop me from doing it,' he snarled. 'No one!' He snapped his hand forward for his driver. 'Go!'

5

Night closed in quickly as the warm summer sun sank below the horizon. High in the sky, rose-coloured clouds drifted by and early stars appeared in the deepening blue.

In the fading light, with his brown hair blowing in the breeze, Harold, the thirty-two-year-old second son of Earl Godwin, stood staring out from the beaked prow of a decorated Polynesian war canoe.

Seated on benches behind him were a dozen bare-chested mariners wearing straw hats and white, half-mast trousers. With barely a splash, their long paddles dug into the waves in unison as they surged across the open sea.

Harold looked round. Sitting among the rowers, gripping the long handle of his oar, lifting and striking the blade with a powerful, seemingly effortless rhythm, was his blonde-haired, bearded brother, Gurth. Although a few years younger than him, he was his closest companion, his confidant and mainstay in the world of politics and power. Level-headed and serious-minded, Gurth could sometimes adopt a gruff exterior—just like their father, Harold reflected, thinking of where they were heading.

With his forehead creased in concentration, Gurth flashed him a happy grin. Harold laughed and pointed ahead. In the distance, coming closer, was the coastline of home.

*

To the torrid, frenzied beat of bongo drums, beneath the flickering, orange glow of flaming torches set on poles, the painted war canoe pulled up alongside the wooden jetty. The waiting crowd of supporters cheered with excitement as Harold leapt ashore and strode along the boardwalk, closely followed by Gurth. On reaching the end of the pier, the joyful, back-slapping throng parted to let them through into an open space, where their family stood waiting to welcome them.

Their father, Earl Godwin, walked forward, holding his arms out wide to greet them as they entered the circle. In his early sixties, he was grey-bearded and heavily built, wearing a worn sheepskin coat draped over his open-necked flannel shirt. His cheerful, booming voice rose above the din.

'Harold! My boy!'

'G'day, Dad!' Harold grinned as they wrapped their arms around each other to a roaring cheer from the gathering crowd.

Pulling apart with a laugh, the Earl took him by the shoulders. 'Let me look at you! You're back! We're all back! And this time it's to stay! Just listen to that welcome! We'll talk later, Harold. We have to make plans. But for now, say hello to your mother and your brothers.' He turned away. 'Gurth!'

As Earl Godwin greeted Gurth, Harold moved on down the line to his stout, homely, perennially anxious mother, Githa.

'Hello, Mum!' he smiled fondly.

'Harold!' she beamed up at him. 'My darling! I'm so glad you're safe!' They hugged each other tightly. 'I just can't believe it! We're all together again!'

'I know! It's wonderful!'

'Except for your sister, of course,' she added, with a note of regret.

'Don't worry, Mum, we'll see her soon,' Harold nodded.

'Oh, I've missed you all so much!' Githa cried with renewed happiness, hugging him to her again.

At that moment, Harold's taller, older brother, Sweyn, stepped forward with his six-year-old son, Haco, beside him.

'Hi, Harold!' he grinned.

'Sweyn! G'day!' Harold exclaimed, laughing and embracing him. 'It's great to be home, isn't it?'

'Yeah, I suppose so.' Sweyn gave a wan smile and sighed. 'It brings it all back though.'

Harold put his hand on his brother's shoulder. 'Come on, mate,' he said gently. 'Let it go.'

'It's no good, Harold, I've tried.'

Harold shook his head in dismay. Not wanting to pursue the subject there and then, he turned to Sweyn's son. 'And Haco!' he smiled, leaning down and hugging his nephew. 'How're y'going, kid?'

'Good,' Haco answered with a shy, disconcerting stare.

Harold ruffled his hair. 'You've grown so tall! Just like your lovely old dad!'

'Hello, old boy!' an aristocratic voice suddenly came from behind them.

Harold turned to see his next-youngest brother, Tostig, standing there, his dyed dark hair permed into tight curls and a large gold ring in one ear.

'Tostig, you old bastard!' Harold laughed. 'How's it been?'

Smaller all round than Harold, with the lean body and sleazy appearance of something half-way between an ex-amateur lightweight boxer and an over-the-hill flamenco dancer, Tostig's taut, hard-muscled frame was dressed in a tight-fitting black velvet suit. From under the wide collars of his white shirt, three long strings of fine silver chain looped down over his low-cut waistcoat.

Closest in age to Harold, he was a mixture of restless contradictions: nervy and nerveless, generous and greedy, at once vainglorious and a hard-done-by victim of life. In childhood they had been constant playmates, but over the years they had grown apart. Although Harold loved his brother dearly, apart from their shared sense of humour and some fond memories they didn't seem to have much in common any more; and he knew from painful experience to keep his guard up whenever he was around.

Tostig's ravaged good looks broke into a fleeting smile. 'Not bad, not bad,' he answered, as they clapped each other on the back. He nodded towards their father. 'Apart from being stuck with that cranky old bugger.'

'Hard yakka, eh?'

'Didn't let up for a bloody minute. Complained about everything. The food. The sanitation. You know what he thinks of foreigners.'

'What do you mean? Dad's always respected other nationalities.'

'Yeah, but he doesn't want them in the family, does he.'

'Ah, yes, I heard you'd got married, mate. Congratulations! I didn't think you'd ever fall in love, Tostig. What's her name?'

Tostig looked round and lowered his voice. 'It's Judith. I don't know about love. Her father's the head honcho over there. He gave her to me.'

'Gave her to you?'

'Well, let's say he smiled on the arrangement. And now, I suppose, I'm stuck with her. Still, she *is* closely related to Duke William, which at least gives me connections in the right circles.' Tostig leant closer. 'And she polishes the old cucumber like you wouldn't believe!'

'Nice one, Tostig!' Harold gave a shuddering laugh. 'You're as revolting as ever!'

All of a sudden, Tostig thrust out his arm with a theatrical flourish. 'And here she is! The light of my life!' he announced loudly, as his wife approached. 'Harold, this is Judith!'

Harold studied his new sister-in-law. Judith was small and compact, her striking Asian beauty marred by the hardness of her eyes and the sharp lines etched around her mouth. A force to be reckoned with if crossed, he thought to himself. Her bobbed, henna-dyed hair, resting in a curl on the padded shoulders of her light blue, corporate suit jacket, swayed from side to side as she sashayed towards them.

'Hello, Judith,' Harold greeted her with a grin, and shook hands. Then, as protocol demanded, he pecked her on the cheek.

'I am pleased to meet you, Harold,' Judith replied, giving him a wide, toothy smile. 'Baby has told me so much about you.'

Harold's eyebrows went up. 'Baby...? Ah...Well, all bad, I hope! Welcome to the family!'

Meanwhile, his fun-loving second-youngest brother, Leofwine, slim, handsome, and sporting a wide, trim moustache, had stepped up beside them.

'Leo!' Harold greeted him fondly.

'Hey, Harold!' They hugged each other with easy affection. 'That was some entrance, man! Where'd you get the paddles?'

'Oh, just something we picked up in the islands. Thought we'd arrive in style! Great to see you, mate!' Harold pointed at his moustache. 'But what's that on your lip?'

'It's his pet caterpillar!' Tostig snorted.

'Don't listen to him, Leo,' Harold nodded in apparent sober reflection. 'I think it looks very dashing.'

'Laugh all you like, y'bastards, the girls love it!' Leofwine grinned, with lighthearted, youthful confidence. 'They say it tickles their fancies!'

Amid their laughter, their youngest brother, fifteen-year-old Wolnoth, walked over to them.

'G'day, Wol!' Harold smiled warmly.

'Hello, Harold,' Wolnoth replied with hesitant formality.

Harold gave him a hug. 'How are you, mate? Had a good holiday?'

'It wasn't exactly a holiday, Harold,' Wolnoth answered. 'Dad did send me to school while we were over there, you know.'

'Oh, right. Anyway, what was it like?'

Wolnoth visibly brightened. 'It was great! I met loads of Normans. And Tostig introduced me to Duke William when he came to visit. That's what I'm going to be when I'm older, a Norman knight. They're the coolest!'

Harold looked aghast at Leofwine.

'Amazing!' Leofwine grinned back, shaking his head in disbelief.

Just then, the commanding voice of Earl Godwin interrupted them.

'My friends!' The Earl threw up his hands for silence. The drumbeats stopped. 'My friends...And my sons!'

The crowd broke into wild, enthusiastic cheering, their faces filled with expectant excitement.

'Now we're all together again, it's time to make up for lost ground, to regain control of our own country and our own destiny!'

There were loud cries of agreement.

'The King is in his palace, no doubt listening to the poisonous advice of his pro-Norman advisors...'

At this, there were angry shouts and general booing.

'And I bet thet're just itching to see what we're going to do.'

The crowd went quiet in anticipation.

'Well, I'll tell you what we're going to do. First thing in the morning, we're marching to the capital!' The Earl smiled at their unanimous roar of approval. 'But that's tomorrow. For now, I thank you all for coming out to greet us, for your vocal and very rhythmic support...'

There was a ripple of good-natured laughter.

'The food is laid out, the beer's on tap, the evening is ready and waiting. Come and get warm, enjoy the music, and let's savour this moment together. Tomorrow, we go. But tonight...we party!'

As a great cheer went up, the racing bongo beat began again.

Watching the proceedings from the edge of the crowd was the sandy-haired reporter, Eric Braithwaite, wearing his familiar safari jacket. He turned away and spoke into a hand-held microphone connected to a small tape recorder hanging over his shoulder.

'Well, there you have it. The Godwins are re-united at last! After a long year in exile, they've thrown caution to the wind and come back to force a showdown. And now the cat is *really* among the pigeons! Tomorrow, Earl Godwin and his army of supporters head for the capital. What awaits them there is anybody's guess. The King, more than anyone, must be fully aware of the gravity of the situation.

'And what a dilemma he's in. Does he give his loyalty to Normandy, where he was raised, or to his subjects here who obviously want the Godwins back? And how will the fact that his wife is the Earl's daughter affect the stormy relationship between these two men? There are great changes on the horizon. Whether for good or ill, the next few days will tell...This is Eric Braithwaite, for the *Anglo-Saxon Chronicle*, on the south coast.'

He switched off the tape recorder and removed the cassette. 'Lenny?' he called over his shoulder.

Moments later, his young assistant, a pimply, freckle-faced youth in a back-to-front baseball cap and an *Anglo-Saxon Chronicle* t-shirt, hurried over to him. 'Right here, Mister Braithwaite.'

Braithwaite handed him the tape. 'There you go, Lenny. Grab your bike and get this back to the office as fast as you can.'

'You bet, Mister Braithwaite!' Lenny grinned with self-importance and rushed off through the crowd.

*

'Damn it, I *know* Godwin's guilty!' King Edward rasped from the head of the oval conference table.

'But that was never proved, Your Majesty,' cautioned Bishop Alred, the President of the Council, seated nearby. Middle aged, with thinning dark hair, his calm face was lined with worldly wisdom and political prudence. He preferred to keep a grip on the tiller of State with a firm hand inside a velvet glove. 'And Godwin denied it.'

'His lust for power's proof enough for me!' the King retorted with a dismissive flick of his hand.

'I agree with you, my Lord,' said the Minister for Homeland Security from the opposite side. Beneath a black, brilliantined quiff, his course red face was chapped from too much use of an electric razor and an astringent aftershave. He leant forward on his elbows, interlocking the ribbed fingers of his black leather gloves, and glared at the Bishop. 'The man's capable of anything!'

'The Minister for Homeland Security is completely out of order, Your Majesty!' Bishop Alred protested. 'Such personal comments are both unhelpful and uncalled for!'

'Well, you only have to look at him!' the Minister scoffed, sitting back and dusting the flecks of dandruff from the lapels of his dark pinstripe suit.

'Why don't you put a sock in it, mate!' snapped Earl Siward, the Commander of the Army, from the far end of the table. A burly, bearded Dutchman in his late sixties, he was fiercely anti-Norman and a staunch supporter of Earl Godwin.

The Minister swiveled round in his seat. 'What? How dare you?'

Siward ignored him. 'Look, Your Majesty, this is getting us nowhere. We know that your brother was killed...'

'Murdered, you mean,' growled the Minister.

'Rubbed out to put the frighteners on his Royal Highness and make him give up the throne!' exclaimed the Treasurer in a heavy Bronx accent, sitting next to him, closer to the King. Small and dapper, with crinkly, lacquered hair, a craggy face, a pencil moustache, and a gold front tooth, he wore a green velvet jacket over a satin waistcoat decorated with playing cards. 'And the finger was pointed straight at Godwin!'

'*Some* fingers were, you mean,' Siward replied sharply. 'There was no evidence that he was ever involved.' He turned to the King. 'All right, you think there was, my Lord, but the fact still remains that in a court of law he was declared innocent.'

'Bah!' King Edward spat with contempt.

'Anyway,' Siward continued, 'none of this has any bearing on why he and his sons were actually banished.'

'Other than to raise the possibility, Your Majesty, that perhaps your judgement of his actions wasn't entirely impartial?' suggested Bishop Alred, coming to the Earl's assistance.

'I beg your pardon?' the King gasped with indignance.

'What an outrageous accusation!' the Minister scowled.

The Treasurer spread his hands in warning. 'Hey, that ain't just slander you're talking there, pal. That's treason!'

'I'll have you know, Bishop Alred, that I'm quite able to tell the difference between righteousness and evil,' King Edward informed him with icy disdain. 'Especially when it comes to Godwin!'

Seated next to Bishop Alred, Archbishop Stigand, the aloof, lantern-jawed Primate of the Saxon Church, nodded his agreement.

'Earl Siward,' he said in a patronising voice, gazing at him over his tinted glasses, 'Godwin and his sons were justly banished because he refused to carry out a direct order from his King to punish a butchering mob. Which you, as Commander of our armed forces, may be required to do yourself in the not too distant future.'

'He refused, Archbishop Stigand,' Siward replied with unruffled tenacity, 'because that mob, as you call them, were local townspeople incensed at having their own families raped and killed by the king's Norman guests.'

'Damn it all! They had diplomatic immunity!' the Minister thundered across the table.

'They were innocently on their way to visit the King!' spluttered the Treasurer.

'And if there was any truth to the charge, which those who survived strongly denied, it was probably just high spirits and too much wine!' the Minister scoffed haughtily.

'Either way, such behaviour can't be condoned,' the Archbishop insisted. 'Killing the King's guests is beyond the pale. They had to be punished, there was no question about it.'

Siward shook his head in wonderment. 'You blokes, you're amazing. To get to the point, Your Majesty, you then called on Godwin to appear before you and he refused, saying he was being set up by the Normans. So, you immediately sent him and his family into exile. Well, now he's back.'

'At the head of an army,' added Archbishop Stigand. 'Don't forget that.'

'An army,' Siward replied, 'made up of nothing more than ordinary citizens who think he's innocent. As I do. And the question remains, what do we do about it?'

'Well, I say we attack!' snarled the King.

'And I say, my Lord, we must listen to them!' Siward demanded.

'People'll think you've gone soft, Sire,' the Minister snorted.

'If we give in, Your Majesty, it'll hurt the economy,' the Treasurer warned. 'The share market would plummet!'

'It costs us nothing to give Godwin a hearing,' urged Bishop Alred. 'An armed confrontation might mean the destruction of the city. It could even lead to civil war.'

King Edward gestured towards the Archbishop. 'Stigand?'

'My Lord, I believe that for people of the same blood and the same culture to kill each other, except under extreme circumstances, is a mortal sin.'

Siward gave a sarcastic laugh. 'What a profound distinction!'

'But these *are* extreme circumstances, Your Majesty,' the Minister objected strenuously. 'Give the signal, not only for war, but for truth, justice, and the rule of law!'

'The truth is all Godwin's after,' Siward insisted. 'To be heard openly and fairly, without Norman-vested interests calling the tune.'

'I damn well take offence at that, Earl Siward!' the Treasurer seethed.

'Take what you bloody well like to it, mate!' Siward answered. He turned towards the King. 'Godwin may be ambitious, Your Majesty, he may be a lot of things, but in all the years I've known him he's never once threatened violence against his own countrymen.'

'Well, what about all those ordinary citizens he's got with him now?' sneered the Minister. 'Don't you call them a threat?'

'One hell of a threat!' the Treasurer agreed.

'We need to call in the troops, Your Majesty,' the Minister warned. 'Strike first and ask questions later. They could go on the rampage at the drop of a hat!' He threw himself back in his seat and folded his arms with truculent finality.

'If I may finish, my Lord,' said the Archbishop. 'Much as I dislike their very presence, I am forced to agree with Earl Siward. These *are* merely Godwin's supporters, and not a paid army. And we do have his word that they'll disband as soon as Your Majesty grants his request for a formal hearing.'

Siward exhaled with relief. 'Thank you, Stigand.'

With a condescending smile, Archbishop Stigand tilted his head and gave a small nod in return.

'All right, all right! You've made your point!' King Edward exclaimed, squirming in his seat. He turned to the Treasurer and the Minister. 'Thank you for your loyalty, gentlemen, but on this occasion, much against our better judgement, we are persuaded that war is not the answer.'

He lifted his eyes to the ceiling and sighed with deep frustration, his knuckles going white as he gripped the arms of his chair. 'Oh, why must I suffer this endless stream of bullying and trivia?' He looked down the table at Siward and gave a vehement laugh. 'Godwin wants the truth? He can have it. And I hope it chokes him!'

*

Iko pounded up the wooden staircase and raced along the corridor, into the depths of the palace. Struggling to pull on a mailed coat over his suit and tie as he ran, he came to the door he was seeking and threw it open, bursting in on the dozen or so Norman knights who had been left to keep a presence at the Saxon court after the Duke's departure. They were sitting around the room relaxing, some dozing, spread-eagled over the arms of their chairs, others reading, drinking, and playing backgammon. They all looked up in surprise as Iko shut the door and leant back against it.

'The King has given in!' he panted. 'It is every man for himself!'

*

Duke William held the phone against his ear. While he listened, his gaze wandered out through the wide plate-glass window of his two-hundred-and-ninth-floor corner office, barely registering the tops of the surrounding office blocks or the sparkling river far down below, snaking through the capital.

'No...No...' he said into the mouthpiece, rolling his eyes, trying to control his impatience. 'I realise it's not your fault, Edward... No, I'm sure you had no other choice...Yes, I know...The worst kind of bullies...You're right, the people *are* gullible. That's why they need a firm hand...Of course you did, Edward.'

He swivelled round in his high-backed leather chair and drummed his fingers on the small stack of folders lying on the desk in front of him.

'Look, don't worry...That's right. Enough to hang themselves! But we'll need some kind of guarantee...No, money's no good... Exactly! It's the only way...Who?...No, not him, much too self-sacrificing! It'll have to be one of the younger ones...'

He opened the cover of a dossier marked *The Godwins* and leafed through its pages. 'Yes, Wolnoth'll do nicely...I agree...And Sweyn's brat, too. What's he called? ...Yes, Haco...Why not? All the more reason for them to behave themselves...Absolutely! All right?...Good...Yes, it'll be fine...But you won't let anything interfere with our agreement, will you, Edward?...That's right. I'm sorry to sound pushy, but...I knew you'd understand!...Yes, it is…For the good of the country…I know you do, cousin…Don't mention it…I hope so!…You, too…Yes, contact me as soon as you know…That's right. Thanks for ringing…Goodbye.'

He slammed down the receiver. 'Damn!' he shouted, thumping the desk with his fist. 'That bumbling idiot!'

*

Iko rushed headlong through the trees. The mob were hot on his heels, their echoing shouts and the crack of breaking branches still in the distance but getting nearer. He skidded to a halt, panting hard. His eyes wild with fear, he looked back for a moment. He held his breath, listening intently, gauging how far away they were. Too close! He ran on.

Coming out of the pine forest onto a dirt road, he turned and sprinted up it. Ahead of him, the way divided. Without hesitation he took the left-hand fork, clutching his sword against his side to stop it from clattering, heading towards a low hill rising up behind the red gums to his right. Fifty metres further on, as he drew level with its base, he stopped beside a wooden gate and leant on it, almost spent, gasping for air. The sounds of the chase were growing louder.

Unseen, beyond the gate, Edith was hiding in the bushes at the foot of the slope, watching him. '*Psst!*' she called quietly. 'Over here!' As Iko looked around in desperation, she stood up and showed herself. 'Quick! Over the gate! Come on!'

Iko stared anxiously behind him once more. Then, a split second before the first of his pursuers broke from the trees, he leapt the gate. As he hurried over to her, Edith dragged him by the hand into the undergrowth and they both threw themselves flat in the grass.

Moments later, a group of men carrying sticks and farm implements ran past. One of them, a huge man with a deep scar running down his cheek from his eyebrow to his bushy black beard, and his shirt sleeves rolled up above his thick, hairy arms, stopped and walked over to the gate. He glared about him, cocking his head, ears pricked for the slightest sound. Iko and Edith held their breath, pressing themselves closer to the ground.

The red-faced, straggling figure of Mr Jenkins came plodding up to the gate, puffing, and holding a stitch in his side. 'What's up, Scarf?' he wheezed, dabbing at his face with a large, spotted handkerchief.

Scarf nodded towards the hill. 'Who lives up there, then?'

Mr Jenkins looked around, getting his bearings. 'That'd be the back of Miss Swanneck's place, I reckon.'

Scarf pondered for a moment. 'I know her,' he sneered. 'She's a Norman, ain't she?'

'When she was a kid, yeah, before she came over. So what?'

'Well, maybe he's gone there to hide? She'd help one of her own, wouldn't she?'

'No way, mate! She's on our side. Remember last year, when that Norman bastard set the police on us?'

'Yeah?'

'Well, she fixed my arm. I might've lost it if it hadn't been for her.'

'So?'

'So, she wouldn't be hiding him, would she?' Mr Jenkins concluded with a testy snort.

'I dunno...I'm not so sure.'

'Look, he's not up there, I tell you. Now, come on. Are you staying here on your own or what?'

Scarf hesitated, scanning the undergrowth once more, then reluctantly shook his head. 'Nah! All right, I'm coming.'

They walked on out of sight.

Lying in their hiding place among the bushes, Edith and Iko watched the gate, listening. Apart from the birds twittering, all remained quiet. After a long moment, Iko let out his breath. 'They have gone!'

Edith rolled over onto her elbow and stared at him. 'So, it *is* you!'

Iko nodded, with a smile of relief. 'Ah, Lady Edith, I hoped that I would find you!'

'Well, did you have to bring trouble with you again?'

'I am sorry.'

Edith sat up. 'It's rare to see a Norman being chased by Saxons. It's usually the other way 'round. Why are they after you?'

'The Godwins have returned, Lady. Now it is open season on all Normans.'

'Returned? The whole family? Harold, too?'

'Yes.'

'Oh, thank God!' she laughed.

'Have you not heard this news?' Iko asked, a spark of hope in his voice. She shook her head. 'Then perhaps there is still time.'

'Why were you looking for me?' Edith inquired, as they both rose to their feet.

'You said you were a Norman, Lady,' he answered, brushing himself down. 'I thought that you might help me.'

'I said I was from that part of the world, not that I was a Norman,' she replied. She turned and picked up her basket of mushrooms from under a bush.

'I do not understand?' Iko frowned.

'There's a vast difference between the two, and I am definitely not a Norman!'

'Lady, this makes no sense!' he blurted in confusion. 'I am from Normandy, so how can I help being a Norman?'

'That doesn't mean a thing,' Edith said scornfully. 'Being a Norman's nothing to do with where you come from. It's a belief, in superiority. That the strong are superior to the weak. That the rich are superior to the poor. That taking's superior to giving and that owning's superior to sharing. Oh yes, and most important of all, that winning is superior to everything! Anyone can be a Norman. All you have to do is believe that crap!'

'We are not all like that,' Iko protested, startled by her scathing tone.

'No?' Edith raised her eyebrows. 'You don't believe there are masters and servants?'

'Well...'

'"Born to rule, up school, up school." Isn't that how your song goes?'

'How do you know that?'

'I told you, I'm from that part of the world. Well, it looks like you're safe now. We'd better get going.'

'I am not sure I want to go with you, Lady. Maybe you will attack me?'

'Can't take the truth, huh?' Edith smiled. 'I forgot, you're all brainwashed!'

'What do you mean?'

'Oh, nothing. It doesn't matter. Let's go.' As she headed off, she called back over her shoulder. 'By the way, your tie's undone.'

Iko's hand went to his throat. 'I am sorry.' He stopped and began to straighten the knot.

Edith looked round at him and shook her head in disbelief. 'Oh, come on!'

*

'Are you certain this is a good idea, Lady?' Iko asked with a bashful grin. He was standing in the middle of the lounge, dressed in a singlet, shorts, socks, and elasticated boots, all of which were much too big for him.

Edith nodded, peering at him, trying not to laugh. 'Well, they're not a bad fit.' She studied his outfit. 'Hm, there's still something missing...I know! Wait right there!'

With that, she hurried out of the room. While she was gone, Iko gazed around the lounge, taking in the various framed photographs, particularly those of Harold, Edith, and little Edmund. His initial perplexity on recognising Harold's face from a newspaper he'd read soon gave way to surprised understanding. A moment later, Edith returned clutching an akubra hat.

'Here you go,' she said. She put the hat on Iko's head and stood back. It was too large and hung down around his ears. 'Perfect! Now no one'll ever spot you for a Norman...from a distance!'

Iko looked down and inspected himself. 'I thank you, Lady...I think!' They both laughed. 'Are you sure your husband will not mind?' he asked, as he adjusted his new outfit.

'My...?' She followed his eyes towards the photographs and smiled. 'No, I'm sure he won't.'

*

In the darkening evening, they stood together on the riverbank. Iko deposited his rolled-up clothes and a bag of food into the back of the rowing boat tied up at the water's edge and stepped aboard.

'Just follow this creek,' Edith said quietly. 'It joins a river that'll take you to a small fishing port. You should be able to get a ship there.'

'Thank you, Lady.'

'And don't speak to too many people on the way!'

'What shall I do with your boat?'

'Leave it tied up near the pub. There's only one.'

Iko bowed. 'I owe you my life, Lady.'

Edith stretched out her hand. 'Good luck.'

'Thank you,' he said, shaking it. He leant down to untie the bow rope, then straightened up. 'Goodbye, Lady Edith. I will never forget you.'

'Goodbye, Sir Iko.'

Iko settled himself on the bench, adjusted the oar handles, and pushed off. 'Who knows,' he called out in a loud whisper, as he pulled away from the bank, 'we may meet again?'

'Nothing personal,' Edith called back softly, 'but I hope not.'

'Ah, I understand!'

She watched the young Norman row off into the dusk, his figure soon fading to an indistinct blob, then disappearing completely. All remained quiet, only the sustained mesmerising ringing of the cicadas, the occasional call of a river bird, and the gentle rattling of the oarlocks disturbing the silence.

'Do you?' she murmured to herself. 'I wonder?'

6

'**R**ead all about it! Earl Godwin cleared!' the newspaper boy called out stridently from the corner of the city block. 'A Norman plot to deceive the King! All charges dropped! Read all about it!'

Some of the pedestrians going past stopped and clustered around him, eager to get the latest news. Leaning against the wall of the building behind him, a sandwich board proclaimed: *Godwin Innocent!*

*

In the cramped kitchen of their small flat, a Saxon labourer dressed in overalls spread out a pack of fish and chips to the delight of his four excited young children, seated in their pyjamas at the formica-topped table. Behind him, over by the stove, his wife was putting tea bags and sugar into two mugs as the kettle started to boil.

Leaving them to tuck in with ravenous enthusiasm, the man picked up his copy of the *Anglo-Saxon Chronicle* and walked over to her. As she turned towards him, he put his arm around her shoulders and showed her the front page. She studied it and smiled up at him.

'Now we'll get these bloody Normans off our backs!' he growled.

*

The cream-painted door of the drawing room opened and a young man in a white tuxedo and black bow tie, and his dark, glossy hair parted down the middle, bounced in with long, eager steps.

The sumptuous interior exuded wealth and sobriety. The large gilt-framed mirror above the marble mantelpiece, the gilded curlicues of the matching upright chairs upholstered in crimson and gold, the delicate English porcelain figurines on the full Empire bookcase, and the quiet ticking of the Louis XVI grandfather clock standing in the olive-green alcove all spoke of status and refinement.

Seated at one end of a lavish Italian settee, flanked by similar armchairs in the centre of the floor, was his plump, red-haired brother, Reggie. Dressed in black formal evening wear, he was leaning back with his legs crossed, absently stroking his ginger moustache, immersed in a volume of poetry. Sitting with prim authority at the opposite end was their elderly mother. Wearing heavy make-up and chunky jewellery, she was tapping the end of a pencil against her teeth, peering down through her lorgnette at the crossword puzzle in a folded newspaper on her lap.

At the back of the room, near one of the two long-draped windows, a second grey-haired woman was pouring herself a drink from a crystal decanter. She turned as the man entered and closed the door behind him. 'Sherry, dear?' she called out.

'Thanks, Auntie,' he answered, striding across the Persian carpet towards the sofa with an excited smile on his face. 'Quick, Reggie, turn on the radio!'

'Right-o!' Reggie answered, lowering his book and reaching out to switch on the bulky cabinet radio standing beside him, next to a lush, spreading aspidistra in a large brass pot.

A newscaster's voice issued from the round, gold mesh speaker: *'and that Godwin's refusal to appear before the King was justified on the grounds that a fair trial had been prejudiced by undue Norman influence.'*

'Hear, hear!' applauded Reggie.

'Therefore, having agreed to send his youngest son, Wolnoth, and his grandson, Haco, to the Norman court as guarantee of his future loyalty to the King, the Earl and his family will now be reinstated with all their titles and possessions.'

'Oh, jolly good!' Reggie cheered.

'Shh, Reggie!' snapped his mother. 'Don't be so silly! Remember your position!'

'In a further, startling development, Sweyn, the eldest of Earl Godwin's six sons, unexpectedly confessed to murdering his cousin three years ago, a crime for which he had already been acquitted on the grounds of self-defence. In an emotional speech, he declared himself unfit to hold office and formally separated himself from his family's claims. Sweyn then vowed to go on a pilgrimage of repentance. Meanwhile, the rioting and attacks against Norman lives and property over the last few days seem to have stopped.'

*

It was after midnight. Walking side by side past the row of ghostly brick warehouses fronting the deserted wharf, Harold and Sweyn approached the waiting ship, its glowing lanterns and obscured outline visible ahead of them through the mist. The occasional shouts of crewmen rang out of the darkness, their hollow cries soon swallowed up by the cavernous stillness. From out on the river came the deep, muffled drone of a foghorn.

On reaching the gangplank, the two brothers halted. 'Well, here we are,' Sweyn sighed, gripping the rail.

'Are you sure about this, Sweyn? There must be some other way you can make amends and still stay here?' Harold protested. 'This has hit Dad really hard, y'know.'

'I know, mate. It's tearing me up, too. But I've worn it for years now. I just can't take it any more. I killed our cousin for the woman I loved and lost her because of it. It's doing my head in, Harold!'

'He drove you to it. He knew you were ready to snap.'

'I'm a murderer, for Christ's sake!'

'No, you're not. You were acquitted. It was self-defence. At worst it was a crime of passion. And what about Haco? How can you do this to him?'

Sweyn shook his head, blinking away a film of tears. 'Don't! When I finally left him at Mum and Dad's, he was sobbing his poor little heart out! He couldn't understand any of it. And now he's going to Normandy! Oh, God! My life is over and I've ruined his! He'll be better off without me.'

'You can't just give up, mate. You won't be gone forever. You'll come back. It can still work out.'

'Maybe. I hope so. Look after him for me, Harold. Explain it to him. Tell him to be strong, that I will be home one day... that I love him!'

'I will. We all will,' Harold reassured him, angry with his brother for what he was doing, wanting to but unable to express more compassion. They held each other in a tight, farewell embrace. 'I still wish you wouldn't go, though.'

'I've got to.' Sweyn's voice began to break. 'Love ya, bro'!'

'You, too,' Harold nodded sadly.

Sweyn pulled away and ran up the gangplank. At the top, he turned. 'See y'later!' he called.

'At least stay in touch.'

'I'll try.'

With a desolate smile, Sweyn gave a final wave and disappeared into the bowels of the ship. Harold stood watching as the gangplank was pulled aboard, then he turned and walked away.

'How touching! Our hero in tears!' a mocking voice suddenly came from the darkness beside him.

Harold spun round.

Over by the wall of a warehouse, a match flared, illuminating a shadowy figure sitting on top of a barrel, his flat, bony face cut into jagged sections by a long, drooping moustache and his black, greasy hair tied back in a ponytail.

'Algar!'

Earl Algar, Harold's long-standing personal enemy and political adversary, grinned with cold malevolence as he lit his cheroot. They'd known each other since childhood. Thrown together at court while their fathers were busy with politics, from the moment they first saw each other a natural antipathy had sprung up between them. There was just something about him, something in his eyes, that had always made Harold's heckles rise.

If truth be known, Algar had always lusted after Harold's sister, but she'd never even *seen* him, wrapped up as she was in her books and her music. As they'd grown up to manhood, Algar had become more ambitious. Since both becoming earls themselves, he'd fought Harold at every turn in the Council, rivalling him for influence and, in Algar's mind, for ultimate power. Now, once more, the Godwins stood in his way.

'That's right. Sorry if I frightened you, Harold,' Algar chuckled coldly. 'Didn't expect to see me, did you, mate?'

'Not at this hour,' Harold answered, casting a quick look around him. 'You're usually in somebody else's bed sleeping it off!'

With an angry growl, Algar jumped down from the barrel, his vulture's eyes flashing. He was garbed all in black, a sheath knife at his belt. 'Oh, that's very witty,' he sneered.

'What d'you want, Algar? Come to gloat?'

'Over Sweyn? Oh, yes! He should've swung for what he did. But you Godwins, you can twist the law round your little fingers, can't you? Well, at least this time you've suffered some pain for it.'

'You bastard!'

At that moment, four of Earl Algar's henchmen materialised beside their leader out of the mist, and Harold braced himself for an attack.

'But wait on!' Algar said with a menacing smile, walking slowly towards him. 'As you rightly guessed it, Harold, I *was* lying in bed with some slut, when a thought suddenly came to me. What if Harold was down at the docks saying goodbye to his poor, remorseful brother, and there he was, all alone, and something terrible happened to him? What if he slipped and fell in? Or worse still, I thought, what an opportunity that would be for some gang of cutthroats to push him in.'

Crushing out his cheroot with his fingers and tossing away the stub, he reached for his knife. 'Well, what else could I do, Harold? I just had to come down and take care of you myself!'

'You're crazy! Just because the Council made you hand back my earldom. You're power mad!'

Just then, back along the wharf, a squad of soldiers led by Gurth appeared out of the fog, carrying lanterns and spears. 'Harold! Are you all right?' Gurth shouted.

'I'm fine!' Harold called back. 'What were you saying, Algar?' he grinned.

Algar gave a cold laugh and let go of the hilt. 'Well, you obviously don't need me anymore. Maybe some other time.'

'I'll look forward to it.'

Algar's thin lips curled in a sardonic smile. 'Welcome back, Harold,' he said, and stepped away. 'Come on, boys!' He and his henchmen melted into the darkness as the soldiers approached.

'Harold! What's happening? Who was that?' Gurth asked, coming up to him.

'Oh, just Algar and some of his mates.'

'Do you want me to go after them?'

'No, don't bother,' Harold sighed. 'There's been enough grief for one night.'

At the mournful sound of a foghorn, they both looked round, staring at the misty river and the fading shape of the ship.

*

Riding out from under the canopy of gum trees spanning the road, Harold took the right-hand fork and continued up the incline, with each thrust of the pedals picturing their reunion. His face told the story. He was almost there!

Had she missed him? Would they still feel the same way about each other? A year was a long time. Up ahead, he could see Vera's house. One day they'd have a house of their own.

As the going grew harder, his bicycle heavy with the sheathed sword strapped to his full saddlebags, he swung out of the saddle and pushed on up the slope. Everything was as he remembered it. To his right, the open fields still stretched away towards the distant line of hills. On the left, up above the raised bank and dilapidated wire fence, was their neighbour's empty paddock. The old horse was still there, munching the cool grass in the shade of the peppercorn tree.

Edith appeared at the front door and shook out a tablecloth. Suddenly, she saw him. Harold stopped and laid down his bicycle. Her face filled with joy as she started towards him.

'Harold!' she cried.

He grinned and walked forward, all his doubts dispelled as she broke into a run and threw herself into his arms.

'Oh, Harold!'

Hugging her to him, he spun her around, then lowered her to the ground, their lips crushing together in reignited passion. 'Edith! My love!'

'You're home!'

'At last!'

Their eyes filled with pent-up longing, they kissed again. Eventually, they let go of each other, laughing with relief. He retrieved his bicycle, and with the tablecloth flapping over the handlebars like the banner of domestic bliss, leaning close together, still touching, they proceeded up to the house.

Coming in through the front door, Harold left his sword propped up against the hall stand and they went into the lounge. Vera was standing in the middle of the room, waiting to greet him.

Although fond of each other, there was still a certain wariness between them. While Vera was a staunch supporter of Earl Godwin, she wasn't completely sure about Harold. She had a natural protectiveness for her daughter. After all, he was a professional soldier, not just an administrator. Yes, Edith obviously loved him, and yes, he was the father of her child, but in the five years they'd been together he hadn't been around all that much.

And then for the past year he'd been away in exile. She worried that he was too much of a man's man, and not the support her daughter needed. For his part, Harold was aware of her underlying mistrust and always felt that he had to prove himself to her. It was understandable enough, he supposed. But his love for Edith was real. In time, he was confident he could win her over.

'So, you've decided to come back, Harold!' Vera smiled.

'Hello, Vera!' Harold grinned, setting down the saddlebags and walking towards her.

'Thank goodness! Now Edith can stop her moping!' she smiled, as they kissed each other on the cheek. She felt his muscular arms. 'You haven't been taking very good care of yourself, have you? You're all skin and bones!'

'I just couldn't stay away from your cooking any longer, Vera. I tried, but...'

'Well, you'll just have to put up with it and like it!'

At that moment, the hall door opened and Edmund, three years old and pyjama-clad, came in rubbing his eyes. 'Mummy?' he blurted in confusion, seeing so many tall, noisy figures standing together.

With a laugh of delight, Edith went over to him. She knelt by his side and kissed him. 'Hello, darling! Edmund, look who's here!'

Edmund peered at Harold for a moment, then his face lit up. 'Daddy!' he cried and ran across the room towards him. 'Daddy!'

Harold gathered his son into his arms and lifted him up high, hugging and kissing him. 'Edmund, my darling! Oh, I've missed you so much! You've grown so big! And you haven't forgotten me!'

'Of course he hasn't forgotten you, Harold,' Edith said.

'It's been a long time.' He crouched down and stood Edmund up on the rug.

'Too long, if you ask me,' Vera said reproachfully. 'A child needs both parents.'

'Oh, Mum, it wasn't Harold's fault.'

'She's right, Edith, I should be here more. And I will be from now on.'

'Did you bring me presents, Daddy?' Edmund asked, tugging him towards the saddlebags.

'Yes, my sweet, lots of presents! For you all!' Harold untied the buckles, then reached in and pulled out a package. 'And this one's...for you!'

While Vera and Edith sat down, with Harold's help Edmund unwrapped his present, a large Polynesian fighting doll. 'A soldier!' he cried.

'And look, his sword comes out...'

Edmund swung the tiny sword around in the air. 'Kill Normans!'

'Well, not exactly...' Harold grimaced. He pulled out another package. 'And this one's for Grandma!'

He leant across and handed it to her. Vera opened it and held up a white cotton nightdress embroidered with tropical flowers and fruit.

'A nightie!' Edmund squealed.

'Thanks, Harold. It's just what I need,' Vera said.

'For those torrid nights!' Edith laughed.

'When a pirate comes to pillage me!'

'It's hand-stitched,' Harold tried to explain, with a bashful grin. Then he reached into the saddlebag again. 'And the next one...is for Mummy!'

He passed the parcel to Edmund, who took it to Edith. With her son hovering beside her, she accepted it and, sharing an excited smile with him, carefully removed the wrapping paper.

'I don't know if it'll fit you...?'

Edith stood up and turned in a circle, pressing the bright, floral, lemon-yellow dress against her. 'Oh, it's lovely, Harold!'

*

Harold stood in semi-darkness on the wooden verandah outside the kitchen, gazing at the warm dusk settling in shades of magenta over the quiet land. Low lights were on inside the house. Edith came out through the fly-screen door carrying two mugs of tea. She handed one to him and kissed him lightly on the lips.

'Mm!' he smiled, taking a sip. 'Thanks, darling.'

She looked out at the view. 'It's beautiful, isn't it?'

He put his arm around her waist. 'It's so peaceful.'

'I'm sorry about Sweyn, Harold.'

'Thanks. This is what he could've done with, y'know. The quiet countryside, a home and a family.'

'Haco, too.'

'Yeah,' he sighed. He pulled her close to him and kissed her hair. 'I'm so glad I've got you, Edith.'

'You're lucky to have me!'

'I know. And I never want to lose you. That's why I think we should get married.'

'Just like that, eh? What about your parents? Your father'd have a fit! Tostig's choice was bad enough, but for his favourite son to marry a Norman?'

'No, Sweyn's always been his favourite.'

Edith shook her head. 'I can't imagine not loving all my children equally.'

'All? Are you planning on having some more?'

'Sometime, yes. I hope so. Edmund'd love a little baby brother or sister to play with.'

'Well, I'll see what I can do about it, then!'

'Typical male arrogance!' she laughed. 'What *you* can do about it! Hah!' She punched him playfully on the chest. 'Listen, buster, no one's having a baby round here till *I* decide!'

Harold raised his arms and backed away. 'Okay! Okay!'

'Anyway, what were we talking about?'

'Marriage, but forget it!'

'Seriously, Harold, you've told me yourself how much your Dad relies on you. With Sweyn gone, he'll need you now more than ever. If you said you wanted to marry a Norman, how d'you think he'd feel?'

'Like his world was ending, probably.'

'You couldn't do it to him.'

'Anyway, you're not a Norman.'

'I would be to him.'

Harold began pacing the verandah. 'I don't care. There has to be a way. I love you and I want you to be my wife. Is that such a crime? We've already got a son, for crying out loud!'

'Your parents don't know that, though, do they?'

'No, not yet.'

'Where do they think you are tonight?'

'I don't know. They probably think I've got a mistress tucked away somewhere.'

'And is that what I am? Your mistress?'

'Of course not. You're the love of my life!'

Edith walked up to him and put her arms round his neck. 'Well, how could you get more married than that, my poor Saxon fool?' She gave him a tender kiss. 'I feel like your wife. You're the father of my child. What possible difference could a piece of paper make?'

'It'd mean I wouldn't have to keep sneaking away down here to see you, for one thing. And Edmund would have all his grandparents.'

'That'd be great. I'd love to marry you, Harold, you know that. All I'm saying is maybe it's not that important.'

'I know, but I still want to do it, as soon as we can.'

She pressed herself against him. 'We can do it whenever you like.'

Harold grinned. 'Get married, I mean!'

*

Moonlight slanted in through the window, splitting the darkness, laying a trail across the carpet and up over the jumble of bed covers thrown off in the heat of their lovemaking.

'Wow!' Harold blew out his breath with a laugh, as he rolled back onto the pillow and pulled up the sheet.

'Did the earth move for you?' Edith smiled, lying naked beside him.

'Everything moved!' As she snuggled against him, he put his arm around her smooth shoulders. 'How about you?'

'Never felt a thing!'

He kissed the top of her head. 'I love you, Edith.'

'I'm so happy, Harold,' she murmured, fingering the small birthmark shaped like a letter *E* on his chest.

'Me too.' He looked down at what she was doing. 'See, your name's even written on my heart!' he chuckled. Edith sighed with contentment.

After a while, as they lay there basking in the afterglow, he shook his head and gave a self-deriding tut. 'I don't know...Do you reckon your mum liked her present?'

'Of course she did.'

'It was a bit personal, though.'

'No, it wasn't. She was tickled pink!'

'I'm sure she'll never wear it. It's almost see-through!'

'Oh, don't worry, Mum'll find a use for it. There's plenty of mileage left in the old girl yet!'

'What? Don't tell me she's got a boyfriend?'

'She's like a rabbit.'

'You're joking?'

'Anything under seventy in trousers is fair game as far as she's concerned.'

'My God!' he laughed. 'The mind boggles!'

Edith stretched out on her back beside him. 'Talking of rabbits, Harold, you could've brought Edmund a stuffed animal or something. That warrior is frightening!'

'No, it's not. You're just a wimp. Boys can handle that sort of thing. He loved it.'

'I know, that's what worries me. You'll just have to try harder with the next one.'

'What did you say?' He leant over her. 'Do you think you might be...?'

'Probably,' she smiled.

'I'd better start looking around for a big fluffy teddy bear, then!'

'Let's wait and see, darling,' she laughed, pulling him down towards her. 'But no more soldiers, please! I want gentle children!'

7

The tree-lined street outside Earl Godwin's home was busy with traffic, as an assortment of pedestrians, riders, carriages, and handcarts went by in both directions. Harold appeared among them on his bicycle. As he made his way through the throng, he acknowledged their greetings with a friendly smile. On reaching the stone entrance pillars of the family home, he returned the salutes of the four policemen standing guard and turned in up the gravel driveway.

Ahead of him, an open carriage bearing the royal crest, with an accompanying military escort, had drawn up in front of the mansion. His sister, the Queen, was just getting out as he approached. He dismounted and leant his bicycle against the ivy-covered wall.

'Harold!' she smiled with unguarded warmth.

'Hiya, Didi!' he grinned, as they hugged each other. He'd been calling her that for as long as he could remember, although her given name was Edith—which simplified matters, he'd realised, when someone else with that name already filled his life. 'I mean, Your Majesty!'

'There's no need to be formal, you dag, just call me Ma'am.'

Harold laughed. 'How's life in the fast lane these days?'

'Oh, monarchial, y'know. Actually, it's pretty dull. All I seem to do is open fêtes and give speeches for charity.'

'Yeah, it must be tough at the top,' he nodded, with an edge of sarcasm.

Younger than Harold by five years, but looking and acting five years his senior, the Queen hooked an affectionate arm through his as they started up the steps to the front porch.

'Now, don't be catty, Harold.'

'And how's Edward?'

'You know the King, he's got such a lot on his mind.'

'Like sending our brother to Normandy?'

'Oh, Harold, that's not fair,' she said, stopping at the top.

'And Haco, after all he's been through.'

'Edward didn't have any choice. Duke William demanded it.'

'And what William wants William gets, eh?'

'Don't be ridiculous. I don't like it any more than you do. But they'll be all right. It won't be for long. Think of it as being like boarding school.'

'Oh, great!' Harold smiled cynically, opening the front door for her.

As they stepped through into the spacious atrium, they could hear muffled pop music and the noise of a party coming from behind double doors to the left. At the far end, beyond a huge, multi-faceted crystal chandelier suspended by a long wire from the high ceiling, a carpeted staircase led up to a three-sided landing and the second-floor bedrooms.

Githa hurried over to them, her face filled with concern. 'Darling! I was beginning to think you wouldn't get here in time,' she said as she kissed her daughter.

'I'm sorry, Mother, I was held up at the palace. We were choosing a new choirmaster.'

'Oh...'

'And would you believe it, one of the applicants actually wanted to jazz up the hymns!'

'But did you speak to the King? Will he change his mind?'

The Queen shook her head. 'No, I'm afraid not. I tried, but you know how Edward is. Affairs of state are his domain. Nothing I could say would alter his decision. He thinks it's best for national security, and there it is.' She took Githa's hands in hers. 'But don't worry, Mother. As I was just telling Harold, Wolnoth and Haco'll be fine. Edward says it'll only be for a short while, just until everything settles down, and then they'll come home again. Now, where is that boy? I must give him his instructions from the King.'

'And what are *they*?' Harold asked drily.

'Oh, just a few do's and don't's. To say sir and please and thank you, things like that.'

'He was in there last time I saw him,' Githa said, pointing towards the party. 'All his friends have come to see him off. It's so lovely of them, don't you think?' Her eyes began to water.

The Queen kissed Githa on the cheek, then swept away through the doors leading into the darkened lounge filled with gyrating teenagers. The music, suddenly loud, became muffled again as they closed behind her.

'Oh, Harold!' Githa sobbed.

Harold held her gently. 'Come on, Mum, don't cry. He'll be all right.'

'But why Wolnoth? And little Haco. What kind of life is it going to be for him with no family around him? To have lost his father, and now this. It's too cruel!'

'Don't. You have to be strong. Wolnoth'll look after Haco. William's the King's cousin, don't forget. He'll take care of them. It'll all work out, you'll see.'

*

An hour or so later, in the quiet of his bedroom, Wolnoth stood beside the bed finishing his packing. There were faint shouts and laughter and the thump of the music coming from downstairs. He closed the lid of his suitcase and gave a last look around the room.

By the light of the single bedside lamp, he gazed fondly at his old toys, his models and mobiles, his desk, his crowded bookshelves, and the pictures on the walls. Two large movie posters for *Iron Conqueror 1* and *2* showed powerful, helmeted Norman knights thrusting large, foreshortened fists towards him.

With a sigh, Wolnoth turned to go. He stopped. Haco was standing in the doorway, his head hanging.

'Haco!' he exclaimed. 'What's up? Are you missing your dad?' Haco stared at the floor in silence and nodded. 'Don't worry, mate, you'll see him again soon. Meanwhile, we're going to have ourselves the best adventure!'

'I don't want to go, Wol,' Haco said in a small voice, biting his lip.

'Of course you do!' Wolnoth laughed. 'It'll be great! Just think of the things we can do over there. Eat lots of junk food. Play the latest computer games.' He pointed at the movie posters. 'And meet all the most famous knights in Normandy! Then, before you know it, you'll be home again and your dad'll be here waiting for you!'

Haco brightened. 'Really?'

'Absolutely!'

'The Normans frighten me, Wol.'

'Ah, don't be silly,' Wolnoth smiled, and gave him a pat on the back. 'They're our friends. I'll look after you!'

*

Laughing with his school mates, shouting to them above the blaring music, Wolnoth made his way across the dark, crowded lounge. At the far end, he stepped through the open doorway into the brightly lit kitchen.

Leofwine looked up from helping himself to the food set out on the table and greeted him warmly. 'Wolnoth! How'y'doin', mate?'

Wolnoth went over to the sink and poured himself a glass of water from the tap. 'Phew! It's getting hot in there!' he said, gulping it down.

'D'you want some food?'

'No, thanks, Leo.'

'It'll stop you getting seasick.'

'I'll take my chances, thanks. I'm too excited to eat.'

'Nervous?'

'A bit, yeah.'

Leofwine put his arm around him. 'You'll be right, Wol. You'll have fun!'

'I know I will,' Wolnoth smiled. 'D'you reckon the Duke'll make me one of his knights, Leo?'

'Is that what you want?'

'More than anything.'

Leofwine shrugged. 'Well, who knows?'

'I don't think Dad would like that idea much, Wol,' said Gurth, standing by the pantry door, next to a curvaceous eighteen-year-old blonde in a figure-hugging dress.

'I know, but he's old-fashioned, Gurth. He doesn't understand.'

'Understand what?'

'That the Normans are the future. You can't live in the past, not if you want to be successful.' Wolnoth grinned at the girl. 'And I want to be successful!'

'D'you want to dance, Wol?' she asked, leaving Gurth's side.

Wolnoth took her hand. 'Sure thing, doll!'

'Hang on, Wol,' Gurth called after him, as they left the room together, laughing.

'Let him go,' Harold sighed, from the end of the room. He was leaning against the dresser, sipping a mug of tea. 'It's his night. He'll find out.'

'And she was so beautiful!' Gurth moaned.

'Face it, Gurth, you're too old-fashioned, mate,' Harold chuckled.

'Too old, full-stop!' Gurth laughed and shook his head. 'This is getting very worrying. In the space of a week we've lost two brothers. One's gone walkabout...'

'And the other's going to be successful,' Leofwine finished for him.

'The bird has to fly the nest sometime,' said Harold. 'Even if it means diving headfirst into the ground.'

'Into a load of shit,' added Leofwine.

'Dangerous shit,' Gurth grunted. 'Norman shit.'

At that moment, the Queen entered the kitchen. 'Hello, boys!' she laughed, twirling her arms in the air. 'I just *love* to dance!'

'Speaking of success,' Leofwine said.

'What d'you mean, y'great creep?' she laughed, tousling his hair.

'Oh, nothing!' he grinned.

'You can't see a thing in there. They didn't know who I was!'

'I'm going out the back for a smoke,' Gurth said, throwing his sister a half-hearted smile and loosening his collar. The Queen gave him a questioning look as he walked away.

'Wait on, Gurth,' Leofwine called out, following him towards the back door. 'I'll come with you.'

As they went out, the Queen turned to Harold with a frown. 'Did I interrupt something?'

'We were just talking about Wolnoth's future.' At that moment, the front door's bell chimed. 'That'll be Tostig. Late as usual!'

'Maliciously late, I sometimes think.'

'No, he doesn't mean to be. He's just a bit insensitive sometimes, that's all.'

She threw up her hands. 'You guys, you're all alike! Always quick to defend each other!' There was cheering in the lounge. 'Here he is, making his grand entrance, showing off to the girls and stealing the limelight. He's always needling!'

'What d'you mean? Needling who?'

'Father, for one.'

'In what way?'

'Oh, in lots of ways. With his marriage, for a start.'

'That's fine coming from you, Didi.'

'Edward may be half Norman, Harold, but he's a Saxon at heart,' she retorted. 'Anyway, Father was pleased about it.'

Harold rubbed his chin and gave a rueful sigh. 'Yeah, I know he was.'

'But Tostig did it just to hurt him. I'm sure he did.'

'Well, what about sending Wolnoth away? That was pretty hurtful. You could've stopped it if you'd tried.'

'You know that's not true! I told you, Edward's mind was already made up.'

'And the non-Saxon half won out, did it?'

'Why must you be so difficult, Harold?' she sighed. 'Why can't you just go with the flow?'

'Perhaps in some ways I'm like Tostig. Maybe the current's a bit too strong.'

'What rot!'

'Is it? What do you think Dad would say if *I* decided to marry a Norman?'

'If *you* did?' she laughed. 'He'd be shattered!'

'Why?'

'It's obvious, isn't it? He's lost Sweyn, he's lost Tostig, and now he's losing Wolnoth. I suppose in some ways he feels that he's lost me, too. If he lost you as well, Harold...Why? You're not intending to, are you?'

With a non-committal smile, Harold set down his mug. 'Come on, your nosiness. Let's go and see the terrible Tostig!'

*

The garden was in darkness. Gurth and Leofwine were standing away from the illuminated back porch, gazing up at the stars. Soft music and occasional bursts of laughter were coming from inside the house.

'So, what d'you reckon, Gurth? Will they be all right over there or what?'

'I dunno, Leo.' Gurth exhaled a plume of smoke towards the sky. 'I don't like it, that's for sure.'

'If they needed a guarantee, you'd think they could've just demanded money or something.'

'Either way it's bloody insulting. Dad's given his whole life for this country.'

'Well, we all know what Edward thinks of Dad,' Leofwine scowled.

'How could he agree to such a thing?'

'Once a Norman, always a bloody Norman!'

'Don't let Harold hear you say that.'

'Oh yeah, I forgot about Edith. Still, it's a bastard of a thing to do, marry the daughter and ship off the son.'

'He wants his revenge,' Gurth sighed. 'He still blames Dad for his brother's death. We should've seen it coming, Leo. Anyone who'd send his wife's whole family into exile without a qualm is capable of anything.' He shook his head. 'What a bloody mess! And Dad thought he'd be able to make a Saxon out of him!' He ground out his roll-up and threw the butt into the bushes.

'Our dear sister was a great help,' Leofwine said with a mocking laugh. 'That's what you call really overplaying the part!'

'She seems to be getting into it, all right.'

'She must take marriage very seriously.'

'Who knows, maybe she loves him?'

'If you don't love your own family, what's any other love worth?'

'Mm,' Gurth nodded.

'Unless you count that blonde in there,' Leofwine grinned.

'What?'

'I saw you chatting her up!'

'Get lost!' Gurth spluttered. 'I'm old enough to be her...' His face cracked into a smile. 'Well, at least her sugar daddy!'

'See, family love, nothing like it!'

'William's family too, don't forget.'

'Oh, yeah,' Leofwine grunted. 'Remind me to send him a birthday card.'

*

The wall lights were turned on, exposing the debris of the party, innocent except for a couple of empty quarter-bottles of vodka among the plastic forks and paper cups and plates strewn about the room. The family were seated around the lounge on sofas and armchairs, regrouping before the next, more painful phase of the departure. Out in the hall the front door was closed and, moments later, Earl Godwin and Wolnoth came back into the room through the double doors.

'That's the last of them,' the Earl said with a weary smile. He put his arm round Wolnoth's shoulders and hugged him. 'Well, my boy, did you have a good party?'

'Yes thanks, Dad,' Wolnoth grinned. 'It was great!'

'Looked like you were doing all right with that blonde bit, Wollo,' Tostig called across to him. 'Pity you're going, I reckon you'd be in there!'

'Don't be cruel, baby,' Judith chided him. 'You'll embarrass your brother.'

'Nah, he's okay. Just think of those sheilas over in Normandy, mate. They'll all be after you!'

'You'll be a big hit, Wolnoth,' Judith beamed at him with a toothpaste ad smile.

Githa pushed herself up from her chair. 'I think I'll start cleaning up.'

'Leave it, Githa. We'll do it later,' said Earl Godwin.

'No, I'd rather get it out of the way. It'll give me something to do.'

Judith stood up. 'I'll help you, Mum.'

Githa hesitated for a second. 'All right, thank you, Judith,' she replied in a brittle voice.

As they headed off towards the kitchen, Leofwine leant over and whispered to Harold. 'That really gets to her!'

'What does?' Harold asked, lowering his voice.

'Her calling her "Mum".'

'Why?'

'Because she's such a pain in the arse!'

The Queen rose to her feet. 'Come on, Leo, lend a hand,' she said, and began to pick things up, moving to the other end of the lounge. Leofwine got up and joined her.

'Harold,' the Earl called from the doorway, 'Can I have a word with you? In the study.' He turned and left the room.

As Harold followed his father out, Tostig watched them go.

'What's that about?' he said.

'Don't know,' Gurth shrugged.

'How come he gets special treatment?'

'What do you mean?'

'Well, neither of us were included,' Tostig scowled. 'What's the big secret? We're both earls, too, aren't we, not just darling Harold? Anyone would think *he* was the one going to Normandy.'

Gurth shook his head and sighed but didn't reply.

With an angry grunt, Tostig walked over to a long sideboard standing against the wall. Surveying the litter of soft drink bottles, disposable cups, and half-eaten plates of biscuits and cheese on its surface, he gave a disparaging tut and bent down to open a small cupboard underneath. He reached in and pulled out a bottle of whisky.

'D'you want a real drink, Gurth?' he asked, looking round.

'No thanks, mate. I'd better start bringing the luggage down.'

'I'll help you, Uncle Gurth,' said Haco, wandering up to them from the kitchen.

'That'a boy, Haco,' Gurth nodded with a cheerful smile.

*

Earl Godwin strode into his private study, waving his hands in the air. 'Ghaagh! That woman! Shut the door!'

Going past a wall of floor-to-ceiling bookcases, he crossed the large oriental mat covering the black floorboards, manoeuvring his bulk between the leather couch and armchairs and his antique mahogany desk, over to an open drinks cabinet on the far side.

'Who?' Harold asked with a grin, closing the heavy oak door behind him.

'Tostig's Judith. Everything about her makes me cringe!'

'Why?' Harold laughed.

'If you'd spent a year listening to that grating voice of hers, you'd know why,' the Earl answered, searching among an array of bottles. 'Baby this! Baby that! Bah! Don't you ever marry a Norman, Harold, they're grabbers the lot of 'em!'

'What did you want to talk to me about, Dad?' Harold asked, an edge coming into his voice.

'Look, you need to go and visit your earldom, Harold,' Earl Godwin informed him over his shoulder as he poured them both a large glass of port. 'You've been away a long time, y'know. You need to start reconnecting.' He turned and held one out to Harold. 'Find out what kind of mood they're in. People can forget very quickly.'

Harold accepted his drink, chinked glasses, and took a sip. 'I know. I already intend to.'

'Algar's had a year now to get his grubby fingers into the pie,' the Earl went on. 'And he's bound to have used it to build up his own power base. Go to them, Harold. Do a tour of the place. Undo the damage he's caused. We can't let him feather his nest at our expense.'

'I'd planned to see Edward about it tomorrow. That is, if I can get past his dragon of a secretary.'

'Good boy. Make sure you see him soon, though. Mid-morning'd be best, when he's not busy boring God. Now, listen, with Algar out of a job he's bound to be looking around for another position...'

'Well, he can wait until his father dies, can't he? He must be on his last legs by now. Algar can take over the family plot. That should be enough for him.'

'Knowing Algar, I doubt it. But I wasn't thinking of him, I was thinking of us.'

'What do you mean?'

'Look, this country's divided into three, right? In the north, there's Siward, who's our friend. When he's gone, who knows? In the centre, there's Algar's family. And in the south, there's us. If we want to go on holding the balance of power, we've got to make a deal with one of them. You can see that, can't you?'

'What are you driving at, Dad?'

'What I'm driving at is that the best way to secure that deal is through marriage. Siward doesn't have any eligible girls, but I was talking to Algar yesterday...'

'That bastard?'

'And he's got a daughter.'

'I know. Aldyth.'

'She's about twenty, pretty, and free.'

'Yeah, pretty free with her favours, so I've heard.'

'That may be, Harold, but anyone can change. And just think how much it'd suit both our families if you married her?'

'Me?' Harold gasped. 'Marry Aldyth? You're joking, aren't you? I don't even know her, let alone love her.'

'What's love got to do with it? I'm talking about securing our power.'

Harold gave a caustic laugh. 'Like my sister's marriage, you mean?'

'Don't think you're the only one who's felt deeply about that, Harold!' Earl Godwin said sharply, setting down his glass. 'I've spent more sleepless nights agonising over her than you'll ever know, believe me. But whether we like it or not, this world is all about power. The getting of it and the keeping of it. Nothing else matters. And we can't let love stand in the way of our mission.'

'Oh, yes? Which is what exactly?'

'To defend our nation's freedom, of course! To protect our values and our way of life. And only power and position, and the funds that go with them, lets us do that. Without that power structure there's nothing, only chaos and heartbreak.'

At that moment, there was a knock on the door. 'Dad, the carriage is here!' Gurth called out.

'Thanks, we'll be right there,' the Earl answered loudly, without turning his head.

Consummate manipulator to the last, even with his own children, he walked up to Harold and laid placating, persuasive hands on his shoulders. 'Just think about it, Harold,' he said, giving him a gentle, reassuring shake. 'Please.'

He let go and crossed to the door. Resting his hand on the brass knob for a moment, he looked back. 'And remember, when I'm gone it's you who'll have to take my place.' He turned the handle and went out.

Harold gave a heavy groan of disbelief and slumped down onto the thick, padded arm of a chair. He let out a long, pensive sigh, his face set like stone, angry and perplexed, as his father's words resounded in his brain.

*

The front door was open and the porch light on. Gathered together at the top of the steps, with sorrowful hugs and kisses, garbled emotion, and words of encouragement, the whole Godwin family said their goodbyes to Wolnoth and Haco. Tostig and Judith, who would accompany them to the Norman court, were also bid farewell, but not with the same mixture of affection and concern.

Taking their leave at last, the four descended the short flight of steps to the driveway. On reaching the bottom, they turned and looked back. Wolnoth gave a happy laugh, while Haco gazed up at his grandparents and uncles in silent distress. With final waves, they all climbed into the waiting carriage.

On the porch above, Earl Godwin stood grim-faced and resolute, his eyes filled with sorrow as he watched them leave. He put his arm around his tearful wife.

'Oh, my babies! I've lost my babies!' Githa cried out as they pulled away. With a great, heaving sob, she collapsed against him and buried her face in his chest.

8

The bare, whitewashed waiting room, one of the recent modifications to King Edward's palace, was filled with light from a bank of high, angled windows running down its length.

Seated at one end, behind her desk, peering at a computer monitor and every now and then fluently tapping on the keyboard with the hard tips of her long, polished nails, was the King's middle-aged secretary. She was wearing a cream silk blouse, pinned at the throat by a large enamel brooch, and had her bronze-tinted, greying hair pulled up into a coiled braid on top of her head. Her plain but attractive face looked stern as she worked, her peach-glossed lips pursed in concentration beneath her magnificent beaked nose, adorned with a pair of bright red horn-rimmed glasses.

Placed along each wall, on either side of the varnished floor, was a line of upright chairs. Perched on the left, halfway down the room, was the Dean of the Royal Chapel, his rotund figure compressed into a dark three-piece suit and his double chin hanging over a clerical collar. His short, stringy hair was combed forward over his balding pate, above a plump, pasty face inset with glaring, piggy eyes. He was clutching a document tube in one pudgy hand, tapping it against the stubby fingers of the other in agitation.

Sitting next to him, his legs tucked under his chair, was a small, dapper tailor, dressed in a black serge jacket, pinstripe trousers, and a large, yellow bow tie. He was gazing at the ceiling, whistling cheerfully to himself, and balancing a flat rectangular cardboard box on his knees, a wad of tissue paper poking out from under its lid.

On one of the seats opposite them, concentrating on filing her nails, was a voluptuous young woman in her early twenties. Olive skinned, with short, spiky, emerald green hair, she wore a short, tight, black leather skirt and a close-fitting black top, unbuttoned to show her cleavage. Her shapely, crossed legs were sheathed in purple, thigh-length pirate boots.

'Oh, this is impossible!' the Dean whined with haughty impatience. 'I've been waiting here for over an hour!'

'His Majesty must have an important meeting,' the tailor answered with an affable smile.

Moving into slow, ominous alignment, like the guns of a warship coming to bear on its target, the Dean swivelled round in his seat and glared down at the man with contempt. 'And you! You're before me! What are *you* waiting for?'

'New robes for the King!' the tailor grinned with pride, patting the top of his box.

'Pah! How could anything be more important than these plans for King Edward's new abbey?' the Dean scowled, smacking the cylinder into the palm of his hand for emphasis.

While he did so, he cast a quick, furtive look across the room at the woman's legs. As if on demand, lifting one over the other with enticing slowness, she crossed them the other way, causing her skirt to ride up over her tanned thighs, allowing him a glimpse of the dark v of her underwear. His throat constricted and the blood pounded at his temples. He glanced at her face to make sure he hadn't been seen. She was watching him with cold amusement. Pursing her wide, fluorescent pink lips, she blew him a kiss. He averted his eyes in shock.

'Well, some might say feeding and clothing the poor is pretty high on the list,' chuckled the tailor.

'Yes, yes,' the Dean replied with mounting irritation. 'But what's more important, the body or the soul?' Unable to resist, his eyes were drawn once more to the silky smoothness of the woman's thighs. 'The soul, of course,' he ploughed on. 'It's eternal. And only the Church can feed it. While bread and cloth merely sustain the body.'

He lifted his gaze and with mouth-watering intensity ogled the swell of her breasts, focusing on the pronounced contours of her nipples. 'The impermanent...ah...body!' he gasped. At last catching hold of himself, he threw another anxious look at her face. Her lambent black eyes bored into his with undisguised loathing. Half-closing their green-glittered lids, she smiled at him with exaggerated sexual longing and licked her lips, sucking and rolling her tongue in his direction. He jerked his head away in angry confusion.

Just then, Harold entered the room and approached the secretary. 'G'day. Earl Harold to see the King,' he said, giving her his most engaging smile.

The secretary looked up at him from behind her desk. 'His Majesty has someone with him at the moment,' she answered in an impregnable, stony voice.

'Oh...right.'

'However, he did leave instructions, Earl Harold,' she informed him, with a condescending arch of her eyebrows, 'that, should you arrive, you were to be admitted at once.' She motioned towards the door at the far end. 'You may go in.'

'Ah, good. Thanks!'

As Harold walked away, she appraised him over her glasses, admiring his broad back, his firm backside, and his strong, trousered legs. Then, emitting a soft sigh and shaking her head at such silliness, she returned to her typing.

Drawing level with the waiting pair, Harold nodded to the Dean. 'G'day, Dean. Sorry to jump the queue!'

The Dean gave a humph and turned away.

'Morning, Earl Harold, and welcome back!' the tailor said with a smile.

'Thanks.'

'Earl Harold?' the young woman called across to him.

He turned towards her. 'Yes?'

With languid ease, she re-crossed her legs, revealing a wide expanse of curvaceous flesh. 'My father said to say hello if I saw you. I'm Aldyth, Algar's daughter.'

'Ah, yes...' Harold replied with an embarrassed grin. 'Well...Hi.'

'Hello!' she laughed, the open invitation in her lingering gaze draining the blood from his brain and setting his pulse racing.

Abashed at his own reaction and its subsequent feeling of guilt, Harold threw her an awkward smile and moved on in haste towards the door. At that very moment, it opened and Earl Algar stepped out into the waiting room. His face was white with anger. On seeing Harold, he instantly regained his composure.

'G'day, Harold,' he said, his small, yellow teeth showing briefly in a lizard smile.

Harold inclined his head with cold disdain. 'Algar.'

'A quiet word with you, mate.' With a jerk of his head, Algar motioned for Harold to follow him down to the far end of the room. They stopped beside a large photocopier and faced each other.

'All right, Algar, what do you want to say to me?'

'Listen, Harold, I know we've had our differences...'

'What, like the other night, you mean?'

'I know, I know, I was out of line. I was angry and hurt, that's all. Nothing would've happened, you know that.'

'Oh, yeah?' Harold laughed.

'Yeah. Anyway, now's the time for us to stick together, mate. And I've been thinking...'

'Really?'

'That if you and I formed a power block, we could end all this Norman arse-licking once and for all. Make the place safe for decent people to live in.'

'And what about the King?'

'Edward's old. He's had enough. We'd be a force to be reckoned with in the world, Harold.'

'Yes, and I'd have to watch my back every second of the day.'

''Course you wouldn't. We'd be a team. But first I need a position, a base to work from.'

'What exactly are you after, Algar?'

'Look, while you were away, I was given your earldom and I did a bloody good job of running it. In fact, I could've held onto it by force if I'd wanted to, but I didn't. I let it go. Now all I'm asking for is something in return. Is that fair or is that fair?'

'Who knows?' Harold shrugged. 'Maybe.'

'What d'you mean maybe? You know damn well it is!'

'It's up to the King.'

'I've already spoken to him. The bastard won't give me a straight answer. So, now I'm making my own arrangements. I was talking to your old man the other day and he agreed our families should be closer.'

'I know, he mentioned it,' Harold said coldly.

'Good. So, I'll make you an offer, Harold. I'm prepared to give you my daughter, my own sweet, innocent Aldyth, to marry, if you'll get the King to give me the earldom Sweyn left? A straight swap. What d'you say?'

'And how does Aldyth feel about being swapped?'

'She'll do as she's told,' Algar growled, giving him a sharp look. 'She'll marry whoever I bloody well tell her to, don't you worry! Well? What's your answer?'

Harold shook his head and smiled with icy contempt. 'Algar, I wouldn't marry your daughter if you offered me all of the money you've extorted from innocent people over the years as a dowry. And be your son-in-law? You must be joking!'

'You're a fool, Harold!' Algar seethed in fury. 'A stupid, short-sighted, bloody fool!' With that, he turned on his heel and strode back down the room.

As he approached, Aldyth rose to her feet. She looked beyond him and gazed into Harold's eyes. Her lips parted in a seductive smile as she slowly ran her hands down the length of her body.

'Put yourself away, girl!' Algar snapped. 'We're leaving!' He strode on past her. Unperturbed, Aldyth sent Harold a final regretful shrug and a languorous wink filled with future promise, then turned and followed her father out of the room.

*

Earl Godwin stood in front of the bathroom mirror, struggling to do up the stud at the back of his detachable wing collar. 'I hate these damned things!' he snarled in exasperation.

'Here, let me.' Githa laughed, hovering behind him.

'Why do I have to have lunch at the palace, anyway?' he moaned, as she reached up to fix it. 'I'd much rather stay here with you.'

'It's an honour, dear. Only the King's favourite gets invited for lunch on Easter Sunday.'

'Favourite, my arse!' he snorted.

'The boys'll keep you company.' She patted him on the shoulder. 'There!'

Lifting up his grey beard, he tugged at the neckband. 'Ghaagh! This thing's too tight! It's choking me!'

'It's the largest one I could find,' she said, disregarding his histrionics, and handed him an elasticated cravat.

The Earl put it on. Then, in shirtsleeves, braces, and suit trousers, he walked into the adjoining bedroom. He sat down on the end of the double bed and slipped his feet into a pair of patent leather shoes, at the same time pulling at his collar, trying to loosen it.

'What a joke!' he scowled. 'Edward can't stand the sight of me. He still thinks I was responsible for his brother's death, y'know.'

'Which you weren't,' Githa replied from the doorway.

'Which, I wasn't. And now this sham! Well, at least we won't have to waste the whole day there.' He stood up and put on his waistcoat, sucking in his stomach to do up the buttons. 'Oof! We'll all get together this evening.'

She walked up to him and patted him on the chest. 'No more goodies for you, my great big Easter bunny!'

'Thank you,' he laughed. 'And I feel a right bunny dressed up like this, I can tell you!'

'Oh, I *so* used to love Easter when the children were little!' Githa sighed with wistful longing. 'Do you remember?'

'What, getting up at dawn to hide all those damned eggs? How could I forget?'

'Yes!' she laughed with excitement. 'But we did teach them the real meaning of Easter, too, didn't we?'

'Jesus versus chocolate? No contest!' Earl Godwin chuckled, as he pulled on his suit jacket.

'Oh, they were such little angels!'

He smiled at her in tender, shared remembrance. 'Yes, they were.' They stared at each other for a long, poignant moment. Then, with a cough, he turned away. 'The trouble is,' he said, checking himself in the full-length wall mirror, 'that in this business one can learn all about the next life first-hand, unexpectedly.'

'Whatever do you mean?'

'Politics is a dangerous game, Githa. I could get bumped off at any moment.'

'Don't talk rubbish!'

'It's a fact. Look what happened to Edward's brother. Someone got rid of *him*, didn't they?'

'You're just feeling sorry for yourself because two of your sons have left. You're tired.' Her eyes filled with tears. 'We're all tired.'

The Earl took her by the shoulders. 'Oh, Githa, I know! But you must listen to me. I'm not saying it's going to, but if something should ever happen to me...'

'Stop it! You're frightening me!'

'That's the last thing in the world I want to do, old girl, but this has to be said. When I'm gone...no, hear me out...when I'm gone, our family's strength mustn't be lost. For the future of this country, it has to continue.'

'Of course,' she replied in a bitter voice, pulling away. 'Business as usual.'

'That's right,' he answered with firm authority. 'Because we do it best. And because we're the only ones with any power who give a damn about ordinary families!'

'But we're *losing* our family!' Githa cried at him in anguish.

'I know! I know!' Earl Godwin nodded, his voice filled with pain. 'And the only way we'll ever get them back is by playing out this game to the end, as well as we know how. Look, all I'm saying is that if it ever comes to a choice between Harold and Tostig, you must support Harold.'

'That's ridiculous! How can you ask me to choose between my own children?'

'Brothers can fight. One can become jealous of the other. We know Tostig's got a terrible temper, and he's ambitious. That's a dangerous combination. For his own good, he has to know we won't stand for it if he acts against the family. Call it a premonition, if you like. I hope it's unfounded.' He gave her a sad grin. 'Maybe I'm getting old.'

'I think you must be,' she said, ignoring his attempt at humour.

'Just remember, Githa, Harold's my natural successor. And, as such, you must stick by him.'

'All right, you've made your point.'

He took her hands in his. 'Don't be angry with me, my love. I'm just voicing my fears, that's all.'

'Well, I wish you wouldn't. Not if it means turning me against my own son.'

'I'm sorry. I won't mention it again.' He pulled her towards him. 'Now, come on, you lovely woman, give us a kiss!' He pressed his lips against hers but received only a half-hearted response. 'That's not a kiss!' he growled in playful persuasion and tried again. This time she kissed him back. 'Mm! I could stay a bit longer, y'know?'

Githa pushed him away, with a small laugh. 'Go on, you old smoothie, get out of here!'

The Earl gave a reluctant sigh. Picking up a thin ivory-handled cane and a flat top hat from a nearby chair, he went to the door and opened it. He turned towards her, snapping open the hat and putting it on at a rakish angle. 'I'll see you later, all right?'

She smiled and nodded. 'And don't eat too much.'

Earl Godwin grinned and shook his head. Stepping out onto the landing, he tipped the brim of his hat to her with his cane, then turned and walked out of sight. Githa remained standing in the centre of the floor, her brow furrowed with concern, staring at the spot where he had been.

*

Holding up the delicate, pale grey balsawood scale model of King Edward's new abbey before his eyes, the Treasurer inspected it with delight.

'Wow! That's incredible!' he exclaimed. 'As your Treasurer, Your Majesty, I gotta tell ya, it'll definitely be worth it. The faithful'll spend up big time to come and see this!'

Looking on from nearby club armchairs were the King and the Dean of the Royal Chapel. Behind them, a warm glow came from logs blazing in the open fireplace.

'My turn!' the Dean squealed with excitement.

Taking great care, the Treasurer passed the model over to him. 'Here you go, Dean.'

'Thank you. Oh, it's absolutely marvellous!'

Meanwhile, King Edward sat preening himself, brushing away some imperceptible imperfection from the front of his robes. He raised his head and looked at them. 'Yes, it is rather magnificent, isn't it?' he said nonchalantly.

'Its power, one can actually feel it!' gasped the Dean in an awed voice. 'I just can't wait to see the real thing. It'll be one of the holiest places in the world!'

'I hope so,' the King shrugged with throw-away modesty. 'It was designed to embody our spiritual identity. Something for people to believe in. Something to treasure and defend.'

'God created the world, Your Majesty, but this makes it even more sacred!' the Dean gushed with obsequious pleasure. 'Would you care to look at it again, Archbishop?' he called out, leaning round in his seat.

'No, thank you, Dean,' answered Archbishop Stigand. Standing beside a tall window on the far side of the comfortable but dingy upstairs sitting room, he parted the net curtains with a finger and stared out. 'You have visitors, my Lord.'

'Who is it?' King Edward said testily.

'Earl Godwin and two of his sons.'

'Why? What do *they* want?'

'Hey, remember what day it is!' the Treasurer laughed. 'They've come for lunch, with gifts for the King!'

The Dean's plump face lit up. 'Maybe they've brought Easter eggs?'

The King slumped back in his seat. 'I'd forgotten. How annoying!' he pouted.

'Send 'em packing, my Lord,' urged the Treasurer.

'Yes,' the Dean agreed. 'Accept their presents and tell them you're too busy to see them, Your Majesty.'

'You have to admit them, Sire,' the Archbishop counselled, walking across the floor towards them. 'It's tradition. Easter lunch is part of the celebrations.'

'Well, I don't see why Easter should be so special,' King Edward grumbled. He tutted and sighed. 'Oh, all right! If I must. Show them into the drawing room, Stigand, and say I'll be along in a minute. And you'd better inform the Queen that I'll be eating separately.' As Archbishop Stigand bowed and moved towards the door, he called after him. 'Oh yes, and send in the chef.'

'Leave it to me, Your Majesty,' the Archbishop nodded and left the room.

'I'll give him lunch, the great Earl. Eggs and fish'll do *him*. That should put him in his place!'

The Dean clapped his hands. 'Oh, jolly well done, my Lord!'

'And his sons can serve the meal!' the King sneered.

'They ain't gonna like that one little bit!' grinned the Treasurer, his gold tooth flashing.

'No, they won't,' King Edward smiled with contempt. 'Humility, gentlemen, is a wonderful thing!'

*

A short time later, in one of the smaller, subsidiary dining rooms of the palace, King Edward and Earl Godwin sat next to each other at a small table covered with a purple embroidered cloth.

Behind them, Harold and Tostig, having laid out plates, cutlery, and glasses, were hurrying to and fro bringing baskets of bread rolls and small bowls of green salad and fruit. They then commenced serving the main course of steamed fish and sliced hard-boiled egg from two silver tureens set on a sideboard in a raised alcove at the back of the room.

Every so often, as he munched on a roll and picked at his meal with a fork, the Earl tugged at his cravat, attempting to loosen it. His face was flushed and damp with perspiration.

'Some more water, please,' the King called over his shoulder.

Harold quickly approached with a stainless-steel carafe and topped up their glasses. On his way back towards the sideboard, as his foot caught on the step of the alcove, he stumbled but regained his balance without spilling a drop. Tostig laughed out loud.

Earl Godwin looked round and smiled. 'Good recovery, Harold! Though you could've helped him, Tostig.'

'As my brother could have helped me, if you'd let him,' King Edward muttered beside him.

'Here we go again,' the Earl groaned, turning towards him. 'How many times do I have to say it to convince you, Edward? I had no part in your brother's death!'

'Yes, yes, so you say,' the King replied, with a dismissive wave of his hand.

In anger, Earl Godwin dug his fork into the fish and shovelled a large piece into his mouth. He tore off a chunk of bread roll and held it up, glaring at him. 'May this bread choke me if I'm guilty, damn it!' He stuffed the piece in his mouth, chewed, and swallowed. 'All right?'

All of a sudden, as a sharp, undetected, needle-thin fish bone caught in his throat, he gagged. He swallowed hard, gulping noisily in an attempt to dislodge it, at the same time clawing at his throat, trying to stretch his collar. The veins in his neck stood out, purple and swollen, as rivulets of sweat gushed down his straining face.

He gasped, clutching at his chest, and broke into a fit of loud, dry coughing. With his eyes bulging in panic, he struggled to stand, then fell backwards, tipping over his chair and crashing onto the floor.

As Harold and Tostig rushed to their father's side, King Edward leaped to his feet, his hand pressed to his mouth. 'My God!' he cried in awestruck horror through his fingers, stifling a laugh of joyful vindication.

*

Bells tolled heavily overhead and pipe-organ music soared from within as the mourners poured out of the cathedral, opening their umbrellas against a cloudburst of fine rain falling from the blue-and-grey patchwork sky. As they came down its deep, paved front steps, the Godwin family members appeared in a group, surrounded by their closest friends. Harold had his arm around Githa. On either side of them, sympathetic crowds looked on in respectful silence.

Seeing the aged Earl Siward approaching across the steps to speak to him, Harold released his mother into Leofwine's care and let the party go on ahead, while he stopped and waited.

'How're you bearing up, mate?' Siward asked with gentle sadness, coming up to him.

'Oh, I'm all right thanks, Siward,' Harold answered, with a weary smile.

'I'm glad. The country needs you to be strong, Harold.' He put a consoling hand on Harold's shoulder. 'If it's any comfort, I'm sure you'll see your dad again, mate. One day we'll all have a beer up there together, eh?'

'That'd be good. As long as he's paying!'

Siward gave a wry laugh. 'Though I doubt if I'll be far behind him. I wouldn't be surprised if he had a pot lined up for me already! Anyway, I just wanted to tell you how I feel, Harold. Godwin was a great man, and for all our rivalry he was one of my closest friends.'

'I know he was, mate,' Harold nodded.

'And after us, you're the only one left to defend the old ways. I know you won't let us down. God bless you, Harold,' Giving Harold a swift, bear-like embrace, Siward turned and walked away.

Harold watched the old Earl stride off through the rain and shook his head. 'I wish people would stop telling me that,' he murmured to himself. He looked up at the mottled layers of cloud, moving across each other like drifting tectonic plates, and let out a deep, sorrowful sigh. 'Oh, Dad!' he murmured softly.

While Harold walked on after the mourners, over to the side, at the foot of the steps, Eric Braithwaite was once again on hand to report the momentous event. Turning his back to the crowd, he began speaking into his microphone in a solemn voice.

'It's the end of an era. Godwin's gone and the nation mourns. While the bereaved family makes its way after the cortège, our thoughts turn inescapably to the future. What will happen next? As Harold takes on his father's mantle, two questions remain to be answered. Will the ambitious Tostig be content to live in his brother's shadow? And where will Algar find the support he needs to be a real contender? The game continues. But don't forget, if none of the main players can win outright power themselves, there's always Duke William waiting in the wings...This is Eric Braithwaite, for the *Anglo-Saxon Chronicle*, at Godwin's funeral.'

He switched off the tape recorder hanging at his side. 'Lenny!' he called out for his assistant, while he opened it and removed the cassette. As he did so, all of a sudden, his face became wracked with dismay. With a moan of dreadful realisation, he looked down at his feet, staring at his brand new, two-tone brogues soaking ankle-deep in a rain-spattered puddle.

9

It was Cup Final day and the city centre was overflowing with football fans, sightseers, and tourists. Making their way back after the match, Gurth and Leofwine threaded a path through the festive crowd across an open plaza, lined on all sides with food stalls, clothing and memorabilia shops, restaurants, bars, and open-air cafés.

All around them, people of all ages were laughing and shouting to each other in the late afternoon sunlight, many sporting scarves, jerseys, and hats in their favourite team's colours. Bright paper streamers were tossed and went rippling over their heads, while large rubber balloons bounced among them, batted backwards and forwards into the air.

On the edge of the square, standing at the curb outside one of the congested bars, Captain Guitaro and The Landing Party, all wearing ponchos and wide sombreros, were playing a jaunty Mexican serenade on trumpets, violin, guitars, and maracas.

As the two brothers squeezed between the revellers, they suddenly spotted Bernard, a close friend of theirs—a bearded, heavyset, high-ranking naval officer in a roll-neck jumper and a blue serge jacket and cap—poised on the corner of a nearby side street, staring about with uncertainty.

'Bernard!' Gurth shouted to him above the noise of the crowd, waving as he looked in their direction. 'Bern! Over here!'

Bernard saw them and gave a broad grin. Leaning forward, and with a seaman's rolling shoulders, he ambled over to join them. 'G'day, guys!' he said with a chuckle, as he reached them.

'G'day, mate!' Gurth greeted him warmly, shaking hands. 'What brings you to town?'

Bernard looked skywards and sighed. 'Came for the game, didn't I.'

'Great, wasn't it?' Leofwine grinned.

'If you call seeing your team get thrashed great, Leo, I suppose it was,' Bernard moaned. They all laughed. 'Hey, how about we get a drink? I'm drier than a cocky's whatsit!'

'Sounds good.' Gurth pointed across the square. 'There's a pub over there.'

In single file, like a conga line at a party, they zigzagged through the throng, over to the far side. Just as they reached the half-dozen already occupied tables on the sidewalk outside the pub, a group of people got up to leave.

'Quick, grab that table, Leo!' Gurth said. 'I'll get the drinks. What're you having, Bern?'

'A beer thanks, mate.'

'Make that two,' added Leofwine.

'Right. Back in a sec'!'

While Gurth went off, Leofwine and Bernard strode over to the table and sat down on benches opposite each other.

As they did so, within the shaded interior of the crowded bar, the dark figure of Earl Algar, his face disguised beneath a black peaked cap and sunglasses, was standing at the counter hunched over his drink, watching them. Slouching next to him, his back against the bar, was a skinny, greasy-haired rocker in a dirty white t-shirt and a studded, leather jacket with its collar turned up.

'So, look who's arrived! Harold's stooges!' Algar whispered with scorn, as Gurth came into the bar and waited in line at the far end.

'What's that to us?' the rocker scowled, only bothering to look round once, then continued texting on his mobile phone.

'Go and listen to them, Raul. Get up close and tell me what you hear.'

'Why bother, Lord Algar? We've got what we came for. The protection money'll keep us going for a year.' Raul grinned and patted his breast pocket. 'And I've made a bundle on the game!'

'Shut it and do it, Raul! There may be something I should know.'

With a grunt of protest, Raul grudgingly pushed himself away from the bar and set off through the crowd.

Meanwhile, outside at their table, Leofwine looked around the plaza with a happy grin. 'What an atmosphere, eh?'

'Yeah, the Final's always a good day out,' Bernard said, dabbing at his forehead with a handkerchief. 'Bloody hell, but it's jam-packed!'

'That just adds to the excitement, mate.'

'I don't know how you blokes live here, it's so noisy.'

Leofwine watched in open admiration as a scantily clad brown-haired woman, with her well-developed body almost bursting out of the tight singlet and hot pants she was wearing, jogged past. 'Oh, you get used to it, y'know!'

Bernard gazed after her. 'Ye-e-es, I can see how it might appeal to one's baser instincts, Leo!'

'Yah, y'old prude! Anyway, how long's it been since your team won the Final, Bernie?'

'It's been ten years. Thanks for rubbing it in, mate! I remember, because it was the year your dad died. Then we came really close again five seasons ago. We should've won it that time. That missed open goal still haunts me. It was against your lot, too, you bastard!'

'What a match!' Leofwine smiled. 'Went right down to the wire!' He gave a sigh. 'It was just after that that we heard Siward had been killed.'

'Yes,' Bernard nodded soberly. 'I was very sorry to hear the news. He was a good man.' He pulled out his tobacco pouch and began to roll a cigarette. 'He and your dad were pretty close, weren't they?'

'Yeah,' Leofwine smiled sadly. 'They were two of a kind.'

'Still, Siward had a good innings. Knowing him, he wouldn't have wanted to go any other way. Killed in action, fighting for King and country.'

'No, I suppose not. Mind you, I've always fancied seeing out my last moments in the arms of some busty brunette!'

Just then, materialising out of the crowd, Raul sidled up to the edge of the footpath behind Bernard and lit a cigarette.

'Well, that has its merits, too, I must admit!' Bernard chuckled, striking a match. 'So, what else has been happening? How's Algar going? Still mixed up with that mad bugger, Gryffyth?'

'Latest word is they're cooking up some kind of plan together to start a revolt.'

'Bloody idiots!'

'And Algar's given Gryffyth his daughter to seal their alliance.'

'Hadn't he already offered her to Harold?'

'Yeah, and Harold told him to get lost!'

'The poor girl.' Bernard shook his head. 'You shouldn't go using your kids like that. It's tantamount to slavery.'

'Oh, don't worry, she didn't mind. Aldyth's as mercenary as her father.' Leofwine lowered his voice. 'Anyway, in order to marry her, Harold would've had to give up his own wife, Edith.'

Bernard's mouth fell open. 'His *what?*'

'They're not officially married yet, but they do live together whenever he gets the chance.'

'Well, I'm blowed!'

'And they've got three children.'

'That's incredible!'

'There was even a hit song about them both, although no one actually knew who Edith was. It came out years ago. 'Harold's in love with a lady'. You must've heard it? No, of course not,' Leofwine laughed at Bernard's blank response. 'I forgot, you don't get radio down there in gnomeland, do you, Bernie?'

'Oh, my old crystal set still manages to pick up the odd bit of classical music and some local gossip, mate. Anyway, I haven't got time to listen to pop songs!'

'Great. That's keeping up with the times for you.'

'What is?' asked Gurth, arriving back at the table, carrying a tray of drinks.

'Ah, wonderful!' Bernard smiled, stubbing out his cigarette.

'I was beginning to think you'd got lost,' said Leofwine.

Gurth sat down. 'Every man and his dog's up at the bar. I had to kill to get these!'

'That's what I mean.' Bernard said, his eyes sparkling with anticipation as he reached for his glass. 'You don't have to queue for anything out in the country.'

Gurth took a long pull of his beer and wiped his mouth on his arm. 'Yeah, well at least it's not as bad as Normandy. You have to queue up for everything over there.'

'Unless you're one of the upper class,' said Leofwine.

'Or rich,' added Gurth, pulling out his tobacco pouch.

'Same thing these days,' Bernard growled. 'Elitism. The Norman sickness. It's happening everywhere, more and more.'

'Getting that way,' Gurth agreed. 'Still, it's better here than anywhere else.'

Leofwine nodded. 'Yeah, we're all broke and we've got no class!'

'So, what d'you reckon on our local brew, Bern?' Gurth said, shaking his head at his younger brother's compulsive wit.

Bernard sipped his beer. 'Mm, not bad. A bit thin.'

'Not like yer real country ale, eh, cobber?' Leofwine said, putting on a broad accent.

'Blood oath, mate! Nothin' like it!'

'Anyway, what were you two talking about before?' Gurth asked, lighting up his cigarette. 'Something about keeping up with the times?'

'Oh, Leo was...' Bernard began.

'I was just filling in a bit of background for Bernie, about Algar's offer to Harold,' Leofwine explained.

'And some song about him and his lady love,' added Bernard.

'You told him about Edith?' Gurth frowned. 'You know that was meant to be a secret, Leo!'

'Yeah, I know, Gurth, but Bernie's okay.' Leofwine turned towards Bernard. 'As I was just about to say, mate, you have to keep this under your hat.'

Gurth leant forward. 'If this ever gets out, Bern, it could be bloody dangerous for Harold's family. No one must know about it.'

'No worries, Gurth, my lips are sealed,' Bernard nodded seriously. Then, swallowing the last of his drink, he smacked his lips together and belched. 'Ah! That's better! Now, I'm afraid I'll have to love you and leave you, my friends. I want to have a word with Harold before I go back.'

'He's probably already left. After visiting our mother, he was heading down to Edith's.'

'You should be able to catch him if you hurry, Bernie,' Leofwine said. 'He can't be far ahead.'

Gurth pointed into the distance. 'Follow that road out of town. Take the first left, and then the second track on your right through the pine forest. Go left at the dirt road and when you come to a fork, go right. If you haven't already caught up with him by then, you'll see a white house with a grey tin roof up on top of a rise. You can't miss it.'

Nearby, Raul tossed his cigarette butt into the gutter and sauntered back into the pub.

Bernard shook his head. 'No, thanks. I wouldn't feel right intruding on him. It's their secret.'

Gurth tipped back the last of his beer. 'Well, we've got nothing planned. Why don't we all go? What d'you reckon, Leo?'

Leofwine leant forward over the table. 'Listen, guys,' he said, lowering his voice, 'I don't want to worry you, but guess who's in there at the bar?'

'Who?' Gurth whispered.

'Would you believe, Algar? And there was a bloke standing behind Bernie, having a smoke, who just went back in and now he's talking to him.'

'Shit!' Gurth exclaimed.

'D'you think he overheard us?' Bernard asked anxiously.

'I don't know. But now that same bloke's gone running off.'

Gurth gave an angry sigh. 'This could mean trouble.'

'And here comes Algar!'

'Right, there's only one thing for it. Come on.' With that, Gurth swung round in his seat. 'Hello, Algar,' he called out loudly, as Algar came out onto the footpath and started to walk away. 'Fancy seeing you here.'

'Well, if it isn't the Godwin boys!' Algar laughed back with derision.

'Where's your mate gone in such a hurry, eh?' Leofwine demanded.

Algar gave a malevolent grin. 'Oh, he just went on a little errand for me, that's all.'

Gurth jumped up. 'Quick, Bern! Get some help and go after Harold! We'll follow you!'

'On my way!'

'After we take care of Algar,' Leofwine growled, while Bernard ran off.

'Come here, y'mongrel!' Gurth commanded, advancing towards him. 'We're going to have a little chat!'

'Like hell we are, you interfering bastards!' Algar snarled.

Pushing aside the middle-aged couple having a quiet drink in front of him, he threw their table over into the brothers' path, knocking them to the ground, then spun round and dashed away through the crowd, sending customers and drinks flying in all directions.

*

Harold came off the forest track onto the un-made, red earth road and pedalled up towards the fork. Far above him, the branches of the ancient redgums interlaced like the latticed roof of a leafy cathedral. On either side of him, amid the fallen limbs and dangling curtains of stringy bark, giant ferns spread out their fronds in the dappled, aquamarine light. The scent of eucalyptus filled the air.

Suddenly sensing something, Harold's ears pricked. He barely had time to register the sudden whirring sound and the flash of metal to his right before, a split-second later, a spear flew out of the bushes and smashed through his front spokes. With a bone-jarring jolt, the wheel buckled and jammed, sending him flying over the handlebars. In one fluid motion, he rolled along the ground and regained his feet, just as Raul and half a dozen armed companions rushed out at him from either side with drawn swords and blood-curdling yells.

In desperation, Harold ran back to his mangled bicycle, dragged his sword out of its sheath strapped to the saddlebag, and charged at them, parrying their blows and swinging in all directions. In a fierce confusion of clashing blades, he downed two of the rebels and broke through their circle. Bleeding from wounds to his shoulder and side, but conscious of keeping them away from the house, he ran along the knoll road to his left, up onto the slope where the trees were wider apart.

With furious shouts, his attackers gave chase. Harold spun round and felled another with a blow to the head, then ran on. Finally, he turned, panting, with his back against the bole of a tree, while Raul and the three remaining rebels closed in. At that moment, with trumpets blaring, Bernard raced up the road behind them at the head of a column of cavalry.

'Who are you?' Harold gasped, as Raul moved in for the kill. 'What do you want?'

'For the revolution!' the rebel snarled. 'Die!'

Lunging forward, he jabbed at Harold's head. As he did so, Harold ducked under his blade and stabbed him in the stomach. Raul let out a yelp, his eyes glaring at Harold in furious disbelief. With a groan he let go of his sword and, dropping to his knees, tipped forward among the gnarled roots of the tree. As he did so, one of the other rebels raised his sword to chop down on Harold's unprotected head.

Suddenly, caught in mid-swing, his body convulsed and his eyes bulged in shock as he was propelled forward a couple of paces and fell face down in the dirt with a javelin sticking out of his back.

Having seen his spear do its work, Bernard dropped his bike and ran up through the trees towards them, pulling out his sword and shouting. The two surviving rebels stared at each other in confusion. Then, as one, they turned and rushed away down the slope. Leaping onto their mountain bikes, they sped off, with the cavalry in hot pursuit.

'Harold!' Bernard called out. 'Are you all right?'

'G'day, Bernard!' Harold laughed, gasping for breath. As he tried to stand erect, his grin turned sickly, his eyes rolled, and he sank forward into Bernard's arms.

*

The evening rain played a soothing adagio on the tin roof of the house. All was quiet in the lounge. Gurth sat on the arm of a chair, his face strained, deep in thought. Edmund, now a young teenager, lay slumped, wide-eyed, in the seat beside him. Leofwine was leaning against the mantelpiece, staring into the fireplace, while Bernard waited nearby, shifting from one anxious foot to the other.

Meanwhile, Gladys was at the open kitchen door, standing behind Harold and Edith's other two children—Magnus, ten, with a dark mop of hair, and Gunhilds, an angelic seven-year-old with her hair in bunches. At the sound of the hallway door opening, they all looked round with concern as Edith and Vera entered the lounge.

Edith gave them a tired smile. 'He'll be fine.'

'Thank God!' Gurth sighed with relief.

'They're only shallow cuts,' said Vera, 'but he's lost a lot of blood. Edith, are you sure you're all right?'

With a weary nod, Edith sat down. 'Yes, I'm fine, Mum.'

Gladys put a hand on the children's heads. 'Come on now, my beauties, let's get you some tea!'

As they followed her into the kitchen, Bernard stepped forward. 'Well, I'd better be going,' he said. 'Goodbye, Edith.'

'Thanks for getting here so fast, Bernard,' Edith smiled in gratitude, shaking his hand. 'You saved Harold's life.'

'No worries. I'm just glad we made it in time.'

'What happened, Mum? How did Dad get hurt?' Edmund asked, coming up to them.

'Some horrible men attacked him on his way home, darling. And Bernard, here, rescued him.'

'Were they robbers?'

'Yes, sort of,' she sighed.

He turned to Bernard. 'Did you fight them?'

'Only a little bit, Edmund,' Bernard chuckled. 'Your dad had already scared them off.'

'I'll see you out, mate,' said Gurth.

'Right. Thanks. Bye all.'

'See ya, Bernie,' Leofwine waved.

As Gurth led the way to the front door, Bernard nodded in the direction of the kitchen. 'I'll just say goodbye in there.' He walked over to the open door and leant his head inside. Magnus and Gunhilds were sitting at the table eating toast and Vegemite, while Gladys stood behind them at the stove, stirring a saucepan. 'See y'later, kids,' he called out.

''Bye!' Magnus replied with his mouth full.

'Goodbye, Mister Beardy!' Gunhilds answered, with a cheeky grin.

Bernard laughed, while the children giggled. 'So long, Gladys. It's been nice meeting you.'

'You, too, Bernie. Come again sometime. It's always good to see a handsome face.'

'I'll make a point of it,' Bernard grinned. 'Bye.' He carried on to the front door, where Gurth was waiting. 'Listen, Gurth, what about the bodies?'

'Don't worry, Leo's taken care of it. We got the last two. There'll be nothing to connect Harold with here.'

'Except for Algar?'

'He's long gone. We'll sort him out later.'

'By the way, mate, how does Gladys fit in?' Bernard asked, as Gurth opened the door for him.

'Oh, she's been part of the family for years. Why?'

'I just wondered…'

'You old dog! You fancy her, don't you?'

'Well, she's a very attractive woman.'

'I'll put a word in for you, if you like?'

'Don't you dare!' Bernard laughed. 'Anyway, the rain seems to have stopped, that's good,' he said, looking up at the clearing night sky.

'Yeah. Bern, look, thanks a lot, mate,' Gurth said earnestly, as they shook hands. 'I'm really grateful. Your speed made all the difference.'

'Oh, I'm a good little mover when I get going!' Bernard grinned.

'Gladys had better watch her step then!'

'See y'later.'

'Yeah. See ya, mate.'

Gurth watched from the doorway as Bernard collected his bicycle, switched on the lights, and wheeled it away into the darkness.

*

Both physically and emotionally exhausted by the tide of recent events, Edith and Harold were taking time out together, sitting on garden chairs under the shade of a pear tree in the backyard. The air felt clean and fresh on their skin and the warm earth smelled good, pungent and sweet in its simple honesty, a balm for their weary spirits.

Harold had his left arm in a sling. On a low, fold-up table between them was a tray with mugs of tea and a plate of biscuits on it—a small island of normality in the sea of ferment and violence that surrounded them. A short way off, Edmund was kicking a soccer ball against the stone wall of one of the sheds.

'Oh, oh, here comes the great footballer!' Edith warned with a smile, as their son turned towards them and booted the ball in their direction.

'It must be genetic,' Harold grinned.

'Yeah, sure.'

'Tell you what, I used to be pretty good!'

'Was that before or after you started playing with swords?' she asked with biting sarcasm, unable to stop herself from forcing a confrontation—not for the sake of a fight, there had been more than enough of that already, but to let him know how she felt. She couldn't just pretend things were alright and that nothing had happened.

'Oh, long after that,' Harold replied with throwaway humour, ignoring her tone.

Then all the pent-up strain of the last few days burst to the surface in Edith's voice. 'Harold, don't! It was frightening!'

'I know,' he said quietly, as Edmund caught up with it and kicked again.

A moment later, the ball landed in Harold's lap, narrowly missing the tea tray. 'Whoa!' he laughed, clutching it to his chest with his good arm.

Edmund trotted up to them. 'Want to have a kickabout, Dad?'

'Not now, darling,' Edith said. 'Dad's not feeling very well.'

Harold balanced the ball on his sling hand and hand-passed it back to his son with his fist. 'Maybe later, Ed,' he smiled. 'You go and score a goal for me, mate!'

Edmund nodded with dismayed acceptance and turned away. Smiling fondly, they watched him punt the ball across the yard and run off after it.

Edith swung back to him. 'You could've been killed, Harold!'

'You think I don't know that?'

'The children were scared stiff!'

The memories flooded by her in a rush: Harold, wounded and unconscious, being carried through the back door of the house and up the narrow hallway by Gurth and Bernard; the sounds of their heavy boots scraping on the floorboards and bumping against the walls; the children standing with Vera in the lounge doorway, their eyes staring, their anxious faces pale and frightened, while she held open the bedroom door for them to carry him through.

'They nearly didn't have a father any more. Have you thought about *that?*'

'Of course I have,' Harold answered sharply.

'You're off with your army half the time, we hardly ever see you. And now you have a running battle outside our home! I can't believe it, Harold, there were actually dead bodies out there! It was hideous! I don't want that in our lives!'

'D'you think *I* do?' he growled.

Stark images of the fight flashed through his mind: the clash of weapons and the ghastly screams echoing among the trees; the grotesque, twisted bodies of Raul and the rebels lying bloody and dead on the ground; the eerie sound of the wind rustling the leaves around their corpses.

'Well, I can't take much more of it! When is it going to end?' Edith demanded.

'God knows!' Harold groaned.

'Which god is that? The god of war?' she asked with derision.

'Give me a break, will you!'

'Well, you obviously don't believe in love.'

'What're you talking about? I love you and the kids more than anything!'

'No, you don't. If you really loved us, Harold, you'd stay here and be with us, not off risking your life playing society's avenging angel!'

'That's not how it is, and you know it!' Harold protested angrily. 'You *know* I want to be with you.'

'Then give it up! How can you talk of love when you carry a sword around with you all the time? What kind of lesson is that for your children? To live in fear of you being murdered?'

'I don't ask people to try and kill me.'

'No, but you know that it's bound to happen, don't you? And that you might have to kill to defend yourself.'

'I can't help that. I love this country, Edith, and I'm damned if I'll just stand by and see it destroyed by rebels and madmen. I'm trying to protect you, too, don't forget.'

'So, leaving us and going off to war whenever the King demands, that's your idea of protection is it?'

'If that's what it takes, yes.'

Edith gave a sad sigh and shook her head at the ground. 'When killing equals love, that's a cold, heartless future we're offering our kids,' she murmured.

'We only kill those who are trying to kill us,' Harold insisted firmly. 'To protect the ones we love. And I make no apologies for that!' He reached down and picked up a biscuit. 'Someone has to defend people against bastards like Algar and Gryffyth, and if the price is high then so be it!' With that, he took an emphatic bite and slumped back in his chair.

Edith lifted her head and stared at him. 'Oh, how noble!' she replied scornfully. 'And who pays that price? It's mothers and babies, women and children, the old and the sick, they're the ones who really pay, not just those wide-eyed, courageous young heroes who get sucked into fighting along with you! Millions more civilians than soldiers have died in every war there's ever been and are still dying!'

'There'll always be accidents in war, Edith. That's just how it is. But no one gets sucked into anything. People fight when they have to, that's all. It's part of men's nature.'

'Men's *assumed* nature, you mean. It doesn't have to be like that.'

'Either way, it's the world we live in,' Harold sighed. 'And we can't change it.'

'I may not be able to change it, Harold, but I'll *never* tell our children to go out and kill or die for it, for such a ruthless, destructive system, or that war is natural and inevitable!'

'It is when when there's no other choice.'

And what about *us*?' she cried out at his obstinacy. 'Don't *we* get a choice? Men have been trying to beat violence with violence for thousands of years, and nothing ever changes. All those wasted lives. All that sacrifice. What's it ever brought us? Just one more war after another. The whole world's become traumatised by it!'

Harold leant down and picked up his mug. 'Well, at least we've tried.'

'For what?' Edith said, doing the same. 'So that one bunch of megalomaniacs can claim the moral high ground over another, for a bigger share of the profits? Come on. They're dysfunctional, the lot of 'em.'

'That's not what it's about. We're fighting for freedom and democracy. Isn't that worth anything?'

'Sure, freedom for some, maybe. Freedom that comes on the back of the misery of countless others. It doesn't matter a damn whose cause is just, Harold, it's always the same. When the dust settles, it's still the rich and powerful who rule while the poor and weak continue to suffer. You call that democracy? Do you think the people want *that*?'

'We all know there's dreadful injustice in the world, darling...'

'Well, I don't hear any of our so-called leaders demanding a stop to it or proposing a new way of doing things. Do you?'

Harold shook his head. 'Not so you'd notice, no.'

'No. They just live off the fat of the land and let others play out their aggressive fantasies for them. Whatever happened to peace and love and giving and sharing? All the things we expect from our own families, for God's sake. They don't even get a mention.'

'Some of us do try to make things better, you know.'

'Not those at the very top, the ones who could actually change things. They're all members of the same club. This is the ultimate boys' game to them, Harold. One full of noble sacrifices and fallen heroes, who think they'll wake up again in some celestial drinking hall with all their mates. In a heaven forged on war.'

'Don't forget the women who'll be there to comfort them, though.'

'That's right, ones who don't argue,' Edith nodded, in bitter recognition of all subjugated women. 'And as long as their system isn't challenged and everyone goes blindly along with them, those rulers remain unmoved, immune in their ivory towers and their paranoid view of the world. They're delusional. They must be. How else can they justify their inaction, living in opulence and playing war games while little children are starving to death, without water or shelter or hope? Don't be naïve, darling, they don't care about people. They've forgotten how.'

'I can't believe that, Edith. My Dad wasn't like that, and nor am I.'

'I'm not talking about you or your Dad.'

'No, but you might as well be. What do you think we've been fighting for all these years? So that one day there *can* be peace.'

'And the end justifies the means, does it? You're living in a make-believe world, Harold. Would you have us all wade through blood to get to your great day of peace? We'd have to wait forever and there'd still be more bloodshed.'

'Well, that's the reality, I'm afraid,' he pronounced with weary finality.

'No, it's not!' Edith insisted, refusing to give in. 'Not *my* reality. It's how we live *now* that's real, not in some hypothetical tomorrow. Don't go to war on our account, thanks, Harold. We've got our love for each other and we're alive. That's all the reality we need. And I'd rather put my faith in that than in some heart-broken future created by paid soldiers and corrupt politicians.'

'Oh, great, I can just see love stopping a Viking from raping Gunhilds or sticking his sword into Edmund's guts.'

'Oh Harold,' she moaned in horror at the awful concept. 'If that ever happened, it'd have to be over my dead body. I'm no saint. I'd use anything I could lay my hands on to defend our children, but it'd be a spontaneous human reaction, not something planned for in advance with armies and defences.'

'If we didn't have those things, Edith, we'd be enslaved within a week. There'd be chaos.'

'Can't you *see*?' she pleaded angrily. 'We're *already* enslaved! *Because* of them!' She banged down her mug in frustration and swept her arm back towards the knoll. 'What d'you call what happened out there in the woods the other day? *Sanity?*'

Harold sighed. 'Look, even if I agreed with you, darling, it still wouldn't change anything.'

'At least you'd be here.' Edith took a deep breath, calming herself down. She looked away for a few moments, watching Edmund trying to bounce the ball up and down on his head, then turned back to him. 'Peace isn't something you can win on the battlefield, Harold. It has to be lived. Otherwise it doesn't exist. And if no one speaks out for it, it never will.'

'The Church doesn't believe that. They bless the troops.'

'Those hypocrites!' She held up her hands and smiled. 'I know! Most of them are basically good, I'm sure. Misguided but sincere human beings. Like you.'

'Oh, thanks a lot!' he laughed.

'Talk about serving two masters. With their false piety. They love their pomp and their power too much to ever dare practise what they preach.'

'Yeah, that's crossed my mind once or twice,' Harold nodded.

'Edmund!' Edith suddenly called out. 'Will you go and tell Gunhi I'm just coming, please, darling.'

'Okay, Mum,' Edmund called back.

Harold smiled after his son, as he kicked the ball away and ran up to the house. 'He's a great kid.'

'Do you know what he told me yesterday? What he wants for his birthday? Guess?'

'I don't know. What?'

'A real sword.'

Harold heaved a sigh of regret. 'All right, you've made your point. I'm a lousy dad.'

'No, you're not, Harold. When you're here, you're a great dad.'

'Oh God,' he groaned, rubbing his face with his free hand. 'It's all so complicated. I don't want to lose you, Edith.'

Edith went and knelt beside him, placing her hand against his cheek. 'Harold, I love you. You can't lose us, not if you hang on to us!' As she put her arms around him and kissed him, he winced. She pulled back. 'I'm sorry, darling. How is your shoulder?'

'A bit sore, that's all,' he smiled. 'Go on, finish your tea. So, tell me,' he asked, as she sat down again. 'If we were ever invaded, darling, what would you do?'

'I'd take the children and run. Why, are we going to be?'

'Not that I know of, but it's always a possibility.'

Edith stared into the distance. 'We'd head for the hills, probably. It'd break my heart for the kids to have to leave their home, but we wouldn't be alone. The world's already *awash* with heartbroken tears.'

'And what would you expect of me?'

She turned to him and smiled. 'To come with us, of course.'

At that moment, Edmund reappeared from the house, closely followed by his little sister, Gunhilds. She was sobbing, her hair and clothes dripping with cake mix. Magnus stood behind them, grinning from ear to ear.

'Look at Gunhi, Mum!' Edmund laughed.

'You said I could make a cake, Mummy!' Gunhilds squealed through her tears, stamping her foot. 'You did!'

'Oh God!' Edith gasped, struggling to keep a straight face. 'I'm coming, darling.' she called back. 'Go back inside, Gunhi, I'll be right there.' As the children re-entered the house, they both burst out laughing. 'I didn't expect her to start on her own.'

Harold face melted in a tender smile. 'She's so beautiful! They all are. All right, Edith, you win.'

Edith looked round at him. 'What do you mean?'

'As soon as I get Wolnoth and Haco back, which I have to do, and there's no reason to hold them now that my dad's gone, I'll hand in my resignation.'

'I'm not asking you to give up your earldom, Harold, only the fighting.'

'I doubt if they'd let me keep it if I refused to defend it.'

She rushed to his side, her eyes alight. 'Oh darling, do you mean it?'

'Yes,' he grinned. 'Then I'll just be your plain old Harold Godwinson. I can't promise to be the man of peace that you want, darling, but I'll give it a go.'

Taking care to avoid his wounded arm, Edith hugged him. 'I love you so much, Harold.' She took his face in her hands and gave him a lingering kiss. 'Now, I'd better go and get your daughter cleaned up!' she laughed. 'Stay here.' She kissed him once more, lightly on the lips, and stood up.

Harold smiled at her, watching as she loaded up the tray and carried it away into the house. Letting out a groan, he unwound his tall frame, climbed to his feet, and sauntered across the backyard. Coming to the soccer ball, he stopped and looked about him. He was alone. No one was watching.

Suddenly, he spun round and side-footed it with dexterous precision through the open doorway of a nearby shed, at the same time lifting his face in silent triumph to an adoring, imaginary crowd. Goal! As the ball sailed through into the darkness beyond, there was a loud crash, followed by a clatter of farm implements and the squawking of chickens. Standing aghast, frozen on one leg, with his good arm out for balance, he screwed up his eyes and grit his teeth in mock horror.

*

The blind was half down, cutting out the sunlight streaming in through the kitchen window. The whole family was sitting around the table having lunch. With his arm no longer in a sling, Harold was using tongs to put salad onto his plate to go with his omelette, when there was a knock at the front door.

'I'll get it!' Magnus cried, with an eager grin. He leaped from his seat and ran out of the room. A few moments later, he returned, followed by a hot and travel-stained Gurth.

'Look! It's Uncle Gurth!' Harold smiled.

'Gurf!' Gunhilds called out with excitement.

'Hiya, kids.' Gurth waved to them. 'Sorry to burst in on you like this, folks, but there's urgent news for Harold.'

He pulled a scroll from inside his jacket and offered it to Harold. Pushing back his chair, Harold stood up and came round the table. After a moment's hesitation, he reached out and took it. Casting a quick look at Edith, he unrolled it and began to read.

'Sit down Gurth,' said Vera. 'Have you eaten?'

'Yes, thanks, Vera,' he answered, squeezing onto the bench next to Magnus. 'I had a quick bite before I left.' He pointed to the jug of lemonade on the table. 'But I wouldn't say no to some of that.'

Gunhilds giggled as Magnus grabbed a glass, held it out for Edmund to fill from the jug, and then passed it to Gurth. They all watched, beaming with pleasure as he noisily gulped it down.

'What is it, Harold?' Edith asked with concern, seeing Harold's stern expression.

Harold gave a heavy sigh and rolled up the scroll. 'It's finally started,' he answered in a hard, flat voice. 'Algar and Gryffyth are on the move. A fleet of Vikings has sailed over to join them. They've ravaged the top end and now they're making their way south, burning and looting as they come.'

For a long moment they stared at each other in silence, their eyes imploring across the yawning chasm of decision—his begging her to understand, hers begging him to stay. At last, he looked away, and the hope drained out of her. His commitment was gone. Gone in a newsflash.

Edith closed her eyes, shutting out his broken resolve, all faith in their union dissolving in the acid of her unshed tears. She heard his voice, as if coming from far away behind an inpenetrable wall of falling snow.

'I'll get my things,' Harold said quietly.

*

On the radio, somewhere in the house, a woman's voice began to sing the blues. With his saddlebags slung over his shoulder, Harold let himself out through the front door and softly clicked it shut behind him.

You're messing my heart around
You're tearing it apart
Can't get my feet back on the ground
Every time you start
To play your little games
Here you go again

He closed the front garden gate and walked across the sunlit road to where Gurth was waiting, already mounted, holding his bicycle ready for him. Strapping the bags onto the pannier, he looked back towards the house and sighed. He swung his leg over the crossbar and raised the pedal with his foot. With a grim nod to his brother, they set off.

You're messing my heart around
You're playing with my life
You keep saying you'll come on down
Then night after night
I know you won't come home
Now I hang my head and moan

Edmund stood alone, watching from one of the lounge windows, his lips tight, his eyes filled with angry determination. Pressed up against the other window, Magnus and Gunhilds

had their arms around each other, staring out. Edith appeared
behind them and gently laid her hands on their shoulders.

My heart
My heart has been true to you
Again and again
I start
I start to get through to you
Then oh then
You pretend
Well...

They all gazed in sadness as Harold and Gurth cycled over to
their waiting cavalry escort.

You're messing my heart around
You're shattering my dreams
How can I trust in this peace I've found
When I don't think you mean
Those tender words you say
Now you've gone away

Are you ever coming back to stay?

Riding side by side at the back of the column, they headed off
down the road.

Like a submarine bursting through the waves, I surfaced from the dream and my eyes flew open. I lay there only partially conscious, drenched in feverish sweat, my body weighing a ton, clinging in desperation to the memory of those last moments, still hearing the song and feeling its plaintive yearning. The anguish of parting poured out of me in a sorrowful moan.

I lay there utterly bereft, like a beached whale, straining as hard as I could to hold onto the threads of the story, clutching at them like the strings of a deflating balloon, receding, evaporating, floating out of my grasp—fighting to keep the images alive, to remember the words and re-live the scenes before they completely disappeared.

All of a sudden, my stomach heaved and a bubble of foul-tasting gas rose up in my throat. I belched. *I was going to throw up!* Letting go of the dream, trusting that it would still be there when I returned, I thrust myself up off the bed and swung my legs over the side. Groaning with self-pity, my head spinning wildly, I staggered to my feet.

The bedside lamp and the television were still on. Close-up shots of Fidel Castro and Chè Guevara flashed on the screen, penetrating my torpid mind. Somewhere in the building, a telephone that had been ringing constantly in the background finally stopped. As my insides churned upwards again, I gagged and held my breath, compressing my lips, forcing the air back down to block the spasm. Racing against a rising tide of nausea, I hurtled from the room.

In a blur, I stumbled up the hall and into the bathroom. Flicking on the light and accidentally slamming the door behind me, I hurled myself to the floor. Skidding across the tiles on my knees, I threw back the toilet seat and vomited into the bowl.

PART TWO

10

I'd made it back onto my feet. The room was still spinning and I was having trouble standing upright without support. I was slumped forward, legs astride, braced against the sink on my outstretched arms, my head hanging down between them and my eyes closed. I breathed heavily, listening to the voice of the television announcer coming from the bedroom.

'Then, on Tuesday night, we continue our controversial award-winning documentary series, 'Invasion!' When the First Fleet landed at Botany Bay, little did their masters back in Whitehall know that they carried with them one of the deadliest viruses ever known to man. Or did they?'

Despite the sour residue in my mouth and nose, and the debilitating post-nausea backwash slapping against the lining of my skull, my interest was stirred. I opened my eyes and lifted my head. Gripping the sink with both hands, I pushed myself up and stared through puffy, half-closed lids at my reflection in the bathroom mirror. My face was ashen and bathed in sweat. My right eye, with its carmine centre ringed by blue and black, looked like some exotic oyster left lying on an old china dinner plate.

'In the 1760s, smallpox had already been used by the British as a military weapon against the North American Indians, transmitted on blankets infected with powdered scabs, as a gift from His Majesty King George!'

I groaned at the miserable, un-remitting cost of history.

'*Was it just coincidence, then, that when those first ships arrived from England, among the medical stores they brought with them were a number of glass jars containing dried smallpox scabs? For inoculation, some might say...But to protect whom? Certainly not the local inhabitants.*'

Lowering my head into the sink, I turned on the tap and splashed water onto my face. Desperate to lie down, I eventually pushed myself away and stumbled back down the hallway to the bedroom. I paused just inside the door, my white shirt damp and undone, rocking backwards and forwards on my feet watching the images on the screen.

Accompanied by ominous music and a mournful sound of moaning on the wind, coloured etchings showed pockmarked Aboriginal men, women, and children lying dead and dying from disease.

'*Either way, within just a few years the whole indigenous population, which some estimates put as high as three million, had been decimated from coast to coast. 'Terra Nullius' was now 'Terra Virulous'!*'

With an exhausted moan, I reached for the remote to turn off the set but fumbled it and dropped it onto the floor.

'*Meanwhile, on Thursday at eight, 'Battle-Zone!' looks at the virtual world of digital violence,*' the voice continued, as a series of clips from action computer games came on the screen. '*Video games. Just good clean fun? Or a cynical plan to prepare the next generation for war?*'

Barely able to keep my eyes open, desperate to escape into oblivion, hoping that the dream would be waiting for me, I fell over to the bed. Kicking off my shoes as I went, I yanked back the covers, threw myself under them, and was instantly asleep.

⁑

Iko stood at the iron railing of the small viewing platform nestled between the bulkheads on the top deck. He stared into the night, watching the lights of the approaching dock. The deck hummed as the engines churned beneath him deep in the bowels of the ship. He leant out and gazed down at the luminous foam rushing past the hull.

His thoughts went back to their last meeting.

He had seen her coming out of one of the rooms in the palace, carrying a pile of towels. Wearing an eggshell blue kimono and a cherry sash, with her hair pulled up like a black satin cushion on her small head, her young innocence and her pale, transluscent beauty, like the finest porcelain, made his heart surge.

He smiled at her, but she turned away and moved to hurry off. He reached out and gently took her hand. 'Don't be angry with me, my love!' he pleaded.

'You promised me you would take me back to our village, Iko,' she reproached him in a tremulous voice. 'I don't like it here.'

'I know I did, Sushi. And I will. But the Duke has asked for me,' he smiled with excitement. 'This is my chance. To make a name for myself.'

'I wish you would not go, Iko. I fear for your life over there.'

'Don't worry, my sweet Sushi,' he grinned. He kissed her fingers lightly and tenderly touched her cheek. 'My sword-arm will keep me safe.'

Oh, how he missed her.

Iko stared into the darkness once more. Then he remembered his mission.

'I want you to check out the situation over there, Iko,' Duke William had said from behind his desk. 'Find out which side's the strongest. If it's the rebels, offer them our help. Very discreetly, mind you. If it's Harold, tell him you've been sent to invite him over to Normandy.' He held out a sealed envelope. 'Give him this letter

to confirm it. Say he can take back the hostages. Dress it up a bit, all right?'

'I understand, my Lord,' he had replied, accepting the letter.

'And remember, Iko, this is top secret. If the Saxons learn you're playing a double hand, they'll hang you for a spy. You're on your own and I'll be forced to deny you if you get caught. Clear?'

The sudden rasp of the heavy steel door opening behind him snapped Iko out of his reverie. He turned quickly to see an old man hobbling through the hatchway, a blanket wrapped around his frail body against the cold. The man raised his hand in greeting. Iko nodded politely in return.

The old man shuffled over to the railing and stood unsteadily beside him, gripping it with both hands. He looked ill. 'Not the easiest of crossings,' he groaned.

'No,' Iko agreed. 'It has been very rough.'

'I wish I hadn't had to come,' the man coughed, his face furrowing with pain.

'Are you all right, old man?' Iko asked with concern.

'Yes, yes, thank you. I have to be.'

'Why do you say that?'

'Because I have a promise to keep. A dying man's request. He asked me to deliver a letter for him. How could I refuse?'

'Ah,' Iko nodded in solemn understanding. 'Who was this man, may I ask?'

'Like me, he was a pilgrim on the road to redemption. He said his name was Sweyn, son of Godwin.'

Iko's eyes widened in surprise. 'Sweyn?'

'Yes. He was on his deathbed with the fever and asked me to deliver a letter to his brother, Harold, for him.' The old man's voice faltered. 'I'm so tired and I don't even know where his brother is. I know that he's a famous person, but I barely have the strength to climb up onto my bunk, let alone wander all over the country looking for him.'

'That is a sad tale,' Iko said, recovering his composure. 'It is also a very fortunate coincidence that we have met.'

'How so?'

'I am on my way to see Earl Harold now, on official business. I can deliver the letter for you, if you like?'

'I don't know...' the old man hesitated. 'Have you some proof of what you say?'

Iko opened his shoulder bag and produced the envelope. 'See. I also have a letter to deliver to him, sealed by Duke William himself.'

The old man inspected it and nodded, satisfied. 'Very well.' With a tired smile, he reached under his blanket and removed a wad of stained, folded paper from within the confines of his dirty clothes. With a trembling hand, he held it out for Iko to take. 'Thank you, young man,' he croaked. 'Now my obligation is over, I can go and lie down.'

'Secure for landing!' a voice suddenly hailed from a loudspeaker behind them. A bell clanged above them in the darkness, the ship shuddered, and the sea erupted into bubbling froth as the engines went hard astern.

*

It was a tranquil, summer morning. With the muffled tramp of marching feet, the jangle of weapons, the soft crunching of wheels on the dry earth, and a square flag flapping in the warm breeze, the small column of Saxon foot soldiers and a bicycle-drawn baggage cart made their way along the valley floor. Bald, brown hills rose up on either side, like the worn molars on the lower jaw of an ancient crocodile.

Riding next to each other on bicycles at the head of the column, were Stavros—a stocky, weather-beaten, dark-bearded captain—and Iko, dressed in a charcoal grey travelling kimono with his long sword strapped to his back.

It seemed to Iko that he had been away a long time and the novelty of the adventure was starting to wear off. The journey was taking forever. He was used to getting where he wanted to go and getting there fast. The man beside him was affable enough, he supposed, although, like all Saxons, too taciturn and gruff, too full of his own self-importance. But he was impatient to get on with his mission. He wanted to meet this Harold, to see if he was all he was reknowned to be. To find out if he was, in fact, worthy of the Lady Edith, for whom he felt the highest, protective, personal regard. Stavros, on the other hand, found his Norman companion to be predictably brash, like all of his kind, and an unwelcome addition to his burden of responsibility.

All of a sudden, Iko banged down hard on the handlebars with the heels of his hands. 'What do you *see* in these things, Stavros?' he moaned in frustration. 'They are so slow!'

'They leave room for the imagination, mate,' Stavros replied with a grin, speaking in a heavy Greek-Aussie accent. 'When I was growing up, every boy in the neighbourhood rode his bike like a horse.'

'In Normandy we prefer powerful machines under us, like roaring tethered beasts!' Iko laughed in fond remembrance.

'Yeah, so loud you can't even think straight!' Stavros growled. 'Anyway, that's it over there, mate,' he pointed ahead. 'Where you said you wanted to stop.'

'Ah!' Iko sighed with relief. He peered into the distance at a squat, square factory, its stovepipe chimney emitting a thin spiral of black smoke. 'But it is so tiny, I had expected something far more impressive.'

'It looks a big enough bloody eyesore to me, mate,' Stavros said sourly.

'You should see our giant factories back home, Stavros,' Iko said proudly. 'All glass and metal and flashing lights. We have created whole towns of them.'

'Well, you can keep 'em, mate. We've got enough great polluting monstrosities messing up the countryside already. We don't need any more.'

'But mass production is essential for economic stability, my friend,' Iko smiled.

Stavros turned and stared at him. 'You ever worked in a factory, mate?'

'Honour forbid!' Iko scowled with distaste.

'No, I thought not. Well, I'll tell you, it's bloody slave labour. Economic stability? Economic rip-off, more like. It's your industrialists and your bloody shareholders, they're the ones who pocket all the money, while the workers just get given the shit end of the stick.'

'That is not very enterprising of you, Stavros,' Iko remarked drily.

'I was taught to work hard for what I get, mate,' Stavros said gruffly. 'And I don't like lazy, good-for-nothing bludgers making a fat living out of my sweat!'

'Ah, so this lucky country of yours is not so lucky then?'

'Yeah, but at least I won't get locked up for saying it, mate, not like back where you come from!' Stavros retorted. Then, seeing how he had offended his companion, he ran his fingers through his thick curly hair and scratched at his short, black beard, knitting his brow, uncertain how to proceed. 'Sorry, mate, nothing personal,' he said at last, baring his strong white teeth in what was meant to be his best winning smile. 'Anyway, what does your friend make?'

'Who?'

'Your mate?' Stavros gestured ahead. 'In his factory?'

'Ties...' Iko replied in a tight voice. 'He makes ties.'

*

Amid a cacophony of clanging machines, ringing shouts, and a loud distorted voice blaring from an old Tannoy system, Iko and his bulky Norman friend, Charles, the factory owner—dressed in a three-piece tweed suit, with a bow tie and fob watch—walked down the centre aisle of the shop floor. On either side of them, workers in overalls stood operating steel guillotines and presses.

'Couldn't be better, dear boy, couldn't be better!' Charles shouted above the din in a suave voice. 'Can't make enough of 'em! It's all formality here now!'

'You are our cutting-edge, Charles!' Iko laughed. 'You prepare the ground.'

Charles smiled and waved his hand in self-deprecation. Suddenly, he spotted a worker sitting by his machine, reading a copy of The *Anglo-Saxon Chronicle*, its headline announcing: *Algar Beaten! Gryffyth Trapped!*

'Jacko!' Charles shouted to a nearby foreman holding a clipboard and pointed at the man. 'Give that chap his cards. He's sacked.'

'But...But...' the worker protested, 'I'm on my lunch break!'

Charles waggled his finger in the air. 'Aah...Yes...Well, think yourself lucky this time. C'mon, Iko,' he grunted, and led the way over to an iron spiral staircase, winding up to a balcony above.

'You run a tight ship here, Charles.' Iko grinned after him, as they began to climb.

'It's what these slack arses need,' Charles called back down. 'Keeps 'em on their toes. It's a competitive world out there, old boy, and if they don't damn well like the conditions, there are plenty more ready and willing to take their place for less money.'

On reaching the top, with their boots ringing on the iron-mesh floor, they strode along the balcony. Going past a line of windowpanes grey with dust, Charles stopped at the low door of an office. He stooped down to open it and they both went in. On closing the door behind them, the sounds from the factory floor below faded into a background hum.

Along the wall opposite, standing between two battered metal filing cabinets, was a chest-high stack of unopened cardboard cartons and a deep wooden shelf piled high with bolts of material and sample catalogues. At the far end, a calendar showing a naked young woman reclining seductively on a motorbike hung next to a wide corkboard covered with order forms, shipment notices, and delivery dockets, all dotted into separate sections with brightly coloured pins. Beneath it stood a cluttered, chipped, enamel-painted desk. They crossed the linoleum floor and sat down on either side of it.

Reaching down, Charles slid open the bottom drawer and pulled out a half-bottle of brandy. He rummaged about, found a couple of china mugs, and poured them both a drink. Passing one to Iko, he raised his own in salute. 'Bung-ho!'

'Cheers!' Iko smiled.

Charles took a long gulp, almost draining his mug. Sucking in the air to cool the tip of his tongue and then blowing out the hot vapour, he smiled with deep satisfaction. 'Aahh! Now tell me, dear boy, what brings you to this godforsaken part of the world?'

'I am on a special mission for the Duke,' Iko replied, sipping his drink. 'He needed someone to be his eyes over here and he chose me.'

'Well, jolly good for you, old boy.' Charles poured himself some more brandy. He offered the bottle to Iko, who raised a hand in refusal. 'A spy, you mean?'

Iko inclined his head. 'Of sorts.'

'Isn't that a bit dangerous?'

'Not at all. I have the perfect cover. I am delivering a personal letter to Harold from the Duke, and also another, from his brother, Sweyn.'

'Sweyn? The axe-murderer? What does it say?'

'Nothing really. Just a few sentimental words written on his deathbed.'

'Ah, so Sweyn's gone has he?' Charles sighed. 'Still, one less bugger to contend with, I suppose. Oh, my life's so boring compared to yours, Iko. The most excitement I ever get is battling for profits.'

'Have patience, my friend, things may change. Now, tell me, Charles, what about Earl Algar and this Gryffyth, what is the situation with them? Are they still a force to be reckoned with?'

'Not any more. Thoroughly beaten, old boy. Harold took on their combined armies and gave 'em a damn good walloping.'

'And their Viking allies?'

'Smashed, by Tostig.'

'I see. And Earl Algar, where is he now?'

'Oh, as soon as he saw that his goose was cooked, he deserted Gryffyth and high-tailed it out of there. Badly wounded, I'm told.' Charles gave a derisive chuckle and leant back in his chair, basking in the warm glow of alcoholic euphoria as he contemplated the rhythmic circling of the ceiling fan.

In his mind's eye he envisaged Algar, with his clothes all blood-stained, being propped up on his bicycle by two impassive officers as they retreated at the head of the bedraggled rebel army. Flailing angrily at them to push away their hands, he nearly fell from the saddle and had to be held upright again.

'A sad end to a most entertaining fellow,' he said at last, with a rueful sigh, as the wave of intoxicated well-being flattened out. He reached for his drink again. 'Which just leaves Gryffyth, trapped up in the hills.'

'Maybe he will fight his way out?' suggested Iko.

'Not a chance. Oh, he'll try to all right, but by now Harold and Tostig will have regrouped. They'll be ready and waiting for him to come down. He's got no other choice. Not unless he wants to starve to death.'

'He could always surrender?'

'No, not Gryffyth. He's as mad as a hatter. He'll never give up. So, there you have it, old boy. As soon as he's finished off, Algar'll be hunted down and then that'll be that.'

'But are you certain Harold has no equal, Charles? What about Tostig?'

'An absolute nut-case!' Charles laughed. 'Totally disliked. It's a miracle he's kept his earldom this long.' He leant forward conspiratorially. 'Look, Iko, where's all this heading? Do you think our great leader is planning to come?'

Iko nodded thoughtfully. 'If he can convince Harold to help him, yes, I think so.'

'That's a big "if". And if not? If he has to use...persuasion?'

'Then, still yes, I suppose,' Iko shrugged.

'Mm. Well, take my word for it, old boy, these people don't like authority, any authority, especially a foreign one. If he invades, they'll fight.'

'And we will definitely win.'

'How can you be so sure of that?'

'Because these Saxons are complacent and avaricious. And because,' Iko smiled, spreading out his hands, 'they already accept the need to wear ties.'

'Well if it's ties they want, the Duke'll put one round their necks all right,' Charles growled with ominous foreboding. 'One they'll *never* shake loose!'

*

While his small column of troops continued on across the high iron bridge, Stavros stopped and dismounted. He looked down over the side. Far below, Iko was standing on the riverbank.

Stavros had decided to let him go on ahead with his business, while he took the longer way around to the fort. At least, it would spare him having to listen to any more of that prattle about 'in Normandy this' and 'in Normandy that'! Although, strangely enough, he'd started to warm to the young knight, what with his naïve enthusiasm and amusing politeness. Still, it was better to keep your enemy at arm's length, he thought.

On seeing him, Iko gave a wave and bowed his head. Stavros threw him a quick salute in return. Then, shaking his head at the folly of his own interest in him one way or the other, he climbed back into the saddle and rode on with his men.

Meanwhile, Iko turned away and strode over to the small rowing boat floating at the water's edge. An old ferryman sat waiting for him with oars ready. He climbed aboard and took his seat in the stern.

Pulling out onto the mud brown river, keeping as far away from the banks as possible, they rowed off down the middle in silence. After a while, Iko reached into his shoulder bag and withdrew Sweyn's letter. He unfolded it and began to read.

Dearest Harold,

Well, it looks like I've come to the end of the road, mate. I'm fading fast. By the time you read this, I'll already know my ultimate fate.

Since we parted that night, I've been wandering the world, searching for some kind of peace of mind. Many times, I've sought refuge in the senses and more than once pitched my tent on the brink of physical oblivion. I've even turned to religion to find salvation and have prayed for forgiveness in every conceivable way!

Iko lifted his head and stared cautiously at the steep, wooded banks on either side. He peered intently into the undergrowth, at the dense, ominous clumps of trees growing down to the water's edge, the perfect place for an ambush. Nothing moved. All remained quiet.

But none of it could ever heal the pain of the memory of what I've done. I just couldn't find the way back. And now it's too late. Crazy, isn't it?

Iko gazed at the tips of the oars rising and dipping in the glistening water as he pondered the words he was reading.

The priests all tell me I've paid for my sins, that I've repented, and so I'm forgiven. Gawd bless 'em. How would they know? They've never put their hands in the fire. If only I could forgive myself.

Sunlight danced on the water ahead of the bow. In the distance was a bend in the river.

I've thrown away everything. My heart and my life. I hope not my soul as well? Oh, how I wish I could come home to see you just once more. I miss Haco so much. I miss you all.

Rounding the bend where the river doubled back on itself, the boat headed across an open stretch of shallow water towards a low headland on the far side.

Look after him for me, will you, Harold? Tell my darling boy that I've always loved him. He must be a young man by now. If only I could have been there to help him through life's storms. But how could I when I couldn't even save myself?

With a gentle bump they drew up alongside a small wooden jetty. Iko quickly put the letter away and, giving a word of thanks to the ferryman, picked up his bag and stepped ashore. Above him, on the fortified riverbank, two Saxon guards stood watching his arrival.

As Iko climbed up the wooden steps to the top, Harold's camp came into view, set back from the river at the far end of an open compound flanked by earthworks. Rising behind the wall of a wooden stockade was the high, gabled roof of a bluestone Edwardian house, while visible through the open gates were numerous rows of small tents.

*

Standing by the window of his quarters in the main house, Harold read through to the end of Sweyn's letter.

Be a father to him, Harold. Protect him with your strength and love. Comfort Mum and Dad for me, too, if you can. Try to convince them that I did find peace. Perhaps soon I will. It's almost time to abandon this wreck, and then who knows?

I hope one day you can all forgive me. Maybe, like they say, we'll all meet again somewhere? I'll believe that if you will. Anyway, until then, I'll just say see y'later, mate.

I miss you all so much.

Your loving brother,

Sweyn.

Dark with a week's growth of beard, Harold's face was filled with sorrow. Clenching his jaw against the painful lump in his throat and blinking away a stinging film of tears, his arm dropped to his side, holding the letter limply in his hand. He gazed out through the window, watching the sun slowly sinking behind the dark, jagged summit of a distant crag rising up from a forest of ghost gums.

He'd been half-expecting something like this, but the actuality of it, although cushioned by distance, still tore a hole in his heart. First his father, then Wolnoth, and now Sweyn. It felt like the foundations of his life had suddenly shifted, that all the old securities were gone, that the walls of his familiar world were crumbling, exposing him to the light of a future in which he, on his own, had to find a place to stand. Thank God he still had Edith.

With renewed determination, resolving to find happiness where his brother had failed, he slipped the letter into the inside pocket of his sleeveless jacket and turned to face Iko, who was standing behind him in the middle of the room.

'Thank you for delivering this, Sir Iko,' he sighed.

'It is an honour, Lord Harold,' Iko replied sadly. 'I am very sorry.'

Harold nodded.

'Lord, I also have a personal letter to you from Duke William, regarding the return of your brother and nephew.' Iko took out his envelope and placed it on the long table that served as Harold's desk. 'I will leave you now.'

'Yes. Thanks. I'll read it later. Come back in the morning and we'll discuss it. Meanwhile, one of my officers out there will show you where you can find a meal and a bed.'

'I am grateful, Lord Harold.'

As Iko bowed and left the room, Harold turned and stared out once more through the window. The sun had gone, leaving the towering rock face and the world below it in shadow.

*

Although the day had been warm, at that altitude the starlit night was cold. The curtains of Harold's quarters had been drawn to keep in the warmth of the fire, gleaming through the small round window of a pot-belly stove over by the wall like the blood-orange eye of some ancient, cast-iron Dogū fertility god.

Harold, Tostig, Gurth, and Leofwine were seated around it on twin two-seater couches, nursing glasses of neat whisky in honour of Sweyn. On small side tables at either end of the room, tarnished brass oil lamps were burning low, matching their mood. Hit hard by their loss, worn out from a long month of fighting and the constant lack of sleep, everyone was on edge.

'So, this old man simply gave the letter to the Norman, did he?' Tostig snorted with suspicion. 'That was very nice of him!'

'It could be an excuse to check out what's going on,' Gurth agreed, sitting next to him.

'What can he learn?' said Harold. 'We haven't got any secret weapons.'

'Not unless you count Stavros...mate!' mimicked Leofwine, in a half-hearted attempt at humour.

There was a brief flurry of laughter, then they all fell silent, gazing into the fire, each occupied with his own thoughts.

'Sweyn sounded pretty depressed,' Gurth said after a while, breaking the silence.

'It's bloody ridiculous!' Tostig scowled, slurring his words, throwing back the last of his drink. 'You've got to get on with life. You can't go around worrying about things you've done wrong all the time.'

'We don't even know if he knew about Dad,' Harold lamented.

'Poor sod!' Tostig banged down his empty glass on the coffee table in front of them. 'Did the Norman say what he died from?'

'No. All we know is that he had a fever.'

'Someone will have to tell Mum,' said Gurth.

'And Haco,' added Leofwine.

Harold nodded, pondering, swilling the liquid around in his glass, staring into the flames. 'Yeah...' He swallowed the last few drops and put it down. 'It's time we sorted out this hostage business once and for all. You've seen the letter from William. He doesn't need them any more. We have to bring them home!'

'Well, at least that'll be some good news to tell her,' Gurth sighed.

'There's still Gryffyth to deal with first, don't forget,' Leofwine reminded them.

'That's right,' Harold nodded. 'We'd better get some sleep.'

Tostig yawned and stretched out his arms. 'I agree. The bastard could show up at any time.'

Harold reached forward, warming his fingers in front of the stove. 'Things must be getting pretty desperate up there. He'll have to make his move soon.'

Tostig stood up and walked over to the desk. He picked up the bottle of scotch and poured himself a large glass. 'Ah, well,' he grinned, 'one more for the road.' He held out the bottle to them. 'Anybody?'

They all shook their heads.

'Well, he'd better not come tonight,' Gurth growled. 'I'm not in the mood for his kind of company.'

'You speak for yourself, mate,' Tostig replied with sudden aggression. 'I'm in exactly the right mood!'

Harold and Gurth looked at each other, imperceptibly shaking their heads and rolling their eyes. Good old Tostig had lost it again.

*

It was the middle of the night. In a cramped storeroom within the main house, Iko was lying fully dressed, minus his boots, on a camp bed, half covered by a light blanket. A red glow from outside, illuminating the whitewashed walls and the shelf racks filled with cardboard boxes on either side of him, flickered across his sleeping figure.

As the incessant ringing of an alarm bell, strident shouts, distant trumpet blasts, and the sound of running feet grew louder and louder, invading his sleep, he rolled over onto his back. A moment later, he woke up with a start.

Throwing off the blanket and leaping from the bed, he squeezed past a two-wheel upright trolley to the window and stared out. With an excited cry, he spun round and hurried back to the bed. Pulling on his black motorcycle boots and grabbing his sword, he strode over to the door and yanked it open. Outside in the corridor, officers and NCOs were rushing past, struggling into mailed jerkins and adjusting their equipment as they ran. Among them was Stavros.

'Stavros. What is happening?' Iko called to him. 'Where is Harold?'

Stavros halted. 'Out there, mate,' he said, pointing away. 'It's Gryffyth.'

'Quick! I have to join in! I need a helmet and armour!'

Stavros paused for a moment, rubbing his beard. 'All right, mate,' he smiled fleetingly. 'Follow me.' He ran on.

Meanwhile, the troops were assembling into tense, excited lines at the main gates, their weapons and equipment gleaming in the light of the flaming torches set in sconces along the palisade. Harold was at the forefront, staring about with concern, as more men ran up from the tents and the main house to join them.

The ringing of steel on steel, blood-curdling shouts, and horrendous screams echoed from beyond the wall. Just then,

Gurth and Leofwine arrived, fully armed, pushing their way through the pack to be near him.

'Ready when you are, Harold!' Gurth shouted above the din.

'Gurth, have you seen Tostig?' Harold called back.

'Bern's gone to find him. He's probably sleeping it off.'

'Damn it, he should be here!'

'Don't worry, he'll make it.'

'Anyway, first in best dressed!' Leofwine grinned, with gung-ho flippancy.

Harold gave him a grim smile. 'Yeah, right.' Then, looking around at his men, he raised his battle-axe on high. 'Ready?' he yelled. 'Open the gates!'

There was a great cheer as the heavy wooden gates were pulled open, and with a ferocious roar, the troops surged out to reinforce the night watch, who were fighting for their lives with their backs against the stockade. A few moments later, Stavros appeared among the stream of soldiers pouring through the entrance. Close behind him came Iko, hastily strapping on a round Saxon helmet.

*

Down the length of the compound, the battle raged as the Saxons fought to repel the night-time assault of the rebel army. Armed with a lethal assortment of knives, clubs, spears, swords, tomahawks, and machetes, the assailants were a hotchpotch collection of malnourished, multi-national separatists and revolutionaries, wearing berets, sombreros, Arabic keffiyehs, black balaclavas, feathered headbands, Chè Guevara t-shirts, white cotton pants, loin-cloths, and army surplus fatigues.

Gryffyth himself led them—a sinewy, bare-chested, glistening-muscled Aborigine in his early fifties, with crazed, flashing eyes, wild frizzy hair and beard, camouflage trousers, and lace-up boots—slashing out to right and left with a short, blood-dripping sword.

An eerie, flickering, orange incandescence from signal fires burning on either side of the battleground lit up the tumultuous scene, throwing the dark figures of the combatants into and out of the light in a kaleidoscopic tangle of jagged, fractured silhouettes. Above the unremitting cacophony of war rose the trilling of bugles, the strident trumpeting of conch shells, and the frenzied blasts of a didgeridoo.

While Gurth led a contingent of men to re-take the earthworks at the far end and stop the flow of rebels swarming up from the river, Harold fought his way through to the middle of the compound. Wielding his long-bladed battle axe at the head of his troops, he began to split the enemy in two.

Meanwhile, just outside the gates, leaving his victims falling about him screaming and groaning, Iko scythed his way into the rebel ranks with swift, sweeping blows of his long sword.

Nearby, busy chopping and jabbing his way through a knot of Saxons, Gryffyth became aware of the furore ahead of him. He lifted his lion-like head and, scrambling up onto a pile of bodies, scoured the mêlée to locate the source of the noise. At the same moment, Iko looked in his direction and their eyes met. Immediately, they began to hew their way towards each other. Eventually, they came face to face.

With a few strokes of their swords, they cleared a space for themselves and engaged, Iko swinging his razor-sharp blade in wide arcs and sudden crosscuts, while Gryffyth darted in and out with quick stabs and short slashes. In just a couple of seconds, to his utter amazement, Iko found himself, although unwounded, with his quilted, mailed jacket ripped apart in three places. Gasping in fury, he lunged at his elusive foe, missing time and again.

Just then, with a heaving shout, the Saxons under Leofwine pushed forward en masse away from the wall of the stockade, forcing the rebels back. Engulfed by the surging press of bodies, Iko and Gryffyth were soon pulled apart and carried, still straining to get at each other, into different parts of the field.

As the sky grew lighter and dawn approached, with the aid of Stavros and a large company of spearmen, Gurth finally succeeded in halting the rebel stream, driving the invaders off the earthworks and into the river. At the same time, having secured the middle ground, Harold sent half of his force down the compound to forge a link with Gurth, while he turned his attention to the battle at the stockade. Taking the rest of his troops, he charged to attack the rebels there in the rear.

Turning to look behind him, Gryffyth saw Harold coming and, with a snarl, rushed to meet him, closely followed by some of his men. As their forces engaged on either side of them, the two came together in single combat—axe against blade, slashing and parrying, jabbing and blocking, ducking and weaving, with neither gaining the advantage.

On an impulse, Harold suddenly changed tactics and hurled his axe at Gryffyth's head. As the rebel leader lowered his arms and leant out of the way, he rushed at him, catching him off balance. Grabbing his sword arm and spinning him around, Harold twisted it up behind him and gripped him by the hair.

'Give up, Gryffyth!' he growled through clenched teeth. 'It's over!'

At that moment, salvos of trumpet blasts issued from right and left, as reinforcements led by Tostig and Bernard charged out of the gates and split down both sides of the enclosure.

Hearing them, Gryffyth struggled with redoubled fury. Snarling through bared teeth, straining and jerking his oiled body this way and that, at last, with a mighty wrench, he broke free.

He wheeled like a cat and prepared to spring again. Just as he was about to launch himself at Harold, the remaining rebels from the stockade came rushing past, having broken off their attack, knocking him aside. Boiling with anger, Gryffyth struggled against them, raising his arms and screaming at them to stop, but he was quickly swept away towards the riverbank by the tide of his own men.

The Saxons gave chase, cutting the rebels down from behind as they scrambled over the earthworks in panic and leaped into the shallow water. They stopped in a line at the embankment, cheering and shouting in triumph, as Gryffyth and his depleted band splashed away towards the opposite bank.

*

The signal fires had been extinguished, leaving a blue haze of smoke drifting over the battlefield in the early morning air, as the bodies of the dead were carried away and the surviving rebels made prisoner.

Meanwhile, with subdued voices, the exhausted, victorious troops filed back into the camp. Among them was Iko, deep in thought, fingering the cuts in his armour as he trudged towards the open gates. Stavros came up beside him.

'Are you all right, mate?' he asked, checking Iko's front for blood but seeing none.

'Yes. I am fine,' Iko nodded.

'Good. Well done, Sir Iko. You fought like a Saxon.'

'That is high praise, indeed, Stavros!' Iko grinned. 'Thank you.'

'Good on ya, mate!' Stavros slapped him on the back and strode away.

A few moments later, approaching the stockade with his axe over his shoulder, Harold spotted Iko and walked across to him.

'Are you hurt, Sir Iko?' he asked with concern, noting the condition of the Norman knight's armour.

'No, Lord,' Iko smiled back. 'Apart from a wounded ego, I am as good as new.'

'I'm glad. Well done. You were a great help.'

Iko bowed his head. 'Thank you.' As Harold turned and started to walk away, he called after him. 'Lord Harold?'

Harold stopped. 'Yes?'

'Should you need someone to assist you in any negotiations with the rebels, if that is your intention, I would be happy to be of service?'

'That could be useful, Sir Iko. Thanks. I'll bear it in mind. Come and see me after you've rested and I'll let you know.'

11

'**W**hat d'you mean late? I wasn't late!' Tostig bristled with indignance. 'It was a deliberate tactic. Wasn't it, Bernie?'

'Well…er…it did give us the advantage of surprise,' Bernard admitted, from the opposite side of Harold's desk.

'It turned the tide of the whole bloody battle, you mean!' Tostig snorted. He was fuming. He wasn't going to be lectured to by Gurth.

'Harold had already beaten Gryffyth, Tostig,' Gurth fired back at him.

Harold shook his head. 'It wasn't quite over, Gurth,' he demurred.

'All bar the shouting, it was.'

'Oh, right,' Tostig raised his eyes to the ceiling and gave a bitter laugh. 'So good old Harold does it again, does he?'

'C'mon, mate, he's only winding you up,' Bernard smiled, trying to calm things down. 'We won in the end.'

'Yeah, well, I don't appreciate it.'

'Anyway, moving right along,' Harold continued, ignoring his brother's outburst, 'the question now is what do we do next?'

'Go after them and finish the job, I reckon,' Bernard answered. 'Before they recover from last night.'

'We can't!' Gurth protested. 'The path's so narrow up there we'd have to go in single file. They'd pick us off like flies in winter. The only way is to starve them out.'

'But that could take months,' argued Bernard.

'And think of the money it'd cost,' Tostig scowled.

Harold sat forward in his seat. 'Gurth's right, an all-out attack's too risky. Anyway, this has dragged on long enough. I want to go home. And preferably in one piece. Their spirits must be broken by now. They're bound to be open to reason.'

'Don't bank on it, Harold,' cautioned Leofwine.

'We have to, Leo,' Harold replied. He looked round at them. 'Therefore, I'm going to make them an offer. A full pardon for those who'll surrender.'

'What!' Tostig exclaimed. 'After all they've done?'

'They've only tried to win back some of their own land,' Harold insisted.

'Not all of them. What about those other ring-ins? They aren't here just to help Gryffyth.'

'A few, maybe, but most of them are genuine sympathisers. If the positions were reversed, we'd accept any help we could get, too, wouldn't we?'

'We wouldn't've lost the bloody land in the first place, mate. Just 'cos they were too piss-weak to hold onto it doesn't mean we have to start feeling sorry for 'em. It's the law of the jungle. The strong survive and bugger the rest.'

'You're being too hard, Tostig. We stole it from them in the beginning, don't forget.'

'Oh, boo-hoo! My heart bleeds for them. Don't be pathetic, Harold, that all happened years ago. Gryffyth and his mob are just living in the past. Anyone who stands in the way of civilization deserves to be crushed.'

'Yes, so we should be civilized. The land's ours now, we can afford to be lenient.'

'Not to Gryffyth, though, Harold?' objected Gurth.

'No. I'll guarantee him his life, but after that he'll have to take his chances with the King.'

'Bah! You're mad!' Tostig spat. 'Let this lot off the hook and we'll have separatists coming out of the woodwork.'

'They did team up with Algar, remember,' said Bernard.

'He wasn't just after his land rights, that's for sure,' Leofwine nodded.

'No, he wanted the whole bloody place for himself!' Tostig snarled.

'I know all that,' Harold answered. 'And Gryffyth was just a means to that end. He was duped. He's a victim. In more ways than one.'

'Ah, you're too soft, mate!' Tostig turned away in disgust.

'Anyway, Algar's finished, thank God,' said Gurth. 'Word is he might not survive.'

'Poor old Algar,' Harold sighed. 'Maybe I should've offered him something?'

'Don't torment yourself, Harold, he was never going to give up.'

'Yeah, you're probably right. Anyway, one thing I do know is that there's been enough killing. It has to stop.'

'Will Edward agree to a pardon, do you think?' asked Leofwine.

'To end the fighting? I'm sure he will.'

'No one in their right mind would risk even taking him your offer!' Tostig scoffed. 'They'd need to have their brains tested.'

'Actually, I've already found a local ranger who's agreed to do it,' Harold smiled. 'He knows Gryffyth well, and the way up to his camp. He'll deliver the message. I only need a volunteer to get my letter to him and bring me back Gryffyth's reply.' Just then, there was a knock on the door. 'Ah. That'll be him now.'

*

With his face perspiring freely in the early afternoon heat, wearing a mailed jerkin over his kimono and his sword tied to his back, Iko threaded his way up a narrow, twisting track between sandstone boulders and soaring gum trees. Walking beside him was an Aboriginal Ranger, wearing a short-sleeved khaki shirt and shorts, and holding a small white cloth attached to a stick.

Climbing up between the rocks onto a level stretch of path, Iko halted. 'Phew!' he whistled, wiping his forehead with his arm. 'It is so hot!' Brushing away the persistent flies, he stared around him. 'Do you think Gryffyth knows we are here?'

'He knows,' the Ranger answered.

'What sort of man is he? Have you ever met him?'

'He's just an ordinary fella. Had his childhood stolen from him. Got given education instead. Now he's back an' mighty bitter. Yeah, I seen him. He's my cousin.'

'Your cousin?' Iko exclaimed. 'Then why are you not up there with him?'

'Cos he don't help our people. The Saxons are here. We got to share.'

'Hm. I see.' Iko nodded.

'Come on,' the Ranger commanded, setting off again.

'I must say, though, this is very beautiful country,' Iko said, gazing at the scenery as they walked on. 'No wonder everyone wishes to own it.'

'We don't want to own it, mate, we want to look after it. This land, she's our mother. You can't own your mother. All we want is somewhere to live our own ways.'

'You are fortunate, then, that the Saxons have given you some.'

'Given?' the Ranger snapped back, bitterly. 'It's ours! They stole it from us!'

'Not from you, personally.'

'From our ancestors. From my people.'

'Everyone's ancestors had their land taken from them at some time or other.'

'Don't try and tick me, Norman. A fact's a fact.'

'Perhaps you would like to take the rest of it back by force, then, like Gryffyth?'

'What are you on about? I already said we have to share.'

'When I walk into danger, I need to know who is at my side.'

'Don't worry, mate,' the Ranger laughed. 'I won't stab you in the back.'

Iko smiled at that. 'Then, permit me one last question?' he said.

'All right.'

'I am confused. If you wish to look after the land, your mother, which the Saxons have...returned...to you, why, then, will you not allow the land to look after you?'

'How d'you mean?'

'By not letting your people benefit from its commercial development?'

'Its exploitation, you mean.'

'Either way, the profits would give you a much better standard of living.'

'Yeah? By whose standards? Our way of life'd be destroyed. Our young kids'd be sucked up into it like through a straw. We'd lose both our children *and* our mother.'

'But they must have offered you a lot of money?'

'Well, they can keep their bloody blood money, mate!' the Ranger retorted. 'Our home's not for sale and neither are we.'

'I am sorry, I did not mean to offend you. But it is still very beautiful.'

'Not just beautiful. She's sacred.'

'One's homeland is always sacred. It gives us our identity and our strength.'

'So, we should treat every place with the same respect.'

Iko shook his head. 'To us, only Normandy is sacred. For the rest, land is just land. To be used to make as much profit as possible.'

'You bloody Normans! You spread your coldness, like your concrete, over everything.'

At that moment, two lanky, bearded rebels in torn clothes caked with dried blood stepped out onto the path ahead of them and pointed their spears with menace.

Iko reached up and gripped the long hilt of his sword. 'Get ready!'

'Keep still!' the Ranger ordered. 'And leave the talking to me.'

*

In the rebel camp, high up on the rocky summit of the crag, a few of the despondent survivors shuffled about with weary fatalism among the branch and stone shelters erected between the boulders, looking for a spot in the shade. The rest lay out on the stony ground in the sweltering heat, many of them wounded, some awake and groaning, others fitfully asleep.

A few women moved among them, giving out sips of water and tending their wounds as best they could, with little more than clumps of moss, handfuls of mud, and torn strips of dirty cloth.

At the far end, out of earshot from the rest, Gryffyth sat amid the rubble of rocks, like a king on his throne. Wrapped in a blanket, his eyes open but unseeing, he was slumped sideways in a high-backed, rickety wooden chair, while munching on a dry piece of bread. Aldyth was seated on a similar chair next to him, her face stern and aloof, staring into the distance. Her hair was now dyed raven black.

Leaning against a granite boulder near them, sipping from a bottle of red wine, was Gryffyth's son, Caradoc. Of lighter build than his father but with the same majestic good looks, he was in his early twenties, with a thick mop of curly hair and a short scraggly beard. A rough, brown cavalry jacket was slung around his shoulders and his bare chest was wrapped in a bandage.

Sitting cross-legged on the ground in front of them all was an aged, weather-beaten Peruvian Indian, wearing worn white cotton trousers and an alpaca hat and poncho. He was plucking dejectedly on a small guitar, its melancholy notes a perfect expression of their overriding gloom.

Meanwhile, a short way off, three mercenaries dressed in camouflage army fatigues, black berets, and sunglasses lay hidden in a hollow between the boulders, observing the group with fierce intensity. One of them, a powerfully built, bald-headed Haitian, spoke with quiet bitterness, giving voice to their common thoughts. 'So, we're to die holed up in this bird's nest, are we? Because of that madman!'

'Don't worry, we'll find a way out,' grinned the lanky, close-cropped, blond Russian lying next to him. 'We've always managed to in the past, haven't we, *tovarich*?'

'I'll slit his throat before they ever get me, I swear it!' snarled the sinewy, fourteen-year-old Arab boy from the other side.

'That wouldn't do us any good,' answered the Russian. 'The Saxons need proof that the revolution's over.'

'This was no revolution, man,' the Haitian scoffed, jerking his head towards Gryffyth. 'That takes passion. *He*'s never burned with hatred for the oppressor.'

The boy thumped the ground with his fist. 'Aiyeee! Or vowed to wash the land clean with the blood of the infidel.'

'The only fire in *his* belly is one fuelled by alcohol!' the Haitian sneered.

'It's revenge that consumes Gryffyth, *tovarich*,' the Russian replied. 'And perhaps jealousy.'

The Haitian turned and looked at his companion. 'For the woman, you mean?'

'What?' spat the boy. 'That bitch?'

The Russian stared at Aldyth. 'Who wouldn't be?' he murmured, an admiring smile momentarily dancing across his cold blue eyes. 'Anyway, it's our own damn fault,' he shrugged. 'We never should've joined him in the first place. It was always too risky going against Harold.'

'Then how do we get our money?' the boy moaned.

'You can forget your money, boy,' the Haitian laughed coldly. 'We'll be lucky to escape with our skins.' He spread his hands out helplessly to the Russian. 'What can we do, man? Even that bastard Tostig wouldn't make a deal with us now.'

'We'll just have to watch and wait, *tovarich*. Choose our moment to take him by force and then hand him over.'

'And then I'll kill him!' snarled the boy.

'Ssh, boy! Maybe,' snapped the Russian, his eyes fixed on the rebel leader, who had stirred himself out of his lethargy and was pushing himself up in his seat.

Crossing his legs and sitting back up, Gryffyth let out a groan and waved his arm at the musician sitting before him. 'Can't you play something happier, Pedro?' he slurred irritably.

Pedro set down his guitar and stared at the ground. The two of them had been together a long time, but now Gryffyth, his old comrade-in-arms, had changed. The once fervent young firebrand, whose star he had willingly followed from the first, was gone. With sorrow and disillusionment, he had watched his friend and leader's dream of an independent state turn to tragedy and his once intoxicating conviction descend into impotent rage.

'I am sorry, Señor,' Pedro sighed. 'I am too sad.'

'What does it matter, anyway?' Caradoc said with a caustic laugh, passing the bottle of wine to the Peruvian. 'We're beaten, aren't we?'

Gryffyth's bloodshot eyes swung round to him. 'Caradoc! Caradoc!' he groaned in angry disappointment. 'What d'you think this is, just some bloody game? I haven't finished with those bastards yet.'

'But we're trapped!' Caradoc blurted, shaking his head in despair.

Pedro took a sip, then held the bottle out to Gryffyth. 'It's true, señor.'

'And your mate Algar won't be coming back to save us!' Caradoc jeered, pushing himself upright from the rock.

'I know Algar isn't coming back!' Gryffyth fumed, gritting his teeth. He grabbed the neck of the bottle and took a swig.

Caradoc lurched towards him. All his tangled emotions, all his filial devotion, all his concern for his father, all of his *own* needs, welled up in him. It was over. Why wouldn't he *listen*? He would have followed him to the ends of the earth, but now he was beyond reason. When he should be protecting them—protecting his *son*—it was all about *him.* The fear and confusion, the hurt and the yearning, blazed out in anger and ridicule.

'Then what d'you plan to do, Dad?' he cried, waving his arms in the air. 'Call on the Great Spirit to fly us all to safety?'

'Don't be so bloody stupid! You're my son, act like it. Show some backbone. We can hold out here for years.'

Pedro pointed to the crust in Gryffyth's hand. 'Señor, that is the last of the bread.'

'The last, Dad. There's no more!'

'And the last of the wine, thank God!' Aldyth snapped beside him.

Gryffyth struggled to focus on the hard crust, took a bite, spat it out, and threw the rest away. 'We've still got the water,' he muttered.

'We can't survive on that!' Caradoc shouted. 'The wounded are dying and the children are starving to death. We won't last a week.'

Gryffyth squirmed in his seat. 'Then we'll make a raid for food and medicine.'

Pedro rolled his eyes. 'Ay. We cannot!'

'Dad, we're surrounded.'

'Well, we'll break out, then.'

'We've already tried that, and it didn't work. We're finished.'

'You have done your best, Señor,' Pedro smiled sadly. 'There are just too many.'

'There must be some bloody thing we can do!' Gryffyth growled.

'We have to surrender,' Caradoc said quietly.

'Never!'

'Maybe you'd like us all to commit suicide, then?' Aldyth spat with sardonic derision. 'That's the traditional thing to do, isn't it?'

Gryffyth turned towards her, spreading his thick lips in a gap-toothed, mirthless grin. 'No, my sweet wife. When the end does come, believe me, it'll be in a blaze of glory. One last great attack, eh, Pedro?'

Pedro hung his head, shaking it in pity. 'Oh, Señor.'

Aldyth twisted away in her chair. 'Either way we die.'

Gryffyth took another mouthful of wine, spilling it down his beard. 'What's the matter, Aldyth, isn't death along with me good enough for you? You're supposed to be my queen.'

'Queen?' Aldyth gave a scornful laugh and snatched the bottle from his hand. She took a long drink and wiped her mouth on her sleeve. 'Queen of what? You've lost everything.'

'What did I ever do to make you so bitter, woman? I thought you wanted me?'

'D'you think I wanted *this*?' she answered, sweeping her arm around the camp. 'Harold wouldn't have me, so I was given to you. That's all. My father's used us both.' She passed the bottle to Pedro. 'Anyway, what does it matter? You're determined to see us all dead, you drunken sot!'

'Maybe I should kill you first, myself, then?' Gryffyth snarled, reaching for the knife at his belt.

Thrusting out her elbows, Aldyth clutched the top of her dress and ripped it open. 'Go on, then! Get it over with.'

'You'd rather have stayed with Harold, you bitch. That's it, isn't it?'

'At least he's a winner.'

Gryffyth gripped her by the breast in fury. 'You'd like it to be him doing this, wouldn't you?' he seethed.

Aldyth broke free and leaped to her feet. 'Don't you dare touch me, you filthy bastard! You're insane.'

'At least I'm not drunk on power!' he shouted after her, as she turned and ran off to a nearby shelter. 'You whore!'

'Stop it, Dad!' Caradoc protested. 'You shouldn't shame her like that. She's your wife.'

Gryffyth rubbed his hand over his face. 'I know, I know. Sit down, Caradoc. Have a drink.'

Caradoc refused Pedro's offer of the bottle. 'No. Someone has to keep a clear head.'

Gryffyth accepted it in his stead and drained it. 'She's never been a real wife to me, anyway. Women. They're all the same, Pedro. Always scheming. Always looking one way, then going another.' He belched loudly. 'Stuff 'em!'

Just then, as he tossed the empty bottle away to smash among the rocks, a sentry came rushing up to them, followed by a group of rebels.

'Well, what is it?' Gryffyth scowled.

'Two messengers from Harold, Gryff!' the sentry panted with excitement. 'Down at the bottom. They want to talk to you, in person.'

Gryffyth looked up at their eager faces. 'Oh, they do, do they?' With an effort, he pushed himself onto his feet. 'Well, I want to talk to *them!*'

*

Waiting at the top of the path, on the shaded edge of a steamy glade, Iko and the Ranger watched in wary expectation as Gryffyth and his men made their way, two abreast, down a narrow ledge traversing a deep cleft in the rocks.

'At last!' Iko whispered. 'Here he comes.'

'Watch what you say, mate,' the Ranger warned softly.

On reaching the ground, the rebels halted. Gryffyth took a few paces forward. He stopped and folded his arms. There was silence.

'You wanted to see me?' he called out, his voice echoing around the small natural amphitheatre. 'All right, I'm here.'

'I've brought you a message from Harold, Gryff,' the Ranger called back.

'Well, I didn't think you'd come from Father bloody Christmas, mate.'

A few of the rebels guffawed. Reaching out behind him for Iko to hand him a scroll of paper, the Ranger unrolled it and began to read aloud.

'To Gryffyth, leader of the rebels, you are beaten. You are surrounded and there is no escape. All you have left is starvation. You must surrender. You have fought a long hard fight, but now you must lay down your arms. I make you an offer. Life and freedom for all who are with you. A royal pardon.'

A buzz of excitement ran through the group of rebels.

'In King Edward's name, I guarantee you your life, Gryffyth, but only he can decide your final punishment. I beg you, save both yourself and the lives of your people.'

The Ranger rolled up the scroll. 'That's all. What's your answer, Gryff?'

Gryffyth stood in quiet reflection for a few moments before speaking. 'And you, Norman,' he said at last. 'We've met before. What do you want?'

Iko put his hand to his ribs. 'Yes, I remember it well,' he smiled. 'I am here to take your answer to Earl Harold. And, for myself, to see what a great warrior looks like close up.'

Gryffyth nodded. 'All right, then, you've had your look. And I've listened to your message. Now hear my reply. Harold's wrong!' he said defiantly, raising his voice. 'I'm not the leader of any rebels. We're an army of freedom fighters. And I say no to his offer. We'll *never* give up the struggle for our independence!'

There were angry cries of protest among his men.

'Tell Harold from me that we're not beaten yet,' he continued. 'And that I'll be back at him before he knows it, to cut out his lying tongue and kill all those who've poisoned our homeland. Now you blokes better leave quick, before I make a start with you.'

'Then you'll be cursed with our own people's blood, Gryffyth!' the Ranger shouted.

'Don't threaten me, you chameleon! The curse is on you and the invaders you've joined, not on those who resist their aggression. Now leave!'

Without hesitation, Iko and the Ranger turned away and hurried back down the path. All of a sudden, a roar of shouting came from behind them. They stopped and spun round.

The rebels were clustered around Gryffyth, jostling each other, all clamouring to be heard at once. Amid a cacophony of furious voices, there were cries of pain and the clash of weapons. Off to one side, Pedro held back the struggling figure of Caradoc as, from the centre of the mêlée, there came a long, heart-stopping scream.

Iko drew his sword.

Seconds later, with a great cheer, the rebels broke apart and surged down the slope towards them, shouting, 'We surrender! We surrender!'

Striding out in front were the three mercenaries. As they approached, the Haitian held up a spear with both hands. 'Here's our answer to Harold!' he laughed, shaking it in the air. Running along beside him, the boy threw up his arms and yelled at the sky, 'Aiieee!'

Iko raised his eyes and stared in horror.

Beneath a blood-clotted mass of tangled hair, his face contorted with rage, his mouth frozen in a hateful snarl, Gryffyth's piercing eyes glared down at him from his gore-dripping head, impaled on the blade.

From somewhere among the crowd came the deep, rasping drone of a didgeridoo.

*

The next morning, leaning on the earthworks above the river, Gurth and Leofwine watched Harold and Aldyth in conversation below them on the jetty, their words audible in the warm, still air. A long, slender skiff with three soldiers sitting in it was tied up alongside the jetty. Harold handed down her suitcase to one of the soldiers, then turned to face her.

'There you go, Aldyth,' he said. 'You're all set. It'll be a bit cramped, I'm afraid, but you should be at the carriage depot in a couple of hours.'

'It'll do fine, thanks, Harold,' Aldyth nodded.

'Good. And you'll be home sometime tomorrow afternoon. I've notified your brothers. I expect they'll be there to meet you.'

'What happens, Harold, now that my father's gone? Will we lose our earldom?'

'No, I'm sure the King won't blame your whole family. I imagine it'll go to your brother, Morcar.'

Her dark eyes lingered on his face, as if caressing him with her lashes. 'You've been so wonderful, Harold. What can I ever do to repay you?' she purred.

'Just have a happy life, Aldyth. And don't get mixed up in any more revolutions.'

'I won't!' Aldyth smiled. She took his hand and spoke in a seductive, husky voice. 'If you ever want me, Harold...for anything...don't hesitate to call me.' She held onto it, not letting go, staring deep into his eyes. 'I mean it, Harold. One word, any time, and I'll come.' At his obvious embarrassment, she gave a bright, light-hearted laugh. 'Now, I suppose I'd better be going.'

'Yes.'

All of a sudden, she reached up on her toes and brushed her lips against his. 'Goodbye, Harold,' she murmured. 'And thank you for everything.'

Recovering from the shock of her kiss and a sudden tightness in his loins, Harold helped her down to the soldier in the stern. 'Goodbye, Aldyth,' he said, his words catching in the dryness of his throat.

As the boat pulled away from the jetty, up on the embankment, Gurth grinned and shook his head. 'I don't believe it! After all she's been through, now Aldyth's actually trying to get her hooks into Harold.'

'Fair's fair, Gurth,' Leofwine laughed. 'Just because her father's near death and her husband's been decapitated doesn't mean a girl shouldn't try and get ahead, y'know!'

Just then, there was the sound of a rider approaching. They both looked round. A messenger was pedalling towards them at speed. He skidded to a halt by the earthworks, dropped his bicycle, and ran down the steps to the jetty. Quickly saluting, he pulled out a scroll from his shoulder bag and handed it to Harold.

'Lord Harold, news just in!'

Harold unrolled it and scanned the contents. He gave a heavy sigh.

'What is it, Harold?' Gurth called down to him.

Harold looked up at them. 'It's Algar. He died last night from his wounds!'

*

That night, Harold had a dream.

Algar was panting for breath, lying on his back on a camp bed. His two officers and an aged doctor were watching him closely, their large shadows thrown up behind them on the walls of the tent by the yellow glow of an oil lamp on the floor. His bare, heaving chest was wrapped in a blood-soaked bandage and his glistening face was twisted with pain.

Kneeling beside him, the doctor looked round at the officers and solemnly shook his head. As he did so, with a sudden loud intake of air, Algar heaved himself up from the bed, arching his body towards the low roof of the tent. Suspended there for a moment, he gave vent to a long, ferocious scream. Then his eyes finally closed

*in death and he fell back down onto the cot in a spray of golden
sweat.*

*

'All right,' King Edward sighed from behind his desk. 'Go yourself
if you have to, Harold. I won't stop you.'

'Thank you, my Lord,' Harold replied, seated opposite him.
'Will you call the Duke?'

'I can't at the moment. The phone's on the blink. I tried to use
it earlier.' The King looked out through the tall windows, at the
trees bending in the wind. 'The lines must be down. Maybe you
should wait a few days?'

'No. If I leave now, I'll get a head start on the storm.'

'Well, if you're sure?'

'I thought I'd go and see Tostig first.'

'Where is he?'

'In Normandy, visiting his wife's family.'

'Oh, that's right, I'd forgotten.'

'He might like to accompany me.'

'Good idea.' King Edward rose to his feet. 'Meanwhile, I'll
let William know you're on your way. There shouldn't be any
problem.'

'That'd be good, thanks.'

Coming around the desk to him, his frail, sparrow-shouldered
frame hunched over, as if carrying the weight of the world, the
King walked Harold towards the door.

'I suppose it is about time they came home,' he said. 'Twelve
years is a long time. And, as you say, neither William nor I require
them any longer.' He laid his hand on Harold's shoulder. 'You and
your brothers have served us well, Harold. You've proved your
loyalty.'

Harold stiffened. 'Thank you, my Lord,' he answered in a tight voice.

'By the way, I was so sorry to hear about Sweyn,' King Edward said, opening the door for him. 'I just don't understand why he did what he did, running off like that? If only he'd made his confession to me, I could have absolved him!'

*

The first photograph had been taken on a golden beach in summer. Lying on a towel, with an open book next to her, Edith looked on with a smile as Magnus tried to bury his father in the sand. Harold pretended to be frightened, wiggling his toes, while Magnus laughed with delight.

The one below it was in early autumn. Leaving their bicycles propped up against the trees, Harold and the children had been collecting blackberries from bushes growing wild beside the track. When Gunhilds' cardigan caught on the prickly branches, she began to tug and squeal. With a reassuring laugh, Harold gently lifted her up to free her and planted a healing kiss on her cheek.

The third was on a winter's morning up in the high country. Rugged up against the cold in overcoats, hats, scarves, and gloves, they had all been playing in the snow. Bending down, with a wide sweep of her arms Gunhilds gathered a clump towards her, compressing it into a large ball with both hands, and then threw it at Magnus but missed. With that, Harold and Edmund began frantically scrambling about, making balls and hurling them at each other as fast as they could. Edmund let fly with one, which hit Harold full in the face. They all laughed uproariously as he wiped the snow from his eyes.

Edmund studied the photo of Harold's spluttering face and smiled briefly at the memory of it. Now sixteen, he was on his knees in the lounge, going through an album of family snapshots. Behind him, in the middle of the room, Magnus was playing with his plastic dinosaurs and superheroes, while Gunhilds sat in front of the open fire concentrating on drawing a picture. Vera was snoozing nearby on the couch, her head lolling, with her knitting on her lap.

Just then, Edith and Harold came in from the passageway and stopped by the open door. Edith stared out through the front windows at the dark clouds gathering beyond the open fields. Heavy drops of rain were starting to splash against the panes. 'I still wish you wouldn't go, Harold,' she said. 'It's not worth the risk.'

Gunhilds looked up from the floor. 'The weather man said there's a storm coming, Daddy.'

Harold gave her a warm smile. 'I'll be all right, sweetheart. It doesn't take long to get there.'

'But couldn't one of the others take your place?' Edith implored him.

'No, it has to be me. I'm the oldest. I have to go. The Duke expects it.' He took her by the shoulders and grinned. 'And, before you start, Edith, I know what you're going to say. Bugger the Duke.'

'Well, how can you be sure it's safe? I don't trust that man an inch. I saw him once and it made my skin crawl.'

'Don't worry, I'll be on my guard. But if I can bring Wolnoth and Haco home, it'll give my Mum such a boost. Anyway, I owe it to Sweyn. I'll be fine. Really.'

'All right,' Edith sighed, 'do it if you must. But I want you back here soon.'

Harold laughed and kissed her. 'I love you! I'd better start packing.'

'I already did most of it for you this afternoon.'

'You're incredible!'

'Dad, if you're going, can I come with you?' Edmund called out to him.

Harold smiled sadly and shook his head. 'No, sorry, mate, not this time. But I'm bound to be going again.'

'Go on,' Edith said, pushing him out of the room and closing the door.

With an angry cry, Edmund suddenly hurled the photo album across the floor, knocking over Magnus's toys. 'Damn! Damn! Damn!' he shouted.

*

The storm broke with full force over Harold's yacht. Hardly making any headway, the vessel was lifted and tossed on the mountainous sea, before being enfolded again, down into the deep troughs between the giant, grey waves—only for it to rise once more and plough on.

12

Duke William stood at the window of his office, staring down at the tower blocks rising up below him, partly obscured by the lashing rain. His lips were compressed into a thin, irritable line, his scheming brain reluctantly resigned to putting his overseas ambitions on hold.

'So, you say he's prepared to come here, do you?' he said over his shoulder.

'Yes, my Lord,' Iko replied, standing erect behind him, halfway across the room, beside the long conference table. 'As instructed, I gave him your letter. On the journey back, he said he would go straight to see King Edward.'

'Hm. Well, he won't chance it till this lot's over.' The Duke turned away from the window. 'You've done very well, Iko,' he said, walking over to his desk, its wide top littered with folders, maps, journals, and sheets of computer printouts. 'I expect I'll hear from Edward soon.'

At that moment, a telephone started ringing somewhere beneath the mounds of paper. The Duke began rummaging through them, becoming more and more frustrated as he searched without finding it. 'Where the? Ah!' he exclaimed, at last exposing an old Bakelite phone, just as it rang again. He snatched up the receiver.

'Well?' he demanded. 'Yes...Yes, I know, Guy...What?...*What?*' He let out a booming laugh. 'You're kidding!' Suddenly, his face grew fierce. 'You've *what?*...Well, I want him out of there!...All right...' His voice turned cold. 'So, what do you want in return,

Guy?...Mm...Mm...Don't press your luck, old chap...All right...I said all *right!*... What?...Bloody hell! But, that's it, Guy, not one thing more! And I want him sent here under escort...Now, of course!...Oh, I don't know, tell him it wasn't your fault. That's *your* problem. And, Guy? Harm him and I'll feed your scrotum to my dogs!...Yes, I do... Hm...Yes...Goodbye!' He slammed down the phone. 'Ha! Ha!' he cried with joy. 'He's mine! He's mine!'

'Who is, my Lord?' Iko asked in surprise.

'Harold!' the Duke laughed. 'The stupid fool's gone and got himself shipwrecked. He's locked up in Guy of Ponthieu's prison. I've just paid a huge ransom for him, which I'll recoup somehow. He'll be here in the morning.'.

He stopped and thought for a moment, then his eyes came alight with renewed purpose. 'Right, Iko,' he said, sitting down behind the desk. 'You run off and get me Odo, while I call my wife.' He picked up the phone again. 'There are decisions to be made...about how best to welcome our unsuspecting hero.'

*

The eye of the storm had passed and its trailing band of rain had died out. In its wake, the morning was cold and grey, the sky heavy with low-hanging clouds. With the roar of their engines rebounding off the walls of the towering office blocks around them, the motorised carriage and its front and back escort of a dozen knights on motorbikes sped along the wet, deserted street.

Filling the view up ahead, at the far end of the echoing concrete canyon, was the Duke's gigantic, steel and mirror-glass skyscraper palace, its massive bulk enshrouded in mist. Moments later, to a fanfare of trumpets from liveried heralds lined up on each side, the column drew to a halt at the foot of its wide front steps.

The carriage door opened. Injured during the shipwreck by a blow to his shoulder from a flying spar as the yacht foundered on the rocks—in shock from his violent incarceration and then his sudden, apologetic, almost respectful release, followed by the cramped, bruising, non-stop overland rush to the Norman capital—exhausted, disorientated, and vulnerable, Harold climbed out and stared about him with dazed uncertainty.

Waiting on a marble terrace at the top of the steps, perched on the front edge and hopping from side to side like some dark bird of prey, was Duke William. Beside him stood his glamorous wife, Matilda. Only as tall as his shoulder, her long wine-red hair, hanging loose at the sides, was gathered up on her head in the middle and fixed with a silver comb. Her full-bodied hour-glass figure was accentuated by a tight-fitting, waisted black overcoat with a thick fur collar. Jutting her pugnacious chin deeper into the soft ocelot ruff, her almond eyes narrowed into slivers of steel and her broad features hardened into a thin, concealed smile of disdain as she watched Harold's arrival.

Standing together behind them were Bishop Odo, Taillefer, Baron Fitzosborne, Iko, and a group of military officers and court officials. On either side of them, serried ranks of Norman knights, wearing high nose-guarded helmets and long chainmail coats, stood to attention behind their grounded, pear-shaped shields.

Right on cue, a formation of helicopters flew past overhead. With a cry of pleasure, as if pouncing on his prize, the Duke swooped down the steps to greet his guest. Shaking his hand with vigorous delight, his face alight with a grin of smarmy confidence, he pulled Harold towards him and embraced him. At that, the company of knights gave a loud cheer, its hollow echo short-lived, deadened by the damp, enclosed space.

*

'Well, it's very big-hearted of you to say so, Harold!' Duke William said with a laugh, as they strode together along the carpeted corridor, closely followed by Baron Fitzosborne. 'But, even if he didn't know, it's still unforgivable behaviour in my book. I've been itching for a reason to get rid of Guy and this could be it. Just wait til I get my hands on him.'

'There's no harm done, William, really,' Harold replied, half-distracted, rubbing at his injured shoulder to ease the pain.

'Hm. We'll see. He knows that I'm furious about it. Perhaps I'll be kind and just let the bastard stew in his own juice for a while.' The Duke stopped at a white, unmarked door. 'Anyway, you're safe and sound now, and that's what matters.' he smiled, his lowered voice oozing patronising concern. He placed one hand flat on Harold's back, at the same time reaching down for the door handle with the other. 'I'll leave you here, Harold,' he whispered. 'I don't want to intrude on your reunion.'

Twisting the knob, Duke William pushed the door open a fraction and stepped back. With a nod for the Baron to go with him, the two walked away down the corridor in silence.

Harold cautiously entered the room and found himself in almost total darkness. Along the far wall, thin chinks of daylight showed between the black drapes covering the windows.

Peering into the interior, beyond the cold, blue luminescence from a ring of computer screens, interspersed here and there by piercing white strips of fluorescent tubing, he made out the figure of a young man in an open-necked white shirt and black trousers, sitting under the compressed beam of a ceiling spotlight.

It was Haco. Now eighteen, he was hunched over a low, smoked-glass table, flipping through a magazine. A short way away, Wolnoth was seated with his back towards him in front of a flat screen, playing a video game.

'Hi, guys!' Harold called out to them.

Wolnoth spun round. Putting the game on pause, he jumped to his feet. 'Harold!'

'Wolnoth, my long-lost brother!' Harold grinned, walking forward. They came together and hugged each other warmly. 'Let me look at you!' he exclaimed, holding Wolnoth at arm's length. 'If I can see anything in this light.'

'Oh, you get used to it after a while!' Wolnoth smiled, shuffling with embarrassed excitement.

Harold ran his hand over his brother's close-cropped hair. 'Hey, that's a good Norman haircut you've got there, Wol.'

'When in Rome!' Wolnoth shrugged. 'You don't look very well, Harold,' he frowned, staring at his brother's colourless face. 'Are you all right?'

'Yeah, I'm fine. Getting shipwrecked's not good for the health, though. And Haco. Bloody hell, you've grown!' Harold laughed, as his nephew approached. They shook hands, and then, somewhat awkwardly, embraced. 'How're y'doing?'

'Very well, thanks, Uncle Harold.'

'Less of the uncle, mate. Makes me sound old.'

'You look old, Harold,' Wolnoth said, pointing at Harold's thick, greying hair. 'You look like Dad.'

'Ah, Wol,' Harold sighed sadly. 'I wish you could've seen him before he died. And Haco, I'm sorry, mate, but I've got some bad news for you.'

'It's all right, Harold, the Duke already told me,' Haco said, with a brave smile.

Harold put his hand on his shoulder. 'Sweyn would've been proud of you, I know.'

'Thanks.'

'Well, now I've come to take you both home.'

'But I don't want to go back, Harold!' Wolnoth said emphatically. 'I mean, I'd love to see Mum and the others, but this is my home now.'

'Come on, Wol...' Harold started to remonstrate.

'No, I mean it. I'll go and see her soon, but not yet. Duke William's about to make me one of his knights. It's what I've always wanted.'

'I know it is, mate, but...'

'It's just so exciting here, Harold. Things are starting to happen. I've got a beautiful girlfriend and I'm meeting all the top people. Hopefully, now that we aren't hostages any more, I can really be of service to the Duke. Dad would be happy for me.'

'Dad would be happy for you if you came home and helped look after Mum.'

'Oh, you can do that, Harold.'

'She'll be devastated, Wol.'

'She doesn't need to be. I'll travel back regularly to see her. And I'm quite safe here, so she needn't worry. Tostig's nearby a lot of the time and I'm with family. I am a grown man, after all.'

'Well, when you put it like that. But I wish you'd change your mind, mate. What about you, Haco?'

'Ready to go when you are, Harold...if we can.'

'What do you mean?'

Haco dropped his voice. 'If the Duke lets you out of his trap.'

'What a load of rubbish!' Wolnoth laughed scornfully. 'What trap? Haco's paranoid, Harold. Don't listen to him. He's still a frightened little child.'

Harold ignored him. 'What are you saying, Haco? Do you think I'm in danger?'

Haco nodded. 'Yes, I do.'

'Oh, shut up, Haco! You do talk nonsense.' Wolnoth snapped.

'Wolnoth! Come on, mate, settle down,' Harold protested.

'It's not nonsense, Harold,' Haco persisted. 'You can't trust the Duke!'

'Utter rot!' Wolnoth laughed with derision. 'Just because you were made to wear a school uniform...'

'They wear uniforms here all the time, not just at school.'

'And suffered a few beatings for being cheeky.'

'All I did was speak out.'

'Against sensible rules. Against the Duke's laws. You deserved everything you got.'

'Guys, guys!' Harold pleaded. 'This should be a happy occasion.'

'I'm serious, Harold. I've been here a long time. Be careful!' Haco warned him again, glaring at Wolnoth.

'I'll keep my eyes open, don't worry, Haco. But you must be mistaken. If the Duke meant to harm me, why would he have bothered getting me out of prison in the first place?'

'Who knows? Perhaps to control you?'

'Well, no one controls me, I can tell you!'

'Of course they don't, Harold,' Wolnoth laughed, and slapped him on his injured shoulder, causing him to flinch. He walked back to his computer and sat down. 'Now, shhh! Just let me finish this game and then I'll show you around.'

*

Seated side by side on a raised bench at the back of an open, motorcycle-powered trishaw, Duke William and Harold rode down the main boulevard of the Norman capital at the head of a procession of mounted knights. Lining the route on either side of them, soldiers with spears kept back the watching crowd of smartly dressed citizens, who were cheering fanatically and waving little Norman flags.

Out in front of the procession strode two heralds, sweeping the air with their large, square banners. Following close behind them were four liveried squires, reaching in sequence into the deep sacks strapped across their chests and throwing handfuls of gold coins, like twinkling confetti, to the crowd.

Glowing with ostentatious pride, the Duke gestured towards the towering, sun-tipped buildings around them. Harold nodded back and lifted his gaze, taking in his surroundings. Rising to the daylight far above him, but with their lower halves deep in shadow, were opulent skyscrapers, a palatial casino, the monumental façade of a bank, the ornate front of a grand hotel, a luxury department store, and the soaring spire of a cathedral, ablaze with a neon sign of a snake entwined around two diagonally-crossed swords.

'What does that symbol stand for?' Harold asked with interest, pointing at the spire.

'It means 'Servants of Xzyatan', the Supreme Ruler of the Universe,' Duke William replied. 'It's the largest church in the world,' he added, with a complacent smile.

'Ah, right...' Harold nodded, pondering the ambiguity of his words and the chilling identity of this Xzyatan.

'Now, look over there...'

While the Duke continued to show off the sights, Harold, maintaining the appearance of polite interest, stared beyond him at the robotic throng of over-enthusiastic citizens lining the road.

Among them, he spotted a knot of shabbily-dressed vagrants with sullen, angry faces, who were not cheering. Suddenly, a squad of policemen appeared behind them and began to pull them out of the crowd. The vagrants resisted, pushing them off and protesting vehemently

As they continued on down the street, Harold twisted round in his seat and looked back, his eyes focused on the group. The police were becoming more forceful, roughly grabbing hold of them and, with blows from their truncheons, violently ejecting them from the line, at the same time glowering at those in the crowd who had stopped to watch, who hastily returned to their cheering and flag-waving.

Harold sat back round. With the beginnings of a doubtful wariness, he inspected the alleyways and side streets hidden between the passing buildings. Within their dark recesses he could just make out rows of slum dwellings and dilapidated tenement blocks, festooned with lines of dirty washing criss-crossing the dank, shadowy lanes.

Further on, down another passageway, squatting amid heaps of refuse and open, running drains, in front of a line of fast food restaurants spewing out clouds of reeking, greasy smoke, he saw beggars flailing their arms and clutching at the legs of heedless revellers.

A few moments later, he caught sight of two middle-aged, stumbling drunks being punched and kicked to the ground by three beefy bouncers outside a strip club. The homeless, derelict men and women looking on shrank away into the doorways, where they huddled out of sight, curling up in fear in their cardboard boxes.

Trying to keep the mounting concern from his eyes, with beads of perspiration pearling on his brow, Harold looked with uncertainty at his Norman host, who was facing the other way. At that very moment, as if reading his mind, Duke William turned towards him and gave him a knowing grin.

*

Rabbits bolted out of sight into the undergrowth as the procession came up the hill along a hedge-rowed lane, the noise of the motorbikes shattering the stillness of the afternoon. Seated together in their open carriage, Duke William was laughing and chatting with Harold, animatedly extolling the virtues of his realm. On his signal, the column halted at the top of the rise. Throttles were closed and engines switched off. Silence reigned.

Harold looked about him at the quiet, rolling countryside and breathed the air in deeply. 'Ahh! It's beautiful, William.'

'Oh, on a private estate I'd agree, absolutely!' the Duke chortled. He shook his head and sighed. 'But out here, I'm afraid it's simply so much wasted space. Completely unproductive. Now, come along with me, Harold. Let me show you my latest pride and joy.'

With that, he vaulted from the carriage and strode away across the slope. Harold climbed down more cautiously and followed after him. Soon, as they made their way over the rutted, chalky ground, a line of giant bulldozers, graders, and other powerful earth-moving machines gradually came into view. At their approach, a foreman stepped forward from a waiting team of workmen and, with a bow, handed each of them a yellow protective helmet.

After they put their hard hats on, Duke William took Harold by the arm and led him around to the front of the hill. As the raw, dusty corrugations gave way to grass, he leant towards him and pointed ahead. 'Now just look at that view, Harold,' he beamed.

Harold gazed out at the pristine countryside lying before them. Under a clear blue sky, pastoral sunny meadows and copses sloped gently down on either side of a meandering river, stretching away through forests and fields towards a distant, sparkling sea. Butterflies floated among the flowers and all was quiet and still, just the soft chirping of crickets and the twittering of birds floating on the warm breeze.

'Just imagine what we could do with an empty, virgin place like that!' the Duke crooned.

All of a sudden, the tranquility was ripped apart by the roar of the earthmovers starting up their engines behind them. Laying his arm across Harold's back, he turned him further around.

'This should give you a better idea of what I'm on about,' he shouted above the noise. 'It's only an artist's impression, mind you.' With a grand sweep of his arm, he proudly presented a giant hoarding looming up in front of them. 'Here, old boy, is my vision for the world.' He peered at Harold out of the corner of his eye. 'For the Norman world, of course.'

As Harold looked up, a sudden wave of dizziness swept over him. He closed his eyes and groaned, his body trembling, as an icy, debilitating shiver ran down his back, followed by a surging tide of heat to his head. He staggered, about to faint, but then the moment passed. Taking in lungfulls of air, he regained his equilibrium. Lifting his eyes to the hoarding once more, with the thunder of the bulldozers pounding in his ears, he stared into the abyss of a future Norman world.

On it, pictured in vivid, sickly colours, was a panoramic evening landscape, lying dark and awful beneath a heavy, grey shroud of pollution. In its centre, a pink and green pall of leaking radiation hung in the air over the four huge cooling towers of a nuclear reactor, squatting, like cyclopean babies among their building blocks, amid a jumble of billowing factory chimneys and bristling coal stacks belching out lung-clogging soot.

Around them, spreading out in all directions, a suffocating, airless city crammed with skyscrapers, high-rise apartments, and glass-domed shopping complexes—littered, here and there, with great mounds of industrial waste and dead stretches of water reflecting the lurid light—sprawled off into the gloom.

Rising out of the smog on the right-hand side, cut through with pipelines and strung down its length with electricity pylons, lay an arid, barren dustbowl of exhausted land, pockmarked with mine pits and swathed in thick, black smoke from a blazing oil field.

On the opposite side, springing up from a bald, scorched hilltop ringed by burning rainforest, a torpid river, poisoned with effluence and chemicals, flowed down through the sweltering urban gridlock and away towards a distant port. There, banks of tall cranes were loading super tankers and enormous container ships as a fleet of giant fishing trawlers, dragging long nets behind them, set off on the tar-slicked sea. Out on the horizon, just visible through the haze, a convoy of battleships sailed past the watery, setting sun with all flags flying.

At the bottom, soaring up out of the clouds into the foreground, was a glittering tower, lit, as if by a thousand jewels, from within. On its rooftop, basking in full sunlight, rich, carefree partygoers, laughing and drinking champagne around a penthouse swimming pool, gazed down over the railings at the view. Along the top of the hoarding, in bold, gold lettering, a caption read: *'Life...The Norman Way!'*

'Well, what d'you think?' Duke William's voice cut through the din, penetrating the nightmarish vision.

Harold turned towards him, his face white with shock. 'It... it's unreal!'

'Oh, it's real all right!' the Duke chuckled. 'Maybe not everywhere, yet, but it's the inescapable future. And all we have to do, my friend, is exploit it to the full!'

13

It was the next morning. From high up near the groined timber ceiling, beams of sunlight streamed down through three arched windows into the lounge bar of the Norman knights' élite private club. Standing immobile, in a pool of light in the middle of the varnished parquet floor, was Harold. Dressed in dark, pinstripe suit trousers and a white shirt, his face remained impassive, his eyes studying the room, as Duke William knotted a grey silk tie around his neck.

The heavy leather armchairs and polished tables had been pushed back against the long bar and the wood-panelled walls bedecked with regimental shields and stuffed animals' heads, to clear a space for the select group of high-ranking officers gathered in a smiling circle around them.

Assisted by Baron Fitzosborne, the Duke helped Harold to put on a waistcoat and suit jacket, followed by a long coat of mail and then a baldric and scabbard, which he adjusted at the hip. Finally, he placed a Norman helmet onto Harold's head. With a satisfied smile, he stepped back to admire his creation, and the assembled knights applauded.

Putting his arm round Harold's shoulders, he turned him towards the court photographer, who had taken up position nearby behind a tripod camera, with a black cloth over his head and a flash gun held up. Keeping very still, Duke William beamed like a hunter with his trophy while Harold grinned at the lense with befuddled self-consciousness.

The flash went off, freezing the moment in black and white.

*

Later that day, the Duke and his wife were taking afternoon tea with Harold in her personal sitting room on the hundred and ninety-eighth floor of the palace, using the occasion for him to become more intimately acquainted with their eight-year-old daughter, Adeliza.

Warm daylight shone in through the net curtains of the balcony sliding door, filling the baby pink and white interior with a soft glow that caught the sheen of the polished bookcases and the glass display cabinets, sparkling on the silver teapot and the tray of scones, jam, and cream.

Matilda was romping with Adeliza on the French rose-print settee, while Duke William and Harold sat nearby on matching chairs, observing their play.

'Silly! Silly! Silly!' Adeliza laughed, throwing herself against her mother and waggling her finger in her face.

'Adi! Adi! Adi!' Matilda cried, turning the tables on her and pushing her down, tickling her ribs and making her squeal. She pulled her daughter up onto the couch beside her and hugged her to her. 'Oh, Adeliza, you're so gorgeous!' she cooed, stroking the girl's thick auburn tresses. 'Don't you think so, Harold?'

'Yes. Yes, she is,' Harold answered politely, crossing his legs and toying with his cup and saucer.

'And she's very talented. She loves to dance. Don't you, Adi?'

To win their affection, Adeliza had learnt very early on to play the confusing role her parents seemed to expect of her. Now, already primed, once again she quelled her inner desire to revolt and followed her mother's prompt.

'I never want to dance for anyone but Earl Harold, Mama!' she exclaimed with a precocious pout.

'Oh don't you, indeed!' the Duke snorted with fond amusement.

'Well, Harold? *Would* you like her to dance for you?' Matilda inquired in an innocent voice, tilting her head, as if challenging him, watching for his reaction with microscopic intensity.

Harold squirmed in his seat, visibly embarrassed and confused.

Seeing his discomfort becoming prolonged, Duke William jumped to his feet. 'I'm sorry to interrupt you, my dear,' he said, 'but I need to talk to Harold for a moment. Would you excuse us?'

'Of course, William,' she nodded.

Harold stood up, trying not to appear too eager. With a formal nod to Matilda and an awkward smile in the direction of Adeliza, he followed the Duke out of the room.

Closing the door behind them and taking his arm, Duke William set off down the corridor towards his private elevator. He halted in front of it and punched a button on the wall. Always on call for him, the doors slid open at once.

As they entered, four panels of fifty buttons each presented themselves—labelled 'Administrative', 'Military', 'Domestic', and 'Residential' in ascending order—with a fifth panel for the top ten floors reserved for the Duke and his family alone. The Duke pressed one of them. There was a sudden jolt and Harold's heart leapt into his throat as, with a soft, rushing sibilance from behind its steel walls, they plummeted in silence for the twenty seconds it took to reach the Military section.

Coming to a gentle, cushioned stop, the doors parted and they stepped out onto the ninety-ninth floor. Pointing the way, Duke William headed off along another corridor, with Harold keeping up on wobbly legs.

'I'm planning a small excursion against some local troublemakers,' the Duke informed him, as they turned a corner. 'It'll be much like your campaign against that Gryffyth chap, same sort of country. I thought you might care to lend a hand?'

'I don't know, William,' Harold answered, shaking his head, finally recovering his balance after what felt like a near-death experience in the lift. 'I was intending to get going pretty soon.'

'It would only take a few days, Harold, and I'd certainly appreciate the benefit of your knowledge. You'd be doing me a tremendous favour. How're you feeling after your ordeal, by the way? I haven't asked you in ages.'

'Oh, you know, not great.'

The Duke gave a cheery laugh. 'You'll be all right, old boy!'

'It wouldn't be very diplomatic of me, would it, to be seen taking part in a foreign war?'

'I'd hardly call it a war, old man. You wouldn't be involved in any of the fighting. In fact, if we plan it right, I don't expect to encounter much resistance at all.'

Coming to the door he was seeking, Duke William stopped and opened it. He paused on the threshold. Inside, standing around a large map spread out on a billiard table beneath a low overhead light, were Baron Fitzosborne and a group of high-ranking officers, all wearing wide, peaked caps and military uniforms adorned with gold braid and rows of medals.

'Well, what do you say?'

Harold gave a weary sigh. 'All right,' he nodded.

'That's the spirit!'

With that, the Duke led him into the room. Harold was introduced and shook hands all round. Then, with everyone crowding about them, they leant forward together over the table and studied the map.

*

As predicted, the campaign had been short and sweet.

On the last day, having made it back to camp early, Iko was sitting on a tree stump near his tent, sharpening his sword. Setting down the whetstone and cloth on the grass beside him and picking up his water bottle, he watched the victorious troops marching back into the clearing in the bright sunlight. The men were jubilant, joking with each other, loud with boisterous relief.

Taking a sip from the flask, he thought back over the things he had seen in the past few days, to the two disturbing events that most stuck in his mind.

The first had taken place up on a grey rock formation at the edge of a windswept moor, when the ragtag force of poorly armed separatists they were attacking had given up and fled. With a confident roar, the Norman infantrymen had charged up the boulder-strewn incline after them. Here and there, dotted around the slope, some of the fleeing men stood their ground for a moment, jeering and waving banners, demanding 'Self-Rule!', 'Freedom!', and 'Independence Now!', before turning and running away.

He had been there with them, riding on motorbikes at the rear of the attack, when Duke William called across to Harold and, laughing with exhilaration, pointed up the hill. Harold, indistinguishable from everyone else in his helmet and mailed coat, knew what he was urging and shook his head.

'Come on, Harold, they're on the run!' the Duke yelled. 'Let's get stuck in!'

'William...'

'Race you to the top!'

With that, Duke William roared off up the slope after his troops. Harold groaned in dismay. A moment later, under the expectant gaze of Baron Fitzosborne and a surrounding audience of grinning cavalrymen, with a reluctant sigh, he revved up his engine and gave chase.

On catching up to the main body of infantrymen, they dismounted together and joined in on foot. Both were carrying shields, the Duke swinging a hexagonal-headed mace with a spike at the top, while Harold was armed with a long sword.

Meanwhile, at the crest of the rise, on the verge of defeat, the separatists suddenly regrouped and turned, surging back down the slope towards them in a final, despairing flourish of resistance. Much to his regret, and angry with himself for being there, Harold was soon forced to defend himself.

As they pushed back the enemy's feeble counter-attack, Duke William kept his eye on Harold, and saw, to his frustration, that he was matching him blow for blow. With bodies falling around them and blood flying off their weapons, they pressed on next to each other towards the summit.

Soon, under the unrelenting onslaught, the demoralised separatists broke and ran for their lives. With glances of mutual respect for each other's prowess, the pair continued on, keeping pace with each other, step for step, cutting down all opposition until they reached the top at exactly the same time.

Panting hard, the Duke looked over at Harold, who smiled back at him, trying not to appear out of breath, while the troops around them laughed in admiration.

Harold wiped his blade clean in the grass and held up the hilt towards him. 'It's not my weapon of choice,' he grinned, 'but it's not bad.'

The second concerning event occurred when a small detachment of Norman soldiers were strung out across a narrow stretch of sandy beach, caught between the sheer cliff face and the spume-blown sea, making a desperate stand against a larger band of separatists.

Behind their thin line, two of their fellows were stuck in a patch of wet quicksand, sinking deeper and deeper as they struggled and screamed for help. One of them was badly wounded.

At that moment, Harold and he had arrived on their motorbikes. Harold stopped and surveyed the scene. 'Damn!' he swore under his breath, furious at himself for having become involved. Quickly dismounting, he leant his machine against a rock and rushed down the beach to help.

As he ran past the back of the Norman line, a knife-wielding separatist suddenly forced his way through. The soldiers wheeled round to grab hold of him, but not before he had slashed out at Harold, who parried the blow, sweeping aside his arm, and with one punch laid him out on his back.

Racing on down to the edge of the quicksand, he then drew his sword, stuck it into the sand and, removing his baldric and scabbard, threw himself flat. Lying at full stretch, he tossed it out to them and dragged the beleaguered men to safety.

Just then, with trumpets blaring, a squadron of mounted knights led by Duke William and Baron Fitzosborne rode down onto the beach. Seeing their arrival, the separatists turned and fled.

While his knights gave chase, the Duke jumped from his mount, handed it to a squire, and ran over to Harold, who was brushing the sand from his clothes. With a broad smile, he took him by the shoulders and held him at arm's length. Tensing against the pain of his grip, Harold shook his head in a mixture of modesty and barely concealed anger, as the soldiers crowded around him, laughing and slapping him on the back.

Duke William stood back from them, watching with shrewd resentment, the smile slowly disappearing from his face as he measured Harold's popularity with his troops.

A loud revving of engines brought Iko back to the present. The Duke and Baron Fitzosborne had ridden into the camp. Harold had also arrived.

Iko watched Duke William dismount and, for a few moments, study Harold, who had removed his helmet and was chatting easily with the men. Suddenly, the Duke's face darkened. With an abrupt flick of his wrist for the Baron to accompany him, he turned on his heel and strode away towards one of the tents surrounding the clearing.

Iko followed them with his eyes. With casual haste, he stood up and went to his tent. Placing his sword and sharpening materials inside, he checked to see that no one was watching and then sauntered after them.

*

Inside the tent, Bishop Odo was sitting at a small folding table, using a calculator to add up a column of figures in a ledger. He looked up from his work and removed his reading glasses as Duke William threw back the flap and stormed in, closely followed by Baron Fitzosborne.

'You look upset, partner?' he smiled, raising his eyebrows with amused concern.

'Damn it, Odo, that man frustrates me at every turn!' the Duke fumed. 'I've spent Xzyatan knows how much on banquets and processions for him, not to mention the ransom I had to pay Guy, and all for what? He's as cocky as ever. Not his weapon of choice. Bah! You should've seen him out there, wowing the troops, absolutely full of himself, the flavour of the month.'

'So I saw!' the Bishop chuckled. 'I must say he's quite an impressive fella.'

Duke William threw himself into a camp-chair. 'Well, I'm damned if I'll let him leave here with that smug look on his face. Not without getting what I want from him first.'

'May I speak, my Lord?' said Baron Fitzosborne.

'Well, what is it?' the Duke growled.

'Wiz respect, my Lord, ze answer is simple. Tell Harold zat if he does not give you his support you will have him tortured and, if necessary, have his eyes put out.'

'Steady on, Fitz! That's a bit rough.'

'Have you ever done that, Fitz?' Bishop Odo asked in amazement. 'Put out someone's eyes?'

The Baron grinned. 'Of course! It's like shelling molluscs.'

'Oh, my God!'

'Well, let's hope it doesn't come to that!' Duke William snorted.

'It's not a bad idea, though,' the Bishop nodded. 'Although we'd better tone it down a bit, I reckon. What d'you think, Billy? Sounds okay to me. Let's give him a fright?'

The Duke spread his hands in innocence. 'Why can't things ever be simple and straightforward? I like Harold. I don't want to have to threaten him. It's not in my nature, you know that, Odo. I just want what's mine, that's all.'

Bishop Odo shook his head and winked at Baron Fitzosborne. 'Of course you do, Billy. We understand.'

'But I'm buggered if I'll let that smooth-talking larrikin get in my way!' Duke William exploded, thumping his fist on the arm of the chair.

Listening outside, without making a sound, Iko stepped away from the wall of the tent.

*

The following day, with their tents taken down and loaded onto wagons along with the rest of the camp equipment, the column of troops headed out of the clearing in high spirits and off down a wide, grassy track through a forest of pine trees.

Harold watched them go. He groaned. His whole body ached. Bruised and buffeted by recurrent violent undulations in temperature, jumping from cold, bloodless valleys of shivering fatigue to ever-heightening peaks of sweltering internal heat, his bloodless face had a sheen of sweat and his lacklustre eyes were becoming glazed. Without being aware of it, he kept scratching at his upper arm.

Deep in thought, he turned away and walked across the open space to his motorbike, taking hold of the handlebars and mounting up. As he pulled on his helmet, Bishop Odo rode over and stopped beside him.

'Congratulations, Harold!' The Bishop smiled. 'You've done a great job.'

'Thank you, Bishop,' Harold nodded.

'But, I gotta tell ya, son, Billy's kinda upset with you.'

'Why? Whatever for?'

'He feels that you're boosting yourself at his expense and not paying due deference to him.'

'What do you mean, due deference?'

'That you're not showing your allegiance to him.'

'Come on, mate. My allegiance isn't to the Duke.'

'Well, he did make you one of his knights, Harold.'

'That was just pretend, Bishop, you know that,' Harold protested. 'It wasn't meant to be taken seriously.'

'Oh, Billy takes it very seriously, believe me. To him it was a real event, with real obligations.'

'That's crazy. I've just helped him win a bloody war!'

'I know. And, don't get me wrong, Harold, he's very grateful to you for it. But I don't think he's going to let you take your brother and nephew home until you've convinced him of your loyalty.'

'And how am I meant to do that?'

'I don't know.' Bishop Odo shook his head and smiled. 'I'm sure he'll think of something.'

'And what if I refuse?'

'I'm not sure, Harold. Like I say, he'll think of something. All I'm certain of is that the Billy I know is capable of doing anything to get his own way. I just thought I'd warn you. But, hey, maybe he's changed!' the Bishop laughed and slapped Harold on the back, making him cry out. 'Aw, sorry, Harold. You okay?' Harold nodded, gritting his teeth against the needles of pain shooting up his arm. 'See you later, then!'

With that, Bishop Odo rode off after the column. Harold watched him go, rubbing his shoulder and growing angrier by the minute. A moment later, Iko drew up alongside him.

'Be careful, Lord Harold,' Iko said in a low voice. 'You are in danger.'

Harold turned towards him. 'Are you part of all this, too, Sir Iko?' he demanded.

Iko looked round to make sure they weren't being overheard. 'No, Lord, I am your friend.'

'Then tell me the truth, as a friend, what does the Duke want from me?'

'I do not know, Lord, but he is planning something.'

'Don't know or can't say?'

'I do not know. I am sorry.'

'Don't worry,' Harold sighed. 'I'll find out soon enough.'

'Lord Harold, my advice is to do as Duke William asks. If you wish to escape, give him anything he wants. Pretend to agree to his demands and you will be safe to go home.'

'Why are you telling me all this, Sir Iko? You don't owe me anything.'

'Because you have shown me kindness in the past, Lord…and because your lady once saved my life.'

'My lady?'

'Lady Edith.'

'Ah, so that was you!'

Iko bowed his head. 'Yes.'

'By the way, what happened to my clothes?'

'I have them in my room. They are cleaned and pressed. I will return them.'

'No, keep 'em if you want.'

Iko bowed again. 'Thank you.' His face broke into a shy smile. 'Sometimes, when I am alone, I put on the hat and remember.'

'Remember what?'

'Some things that Lady Edith said about being a Norman, and the strange sense of freedom I felt hidden away in your countryside. I am lighthearted when I wear that hat.'

Harold gave a mirthless laugh. 'Well, maybe you should start importing them then. Things could do with a bit of lightening up around here.'

*

In a cramped, high-walled courtyard at the back of the towering palace, Haco sat on a bench reading a book. He looked up as a helicopter raced across the patch of blue sky overhead and then flew out of sight. On the other three sides, beyond the barbed wire-topped enclosure, the sheer faces of office blocks rose up to the afternoon sunlight, leaving the area in deep shadow. Police sirens wailed in the distance.

A door at the back of the palace opened and a young kitchenhand carrying a garbage bag came out, followed by Harold. With a bored shrug, the youth pointed towards Haco, then walked across the concrete space to a large dumpster, lifted up the lid, and tossed the bag inside.

'Harold. Thank God you're back!' Haco exclaimed as Harold approached.

'G'day, Haco.' With a weary sigh, Harold sat down on the bench next to him.

For a few moments, they watched in fascination as the kitchenhand clambered up onto the bin, jumped up and down a number of times to squeeze the bag in, then leaped off, slammed the lid shut, and sauntered back into the palace.

Haco closed his book and put it down. 'Harold, you look awful. Are you injured?'

Harold shook his head, scratching at his shoulder. 'No. It's this damned shoulder. It won't stop itching...What is this place? It stinks!'

'This is our exercise yard. We're not allowed to leave the palace.'

Harold shook his head in disgust. 'The sooner I get you both out of here the better. Where's Wolnoth?'

'Inside.'

'Playing those mind-sapping games again, I suppose?'

'That's a bit cynical.'

'The ones I've seen are nothing but violence.'

'Talking of violence, Harold, how was war with the Duke?'

Harold looked sideways at him. 'Hm. Point taken,' he grunted, with a self-reproachful laugh. 'It was touch and go there for a while.'

'What do you mean?'

'William sucked me right in, the bastard. I could easily have been killed. He must've known that. I should've listened to you, Haco. I never should've gone. And just to top it off, as we were getting ready to come back Odo virtually gave me an open warning.'

'About what?'

'That I won't get out of here in one piece unless I prove my loyalty to the Duke.'

'How are you supposed to do that?'

Harold groaned and rubbed the back of his neck. 'Oh, my head!...I don't know yet. Apparently, we're going on a trip tomorrow. He'll probably tell me then. I've got half a bloody mind to make a run for it.'

'Harold, you mustn't! That'd give him the excuse he's been looking for. Anyway, there *is* no escape. I've been trying for years.'

'Hm. I'll just have to wait and see what he's got to say, then.'

'Promise him anything. Lie if you have to. Only, don't lose your temper.'

'That's easy for you to say.' Harold groaned again and slumped back on the bench. 'What the bloody hell is he after, Haco?'

14

'**T**he throne!' Duke William smiled. 'There, I've said it! That's why I've brought you here, Harold. Edward first promised it to me on this very spot, over ten years ago.'

They were sitting alone together in dappled, afternoon sunlight, on a large flat boulder above a shallow rock pool beside a secluded, gurgling waterfall.

'I didn't know that,' Harold answered, hiding his shock.

'In fact, he reaffirmed it the last time I saw him. And putting your brother and nephew in my safekeeping clearly demonstrates his faith in me, wouldn't you say?'

'Yes, I suppose it could look that way,' Harold nodded, fighting off a wave of dizziness. His face was flushed with the onset of fever. He picked up a small pebble and tossed it into the crystal clear water, watching the ripples spread out across the surface. 'There still might be others with a claim, though?'

'No, the only possible contender was Algar, and he's dead. Which just leaves you and me.'

'What about Tostig?'

'From what I hear, your brother's on the verge of being chucked out of his earldom. He's not half the man you are, Harold.' Duke William stared at him, like a hangman dangling a noose. 'You know I could have you locked up and do this alone, don't you?'

'I suppose so, if you wanted to.'

'But I respect you too deeply, Harold. I dearly want us to be friends. As prince to prince, all I'm asking for is your help.'

Fighting down his anger and a sudden urge to push the Duke off the rock, Harold pretended to be interested. 'What would you want me to do, William?'

'Just speak on my behalf to your Council, that's all. Give your full support to my claim. Tell them the truth, that as well as being the rightful king, I'm also the best man to defend your people and improve their lives. It's as simple as that.'

'That could prove more difficult than it sounds.'

'You can convince them, I'm sure.'

'Mm. And, what would I get in return?'

'Now, you're talking!' the Duke exclaimed, with an eager grin. 'Obviously, you'd keep the earldom you already have, plus I'd give you part of the north. And whatever else you can wring out of me over a bottle of scotch. What do you say?'

'On reflection, that I couldn't expect anything more. And I certainly don't relish the idea of prison. I've already tasted the food, thanks. But, in the end it's the Council who decide.'

'Yes, but they'll listen to you. And, if they don't, it's my loss. Just help me as much as you can, that's all I ask.'

Harold dropped another stone into the pool, pondering as it plopped and drifted to the bottom. 'All right, then,' he replied at last. 'I agree.'

'Really? You promise?'

'Yes. I promise.'

'Wonderful! That's splendid!' Duke William laughed. 'Of course, I'll need you to make some kind of public declaration of all this,' he added. 'An oath of allegiance in front of my barons should do it. Merely a formality, you understand. All right?'

'If that's what you want,' Harold nodded.

'Good. And one other thing. You'll have to leave me some kind of security. Just in case you're persuaded, much against your will, of course, to see things differently once you get home.'

Harold's voice tightened. 'What had you in mind, William?'

'Oh, I should say someone to stay here on your behalf would do the trick.'

'Is that really necessary? You have my word.'

'I'm sorry, Harold, but that's not quite enough, I'm afraid. I need something more concrete to use as collateral with my bankers. This could be a costly exercise and you know what money men are like. They never want to take risks.'

'A hostage, you mean?'

'I do so dislike that word. No, I'd much rather look on him as being a special guest. A living token of your trust in me, what! You do trust me, don't you, Harold?'

'Yes, but...I didn't expect...Who?'

'It's no big deal. Your brother likes it here. In fact, I'm thinking of making him one of my knights.'

'Wolnoth?'

'He'd fit the bill perfectly, I'd say.'

Harold rubbed his pounding forehead. 'Aah!'

'Have you a problem with that, Harold?'

'No,' Harold answered, recovering himself. 'But...well, obviously I'm concerned about my brother.'

'No need to be, old boy. No need at all. Actually, I already took the liberty of mentioning it to him, I hope you don't mind, and he was absolutely over the moon at the prospect of staying on here.'

'But what if I support you and the Council rejects your claim? What happens to Wolnoth then?'

'In the unlikely event of that happening, of course he'd be allowed to go home whenever he wanted.'

Harold stared at the gushing waterfall. The sound of its flow roared like a torrent through his brain, magnified by the horror of what he was agreeing to.

'I don't know...'

'What is it now?' the Duke said testily. 'Don't tell me you still have reservations?'

'I was thinking about my mother. She can't wait to see Wolnoth. She'll be heartbroken.'

'Yes, yes, very commendable, I'm sure. We should all love our mothers. But you can tell her from me she needn't be unhappy. She'll have her boy home safe within a year.'

'How do you know that?'

'Because, much as it saddens me, I have it on the best authority that Edward is terminally ill. He's got twelve months at most.'

'My God!'

'So, don't worry. She'll understand.' Clapping Harold on the back, making him groan, Duke William climbed to his feet. 'And you can cheer her up with the good news of your impending marriage.'

'What?' Harold gasped in feverish pain as he stood up.

'Oh, didn't I mention it? I was sure I had. Well, Matilda and I thought it only fair that the final condition should be on us, to provide you with some token of *our* good faith in all this. And so...well actually she came up with the idea and I'm all for it... we've decided to give you our most cherished possession, our beautiful daughter, Adeliza, to marry as soon as I'm crowned king. I do hope you're pleased?'

'But, she's only a child!' Harold laughed.

'The younger the better! All the more mileage, what!' the Duke chortled. 'In a year or two she'll be ready to start giving you babies. Think of it, Harold, we'll be united by blood.' He thrust out his hand. 'We'll have the betrothal ceremony tonight.'

'Fine! Why not?' Harold shrugged, with an inane grin, shaking it.

Duke William gripped his hand tightly. 'Then you agree to everything?'

'Yes.'

He leant forward, peering into Harold's eyes, searching his face for duplicity. 'You wouldn't try to deceive me, would you, Harold?'

'No,' Harold nodded, meeting his gaze. 'Whatever I can do, I'll do.'

With a cry of success, the Duke clamped him in a bear hug embrace. 'Oh, splendid. Absolutely splendid!'

Harold stared over his shoulder, his face agonised, his mouth open, crying silently, hot tears springing to his eyes.

*

The scenes rushed by Harold in a blur, sweeping him along, as if down a waterslide, from one event to the next.

Beneath a glittering chandelier, all seated around a white-clothed dining table gleaming with silverware and crystal glass, Duke William, Matilda, Bishop Odo, Taillefer, and Baron Fitzosborne were engaged in raucous banter as they ate their dessert.

At the far end, Harold sat slumped in his seat, his face flushed and sweating, his head lolling, his eyelids heavy, opening and closing as he tried to focus on them all. The distorted echo of their booming voices, the chinking of glasses, and the spoons scraping on their bowls became amplified in his head, making his nerve endings scream.

The room spun about him. His vision swung from side to side across the table. Their faces appeared large and grotesque as each in turn looked towards him, laughing and sniggering.

He shut his eyes.

*

Lit from both sides by radiant tiers of black altar candles, Harold and Adeliza stood on the chancel step, facing each other in the claustrophobic darkness of the chapel. Their arms were outstretched, and they were holding hands. He was semi-delirious, swaying on his feet.

Standing above them, like a praying mantis, the long-limbed figure of Bishop Odo—dressed in his full regalia of a gold-bordered, black surplice over flowing white robes, a purple bib with a golden collar, a plain gold mitre on his head, and a gold medallion and ring—was conducting the ceremony.

Peering down through his half-moon, silver-rimmed glasses, while intoning from an ancient leather-bound book lying open on a lectern beside him, he reached out and laid a woven gold sash over their joined hands, then wrapped it around. The meaning of the Bishop's words were lost on Harold, obscured and obliterated by the piercing whistle of tinnitus in his blocked ears and the tight pressure bubble threatening to burst through his skull.

Behind Bishop Odo, set in the centre of the altar and gleaming under an overhead spotlight, was a large gold statue of a snake entwined around two diagonally crossed swords, with its coiled tail forming the base. Its black obsidian eyes glared out at them, above the forked tongue flicking from its snarling mouth.

Standing next to Harold, close enough to make their menacing presence felt, were Baron Fitzosborne and Taillefer, witnessing the betrothal with malevolent grins.

Barely able to stay upright, in a haze of delirium Harold looked round at Duke William and Matilda, who were observing the proceedings from their young daughter's side. The cunning, almost animal intensity of their faces, the depraved mixture of their scheming smiles, and their warped parental pleasure made him physically recoil. As the ceremony reached its climax, he saw her take hold of the Duke's arm and gaze up at him in adoring excitement.

Suddenly remembering the girl, with protective concern Harold looked down at Adeliza, half-expecting to see her smiling to herself, in the first flush of power and possession, without a trace of innocence or uncertainty. Instead, she was looking up at him, clutching his hand as if it was a life raft, adrift in a world that she didn't understand, lost, alone and unsafe, her eyes watering with fear and bewilderment.

*

In a corner of the nave—decked out on all sides with suspended shields and tasselled flags, and curtained off from the rest of the cathedral by a huge, black and gold tapestry depicting the snake-swords emblem of Xzyatan—seated on a carved white marble throne, high up on a stepped platform built into the foot of one of the giant piers supporting the inner wall and the side aisle vaulting, Duke William stared down at the assembly, drumming his fingers on the arms with impatience.

Standing erect and forbidding on the flagstones below him were Bishop Odo and Baron Fitzosborne. In front of them, out in the middle of the floor, were two large chests draped with the Norman and Saxon flags—one, an embossed silver disc on a navy blue ground; the other, a yellow sun in the centre of turquoise and red ochre halves, with a black and white border. Set on top of each chest was a small, square casket topped by a golden crown studded with precious gems.

Drawn up along three sides of the nave, Norman knights stood in ranks, their faces devoid of expression, waiting in silence. Positioned some way apart, flanked by a pair of burly, grim-faced officers, was Wolnoth. All of a sudden, the sound of wood scraping on stone echoed between the pillars as the porch door was opened and, moments later, semi-conscious, Harold was led in like a criminal by two Generals.

On his entry, a sudden flourish of trumpets resounded throughout the vast interior, startling Wolnoth and making him smile. The officers looked round at him and frowned with threatening displeasure.

'Enter, Earl Harold!' Baron Fitzosborne's sepulchral voice boomed about the stone enclosure as Harold was forced to a halt. 'You are called here to swear allegiance to Duke William, Lord of ze Norman Realm and Guardian of ze True World Order. Do you appear here of your own free will?'

His face ashen and his brain numb, Harold's eyes went rolling as he was nudged awake by one of the Generals. 'I do,' he croaked.

'Welcome, Harold!' the Duke called down to him. 'I have brought you here to repeat, in front of these witnesses, the promises you made to me recently concerning my inheritance of King Edward's royal estate. Are you prepared to do this?'

Harold's bleary eyes travelled around the watching assembly. 'I am.'

'Very well. Bishop Odo will now administer the oath.'

The Bishop walked over to the twin chests and turned towards him. 'Step this way, Harold.'

Guided by the Generals, Harold stumbled after him.

'Before we begin, Harold,' Bishop Odo said, raising a cautionary finger, 'I can't impress upon you strongly enough the seriousness of the oath you're about to take. Within these caskets lie a collection of our holiest symbols, the most sacred objects in the Norman realm, all gathered together in a fusion of awesome power. That this oath is binding, let there be no doubt in your mind.'

He peered closely at Harold, who nodded his head. 'If you break it, not only will you suffer the harshest material punishment, but your soul will be damned to absolute destruction. You will have mocked the name of the Great God, Xzyatan.' He made the sign of the swords and snake on his chest. 'For which there is no forgiveness. You will be called to account and declared bankrupt in both body and spirit. Like a bad debt, you will be struck from the ledger of the Supplier of Life. Do you understand?'

'I do.'

'For your sake, I hope so.' The Bishop nodded for the Generals to release him. 'Okay. Come closer, Harold. Now, turn and face the assembly and place a hand on each of these caskets.'

Swaying on his feet, Harold complied, stretching out his arms and touching the crowns.

'I will now read you the oath... I, Harold, son of Godwin, do solemnly swear that, upon the death of King Edward, I will support Duke William in his just claim to the Saxon throne and that I will use all my power, both in word and deed, to bring him to his rightful inheritance. In token of this, I leave my brother, Wolnoth, in his charge...'

Wild-eyed, Harold threw a tortured look at Wolnoth, who smiled cheerfully back at him.

'And I agree to take Adeliza, his daughter, as my bride as soon as he is crowned king. I take this oath in the name of all that is holy, and in full knowledge of the terrible curse I will suffer should I break it...Do you accept the oath, Harold?'

Harold took a deep breath. 'I do.'

Bishop Odo turned to the Generals. 'Remove the crowns.'

Harold moved away as the two men, acting in unison, lifted off the caskets, pulled away the flags, and opened the lids of the wooden chests hidden underneath.

'Look inside, Harold,' the Bishop instructed him with ominous gravity. 'And behold the dreadful symbols of Divine Law!'

Harold staggered across to one of the chests and peered over the edge.

An almost tangible heat rose up from the treasure that greeted his eyes. Piled up inside was a dazzling collection of gold and silver coins, bank notes, and money-printing plates. A jewel-encrusted, gold snake-swords sculpture pointed up at him, as if in accusation, from a sparkling heap of diamonds, rubies, emeralds, opals, and sapphires.

There was jewellery of every conceivable kind, along with ancient congealed coins from under the sea, diamond credit cards, an album of rare postage stamps, and a golden lottery ticket. Spread along the sides were bars of gold bullion, silver ingots, bags of gold dust, and thick wads of gilt-edged share certificates.

In the middle of the central mound, a glittering gold mask decorated with peacock feathers and precious stones, a silver winged helmet, a diamond tiara, and a gem-studded sword and scabbard lay in a ring around an enormous gold nugget. Propped up against it, in an elaborate gilded frame, was a sepia photograph of the front of the World Bank.

With his head swimming, struggling to keep his eyelids from closing, Harold turned away and lurched over to the second chest. As he stared down, his eyes jolted open in surprise.

A crystal soccer ball sat balanced on the strings of a silver tennis racquet, next to a set of golden golf clubs, a pair of gleaming running spikes, and a solid gold cricket bat. Surrounding them, among heaps of poker chips, onyx dice, and scattered packs of playing cards, was a spinning roulette wheel, pearl-inlaid backgammon and Monopoly boards, a jockey's silk cap and riding crop, all kinds of medals, ribbons, rosettes, gold cups and winners' trophies, and a handcrafted replica of a Rolls-Royce 'Silver Ghost'.

Running around the walls made of blank plasma screens, making a quiet motorised buzzing sound, half a dozen brightly coloured miniature cars were racing on a black, two-lane track. Meanwhile, jutting out of the centre of the pile, tilted at a carefree angle and encircled by a toy gun and holster inlaid with plastic jewels, was a jeroboam of vintage French champagne.

Harold stood there in shock, gripping the edge of the box, his face white, his body trembling with both fever and locked-in, hysterical mirth at the dreadful insanity of it all. Giving a pitiful moan, he let go of the lip and fell backwards, oblivious to the Duke's stern command ringing out behind him.

'Close the chests!'

As his head hit the flagstones, the lids were slammed shut.

15

Out of black inner space, Wolnoth's smiling face materialised. 'Wolnoth!' Harold shouted to him in anguish, but his brother's image faded away, back into the darkness.

There was the sound of falling rain. 'Harold?' Bishop Alred's voice called above it. 'Harold?'

Harold opened his eyes. His haggard face was pressed up hard against the rain-soaked window, bumping on and off the glass to the swaying motion of the carriage. As he came to, he stared out, focusing on the line of passing fish stalls setting up along the quay for the early morning trade.

'Harold?' the Bishop's insistent voice spoke again, beside him.

Harold turned back into the carriage. A raincoat was draped over his shoulders. Bishop Alred was sitting on the bench next to him, wearing a black overcoat. Collecting his wits, Harold peered out through the opposite window at the dockyards splashing by in the wet, grey dawn, where stevedores were unloading the cargo from a ship lying at anchor. He looked across at Haco, lying asleep on the other bench.

'Sorry, father,' he groaned wearily. 'After what I've already told you I don't remember anything, not until you woke me in my cabin.' He rubbed his face in torment. 'How am I ever going to tell my mother?'

'Don't worry, my son,' Bishop Alred said. 'Githa knows only too well what sacrifices have to be made for one's country. She won't blame you.'

'But I left Wolnoth behind!'

'He wanted to stay, you said so yourself.'

'I know,' Harold sighed. 'But he's got no idea what he's getting himself into. The Duke will never let him go.'

'You don't know that, Harold, not for sure. William can't gain anything by keeping him against his will. Anyway, you had no choice.'

'And what about my oath?'

'What oath? To sell out your country? You can't swear to that. No. All in your power, you said. Well, it's not in your power to decide who'll be king. That decision, thank God, rests with the Council, of which I'm the Head. Take it from me, my son, they won't hold it against you.'

'That oath!' Harold moaned in anger. 'If it hadn't been so heavy it would've been laughable. Boxes full of baubles and playthings.'

'Don't underestimate the importance of wealth and the desire to win, Harold,' the Bishop cautioned. 'They can make kings and bring down empires. And there are some courts that would say you've entered into a very binding contract. But it's Edward's promise that really disturbs me. It could complicate matters.'

'Ain't that the truth!' Harold slumped back heavily in his seat. 'Is he really as sick as William said?'

'Oh yes, the chariot's coming for him, all right, and he knows it. In fact, he welcomes it. In terms of faith, Edward's a saint. It's his practical side that's the problem. Anyway, you'd better go and see him. You can judge for yourself. Meanwhile, we'll get that arm properly looked at.'

'Thanks.'

'And, at least, we can give thanks that you got Haco back.'

Just then, Haco sat up and rubbed his eyes. 'Hi.' he yawned, with a grin. 'I must've fallen asleep.'

As they both yawned in response, they all laughed.

'Don't worry, Harold,' Bishop Alred said, turning towards him. 'Githa will understand. Now, I've got news for you about Tostig...'

*

'But I don't understand!' Githa cried in confusion. 'You all told me he'd be safe! Even your father. And, now you're saying the Duke won't let him go?'

'I know we did, Mum,' Harold nodded grimly, sitting beside her at the kitchen table. 'But he's not a prisoner.'

'Then why does he have to stay? Wolnoth's no threat to anyone. He *must* be a prisoner.'

'No. He's there as a guarantee that I'll help William get the throne.'

Githa turned to him in horror. 'Harold, you can't. Your father would turn in his grave!'

'I know he would.' Harold sighed. He took a sip from his mug of coffee. 'Anyway, the Council wouldn't let me, even if I wanted to. And once the Duke knows that, he'll have to send Wolnoth home.'

'Are you sure?' she asked with a doubtful frown, pulling out a large handkerchief.

'That's what he told me, and I have to believe him.' As Githa blew her nose, Harold exchanged a quick, doubtful look with Haco, who stood leaning against the nearby bench. 'So, there's nothing to worry about, Mum. Wolnoth will be well looked after. In fact, he's having the time of his life. He's even got a girlfriend over there.'

'Well, he'd better not be thinking of marrying her! I couldn't stand another Judith in the family. That conniving little witch, she's totally mesmerised Tostig.'

'Oh, I think Tostig knows what he's doing, Mum.' Harold turned in his chair. 'You've met them both, haven't you, Haco?'

'Yes,' Haco grinned. 'The first time was when Grandpa brought us back from exile.'

Githa looked up, her face brightening. 'That's right!'

'I remember Tostig had curly hair and wore loads of jewellery, while Judith jumped around a lot telling him off!' They all laughed at the picture of it. 'And they hadn't changed much the last time I saw them.'

'She's got a real tongue on her, that girl,' Githa said with disdain.

'So has her big sister, I reckon,' added Harold.

Haco pulled a haughty face. 'The Empress Matilda, that's what I call her.'

'Yeah, in her dreams!' Harold laughed coldly.

'If they're that power-hungry, Harold, how on earth can you trust them?' Githa said, shaking her head.

'I don't trust them, Mum. Either of them. But at least I know the Duke's actions are bound by a code of honour. He won't break his word.'

'Good people don't need a code of honour,' Githa snorted.

'No, but bad people do. And I'm glad they've got one. It'll keep Wolnoth safe.'

Githa put her head in her hands. 'Oh, these Normans!' she cried. 'They've ruined our lives. Your father gave up everything to protect us from them. He lost touch with Sweyn...and our only daughter...Tostig's been seduced by that harridan... and now they've taken my little boy!' She sobbed into her handkerchief.

Harold put his arm around her. 'Oh, Mum, don't! Wolnoth'll be all right. In fact, Duke William told me to tell you that he'll be home within a year.'

'How can he possibly know that?' she snapped, staring round at him.

'Well, according to him, Edward's dying. He's only got a year to live.'

'Is that true, Harold?'

'Bishop Alred confirmed it.'

'Your sister never mentioned it?'

'Maybe she doesn't know. I'll try to find out this afternoon when I visit him.' He gave a heavy sigh. 'Then, I'd better sort out this business with Tostig.'

Githa shook her head. 'Oh, he's just been a bit headstrong, that's all.'

'I don't think so, Mum. Not this time.'

'Don't be too hard on him, Harold, he's had a difficult year, what with you being away for so long and having to be at the beck and call of the King all the time. With that wife of his nagging in his ear. He doesn't have your experience.'

'I know all that, Mum, but he's been accused of conspiracy to murder.'

'What? It must be a mistake?'

'I hope so. I know he's got one hell of a temper, but surely he wouldn't go that far?'

*

The rain had stopped. Out in the bright, early-afternoon sunlight, couples in long dresses and frock coats were strolling arm in arm around the lawn at the back of King Edward's palace. Baroque harpsichord music came from a quartet seated under a scalloped canvas awning at the far end. In the middle of the space, a game of croquet was in progress. Everyone watched in silence as Harold appeared and strode across the grass towards the large wooden rotunda. He climbed up its short flight of steps and entered the shaded interior.

Sitting on a bamboo couch, in semi-darkness on the far side, was King Edward, dressed in loose white robes, down which flowed his long, unkempt white beard. He had his eyes closed and his hand on the bowed head of a small choirboy kneeling in front of him.

Harold announced his presence with a loud cough. The King suddenly opened his eyes and gave a startled cry. 'Aah! That'll do, now, boy. Off you go.'

The choirboy jumped to his feet, bowed, and left, going past Harold with a roll of the eyes and a 'you're all a bunch of loonies' smirk on his face.

King Edward crossed his legs and adjusted his robes. 'I was just hearing the child's confession,' he explained. He picked up his sherry glass from next to some travel brochures on a low table beside him and leant back on the couch. 'So, you've decided to return to us, Harold?'

'Does that surprise you, your Majesty?'

The King waved a limp hand. 'No, no...'

'What happened to your call to the Duke, my Lord? He wasn't expecting me.'

'Ah, yes, I'm sorry about that, Harold. But, what with the terrible storm and then events here, I totally forgot.'

'Oh, right.'

'Still, never mind. At least you're home again, safe and sound,' King Edward smiled. 'As, of course, I knew you would be.'

'Of course.'

'Would you like a sherry?'

'No, thanks,' Harold sighed.

'It's very fortifying, y'know.' The King held up his empty glass. 'Would you mind?' Harold took the glass and refilled it from a decanter on a side table, then handed it back to him. 'Thank you. Now, tell me, how did it go?'

'Oh, fine!' Harold nodded sarcastically. 'Apart from the fact that I was forced to swear an oath, under threat of imprisonment, that I'd help William get the throne.'

'After I'm gone, I hope?' King Edward laughed.

'And he's keeping hold of Wolnoth to guarantee my support.'

'Oh dear.'

'Yes. Because, apparently, you've already promised him the crown?'

The King squirmed in his seat. 'Oh dear, oh dear! I did do that, didn't I? It was so long ago, I'd forgotten. Trust William to remember. He's such an overpowering man, as well you know, Harold. I never really meant it.'

'Oh, that's all right, then.'

'What did you say, forced to swear an oath?'

'Well, obviously I can't stick to it.'

'No, no, of course not. He won't be very happy about it, though. I see dark days ahead. No, we'll just have to carry on as if nothing has happened. But it's a pity about your brother.'

'Yeah, it is. My mother's totally distraught.'

'I'm sure she must be. I'll send the Queen to her. Now look, Harold, the North's in turmoil. Tostig's gone and got himself into a spot of bother over some woman, so I'm told. Some nonsense about him planning to have her husband killed. Thank God I'm celibate! They're such strange creatures, women, don't you think?'

Harold shook his head, disregarding the comment. 'I don't believe a word of it,' he answered. 'Tostig wouldn't be that stupid. Anyway, he's already married.'

'You don't know your brother very well, then, Harold!' King Edward snorted. 'Anyway, the locals have raised an army against him and they've called on Algar's son, Morcar, to lead them. It might just be a power play. Who knows? But you'll have to go up there and sort it out for me. Help Tostig as much as you can.'

'I'll try,' Harold answered tiredly.

'Good. Then, when you return, you should be just in time to watch me give up the throne.'

'What d'you mean?' Harold pointed to the travel brochures. 'Are you planning on abdicating, my Lord?'

'Oh, those!' the King chuckled. 'I confiscated them from that choirboy.' He picked one up and flipped through its glossy pages. 'Sun, sea, sand, and sex, that's all they are. As I told him, there *is* no paradise on Earth.' He dropped the brochure back on the table. 'No, my doctors have informed me that I only have a short time to live.'

'I'm so sorry, Edward,' Harold commiserated, surprised at his own sincerity.

'Don't be, Harold. I'm glad of it. I've confessed my sins and I'm ready for much higher things than men's mere lust for power and the trivial complaints of women.'

'What was that about women, Edward?' the Queen smiled, approaching out of the shadows, having entered unnoticed.

'Ah, my dear. Look who's here!' King Edward pointed.

'Harold!' she cried with delight.

'G'day, Didi!' Harold grinned as they hugged each other.

'Harold was just saying how your brother Wolnoth's been detained by Duke William. And that Githa's very upset. You must go and comfort her, my dear.'

'Oh, no! Will he be all right, Harold?' she asked anxiously.

'He'll be fine,' he nodded, with a weary smile.

'Harold will tell you all about it.' The King waved his hand. 'Now off you go, you two. I need to rest.'

The Queen went over to her husband and, placing a hand on his shoulder, kissed the top of his balding head. 'Edward, you mustn't over-tax yourself. Is there anything I can get for you? A blanket? Or a book? Would you like a warm drink?'

'No, no, nothing, my dear, thank you,' he replied, patting her hand. 'Except, perhaps, another sherry?' He held out his glass to her, with a helpless, innocent smile.

*

Edith pulled up the blind above the kitchen window and gazed out at the view. The summer sun, just rising over the distant wooded hills, was already hot, turning the morning haze into a glistening filigree of evaporating dewdrops. On all sides of the vegetable garden, birds sang out their dawn chorus to the echoing cry of a cock crowing in the backyard. With a sigh of yearning for the simplicity that should be theirs, yet remained elusive, she turned and went back to the stove, where bacon was sizzling in a pan and the kettle was starting to boil.

The door opened, and Harold came in. He walked over to her and wrapped his arms around her from behind, squeezing her against him and kissing the side of her head. 'Good morning, my love!' he said brightly.

'Sit down, darling,' she smiled, gently shrugging him off. 'Breakfast's almost ready.'

Harold left her and crossed to the window. 'It's so beautiful!' he said, looking out. He took a deep breath and exhaled with contentment. 'I love this time of day.'

'Here you are,' she said, placing a loaded plate onto the table. He went over to her, pulled out a chair, and sat down.

'Mm! Thanks,' he grinned, savouring the sweet, succulent aroma of the bacon and eggs. 'This is sheer bliss, Edith. I could stay here forever.'

'Why don't you, then?' she said, putting a mug of tea down beside him.

'I knew you'd say that!'

'Well?'

'You know why, darling. The country has to be made safe first. I can't just walk away. All I have to do is sort out this Tostig business, then make the centre secure...'

Edith shook her head angrily. 'I don't want to hear it, Harold! There's always just one more thing to do, then another and another. I don't think we're ever going to be a real family!' She turned and strode back to the stove, moving around in agitation, clattering the saucepans and throwing things into the sink.

Harold got up from his seat and followed her. He took her gently by the shoulders. 'Of course we'll be a family, darling.'

'It's crazy!' she laughed in frustration. 'When we are together, all we seem to do is fight.'

'No, we don't. It'll be all right.'

'We need you so much, Harold!'

'Oh, darling, don't give up. We're almost there. We have to see this through. We have to!'

'I know. I know.' She pushed him away. 'Go on, finish your breakfast.'

Harold sat down again. 'Everything'll work out, Edith, really. I promise you, it'll all be over soon. Then I'll be home for good.'

'But what if the Duke tries to take the throne by force?'

'He can't, not if we're united. And, for the moment, I'm the only one who can achieve that. That's why, as I told you last night, when Edward's gone I think they'll offer me the crown.'

'That was some bombshell!'

'Yeah,' he chuckled. 'Then William'll have to swallow his ambition and send Wolnoth home. The only problem could be that fiasco in Normandy, although Bishop Alred predicts the Council will back me.'

'But if your presence is all that holds him in check, how will you ever be able to leave?'

'I'd have to appease him somehow. Send over a delegation to negotiate. Make it all public if I have to. He wouldn't dare risk a trade embargo. Maybe I could even get their Grand Pontiff to intervene. And in the meantime, I'd find a successor.'

'Like who?'

'I've been thinking the Council might accept Gurth. How does that sound, King Gurth?'

'Poor Gurth!'

Just then, the kitchen door opened and Edmund entered, puffy eyed and walking sluggishly, followed by Magnus, half-asleep, and Gunhilds, clutching a small piece of sheet, with her thumb in her mouth.

'Well, look who it is!' Harold laughed.

'Hi, Dad. Mum,' Edmund nodded, going to the far end of the table.

'Good morning, darling,' Edith called over her shoulder.

Gunhilds stopped next to Harold's chair, while Magnus, yawning, sat down and grabbed the box of breakfast cereal.

'Morning, Daddy,' she said.

'Hello, angel!' Harold smiled, kissing her cheek. 'Wakey-wakey!' he laughed to Magnus.

'Oh, hi!' Magnus grinned, yawning again.

Gunhilds went over to Edith, put her arm around her legs, and leant against her, sucking her thumb, watching them all in silent contemplation.

Harold looked at Edmund and smiled. 'How d'you feel, mate?'

'Oh, my head!' Edmund groaned. 'Does wine always do this?'

Edith looked round at him. 'When did you have wine? You told me that was blackcurrant juice you were drinking. I thought you were acting strangely!'

'I only gave him half a glass,' Harold laughed. 'He must've sneaked the rest himself!'

'Harold, how could you?' she scolded him.

'I didn't think it'd do him any harm. After all, it was a special occasion.'

'If you didn't keep going away, Dad,' Magnus threw in, between spoonfuls, 'we wouldn't have to have a party every time you come back.'

'Or get up so early to say goodbye,' Gunhilds moaned.

'Well, I'd better make sure it doesn't happen again, hadn't I? Only, this time, I have to go and help good old Uncle Tostig.'

'Take me with you, Dad,' Edmund pleaded. 'You said you would next time.'

'Me too!' Magnus grinned with excitement.

'You're too young, silly!' Gunhilds chided him.

'I wouldn't get in the way, Dad,' Edmund persisted. 'I could just watch how you do things. After all, I'm going to join the army when I leave school.'

Edith banged down a plate of food in front of him. 'No way! Eat!'

'Why not? I'm not a child any more, I'm sixteen!'

'Only just. And the answer's still no! One soldier in this family is more than enough.'

'Dad?'

'You heard your mother, Ed,' Harold smiled sadly at his crestfallen son. 'Eat your breakfast, mate. Anyway, soon, even I won't have to be one,' he said, looking cheerfully up at Edith.

She turned away without response.

*

The spitting image of his violent father, only weaker-chinned and more sallow, Morcar, the dark-haired, drooping-moustachioed son of Earl Algar, sat out of the morning sun under the shade of his tent awning, gazing at a small photograph of him in an oval silver locket he held in the palm of his hand.

All of a sudden, disturbing his reverie with a clatter of sword pommel against armour, one of his captains ran up the low incline towards him. 'There's an army coming, Morcar!'

Morcar closed the locket and put it away in his pocket. 'Which direction?'

'Over there,' the captain pointed.

'We've just come from there ourselves.' Morcar peered into the distance and gave a laugh. 'It must be Edwin!'

A few moments later, Edwin, his clean-shaven, slower-witted younger brother, rode into the armed camp on his bicycle, followed by his men. He dismounted and ran up the slope. 'Hiya, Morc!' he panted.

'Edwin!' Morcar smiled and embraced him. 'Great. You made it!'

'Not too late, am I?'

'No, you couldn't've timed it better, mate.'

'Good. So, what's the order of play, Morc?'

'As soon as Harold arrives, we'll send him our list of complaints against Tostig.'

'D'you think he'll listen?'

'Yeah. If nothing else, Harold's a fair-minded bloke. He'll hear us out.'

'Tostig won't like that!' Edwin snorted. 'Hey, you wouldn't believe the trouble I had getting away from Aldyth. She wanted to tag along, too.'

'Our sister always loved a good fight.'

'Nah, it wasn't that. I just happened to mention that Harold might show up. She's really got the hots for him.'

Morcar raised his eyebrows. 'Has she? Well, maybe we can turn that to our advantage.'

'How d'you mean?'

'Harold's single, isn't he? What could be more logical than...?'

Just then, a burst of shouting erupted from the entrance to the camp. Seconds later, the captain rushed up the slope again. 'It's the King's army!'

'Okay, get the men ready,' Morcar nodded, and the captain ran off. 'And here comes lover boy, right on time!' he chuckled coldly.

*

At the far end of the town hall meeting room, behind a table loaded with documents, Harold sat listening. His face was stern. Standing next to him was Bishop Alred.

Bernard was on his feet. 'Blackmail, extortion, sexual assault, and now attempted murder! The list goes on and on!' he fumed, shaking a wad of papers in the air.

The members of the Council and the numerous high-ranking Saxons, seated around him on three tiers of benches, growled in angry agreement.

On the opposite side of the floor, Tostig lay sprawled on a bench with his legs sticking out and his arms folded, sullen and glowering, surrounded by a dozen of his cronies. 'I already told you, mate, I'm bloody innocent!' he shouted back. 'How the hell could I know they were planning to kill him?'

Bernard shook his head and turned away. 'I'm sorry, Harold, I know he's your brother, but I say the evidence against Tostig is overwhelming.'

At this, there were loud cheers and yells of agreement from the rows of townspeople filling the hall.

'Bah!' Tostig spat with contempt and jerked his head away.

As Bernard sat down, Bishop Alred leaned closer to Harold and conferred with him.

Meanwhile, sitting at the back of the hall, was the familiar figure of Eric Braithwaite. He turned around in his aisle seat and spoke quietly into a microphone. 'The mood of the people is obvious. And that last outburst shows just how appalled the Council is by the extent of Tostig's crimes. I wouldn't like to be in Harold's shoes now. Does he deliver his brother up for trial and possibly the hangman's noose or will family loyalty win out?' He looked round for a moment, then quickly turned back. 'But, wait! Bishop Alred is about to speak.'

The townspeople quietened down as the Bishop walked forward.

'Your actions have taken you beyond the pale, Tostig,' he said, raising his voice for all to hear. 'By rights, you should be stripped of your earldom and made to face the full penalty of the law.'

There was a resounding cheer of assent from the crowd.

'However, the King has already expressed his wish that, for services rendered in the past, should you be found guilty you are to be shown leniency.'

There were angry gasps of disbelief. 'Therefore, according to the power vested in me by His Majesty and by this Council, you are hereby ordered to take your possessions and immediately leave this country forever!'

There was uproar at this, as a pandemonium of shouting and booing filled the hall. 'No! No!' yelled the crowd. 'Don't let 'im off! He's bloody guilty! Hang 'im!'

Amid the tumult, Tostig leapt to his feet. Livid with rage, he stuck his middle finger up at the array of Councillors. 'You can stuff your verdict up your arses, you bastards!' he snarled. He spun round to Harold. 'You've paid your lackeys well, Harold, but you won't get rid of me that easily. I'll be back, mate. You mark my words, I'll be back!'

With that, shaking his fist at the furious townspeople, he turned on his heel and stormed out of the room, followed by his men.

Amid the ensuing furore, Eric Braithwaite looked round again and lifted the microphone to his mouth. 'Well, Harold certainly hasn't made any friends here today! And, at a time when the country urgently needs to build bridges between its warring factions, with rumours of King Edward's ill health gaining credence, and with the ever-present spectre of foreign invasion lurking just over the horizon, this outcome can only serve to fuel the resentment between the parties.

'Who around here will ever completely trust either the King or Earl Harold again? If the time ever comes when Harold has to rely on these people's support, he may find that today's decision costs him more dearly than he thought…This is Eric Braithwaite, for the *Anglo-Saxon Chronicle*, in the shifting centre of the kingdom.'

*

A few hours later, once the formal process of his brother's exile was completed, Harold managed to escape, to make sense of what had happened and come to terms with his disparate feelings. Finding safe haven in the hushed darkness of the local parish church, he sat slumped in a pew halfway down one side, alone and dejected, watching the few aged parishioners and a pair of altar boys preparing for the evening service.

There was the sound of the heavy porch door closing behind him. A moment later, the dark figure of Bishop Alred appeared like a wraith out of the gloom by the vestibule. He stopped and looked around. Spotting Harold, he advanced down the central aisle, the click of his heels on the stone floor echoing around the dimly-lit interior. Drawing level, he genuflected, then squeezed himself in and sat down beside him.

'I didn't expect to find you here, Harold?' he whispered.

'I just needed a quiet place to think, father,' Harold sighed.

'Are you all right, my son?'

'No, not really. Feeling a bit lost, to be honest.'

'Why? Because of Tostig?'

'Among other things,' Harold said quietly. 'He should've stood trial for what he did.'

'And yet?'

'And yet I couldn't do it to him. I sold out. The people deserved justice and what did they get? Double standards.'

'Don't be so hard on yourself, Harold. You did what you had to do. You were only following the King's instructions.'

'And what if they were wrong?'

'What if they were right? It's our duty to save souls, isn't it? Maybe, by being given this chance, Tostig can find peace and redemption. After all, the King is a man of compassion.'

Harold gave a cynical laugh. 'Some might say Edward was just playing politics. That he didn't want to upset the Duke by hanging his brother-in-law. And if there's one thing I know about Tostig, Father, it's that he won't take this lying down. You were there. You heard what he said.'

'I know,' Bishop Alred sighed. 'And I pray they were just words spoken in anger. But if he does decide to cause more trouble, the law will deal with him, you can be sure of that. And in that event, my son, you can take comfort from the fact that you've tried to help him. Now, what else is bothering you?'

'The oath I took.'

'Well, you know the answer to that one already. By protecting yourself you were protecting us all.'

'How could I have let myself get backed into a corner like that? I never should've gone.'

'It doesn't matter. What's done is done. And, anyway, with you as king William'll be forced to give up his plans.'

"Maybe. If I'm chosen.'

'Well, actually,' the Bishop smiled, 'I've just come from a full meeting of the Council. Their decision was unanimous. You must succeed Edward, Harold. Congratulations.'

'Thank you,' Harold answered without enthusiasm. 'How is Edward?'

'On the decline, I'm afraid. The doctors are with him now. It doesn't look good.'

'He could still name William, though.'

'If he does, the Council will override him.'

'That could cause a split.'

'We'll deal with that when the time comes. No, you're the man the country needs, my son.'

Harold rubbed his forehead. 'Oh, God!..I'm sorry. It's just that sometimes I think I'm never going to be with Edith and the kids.'

At that, Bishop Alred's face visibly hardened. 'Look around you, Harold,' he directed in a stern voice, pointing about him. 'That plaque. Those tombstones. These windows. What do you see?'

Harold stared at a brass plaque listing those killed in action; a flagstone bearing the names of officers who had died in battle; and a stained-glass window depicting a heroic figure carrying a sword and shield, standing among the bodies of his fallen comrades with grateful women clinging to his legs.

'War heroes?' he suggested.

'No. They're more than just war heroes, Harold. Those men didn't only give up their lives, they also sacrificed their own personal happiness to defend their country and their loved ones. Would you be prepared to do the same?'

'Yes, I think so.'

'You only think so? I need to know, my son.'

Harold frowned. 'All right, then, Father,' he answered in a tight voice. 'Yes, I would.'

'Very well, then, Harold. As you know, apart from the King, you, Morcar, and Edwin are the three most powerful men in the country. And, on Edward's death, it's more than likely they're going to resent you being given ultimate power. Therefore, now more than ever, given this new threat from the Normans, it's imperative that you make an alliance with them. To that end, Morcar has asked me to arrange a meeting.'

'Good. Thankfully, so far, they don't seem to be taking after their father.'

'Time will tell. Ambition does strange things to people. Nevertheless, the fact remains that unless you can forge an iron link between you and the sons of Algar, on your accession there could well be civil war. And there's one way, and one way only, to prevent that, Harold. You must marry their sister, Aldyth.'

'What is this, déjà vu?' Harold laughed out loud with bitter incredulity, remembering his father's same demand. 'Don't be ridiculous! I've got a family, you know that. I can't just chuck them aside.'

'I know what they mean to you, my son. Don't think I haven't anguished over this, but there is no alternative.'

'No! Never! Forget it. I'd rather give up the throne.'

'And see your country torn apart? Well, of course, if that's your decision?'

'You'll have to find someone else.'

'Who? Gurth? Morcar? Neither of them commands the respect you do. William would have them for breakfast. Like it or not, Harold, you're the people's choice. It has to be you.'

'I don't believe this! Since when has the Church condoned adultery?'

'Technically speaking, my son, in the eyes of the Church your relationship with Edith is a sin.'

'Oh, thanks a lot. You're a real friend!'

'I am your friend, Harold, believe me. But this is more important than either family or friendship. Sometimes the sword that we use for defence...'

'That *we* use?' Harold queried with scathing sarcasm.

'*That's* used for defence,' the Bishop clarified with a patient sigh, 'must also be used to sever the ties that bind us from our duty.' He rose to his feet. 'I'll leave you to consider what I've said. Only don't take too long, Harold, the King doesn't have much time.' Stepping out into the aisle, he bent his knee to the altar, crossed himself, then turned and walked away.

Harold slumped back in his seat.

King? He couldn't even begin to think about *that*. His emotions were already stretched to the limit. It was all getting away from him, spinning out of control. For each new problem he'd found a solution, only to find himself facing an even greater problem. Up until then, he'd somehow managed to keep his balance, to remain in control, to see his way out of the morass, back into the light. But now *this!* For the first time, he felt the real edge of fear. A wave of panic gripped his throat, crushing his temples in a vice. Oh, not *that!* he pleaded in the vault of his mind. Please, God, not *that!*

Letting out a tortured groan, he threw himself forward, screwing up his eyes in torment against the white-knuckled pyramid of his clasped hands.

16

At the sound of knocking, Edith put down her basket of ironing and hurried out of the laundry to the entrance hall. She opened the front door. Gurth and Bernard were standing outside on the porch. Beyond the garden fence, on the other side of the road, a carriage and riders waited in a line.

'Gurth!' she cried in surprise.

'G'day, Edith.'

'It's been so long!' she said as they hugged. 'How are you?'

'Good, thanks. You look great, as usual.'

'That's what family life does for you. You should try it sometime.'

'Still searching. A good woman's hard to find. Talking of which, I've brought Bernard along with me. He was hoping to see Gladys.'

'Thanks for your concern, Gurth,' Bernard smiled. 'G'day, Edith.'

Edith stepped back. 'Come in. Come in. Nice to see you again, Bernard,' she said, as they entered. 'She's out the back, I think. Go on through. You know the way.'

Bernard grinned at them both. 'Right, then. Thanks.'

They watched as he crossed the lounge and headed off down the hallway. 'Well, he seems to be quite at home here?' Gurth queried with a laugh.

'Oh, Bernard's dropped by a couple of times lately.' Edith put on a deep southern drawl. 'Ah do believe he's sparkin' Miss Gladys.'

'The old devil!'

'Anyway, what brings you all the way down here, Gurth?' A look of concern rose in her face. 'Has something happened to Harold?'

'No, no, nothing like that. He's fine. In fact, it was him who sent me. He wants me to take you to him.'

'Take me to him? I'm sure Mum'd look after the children, but why the urgency?'

Gurth shrugged. 'I don't know. He wouldn't tell me. Edward collapsed yesterday, maybe that's the reason?'

'Oh, dear! So, it's finally happening?'

'Looks like it. And the Council's chosen Harold to succeed him. He probably wants you there to celebrate.'

'Oh, sure. With Edward on his deathbed, I can really see that. Come on, Gurth, you're hiding something?'

'He asked me to fetch you, that's all.'

'You can't lie to me, I know you too well,' she smiled at him. 'Please, tell me?'

'I'm not supposed to, Edith. Harold wants to explain it to you himself.'

'Explain what?'

'Just that...now he's been chosen...they want him to marry.'

Edith laughed with relief. 'Is that all! What's wrong with that? There's nothing in the world Harold wants more than for us to...' Seeing Gurth look away and remain silent, she suddenly understood. 'Oh, God! Oh, no! It isn't me, is it?'

'I'm so sorry, Edith...'

All the breath went out of her, as she sank down onto the couch. 'Who?' she asked in a lifeless voice.

'Aldyth.'

'Ohh!' she moaned. She lifted her face to the ceiling and gave a sobbing laugh. 'Aldyth!'

*

Out in the backyard, Bernard and Gladys stood wrapped in each other's arms, sharing a passionate kiss while chickens strutted around them, pecking at the corn, staring up at them with watchful eyes. A basket of eggs dangled from her arm.

Gladys pulled away, panting. 'Stop it, you hairy old man, you'll break the eggs. No, don't stop!' she commanded as he hesitated, grabbing his shirtfront and pulling him closer for another kiss. Gasping for air, they finally separated.

'Well, you're a fast worker, I'll say that!' she laughed.

'I have to be!' Bernard grinned. 'There isn't much time. Gladys, I haven't stopped thinking about you since the last time we met.'

'Me, too,' she admitted. Like magnets, their mouths flew together once more. 'Oh, this is silly!' she said, pushing him away at last and straightening her skirt. 'I'm acting like a schoolgirl. You must have plenty of women in your life, an important man like you?'

'No, none. Really. Not since my wife died. How about you? Gurth told me you're a widow. Do you think…I mean…are you… available?'

'What? Oh, goodness. Available? Of course, I'm available!' she laughed. They kissed again. She broke free and grabbed his arm. 'Come on,' she said, her eyes twinkling with delight. 'I have to take these in.'

'Here, let me carry that for you,' he offered, as they started back towards the house. She passed him the basket. 'Well, would you mind if I came to see you sort of…you know… seriously?'

'What're you trying to say, Bernie? You weren't so tongue-tied a minute ago.'

'Damn it, woman, I want you! I mean, I don't want to rush you, but...'

'Rush all you want. I like it.'

'Then...?'

'Yes, you gorgeous great hunk! I want you too.'

Bernard put his arm around her thick waist. 'I don't even know where you live or what you actually do here, Gladys?'

Gladys smiled and thought for a moment. 'Well, I live just down the road in a little old house,' she began. 'And I work here a few days a week. Part-time nurse, part-time babysitter, things like that. For all her qualities, Edith's a lousy cook, so some days I do that, too. Next time you're here I'll make you a meal, if you like?'

'I'd like to eat *you!*' he grinned.

'You saucy beast!' Gladys chuckled. 'Mind you, I've got a lot of old meat that hasn't been chewed on in a long while, I can tell you. What am I saying? Enough of this! Anyway, why are you really here, Bernie? Apart from seducing me, of course.'

'Gurth wouldn't let on. All I know is that Harold wants to see Edith.'

At that moment, Gurth appeared at the back door. 'Come on, mate,' he called out. 'We're off!'

*

Harold sat forward in his armchair, resting his chin on his hand, deep in thought. His eyes were wild and staring, lost in the patterns on the wood-panelled wall of the study, as he wracked his brain for some other solution. He turned with a start as the door opened behind him and Gurth came in, followed by Edith. Pushing past his brother, she rushed towards him. Harold jumped to his feet.

'Edith! Thank God you're here.'

'Oh, Harold!' she cried, coming into his arms.

'Edith knows, Harold,' Gurth said from the doorway, as they clung to each other. 'I'm sorry. She made me tell her.'

'It doesn't matter, mate. It's all right. Thanks for bringing her.'

'No worries.' Gurth gave them a sad smile and went out, shutting the door.

Harold held Edith close, kissing her hair. 'My love!'

'Oh, Harold! I'm so frightened.'

He stepped back from her. 'Come on, let's go outside. We have to talk.'

Exiting through another door leading out into the chill night air, beneath the pale glow of frosted lamps set on poles at intervals along the balustrade, they set off down the paved terrace overlooking the lawn with Edith gripping his arm.

'What did Gurth tell you?' Harold asked.

'That they want you to marry Aldyth,' Edith answered coldly, a perilous tone rumbling like magma beneath the surface of her words.

'Did he say why?'

'To make the kingdom secure or some such rubbish.'

'Yeah,' Harold sighed. 'And to prevent civil war on Edward's death.'

'Harold, you can't!' She stopped and turned towards him, clutching his sleeve. 'You're mine. We need you.'

'I know, Edith, I know!' he moaned. 'But what can I do?'

Enraged, she stepped back to face him. 'What d'you mean what can you do? Tell them all to go to hell and leave with me right now!'

'I want to! You know that.' he insisted in anguish. 'But if it means the country'll be safe? And it's my only chance of getting Wolnoth back.'

'I can't believe I'm hearing this! You're actually thinking of doing it. This is insane, Harold. I'm sorry about Wolnoth, but we matter more! Anything that tears us apart is wrong.'

'It wouldn't have to tear us apart, darling. It wouldn't change the way we feel about each other. It'd be a diplomatic arrangement, that's all. It'd never be consummated.'

'Oh yes? And how would you explain that to Aldyth?'

'I'd tell her about you and the kids. She'd understand. Then, as soon as this Norman business blows over, I'd get an annulment.'

'And then you'd have your civil war. She'd understand!' Edith laughed with contempt. 'What d'you think she is? Little Miss Nice? She's her father's daughter, out for what she can get. Do you really think her brothers are just going to stand by and watch their sister be made a fool of? And lose their grip on the throne? You'd have to deny us, Harold. You'd have no other choice. We'd be pushed right out of your life. We'd be lost to each other forever.'

As her voice broke, Edith turned away and leant against the balustrade, staring out at the night through glassy eyes. Harold went to her and put his arm around her. 'My love, I won't let that happen. I couldn't.'

'Do you remember how all this started, Harold?' she said, fighting back her tears. 'You were just looking for a way to marry me without hurting your father. And now it's come to this. We won't even exist.'

'Edith, I love you...'

'And I love you, too.' She pulled away from him. 'You have to decide, Harold. Now! Is it us you really want or this abstract madness you call duty?'

Like a bolt of electricity, the bleak despair in her voice shocked his emotions into life and his heart rushed out to her.

'Come on,' he growled, suddenly grabbing her hand. 'We're leaving!'

Pulling Edith after him, Harold strode across the balcony to a nearby glass door. Opening it and pushing aside its long net curtain, they entered a small dining room. A uniformed waitress was busy spreading starched white cloths onto the tables, while a male cleaner vacuumed the polished floor. Both of them stopped what they were doing and stared in surprise, as he led her across the room and out through the open internal door.

Coming into a dark, narrow passageway lined with cedar panelling, they stopped. All was quiet. Off to their right, the musty corridor stretched away past the bannister of a wooden staircase. Seeing Gurth and Bishop Alred approaching along it in the distance, they turned in the opposite direction and headed towards the palace entrance.

'Harold!' Gurth shouted after them.

Gripping each other's hand, they hurried on. There were the sounds of running feet behind them, getting closer.

'Harold!' Gurth called out. 'Wait up.'

With a weary sigh, knowing it was futile to ignore them, Harold stopped and closed his eyes, bracing himself for the inevitable showdown. Edith tried to drag him on, but he resisted. As they arrived, he grit his teeth and turned to face them. Gurth ran up to him, with the Bishop a few paces behind.

'What d'you want?' Harold said.

'Where are you going?' Gurth exclaimed. 'We've been looking everywhere for you.'

'So?'

'The King's dying. He's been asking for you.'

'You are needed, my son,' Bishop Alred said with solemn sadness.

'He's not your son!' Edith snarled at him with contempt, tugging at Harold's hand.

'You must come with us, Harold,' the Bishop commanded.

In frantic defence, Edith tried even harder to pull him away. 'Don't listen to them, Harold!' she pleaded. 'Come on.'

Harold didn't move. She yanked at his hand, but he wouldn't budge. She turned and stared at him. For a moment, the pulse of time seemed to stop beating as they gazed into each other's eyes.

'Darling...' he murmured, his voice imploring, cracking with despair, yet fixed in its resolve. She could see it in his face, the phoenix of national salvation rising from the ashes of their aborted escape, already decided, enclosed and unreachable, like the lost world trapped inside a whirling cyclone. 'I can't!'

'Let him go, Edith,' Bishop Alred instructed her with a gentle smile. 'Let him go. His destiny calls him.'

'Edith, the country needs him,' Gurth tried to explain.

'*I* need him!' she roared back, clinging onto Harold's hand, feeling it slipping out of her grasp. 'Don't, Harold! *Don't!*'

As if in slow-motion, finger by reluctant finger, Harold pulled his hand free. In an instant, they took hold of his arms.

'Harold!' Edith cried out, in tears, as they led him away. '*Please!*'

Harold looked back over his shoulder, sending her a twisted, reassuring smile. 'Don't worry, Edith. It'll be all right.'

'Oh, God! No! *No!*' she screamed after him with all her force, but it wasn't enough. Harold was gone, swept on up the corridor by Bishop Alred and Gurth.

She slumped back against the wall, burying her face in her hands, sobbing her heart out, and slowly slid down to the floor.

*

There was a hushed stillness in the bedroom of the royal apartment. The atmosphere was intense, charged with emotion, the respectful silence pregnant with anticipation. The wings of the Angel of Death spread over the room, hovering in the shadows on the ceiling, just beyond the reach of the lowered oil lamps.

Lying under the covers on his canopied, four-poster bed, to all appearances King Edward was unconscious. His cheeks and eye sockets were sunken, and his skin, like yellowed parchment, was stretched tight across his bony face. Intermittent breaths came out of his open mouth in small, bubbling gasps, causing the minutest fluttering of his colourless lips. The Queen sat beside him with her head bowed, holding his white-veined, emaciated hand in hers.

On the opposite side of the bed, clustered together in their dark garb like a pack of expectant vultures, were Archbishop Stigand, the Dean of the Royal Chapel, the Minister for Homeland Security, and the Treasurer.

Meanwhile, standing near the door at the back of the room, Leofwine and Bernard were talking in low tones to the King's ageing doctor. They all looked round as Bishop Alred and Gurth entered with Harold.

'How is he?' the Bishop asked quietly.

'No change,' Leofwine answered.

'He may be in a coma,' said the doctor.

Harold walked over to his sister and put his hand on her shoulder. 'Hiya, Didi,' he said softly.

She turned and looked up at him through her tears. 'Oh, Harold!'

All of a sudden, King Edward opened his eyes. He looked round at her, squeezed her hand, and gave her a feeble smile. 'Ah, my Queen!'

'Oh, Edward!'

'I have been a good husband to you, haven't I, my dear?' he frowned. 'In my own way?'

'You have!' she nodded, crying openly.

He held out a shaking hand. 'Harold.'

Harold smiled with gentle, mixed affection, taking hold of it. 'G'day, Edward. How're y'going?'

'Nearly there...Nearly there,' the King answered, with a tired smile.

'Quick! While he's lucid!' the Treasurer exclaimed.

Archbishop Stigand moved in haste to the bedside and leant over the dying monarch. 'Your Majesty,' he crooned, 'before you leave us for your heavenly throne, you must tell us who you wish to succeed you? Surely Duke William would be best?'

'The Council would never support that,' said Bishop Alred, walking forward and standing next to Harold. 'My Lord, only someone strong and popular can lead us through these troubled times. You must choose Harold.'

'Just give the Duke your blessing, Your Majesty,' the Archbishop urged. 'And let *him* deal with the Council.'

'Duke William would bring us security, my Lord,' the Minister added, leaning forward.

'And it would finally put an end to the Godwins' ambitions, my Lord!' sneered the Dean, from the back of the group.

The Queen and Harold raised their heads and stared at him in cold fury.

'How dare you!' she exclaimed, lashing out at him with indignant loathing.

'You want ambition, Norman, just look to your master!' Harold snarled.

The Dean recoiled in shock, as if he'd been physically struck. King Edward gave a world-weary, pitying chuckle and turned towards the Queen. 'What do you say, my dear?'

'Not the Duke!' she pleaded, lifting his hand to her cheek.

A faint smile flickered across his face. 'No?' Suddenly, he winced and his body convulsed. 'Aah!' he gasped, writhing and groaning in pain. Fighting for breath, he raised his head off the pillow, staring into the distance. 'You...want...Harold?' he croaked. 'So...be...it!' Giving a tortured cry, a shudder ran through his frail body, his chest heaved, his eyes closed, and letting out a final, long, rattling breath, he fell back on the bed.

With a loud sob, the Queen laid her head against his lifeless hand, weeping, while the doctor quickly pushed his way through to the bedside. He listened to the King's heart, felt for a pulse, and then held a mirror over his mouth. Eventually, he looked up at them all craning over him. 'He's gone!'

With a scowl, Archbishop Stigand spun round to his companions. 'Come on!'

Followed by the Minister, the Treasurer, and the Dean, he swept away across the room, his chin raised in haughty disgust.

Leofwine moved to block his path. 'You've had your day, Stigand,' he grinned coldly. 'You and your mates'll be in opposition now, for a long, long time.'

'Don't crow too soon, Leofwine,' the Archbishop sneered. 'There's a new broom coming, one that'll sweep you and your kind away for good! Now let me pass.'

With a flamboyant twirl of his arm and an exaggerated, low, courtly bow, Leofwine stepped aside, allowing him and his party to stride on in fury towards the door.

*

Resonating throughout the theatre auditorium, a sustained chord of organ music reached its ear-splitting crescendo and ended abruptly in a ringing silence.

Holding aloft a glistening, gem-encrusted gold crown with both hands, Bishop Alred began to speak in a loud, solemn voice. As he did so, he very slowly lowered his arms.

'Following, without question, the time-honoured custom handed down to us, whereby one amongst us is chosen to represent the spirit of our nation, invested with power and authority, bestowed with great wealth and comfort, held in reverence by both Church and Man, the embodiment of our laws and institutions, a figurehead for whose grandeur and sustenance we gladly offer our labour, and in whose defence we willingly sacrifice the lives of ourselves and our children, so we take you, Harold, as our anointed King!'

Seated below him, Harold, now with a full, greying beard, stared out from a scallop-backed, intricately carved throne, holding twin sceptres across his chest. His face remained expressionless as the Bishop reached down over the back and placed the crown on his head.

Bishop Alred then turned away and stepped down from the dais on which the throne was set to join the Saxon notables gathered below, standing in two groups, beneath Corinthian columns on either side of the stage. As the Bishop took his place among the members of the Council, all wearing their long robes of state, the large collection of military officers, clergymen, and senior politicians on the other side—Gurth, Leofwine, Bernard, Morcar, and Edwin among them—drew their ceremonial swords and pointed them on high, all shouting together in affirmation, 'We take Harold as our anointed King!'

Behind them, hanging at the back of the stage, was a large drop cloth painted in bright pastel colours, depicting the tops of gum trees in the foreground, with a carpet of forest stretching away into the distance beyond, creating the illusion of the stage being set high up on top of a hill.

Fluffy, peach-coloured clouds and little, pink, half-naked androgynous cherubs, with tiny wings and Cupid bows and curly mops of hair like Harpo Marx, floated above in a powder-blue sky. Giving the appearance of evening mist, white vapour from a dry-ice machine wafted around the foot of the dais and across the floor.

Out in the darkness of the packed stalls, the invited guests stood up, rising in silhouette against the brightly lit stage, and with one accord cried out their allegiance, 'We take Harold as our anointed King!'

Immediately, there was a loud organ blast, followed by a bright fanfare of trumpets and the rapturous singing of a choir, as the coronation anthem began. While the audience applauded, a follow-spot came on, picking out a young, blonde usherette, with an ice cream tray strapped around her neck, standing below the corner of the stage. Straightaway, one of the guards standing in a line at the front of the auditorium hurried over to her and quickly steered her back towards the green neon exit sign and velvet drapes of a side door. The spotlight went out.

Meanwhile, Harold had risen to his feet and descended the steps of the dais. As he walked forward, with a smile, to the front of the stage, the audience gave him a rousing cheer and a standing ovation.

*

On the radio in the lounge, the commentator's dramatic voice broke in over the anthem and the noise of the cheering crowd.

'And so, Harold is crowned King. As he steps forward, waving to the crowd, the assembly rises as one to acclaim him. He is the people's choice. Long may he reign! And may this auspicious

occasion mark the beginning of a time of peace, prosperity, and happiness for us all!'

Across the room, Edith and the children were huddled together on the sofa, listening to the broadcast. Gunhilds was curled up on Edith's lap, worriedly sucking at her piece of sheet. Their faces were blank, lost, and abandoned. With a barely audible sigh, Edith shut her eyes to block out the pain of their shattered world.

*

Beneath its vaulted ceiling, the chapel was packed to capacity with all the most notable Saxons seated in rows on either side of the centre aisle. At the far end, Bishop Alred stood in front of the altar, clasping a prayer book and reciting a blessing.

Standing before him were Harold and Aldyth, her face covered by the veil of her white wedding dress. Watching the ceremony from the front pew behind her, Morcar and Edwin were smiling with pleasure.

Suddenly, half-pulling away as if trying to escape, Harold leant round and stared back down the aisle with a look of sickly, horrified despair on his face. A moment later, he turned to face the altar again as, with a commanding flourish, the piercing pitch of a pipe organ sounded the opening bars of Mendelssohn's *Wedding March*.

*

Vera was standing at the open kitchen window, gazing out at the treetops and puffing on a small cigar. The *Wedding March* was coming from the transistor radio behind her. Blowing out an angry cloud of smoke, she turned and strode back to the table. With a sharp flick of her finger, she switched off the music. Stubbing out her cigar in the ashtray, she looked down at the copy of the *Anglo-Saxon Chronicle* lying beside it. The headline read: *Long Live Harold and Aldyth!*

With a growl of resignation, she walked over to the fly-screen door and opened it. She stared out at the garden. Her shoulders drooped and she let out a long, sad sigh. Then, taking a resolute breath, she threw back her poncho and stepped outside.

*

Edith was busy loosening the soil around the strawberry bushes with a spade. On the edge of the vegetable patch, Magnus stood, bored and listless, scratching at the earth with a stick, while Gunhilds sat cross-legged on the grass nearby, putting a dress on one of her dolls. A short way off, Edmund lay on the low stone wall, his hands under his head, staring up at the sky.

Magnus walked over to him. 'Want to play a game, Ed?' he asked with a hopeful grin.

Edmund shook his head with glum indifference. 'No, go away. I'm not in the mood.'

Magnus wielded his stick like a sword. 'Oh, come on. We've got to do something. I'll be Duke William.'

'Leave me alone. I said *no!*'

'You can be King. Gunhi can be your Queen!' Magnus laughed, as Gunhilds came up to them, clutching her doll.

Edmund sat up, scowling. 'What're you going on about? Dad's the King. He hasn't got a Queen.'

'Mummy should be Queen,' Gunhilds stated sadly.

Magnus waved the stick in Edmund's face. 'It's only pretend.'

With an angry growl, Edmund suddenly reached out and grabbed a garden rake leaning against the wall, parried the stick, and poked Magnus in the chest with the handle. 'Get lost!' he shouted.

Magnus dropped his stick and held his chest, his eyes watering. 'Ow! You didn't have to do that, Edmund!'

In a surge of remorse, Edmund threw aside the rake and jumped down from the wall. 'I'm sorry, Magno,' he said, putting his arm around his brother. 'Are you all right?'

Magnus nodded, his bottom lip quivering. At that moment, Vera approached. 'Come on, you children, off you go and do something constructive,' she chided them, with a smile. 'Give your mother some peace.'

'But there's nothing to do, Nanna,' Magnus moaned.

'Oh yes there is,' Vera laughed. 'Someone has to bring in wood for the fire, the tyres on the bicycles need pumping up, and there's a rabbit loose in the front garden.' She clapped her hands. 'Go on, now, off you go. Shoo!'

'I'll get the rabbit!' Gunhilds cried with excitement, while the two boys groaned. 'I bet it's Mr Floppy!' she laughed.

Vera watched them disappear around the house. She smiled fondly after them and shook her head. Turning away, she walked over to Edith. 'There you are, darling,' she said, unable to keep the sadness out of her voice.

Edith nodded, staring at the earth with a detached, wan frown. 'Hello, Mum.'

'Edith, I...'

'Will you look at these strawberries? We're halfway through summer and they still won't ripen.'

Vera stepped closer. 'Edith, I just heard on the radio...'

'And the lettuces, they're tiny! Maybe something's affecting the weather?'

Vera took her by the shoulders. 'Leave the garden, Edith, and listen!'

'I don't want to hear it, Mum.'

'You must,' Vera said firmly. 'Darling…Harold has just married Aldyth!'

Like a frightened doe, Edith's eyes filled with hurt confusion.

Vera pulled her to her and held her in a tight, protective embrace, trying to staunch the wound and absorb her daughter's pain. 'Oh, my darling girl! I'm so sorry.'

Emitting a small, lost laugh, Edith prised herself free. With her bleak smile cracking under the weight of her sorrow, she turned away and continued digging at the ground.

⁑

Twisting and squirming like a pike on a pole, writhing in agony, jerking this way and that, frantic to escape the piercing skewer of crucified love—as if I were Harold, as if I had done it—desperate to negate the horror of that irrevocable breach, in my sleep I threw myself backwards…and came to my senses sitting bolt upright on the bed, my eyes wide open and staring, panting for breath.

PART THREE

17

My face was pouring with sweat, my chest heaving in panic. My eyes, although open, were delirious and unseeing. Sitting up on the bed, my body rigid, locked in my fear, I stared back into the rapidly receding nightmare. As the images finally faded, tumbling away down the ravine of sleep, to become lost in the shadowlands, I became conscious of my surroundings. With a gasp of trembling relief, like a mountaineer who had somehow survived an avalanche, my muscles unwound and my breathing settled.

I looked around me. It was the dead of night. The room was half in darkness, semi-lit by the bedside lamp. I wanted to turn off its intruding brightness but could do nothing about it. I was too weak. My head was still spinning, the weight of my eyelids pulling them down, my brain telling me I needed to collapse.

Punk music was blaring from the television. The noise was excruciating, seeming brash and ridiculous, an insult to the heartwrenching emotions I'd felt in that other world. I struggled to focus on its source, finally deciphering the colour and motion on the screen as a five-piece band of scrawny, vitamin-deficient adolescents with spiked Mohawk hair, face-rings, and ripped t-shirts, prancing around on stage in wired, aggressive agitation. The effort of watching them slamming their guitars and storming about with frenzied, unrhythmic abandon was too much for me. I groaned and fell back on the bed.

Screwing up my eyes against the glare of the light, I rolled over onto my other side. As the clanging and crashing slowly melded into a dissonant wall of evaporating sound, with a fateful, yearning sigh I let go and dropped into the void.

∷

In the hot, sultry, south-eastern corner of the Norman empire, a young woman wearing a pale pink headscarf and a threadbare, baggy blue cotton jacket, with a swaddled baby strapped to her back inside a woollen cocoon, stood bent over at the waist, knee-deep in water on the edge of a rice field. Behind her, a rustic track stretched off into the distance along a rutted causeway, before climbing a jungle-clad hill towards the curved eaves and dragon-headed gables of Tostig's ebony and stone mansion.

At the clatter of an approaching motorcycle, the woman straightened her body and looked round. Her tired face remained expressionless as, seconds later, a messenger riding an old moped, with a satchel strapped across his back and a bamboo cone hat on his head, rattled past in a cloud of dust and bumped away up the road.

*

'The bastard! The double-dealing bastard!' Tostig shouted in fury, staring at the letter in his hand. Lifting his head and seeing the messenger still standing there, he paused in his tirade. 'Well, what're you waiting for?' he snapped. 'A tip?'

'For any reply, my Lord?' the man answered in apprehension from the doorway.

'There *is* no reply!' Tostig exploded. 'Now get out!' With mounting anger, he bent his knees and swung his arms about from side to side, imitating a chimpanzee. 'Go on. Don't just stand there like a monkey, get out!' he roared, shooing the terrified man away. 'Get out!'

'What is it, baby? What's happened?' Judith called out to him with concern, craning her head over the back of a dark rattan couch halfway down the room.

'Edward's dead!' Tostig fumed in her direction. 'His body's not even cold yet and Harold's been crowned king!' He stormed about the room, waving the letter in the air. 'But is he content with stealing the throne?' He widened his eyes and threw a sardonic laugh at the ceiling. 'Oh, no, not my dear brother. Now he's gone and married Morcar's sister!'

'Has he no bloody family loyalty?' Judith spat with venom.

'All right!' Tostig snarled, grinding his teeth. 'No more Mr Nice Guy!' He screwed up the letter and flung it away. 'Just wait till William hears about this!' he laughed. 'He'll be furious! Harold wants to raise the stakes? Oh, I'll raise 'em, all right. Pack my winter clothes, Judith. I'm going to the palace!'

*

Pulling the bowstring back to his cheek, Duke William squinted along the shaft of the arrow. With slow deliberation, he swivelled round, selecting and then taking aim at one of the terrified servants running between the bare, frozen trees while holding up small, round, straw-filled targets on sticks. He fired.

At that very moment, the man lost his footing and fell to the ground in a flurry of snow, still holding up his target with both shaking hands. There was a powerful jolt, almost breaking his grip, as the missile struck home. With his eyes rolling in fear, he looked up and stared in amazement at the arrow embedded in the centre.

'Missed!' the Duke laughed.

'Get up, you idiot!' Baron Fitzosborne shouted at the terrified man.

'Some hunting party this is!' Taillefer complained, stamping his boots against the cold. 'Not an animal in sight. Nothing but bloody targets to shoot at.' He pointed at the servants. 'Maybe we could string out a few of those fellows? They're not much good for anything else.'

'Zat would make life interesting,' the Baron grunted, warming his hands over the glowing red coals of a nearby brazier. Behind him, court attendants were preparing hot refreshments on the tailgate of a wagon—pouring hot chocolate from an urn into a silver jug and loading up plates with savoury pastries.

Just then, the air was split by the jarring, high-pitched whine of a labouring moped coming towards them through the woods.

'Who the hell's making that racket?' snapped the Duke.

'They'll frighten away the targets!' Taillefer grinned.

A few moments later, Tostig rode into the clearing. Wearing a black cap and coat, with tight white oilskins tucked into brown fringed boots, his face was swathed in a thick woollen scarf. He came to a halt and switched off the engine. As he dismounted and handed his motorcycle to an attendant, Duke William strode over to him, hiding his annoyance behind a disarming smile.

'So, it's you making all that noise, Tostig.'

'Sorry, William, but it's bloody hard going through this snow!' Tostig smiled, brushing the ice from his coat with his gloved hands. 'But I thought I'd better bring you the news myself.'

'What do you mean? What news?'

Tostig took the Duke by the arm and led him aside. 'Edward's dead and Harold's been crowned king.'

'What?' Duke William thundered quietly. 'That throne is mine! Edward promised it to me.'

'Well, I guess they must've forced him to change his mind.'

'Harold swore an oath to help me, in front of witnesses.'

'You didn't really expect that to mean anything to him, did you, William?' Tostig laughed coldly. 'Harold's not giving up the throne for anyone, least of all you or me.'

'Is that right?' the Duke growled. 'Well, we'll see about that. I'm sorry to have to say this, old boy, but your brother's a liar and a thief. And he's going the right way to getting his bottom smacked!'

'You don't have to mince words with me, mate. My brother's a greedy, conniving bastard.'

'Ah, yes, I heard you two had a falling out. So, what is it you want, Tostig? You haven't come here simply to tell me this happy news, have you?'

'No,' Tostig shook his head. 'I just thought we could be of service to each other, that's all. After all, we both want the same thing, only to different degrees. You want the lot, I want a bit. I'll scratch your back if you scratch mine.'

'Well, I'm blowed!' Duke William laughed out loud, staring at his brother-in-law, cogitating, sizing him up. 'Maybe you're right. Just let me get rid of this thing.' He pulled the last arrow from the quiver strapped to his waist. 'Then we can go home and compare itches.'

Looking around and spotting a servant dashing among the trees, he put the arrow to his bow. As he lifted his arm and took aim, the man froze on the spot. Trembling in panic, he dropped to his knees. Quickly crossing himself, he held the target above his head and shut his eyes.

The Duke let the arrow go. With a *whirr*, it flew straight towards the cowering figure and smashed into the bull's eye.

*

Swimming with long, languid strokes, Duke William glided up to the shallow end of his heated, indoor pool and gripped the wall. He turned and leant back, resting his elbows up on the side. A few moments later, Tostig approached, splashing and spluttering, then dived down and surfaced beside him.

'I won!' the Duke laughed.

'Yeah,' Tostig panted, wiping his eyes. 'You're lucky I'm out of condition, mate.'

For a while they both stood there catching their breath, watching the artificial light playing on the steaming surface of the turquoise water and gazing at the courtyard garden outside, beyond the wall of tall plate-glass windows.

'I'm sorry I can't give you any firmer commitment than that, Tostig,' The Duke said, his voice reverberating around the domed interior. 'But leave it with me and, as soon as I've run it by a few people, I'll be in touch.'

'All right, William, but don't leave it too long,' Tostig replied, pushing himself away from the edge and floating back in the water. 'You're my first choice, but this is a high-stakes game, don't forget.'

'What're you saying?' Duke William frowned at him. He turned and waded over to the short flight of curved, tessellated steps leading from the pool.

'That there may be other players who'd like a piece of the action,' Tostig called after him.

As the Duke walked out of the shallows, two servants hurried across the granite floor towards him. Taking the outstretched hand of one of them, he allowed himself to be helped from the water, while the other held out a large, white bath towel for him.

'You don't say?' he nodded, drying himself down and wrapping the towel around his waist, as the servant offered him a second, smaller towel.

'After all, I have to look after my own interests, don't I?' Tostig grinned, following him out of the pool.

'Of course,' the Duke flashed him an ominous smile, rubbing vigorously at his hair. 'Just don't do anything too hasty, Tostig, that's all. We wouldn't want to get in each other's way, now, would we?'

*

It was well after midnight. Apart from the background hum of the air-conditioning, all was quiet on the hundred and forty-ninth floor of the palace. As Wolnoth padded down the silent, carpeted corridor in his socks, all of a sudden a door opened ahead of him and a chambermaid stepped out backwards, pulling a food trolley.

A couple of years older than him, she was tall and willowy, almost flat-chested, wearing a white pinny over her figure-hugging, crumpled black cotton uniform, with a short skirt and black stockings that highlighted her long slender legs. She looked round at him in surprise. On seeing her, Wolnoth's eyes ignited, but the sympathetic smile she gave him doused all his hopes, consigning his lovesick heart to the blue depths of rejection.

At that moment, Tostig appeared in the doorway behind her, naked except for a sarong. The chambermaid turned towards him with a welcoming smile. A lecherous grin spread across his face as he grabbed her, pressing his lips to hers, their mouths open, tongue to passionate, slobbering tongue, and squeezed the tight cheeks of her bottom through the flimsy material of the skirt. Letting out a squeal of laughter, she pushed him away. Blowing him a final good night kiss, she set off down the corridor.

Tostig watched her go, feasting on her body with his eyes, devouring it again in his mind. As she disappeared round a distant corner, he turned to go back in, then saw his brother standing there.

'Hey, Wollo!' he exclaimed. He nodded after the maid. 'Now, that's what I call room service...What? Don't tell me you know her?' he said, seeing the pained look on Wolnoth's face.

'Yes...Yes, I used to.'

'And I suppose you've had your wicked way with her, have you?' Tostig chuckled.

'No...no...that is...she said she wanted to wait.'

'Ah, yeah, well, women are like that, mate, they say one thing and do the opposite. Still, plenty more fish in the sea, eh? Don't worry, she's probably got the pox anyway. Come on in!'

'How can you talk about her like that when you've been...you know...doing it with her?' Wolnoth protested, following Tostig into the small lounge of his apartment and shutting the door behind them.

Along with the acrid smell of tobacco, the musty odours of perfume, perspiration, and sex still hung in the air, somehow made more pungent by the subdued lighting of the dimmed oyster-shell wall sconces and the low table lamp over in the corner by the window. Through the open bedroom doorway, he could see the rumpled double bed and scattered clothing.

'Only joking, mate!' Tostig laughed, moving across and discreetly closing it. 'Just trying to cheer you up. Look, you'd better get used to it, Wol, sheilas are all the same. They've got one use and that's how it's meant to be, nothing wrong with that. It's the nature of life.'

'But what about Judith? What if she found out?'

Tostig hung an arm around Wolnoth's neck and rested his fist against his chin. 'Mate,' he smiled, with a hint of menace, 'what Judith doesn't know, Judith doesn't know. Right? Anyway, what're you doing up at this time of night?'

'I couldn't sleep.'

'Take a seat. D'you want a beer?'

'Yes…yes, thanks.' Wolnoth sat down on one of the two low-backed couches.

Tostig went over to the small bar fridge and returned with a couple of bottles, which he placed on the glass coffee table between them. Arranging his sarong, he settled himself down onto the opposite couch and lit a cigarette. Through the vertical blind covering the window beside him, the multi-coloured lights of the city glowed in the night. 'Now, what's up, mate?' he asked.

Wolnoth rubbed his hand over his face. 'I'm so homesick, Tostig!' he moaned.

'Oh, Wol.'

'It's like I've spent my whole life here. It was so exciting at first, you know. Even when Harold was here last year, I still thought it was the hub of the world. The place to be. But now I just want to go home.'

'Home.' Tostig blew smoke up at the ceiling and gave a wistful sigh.

'I want to see Mum again.' Wolnoth smiled, his eyes watering. 'Taste one of her breakfasts.'

'Mm. Those mushrooms!'

'I've been here nearly fourteen years, d'you know that? Fourteen bloody years! Wasted on a stupid mirage. This isn't how life's meant to be. It's a machine!'

'What d'you mean?'

'People don't count for anything here. It's a heartless system run on snobbery and lies, ruled by a tyrant who demands absolute obedience and gives nothing in return.' Wolnoth sipped his drink and gave a bitter laugh. 'I'm sorry. It must be the beer. Like I said, I just want to go home.'

'Ah, mate!' Tostig shook his head with sadness. 'There is no home, Wollo. It's just a dream our parents had. One they brainwashed us with when we were kids. It died when we grew up. It doesn't exist.'

'Of course it does.'

'No, mate, it's gone. Mum's planning on selling the house. Dad's dead. Sweyn's dead. You're in exile. I've been banished. And, sooner or later, Harold and I are going to be at each other's throats. Where's the home in all that?'

'You're scaring me, Tostig.'

'I don't mean to, mate. I just want you to know the truth.'

Wolnoth drained the last of his beer. 'Well, anyway, I'm going to speak to the Duke. See if he'll let me leave.'

'I wouldn't do that if I were you, Wol. There's a lot of jockeying for position going on at the moment and, believe me, you're safer here out of the road. Just give it a couple more months. Wait till it all blows over and then we'll get you out, I promise.'

*

On the back wall of the light, airy, polished chrome and tile foyer of the palace, a bell rang and the doors of one of the eight elevators opened with a hiss. Duke William and Tostig stepped out together and walked towards the sheer plate-glass entrance.

'All I'm saying, William, is you'd better be quick,' Tostig said. 'I'm determined to go back and I'll do whatever it takes to get there.'

'Don't worry, old boy,' the Duke replied with an amicable laugh. 'I'm sure we'll be able to come to some kind of mutually beneficial arrangement.'

'I certainly hope so, mate.'

As the doors slid open, the guards on either side of them came to attention. They walked out into the bright, cold morning and halted on the terrace at the top of the steps.

'Well, here we are,' Duke William smiled, his breath blowing out in a cloud of vapour. He held out his arms for a hearty embrace. 'Now, off you go, Tostig. Have a safe trip. And, once again, thanks for coming.'

'No problem,' Tostig nodded.

'Give my best to Judith, won't you?' the Duke called after him as he trod carefully down the frosty steps to his motorbike, parked ready and waiting for him.

'I will. Hear you soon, then?'

'Absolutely!'

Tostig pulled his cap down over his ears and kicked the engine into life. With a wave of his hand, he set off.

As his brother-in-law rode away, Duke William stood staring after him, the smile slowly receding from his face. A moment later, Baron Fitzosborne came to his side. He looked at his leader, noting the tight set of his jaw and his narrowed eyes.

'Are you all right, my Lord?' he asked.

'That over-inflated little upstart!' the Duke seethed. 'How dare he give ultimatums to me?'

'Tostig's a mosquito, my Lord. We don't need him,' the Baron's voice rumbled in reassurance. 'Ze most he can do is irritate Harold.'

'Hm...' Duke William murmured, pondering. 'And maybe distract him long enough to be of some use. Of course, it all depends on who's with him.'

'Who is wiz him?'

'Yes. He's on his way to get help now.'

'Who would want to help Tostig, my Lord?'

'Oh, he's got a few connections all right. And I know of one man who has both the balls and the gall to take a chance on him.'

'Who, my Lord?'

'The terror of the north…Hardrada, King of the Vikings!'

With that, the Duke spun round and called across to a group of lawyers and clerics gathered in conversation at the far end of the steps. 'Lanfranc!'

One of their aged members—a slender figure with shoulder-length grey hair, and rimless glasses, a black academic gown, and a floppy felt beret—separated himself from his peers and approached with haste, halting on the step below.

'You called me, my liege?' he inquired in a mellifluous French accent, sweeping off his beret and clutching it to his chest, bowing his head to the side.

'You're an expert in Church law, aren't you, Lanfranc?'

'I can truly say that I am, my Lord. I know it inside and out.'

'And I'm told you have influence with the Grand Pontiff? That he listens to you?'

Lanfranc nodded and smiled. '*Oui*, my Lord. He knows me very well. We are very close.'

'Good! Then come along with me, my friend.' As Lanfranc climbed up to join him, Duke William put his arm around his thin shoulders and led him back towards the building. 'I've got a job for you, Lanfranc. One that requires your particular talents.'

The glass doors opened to let them through, then slid shut again behind them.

*

Sitting comfortably in her favourite late Rococo armchair, enjoying the even flow of warmth from the wide, stainless steel, imitation log fire set in the rear wall of the recess beside her, Matilda was humming to herself as she worked at the small round needlepoint on her lap. She looked up with concern as her husband entered their private apartment, shutting the heavy door behind him with a bang. He leant back against it and heaved a sigh of relief.

'Thank Xzyatan he's gone!' Duke William gasped. 'I don't know what your sister sees in that chap, Matilda,' he said angrily. 'He's utterly uncouth. And arrogant beyond belief!'

Pushing himself upright, he strode across the lounge—an enormous, open-plan space furnished with Persian carpets, heavy sideboards, antique and modern seats, abstract granite sculptures, and tapestries of hunting scenes hanging from brass rods on the walls—over to a small cocktail bar in the corner.

'I need a stiff drink! Can I get you something, my dear?' he asked.

'No, thank you,' Matilda replied, applying another stitch. 'Judith's not blind, you know. She's just using Tostig as an investment.'

'Well, it's a pretty poor investment, if you ask me!' he barked, with a cold laugh, pouring himself a large whiskey from a cut-glass decanter. 'Good riddance to their whole family, that's what I say.'

'Before you settle in, William, aren't you forgetting something?'

'And what might that be, my dear?'

'You still have to deal with Wolnoth, don't you?'

The Duke slapped his hand to his head. 'Blast it! I'd clean forgotten about him.'

'Do you know, this morning he actually had the nerve to come and ask me if he could leave!' Matilda snorted, with a haughty click of her tongue.

'Oh dear,' he tutted.

'You'll have to get rid of him, you know,' she said, carefully laying down her needlework on the small table beside her.

'Mm. Maybe later. You never know, he still might be useful to me one day. Poor Wolnoth,' he laughed. 'I'd almost feel sorry for him if he didn't try so hard to fit in.'

'Oh, he's pathetic, William!'

'Yes. Well, I suppose I'd better have him locked up, then.' He put down his glass. 'I'll go and do it now.'

'You don't actually have to go yourself, do you? Couldn't Fitzosborne do it for you?'

'Well, there is a certain protocol...'

'Oh, bugger protocol! You deserve a rest.'

'Damn it, you're absolutely right, my dear!' He picked up a telephone from a Queen Anne side table nearby and pressed a single number. 'Hello? Fitz? Look, do me a favour would you, old boy? Chuck Wolnoth in the Black Tower...That's right!' he laughed. 'Yes, *and* throw away the key!...Absolutely!...Good man... Thanks, Fitz. Bye.' He replaced the phone and let out a long, self-satisfied sigh. 'Now can I have that drink?'

*

Illuminated by the strip light over the bathroom mirror, Wolnoth stood at the sink shaving off the last of his moustache. He was bare to the waist and wearing boxer shorts. Rinsing off the razor and putting it to one side, he leant down and scooped water onto his face. Then, lifting his head and wiping his eyes, he looked in the mirror again.

He recoiled in shock. Two Norman soldiers were standing close behind him. As he spun round, they grabbed him by the arms and tore him away from the sink, then frog-marched him out of the windowless closet towards the lounge.

Meanwhile, Baron Fitzosborne watched impassively from the doorway. As they went by him, Wolnoth pulled against his captors, forcing them to stop, trying to remonstrate with him. The Baron ignored him. Motioning for his men to continue, they pulled Wolnoth on, dragging him, still struggling, across the carpet and out through the open door.

*

High up in his corner office overlooking the city, Duke William and Bishop Odo sat together at one end of the conference table, sharing a bottle of cognac. Although the lamps had been left off, the room was illuminated by the glow from the rooftop lights of the surrounding skyscrapers, playing a kaleidoscopic symphony of overlapping, watery colours on the ceiling.

The Duke swirled the amber liquid around the inside of his brandy balloon, studying its shimmering refractions, and took a sip. 'Well, it looks like we'll have to do it the hard way, then,' he said.

'I must say you don't seem very perturbed about it, Billy?' the Bishop frowned in surprise.

'Why should I be? It's not as if it's totally unexpected, is it?'

'Huh? I thought you were counting on Harold?'

'Oh, no, no!' Duke William chortled, with an airy wave of his fingers, dismissing the very idea of it. 'Obviously, I had hoped he'd stick to our agreement, but I never actually believed he would. Anyway, it's not important now. In fact, in the long run, it's probably better this way.'

'But he's broken his sacred oath. The man's a traitor and a heretic!'

'Odo! Odo! You're looking at things in black and white. At appearances. Reality's neither one nor the other, you know that. Under the surface it's grey, pure grey.' The Duke tapped his forehead. 'And to deal with it, you have to use the old grey matter.'

Bishop Odo threw back a mouthful of his drink and blew out his breath at its heat. 'Well, there's no doubt you're the master of that, Billy!' he coughed.

'Thank you. I've been doing it since I was a boy.' Opening the lid and lifting a thick cigar from the black walnut humidor on the table, Duke William ran it under his nose, savouring the aroma. 'I'm not interested in saving people's souls, Odo. Or in chastising them. Those are just tools, the means to an end.'

'Which is?'

'To get power. I can find a hundred uses for a heretic who has power, but I've got no time for saints.'

'Like cousin Edward, you mean?'

'There you are, a perfect example! Dear Edward was a nice enough chap, but he was absolutely useless. No power whatsoever. More of a hindrance than anything.' The Duke lit his cigar and blew out a plume of smoke. 'Anyway, even if Harold had supported my claim with their Council, I still mightn't have got what I wanted. But now he's broken his promise, he's given me the leverage I need. Not only with my bankers but with my barons as well.'

'Fitzosborne and the rest, they'd do anything for money,' the Bishop said with contempt.

'That's right. But you and I are different, brother. We don't spend our time yearning for gold, or glory, or the pleasures of the flesh. We simply serve Xzyatan.'

Bishop Odo made the sign of the swords and snake on his chest. 'I'll drink to that.'

'Because we can have all those things, automatically,' Duke William grinned, tipping the bottle and replenishing their glasses, 'when we follow His Spirit. Which is all-encompassing, indiscriminate, sheer, grey...*Power!*'

*

Under the burning midday sun, Harold pedalled laboriously across the baked brown stubble of the paddock. The band of his straw hat was wet with perspiration and his damp t-shirt itched and clung to his back, while below his rumpled shorts his exposed knees felt like seared barbecue chops. Off to his right, high up in the blackened branches of a dead tree, a solitary large crow began to caw.

Harold's wheels crunched in the dust as he braked and pulled to a stop. Waving away the flies buzzing around his bearded, sweating face, for a few moments he sat still, observing the bird with an uneasy feeling of dread. Its desolate triple cry—*craaa, craaa, craaaaa*—seemed aimed directly at him. He turned away and peered ahead into the distance, staring at the glowing white fascia of the house. He sighed and rode on.

Coming to the edge of the field, Harold opened the gate and pushed his bicycle out onto the road. He climbed back into the saddle and carried on up the long incline to the top. On reaching the house, he dismounted. Propping his bicycle against the fence, he walked up the garden path and knocked on the front door. After a short wait, there was the sound of someone inside, coming down the hall. Seconds later, it was opened by Edith. On seeing him, her face visibly tightened.

Harold gave her a sheepish smile. 'Hello, Edith.'

'What do you want, Harold?' she asked in a hard, toneless voice.

He was taken aback. 'I want to see you, of course! Darling, we have to talk. You've got to let me explain.'

'There's nothing to explain,' Edith answered. 'You've made your choice. Now all we have to do is learn to live with it.'

As she turned to go, he cried out in desperation, 'Edith, I love you!'

The door closed on his words. Harold looked around, shaking his head in amazement. In anger, he banged on the door with his fist. There was no reply. He thumped again. Moments later, he heard heavy footsteps approaching and Vera opened the door.

'Stop your noise, Harold!' she commanded. 'Edith doesn't want to see you. She's hurt and confused. You'll have to go away.'

'No! I need to speak to her! I want to see the kids.'

'They're at school. You'll have to arrange another time. I'm sorry, Harold.'

She shut the door in his face.

*

Tostig listened to the thrashing, hypnotic rhythms of Asian punk music, interspersed with raucous laughter, drunken shouts, and female squealing, coming from the wild party taking place in a long wooden hut perched below him on a rocky outcrop. Beggars can't be choosers, I suppose, he reflected sourly.

In the distance, beyond the jungle-clad island cove, the summer sun was setting in brilliant gold over the sea. Closer in, partly obscured by palm trees, two large Thai fishing boats were riding at anchor.

Seated at a small, round raffia table beside the bamboo balustrade, flanked by lush foliage and scented tropical flowers, Tostig gazed out at the view, a drink in his hand, waiting for an answer. Summoning his courage, he took a deep breath and looked round at his host.

'So, what's the problem?' he asked with a nervous laugh. 'Isn't it tempting enough for you?'

Standing at the far end of the balcony, the giant figure of Lord Hardrada, the Viking king, turned towards him. Two and a half metres tall, he easily dwarfed his Saxon visitor. Beneath the fur coat draped around his mountainous shoulders, his bulging, muscled, tattooed torso was naked to the waist, around which was wrapped a broad yellow sash. His hard, flat face, with its drooping moustache and forked beard, was adorned with large, pendulous gold rings hanging from the lobes of his jewel-studded ears.

Two necklaces—one made of boars' tusks, the other of tiny skulls carved from human bone—circled his thick neck. A long mane of iridescent, metallic blue-streaked, grey hair, strung through with beaded rats-tails, hung down at the back of his head, which was closely shaven at the sides. Floating high above the broad orange scarf tied around his forehead and knotted at the side, a rigid Mohawk crest curved back in a bristling, waxed arc like a chainsaw blade embedded in his cranium.

'Half-shares in a kingdom adrift with no rudder?' Hardrada queried, raising a scornful eyebrow. Like a thin scraping of molasses over dry rock, the tuneful cadence of his voice—with its part-Asian, part-Irish accent—had a cold, rough edge to it. 'Oh, the idea's tempting enough, to be sure.'

He gave a deep, rumbling, world-weary chuckle. 'But I've been too long in this business to get careless now.' His eyes narrowed into dangerous slits. 'I've heard all about your famous brother, Tostig. And I also know what you and he did to some of the other raiders who went after so-called easy pickings with Algar.'

Tostig spread his hands in helpless innocence. 'I had no choice, Lord Hardrada!' he blurted. 'You must know that? I had to obey King Edward.'

Hardrada let out a booming laugh. 'Don't worry, me boyo! I didn't like the competition anyway! No, only one thing concerns me now. What are the chances of winning?'

'They're excellent, mate, believe me,' Tostig smiled with relief. 'They couldn't be better!'

'You seem pretty sure about that?'

'I am. I've got friends and supporters everywhere just itching for me to come back. Enough to put together a large army. So, when you arrive with your men, if they fight on land as well as they do at sea...'

'They do,' Hardrada replied coldly.

'Of course they do,' Tostig agreed quickly. 'With our combined strength, we'll be unbeatable! Morcar and Edwin'll run like the rats they are, leaving Harold to face us alone. One battle is all it'll take. It's as simple as that. We can't lose.'

'What about your brother-in-law, the Norman?' Seeing Tostig's surprised look, Hardrada gave a mocking laugh. 'Don't worry, me boyo, I hear everything!'

Tostig stood up and began to pace the balcony. 'Oh, he wants the throne all right, no doubt about that. But he's a stickler for formality is our William. He does everything by the book. He won't make a move without permission from the top.'

'From the top? Who does a Norman duke answer to?'

'I don't know,' Tostig shrugged. 'His bankers, maybe? The Grand Pontiff? Who knows? Who cares? What's important is that that all takes time.'

Hardrada lifted a bottle of beer from the ice crate at his feet, opened it with his teeth, spat out the cap, and gulped some of it down. 'And meanwhile, your brother has to keep his army ready, on edge, with no sleep, in case William comes. In case I come! It can be very tiring looking two ways at once.' He gave a loud, exaggerated belch and brushed away the froth running down his beard. 'You never know,' he mused, 'when we land, he might even risk splitting his force?'

'All the more reason for us to strike quickly while we've got the chance,' Tostig said eagerly.

'Hm...' Hardrada grunted, savouring the proposition. 'It'd have to be timed just right. Not too soon, but before the Normans arrive.'

'Exactly!' Tostig's eyes shone with mounting excitement. 'So, what d'you say?'

Hardrada lobbed his empty bottle over the balcony and belched again. Grinning broadly, he held out a massive hand. 'That you've got yourself a deal, me boyo!'

18

The doom-laden voice of the Norman envoy echoed across the wide, parquet floor of the audience chamber, rebounding forward along the walls, compressed by the low ceiling into a hard, blunt chisel of threatened violence.

'Lord Harold, Duke William hereby offers you one last chance to renew your oath of allegiance to him or suffer the consequences!'

For a few moments, his words hung in the air, then there was silence.

Seated next to each other on carved thrones, up on a dais in front of him, Harold and Aldyth stared down at him with glacial intensity. Meanwhile, standing in a group to one side, among the gathered members of the Council, Gurth, Leofwine, Bernard, Haco, Morcar, and Edwin looked on with stern contempt. On the opposite side of the room, sitting upright and alone, a sour-faced clerk dressed in a grey suit and tie had his legs crossed and a notepad on his knee.

Resembling an undertaker in his black coat and tails, with a supercilious sneer on his pock-marked face, the thickset, pugnacious envoy continued reading from the scroll he held out in front of him.

'The Duke demands that you forthwith acknowledge his right to rule the Saxon people, that you hand back the crown, which you have stolen from him, and that you take his daughter as your bride. What is your reply?'

Harold gave a thin smile. 'You can tell the Duke,' he answered in a calm voice, 'that since that oath was made under threat of violence, both the law and my conscience release me from it. The crown belongs to the people. Only they can decide who wears it and they have chosen me. As for taking his daughter as my bride, that's impossible. I am already married. My queen sits here beside me.'

'Is that your final answer?'

'It is.'

'Then, sadly, I must inform you that Duke William, Lord of the Norman Realm and Guardian of the Free World, hereby declares war on you and all those who are with you, and that, forthwith, he will come to take possession of his land.'

'Then you can tell him from me that he'll regret that decision,' Harold retorted, amid angry exclamations from those watching. 'And that if he tries to invade us, our army will be there waiting, ready and able to stop him...Now, leave in safety.'

With a stiff bow, the envoy rolled up the scroll and turned away. Motioning for the clerk to follow him, they left the chamber.

Gurth let out a low whistle. 'Wow! That was short and sweet.'

'A nice bloke, that envoy,' Leofwine said, walking out onto the floor.

There were a few wry chuckles and then everyone started talking at once. Harold sat in silence, gripping the arms of his throne.

Aldyth put her hand on his sleeve. 'Don't let that Norman get to you, Harold. He's all mouth!' she said contemptuously.

'Somehow I doubt it, but thanks for your concern, Aldyth,' he replied, stiffening at her touch.

'Will I see you for dinner?' she asked, as they both rose to their feet.

'No, I'll be working late. I'll have something down here.'

'You're always working late,' she complained, lowering her voice. 'You never spend any time with me.'

'Can't you see I've got things to do, damn it?' Harold whispered sharply. 'I've got a country to defend! Now, back off.'

'Oh, I'll back off, all right!' Aldyth snapped. 'Right back home. And I'll take my brothers with me!'

'Look, we'll talk about all this later, Aldyth,' he said, simmering down. 'I'll be up to see you as soon as I can.'

'And will you spend the night with me?'

'For God's sake!'

'Well, will you? You hardly ever do.'

'All right!' he growled, grinding his teeth.

'When d'you think you'll be there?'

'I'll be there when I'm there! Now, will you please leave me to get on with my work?'

'Of course, my love.' Aldyth smiled brightly, her eyes sparkling with success. 'Meanwhile, I'll slip into something more enticing for you. I'll be waiting!'

With that, she stepped down from the dais and walked away towards her two ladies-in-waiting, standing at the side door. As she went past him, she gave Morcar a wink and a quick, meaningful nod.

'Come on, let's get to business.' Harold said with a smile, joining the others. 'Go on through to the other room.'

'Bit of a lovers' tiff, eh, Harold?' Morcar grinned, as they all began to file out.

Harold forced a laugh. 'Oh no, it's nothing! Nothing time won't fix, anyhow. Go on, mate, after you.'

As Morcar walked away, Gurth approached. 'Are you all right, Harold?' he asked with concern.

'Gurth! Gurth!' Harold moaned in anguish, once they were alone. 'I can't believe this is happening. I've lost them. I've lost Edith and the kids!'

'No, you haven't.'

'I have! It's like I've sold my soul to play insane games with Aldyth and the Duke.'

'The Duke's not playing any game, mate,' Gurth scowled.

'She's using me! They both are. And there's not a damn thing I can do about it. I've become a whore to power!'

'Don't worry, Harold. We'll fix the Duke and then you'll get them back.'

'I won't!' Harold cried, clinging to his arm. 'She won't let me in the door. I've slept with her, Gurth. I've slept with Aldyth.'

'So what? That's what you're supposed to do, isn't it? You're married.'

Harold pulled away. 'Oh, great! I destroy my family and you tell me what a fine job I'm doing as an adulterer.'

Gurth grabbed his shoulder. 'Stop it, Harold! You're torturing yourself. You had no choice. Edith knows that. She'll forgive you.'

Harold closed his eyes and shook his head. 'God, I hope you're right!'

'I am. Believe me, mate, it'll all sort itself out.'

Harold gave a resolute sigh. 'Come on,' he said. 'We haven't got time for this.'

Without further word, they followed after the rest.

*

'Well, I think that covers just about everything,' Harold said, from the head of the planning table. 'Tomorrow morning, I'll head for the coast to inspect the ships. As admiral of the fleet, Bernard, of course you'll come with me.'

'Right,' Bernard nodded, seated close to him.

'Gurth,' Harold said, shuffling through a stack of papers and tossing a folder over to him. 'Take Haco with you and get the southern defences ready, all right?'

'No worries, Harold.'

'Good.'

'If the reports are true, Harold,' Haco said, 'do you reckon Hardrada will back Tostig?'

'We have to assume that they are, Haco. Going by Hardrada's reputation, it'll be too good an opportunity for him to miss. He'll know we have to keep ourselves ready for the Normans, so he'll be banking on us only being at half-strength when we meet.'

'Which we may very well have to be,' said Gurth.

'Only if they both come at once, which is unlikely. With a bit of luck, we'll have time to get a full army up against the Vikings and then back down to welcome the Duke.'

'Why do you expect Tostig to arrive in the north, Harold?' asked Morcar.

'That's where most of his supporters are. It's where he'll raise his army. His side of the bargain, no doubt.' Harold smiled at Leofwine. 'So, I've got a job for you, Leo.'

'Are you sure you mean me?'

'Yes,' Harold laughed. 'I know you like travel and adventure!'

'Not if it involves hard work.'

'I want you to secure the north. Go up there and give them a warning.' He slid a bundle of envelopes across the table. 'Here are letters to the main landowners and civic leaders. Tell them that we know what Tostig's planning and that they'd better not get involved.'

'I doubt if it'll do much good, Harold,' said Gurth. 'That's real redneck country up there.'

'I know. Still, it might make one or two of them think twice before joining in. It could be dangerous, Leo, so be careful.'

'Oh, great!'

'You'd better take Stavros with you,' Gurth grinned. 'He'll protect you, mate!'

'Good idea, Gurth,' Harold agreed.

Leofwine rolled his eyes. 'There goes the holiday, then!'

'Right, that just leaves the lookouts,' Harold continued. 'Morcar, Edwin, I'll need you to take your separate forces and set up alarm posts along the north and central coasts. It's a big ask, I know. Keep your men on alert. As soon as you know where Tostig's landed, I want you to link up and head towards him. Wait for me and I'll join you as soon as I can. With any luck, I'll only be a day or two behind you.'

'Consider it done, Harold,' Morcar answered, while Edwin nodded in agreement.

'That's it, then,' Harold sighed. 'All we can do now is wait.'

*

As soon as the others had gone, Harold started drinking. After an hour or so wrestling with his desire and staving off the inevitable for as long as possible, clutching a three-quarters empty bottle of red wine in his fist, he stumbled up the wooden staircase leading to their apartment.

Just before the first landing, he tripped and lost his balance, pitching back down a few steps with a clatter and finally stopping himself by clinging to the bannister. On the floor below, a door opened. A palace guard stuck out his head and looked up. Harold grinned down at him and put a finger to his lips. 'Sshhh!' he giggled in a loud whisper. As the guard shook his head reprovingly and went back inside, he shrugged drunkenly and continued climbing the stairs.

On seeing the portrait of King Edward hanging on the wall above him, he raised the bottle in salute. 'Cheers, me old mate!'

Taking a swig, Harold lurched on up to the top landing. He stumbled across the narrow stretch of floor and entered their apartment. Traversing the dimly lit lounge, bumping into pieces of furniture on the way, he staggered over to Aldyth's door and leant back against the wall beside it. Gasping for breath, his head pounding, he screwed up his eyes in self-loathing. Then, with a final, capitulating groan, he pulled himself erect, took another long gulp of wine, and turned the handle.

Inside the softly lit bedroom, standing at the end of her four-poster bed, was Aldyth, wearing a diaphanous black negligee. 'I thought that was you, Harold,' she smiled seductively. 'Come in.'

As he stared at her, she slowly untied the thin covering and let it fall to the floor. Beneath it, her voluptuous body was encased in a shimmering violet corset, with panties, suspender belt, and stockings to match.

'Shut the door, my Lord,' Aldyth cooed in a husky voice, running her fingers up through the thick waves of her glossy black hair, letting it cascade through her fingers, and licking her lips. 'Then come and enjoy your wife.'

With a moan, Harold reeled into the room.

*

Edith pulled the door of the greenhouse shut behind her and stepped out into the crisp, clear, autumn evening. She walked her bicycle across the stretch of garden at the side of the house and onto the gravel path, then out through the front gate. She halted, watching in fascination as a flight of pure white cockatoos screeched across the deepening sky, landing and swaying, their wings outspread, in the upper branches of a majestic gum tree.

With her face catching the last rays of the setting sun, she mounted up, adjusted her woollen hat and gloves, and pushed off down the road. In the distance, rooftops were visible here and there among the russet and gold leaves, where blue spirals of smoke drifted up into the frosty air, redolent with the sweet, earthy scent of burning eucalyptus.

Entering the forest at the bottom of the slope, Edith turned off onto the grassy track to her right. After a while, in the distance, the main street of the small, neighbouring town, lined with red-brick buildings and picturesque shops, came into view. The store lights were on and pedestrians, bicycles, and wagons could be seen moving to and fro.

As she rode onward in the fading light, she lifted her eyes to the early night sky, dominated by a bright, sparkling star with a pink halo around it.

*

Illuminated by the light from the shops and the pulsating, pink glow from above, all along the wooden sidewalk townspeople were gazing up at the sky in various states of awe, fear, and excitement.

A middle-aged woman clutched onto the arm of her mother and pointed in alarm. 'Look! There it is.'

A man crouched down next to his little girl and boy and raised his arm. 'Up there.' he smiled at them. 'It's the comet!'

On the opposite side of the road, two drunks came down the steps from the pub and started across the dusty street, weaving their way erratically through the traffic.

'Wha's all the fuss?' the one in front said, staring at the gesticulating people through bleary eyes.

'I's the comet. I's back!' his friend answered, pointing upwards.

The first drunk looked up, staggering about, trying to get his balance. 'Gor. 'S a bloody monster!' he laughed and began waving his arms and cavorting about. ''S gonna eat the world!'

'Shuddup, y'great drongo!' cackled his mate.

On the far side, by the shops, two young women with big Afro hairdos, wearing tight jeans, fringed jackets, and tie-dyed, rainbow-coloured tops, climbed up the few steps to the sidewalk, laughing together as they went. Linking arms, they headed for the open door of an organic health food shop. Below them, at the foot of the steps, their companions—a pair of young hippies and an Aboriginal youth—were busy loading sacks and boxes onto their hand-pulled cart. The hippies were sharing a joint.

One of them stopped what he was doing and gazed up at the comet, his mouth hanging open. 'Wow! Far out, man!' he exclaimed. He sucked deeply on the cigarette and passed it over to his friend. 'It's like the Star of Bethlehem, man.' he gasped in a tight voice, holding in the smoke.

Accepting the joint, the other laid down the small sack he was holding and looked up. 'Life's a trip, man!' he nodded, putting it to his lips and inhaling. 'What a drag we don't all groove on it.'

'Peace on Earth to all men, man!' the first hippy said fervently, blowing out a stream of pungent vapour towards the fiery, three-tailed comet, watching it move rapidly over the town, with the Southern Cross floating in the sky above it like a starry kite.

'Nah, him's just a lump of ice, mate,' the young Aborigine interrupted them in a serious voice.

The hippies turned and stared at him. He flashed them a broad, innocent, toothy grin, and they all burst out laughing. The second hippy picked up the small sack he'd just put down and threw it at him. As the Aborigine caught it on his chest, it burst, covering him in flour. Still laughing, he threw it back at them, engulfing them both in a wholemeal cloud.

Further along the street, below the front window of a general store, were two headline boards. One, for the *Anglo-Saxon Chronicle*, asked in alarm if it was *The End of Civilization?,* while the other, for *Farmers' Weekly*, reported with comparative optimism that *Comet Stampedes Herd!*

Edith came out of the store carrying a full shopping bag. She crossed the boardwalk and stepped down to her bicycle. Standing outside his hardware shop next door, observing the comet, Mr Jenkins, now in his sixties, portly, and wearing a grey dust-coat, spotted her as she began to load up the front basket.

'G'day, there, Miss Swanneck!' he called out to her.

Edith turned to him with a smile. 'Evening, Mr Jenkins.'

He pointed at the comet. 'Quite a spectacle, don't you reckon?'

'It sure is,' she agreed, looking up.

'A whole week it's been here. Never seen anything like it. Mrs Jenkins says it means something terrible's going to happen.'

'What, like the end of the world, you mean?' she half-laughed.

'Yeah, silly isn't it? I keep telling her it's just a quirk of nature. Better not be the end, I can tell you, business is booming!'

Mounting her bicycle, Edith scanned the street. 'Well, it's certainly brought everyone out to have a look.'

'That it has,' Mr Jenkins nodded. 'Still, mustn't dawdle,' he added, seeing some customers going into his shop. 'Time's money, as they say.' He rubbed his hands together. 'Got to make hay while the sun shines.'

Edith adjusted her basket. 'Yes, I'd better get going, too.'

'You do that, Miss Swanneck. Can't keep the little ones waiting, eh?'

'Not so little any more,' she smiled.

'No, of course they're not,' Mr Jenkins laughed. 'Your boy, Edmund, came in just the other day. How he's grown! I remember when you fixed my arm for me, he was just a little tacker.' He rubbed his chin. 'What was that? Twelve? Fourteen years ago? Blimey, how time flies!'

'Yes,' she answered with a wistful sigh. 'They're growing up fast.'

'They do that all right!' he chuckled.

'Ah well. See you later.'

'Good on ya, miss. Take it easy.'

She pushed off. 'Bye!'

'Steady as she goes!'

As Edith cycled away down the street, Mr Jenkins lifted his gaze once more to the sky.

Meanwhile, standing in the shadows, observing all this, was the menacing, bearded figure of Scarf. Fingering the scar running down his cheek, he stared after her with leering malevolence, ogling her buttocks as she bent over the handlebars and pressed down on the pedals. Then, seeing Mr Jenkins turn to go back into his shop, he called out to him.

'Getting a bit chummy with the enemy aren't you, mate?'

Mr Jenkins started and spun round. 'Oh, it's you,' he said with a resentful sigh, as Scarf stepped forward out of the darkness. 'What're you going on about?'

'Her,' Scarf sneered, jerking his thumb after Edith. 'That Norman tart.'

'I already told you before, Scarf, she's one of us. She's as Saxon as you or me. And she's not a tart!'

'Yeah? Well, in my book leopards don't change their spots.'

'Then you want to stop reading fairytales don't you, mate!' With a loud tut and an angry shake of his head, Mr Jenkins went back into his shop.

As Scarf continued to stare after Edith, a gaunt, sallow-skinned preacher with a thin, dark strip of beard around his chin and his eyes shining manically behind gold-rimmed pebble glasses appeared silently at his shoulder. He was wearing a flat-brimmed, domed hat and a long, black, buttoned-up coat, with a light blue armband displaying the acronym F.U.N. Under his arm was tucked a blue folder. 'I know how you feel, friend,' he said quietly.

Scarf turned in surprise. 'What d'you mean?' he said aggressively.

The preacher gestured towards the street. 'The heathen are inside the gates and decadence abounds!'

Scarf looked round. 'Drug-crazed pacifists and foreign scum, you mean!'

'Yea, sinners all! But the hand of the Lord is mighty, friend. He has sent us a sign.'

'What're you talking about? What sign?'

'Up there!' The preacher pointed at the comet, now moving away from the town. 'A curse on the son of Godwin for making a pact with the devil.'

'Bloody Harold. Weak as piss!' Scarf scowled. 'Maybe you're right.' He stared at the man intently. 'And maybe you're mad?'

'Have faith, friend,' the preacher confided, with a sly smile. 'It's written in the scriptures. Iniquity reigneth but for a short season, and then...'

'And then what?'

'And then, friend, for all God-fearing patriots, for all true homegrown sons of the land, our moment will come!'

'Oh yeah?' Scarf sneered. 'And how's that going to happen?'

'We have a champion.'

'Who?'

'Morcar,' the preacher answered, lowering his voice.

'Morcar? Get lost!' Scarf laughed with derision. 'I was right, you are mad. His dad, Algar, was a man's man, but Morcar? He's just a pup! Another politician with a grudge, that's all, out for what he can get.'

'But that's what we need, friend. That's exactly what we need. A back to ride on to bring us to power.'

'I'll believe it when I see it.'

The preacher opened his folder and offered Scarf a pamphlet. 'Here, take one of these. It'll answer all your questions.'

Scarf accepted it and read out the heading on the cover. 'F. U. N. Fun?'

'Yes,' the preacher said, with an almost bashful smile. 'A good name, don't you think?'

'Yeah, very catchy! "The Fundamentalist Ultra Nationalist Party". Doesn't sound much like fun to me.'

'We believe in good, clean fun.' The preacher pointed at the approaching hippies. 'Not this dirt! Mark my words, friend, the land will be purified and the idolaters purged. Just wait and see.'

'No, you wait and see, mate,' Scarf snarled. 'I've got my own way of dealing with trash!'

With that, he dropped the pamphlet and jumped down from the sidewalk. As he started to walk away, the preacher called after him. 'Wait, friend! Why don't you come to one of our meetings?'

'I'll give you a call,' Scarf laughed back. He rolled his eyes, searching for a clever reply. 'When it all comes to pass!'

With a guffaw, he turned and headed off across the street, just as the two hippies and the Aborigine, all covered with flour, came past with their cart, followed by the two young women. The first hippy gave him a stoned smile and made the v-sign. 'Peace and love, man!' he grinned.

With a growl of disgust, Scarf pushed him over into the dust and strode on, his eyes blazing in anger, towards the pub.

*

Kneeling up on the back of the armchair, Edith gazed out through the window at the comet, now just a distant, flickering light slowly disappearing among the stars above the fields. Her eyes were filled with tears.

Behind her, she heard the front door shutting and the noisy tread of feet. At the sound of footsteps approaching, she turned to see Gunhilds coming towards her across the carpet. Her face lit up and she put her arm around her daughter. 'Hello, Gunhi!'

Gunhilds knelt on the arm of the chair. 'The comet scared the animals, Mummy. Where is it?'

Edith kissed her cheek and pointed through the window. 'Over there, darling,' she said, as Gunhilds put her face to the glass. 'See? It's going away.'

Meanwhile, Vera walked over to the open fireplace. Moving aside the fireguard, she picked up the poker, prodded the coals, and threw in a small log from a pile on the hearth. Hanging the poker back on the rack, she replaced the wire mesh guard and straightened up.

'Well, we had a lovely walk,' she said, with a smile.

'Boring, if you ask me!' Edmund said in a sour voice, making for the hallway door. Vera laughed.

Magnus, having stretched himself out on the couch, sat up eagerly. 'Where're y'going, Ed?'

'Why?' Edmund asked in a wary voice.

'Just wondered, that's all.'

'I'm going to listen to some music, if you must know.'

'Can I come?'

There was a pause, as Edmund relented. 'All right.'

Magnus jumped up to follow him. Vera tousled his hair as he went past and he writhed away with an embarrassed grin.

'I'm coming, too!' Gunhilds called after them.

'No, you're not!' Magnus shouted.

'Yes, I am!'

She skipped across the lounge and followed them out through the door. With a groan of relief, Vera sat down on the couch. 'How's the comet doing?'

'It's fading fast,' Edith answered.

'Gladys reckons a disaster's coming.'

'So do a lot of people,' Edith sighed. 'Anyway, what more disasters could there be in our lives?' She climbed down from the chair. 'There, it's gone!'

19

Lanfranc gazed across the chalet stateroom, drinking in the view outside. Framed by the curved expanse of its wide tinted window, snow-covered mountain peaks stretched away, ridge upon serrated ridge, into the crystal-clear distance. It felt like he was on the roof of the world!

In front of the window, facing out, was a single, empty golden throne, its high back covered with mysterious geometric designs. Over to the left, in an alcove, a white marble fountain in the shape of a naked, horned devil holding its penis and urinating splashed into a pool. Spaced around the otherwise bare walls were luminous glass globes, balanced on silver tripods, each pulsating with the rotating colours of the rainbow. In the background, an eerie, synthesised, liturgical singing—as if playing backwards or in some strange unknown language—issued from speakers set flush in the low ceiling.

Standing at the foot of the raised enclosure before him, its interior screened off by voluminous, cream net curtains, Lanfranc waited with trepidation to learn the outcome of his mission. Through the folds in the gauze, he could make out the indistinct figures of the Grand Pontiff and the Chief Banker. They were hovering before a third figure, who was seated and partially hidden from view.

As he peered at them, they made low bows of obeisance and turned to leave. Lanfranc gripped his hands together to stop them from shaking. The Grand Pontiff walked towards him carrying something in his arms and pulled aside the curtain.

Despite the unlined smoothness of his Asiatic face, Lanfranc knew that the Grand Pontiff was very old. Tall, lean, and completely bald, without any eyebrows, he was wearing a pharaonic mitre and a long-sleeved, purple robe with a high wing collar. He held up the netting to let through the younger, corpulent Chief Banker, who was also bald, and dressed in an immaculate dark suit with a grey silk cravat and a diamond pin.

As the pair stepped down onto the polished quartz floor, Lanfranc caught a glimpse of the small, wizened alien being beyond them, inside the enclosure—the one he had been told about, the one he had been taken to see, the Emissary of Xzyatan!

Wrapped in a dull khaki-green toga, the Emissary was leaning over a thick telescope that protruded up through the ceiling. As if sensing he was being watched, the Emissary lifted his head. His hairless face seemed strangely blurred, covered by what looked like a thin film of greasy plastic. For a few moments, his unblinking, ovoid black eyes stared directly into Lanfranc's, then he turned away and bent once more over the eyepiece. The curtains swung closed.

The Grand Pontiff approached Lanfranc, who fell to his knees before him, trembling with fear and excitement. With a sympathetic, understanding smile, he reached out his arms and presented Lanfranc with a large, folded cloth. He then held out his hand. On his bony finger was a diamond-studded, skull-shaped ring. Struggling to keep hold of the bulky material, Lanfranc leant forward and kissed it. The Grand Pontiff removed it and gave it to him.

At that moment, without making a sound, a blond-haired, dark-skinned servant—wearing a white, knee-length chiton—appeared, as if out of nowhere, at their side. A silver tray with an open chequebook and a gold pen lying next to it was balanced on his hand. Taking up the pen, the Chief Banker filled out a cheque, signed it, and tore it off. He walked over to the still kneeling Lanfranc and handed it to him.

The Grand Pontiff motioned for Lanfranc to rise. With a nod of approval and dismissal, he gestured towards the open double doors at the back of the stateroom. Giving deep bows of thanks, Lanfranc backed away and continued on out of the room. The doors closed in front of him, leaving him alone in a small anteroom.

Clutching the folded cloth, the ring, and the cheque to his chest, he spun round, a look of stunned amazement on his face.

*

Standing on a clifftop, on the tropical north coast, one of Morcar's lookouts wiped his watering, red-rimmed eyes. Gripping his spear more tightly, he tugged down the rim of his tin helmet and stared out to sea. With his cloak billowing up behind him in the blustery, winter wind, he scanned the empty, grey horizon.

*

In the chilly, salt-laden air of the central coast, two sentries stood together on a grassy track high above the sloping sand dunes. Below them, the wind-blown surf was pounding onto the beach. As they peered out beyond the crashing waves, a third guard rode up to them on a bicycle. Handing each of them a lunch box, he raised his eyebrows, questioning whether they had spotted anything. With glum looks, they shook their heads.

*

With their spears resting over their shoulders, three guards ambled slowly along a sandy, southern beach. Calling out to each other and laughing in the bright, spring morning air, they lazily skimmed pebbles into the breakers as they went. One of them halted. Shielding his eyes from the sun, he once again checked the sea for ships. Still nothing!

*

Seated at the far end of the vast, highly polished First Empire table taking up most of the floorspace in their austere, oak-beamed dining room, Matilda patted her thick, dark tresses, braided and coiled like earmuffs on the sides of her head, and delicately slid off her silver napkin ring. Tucking the starched white cloth into the neck of her long-sleeved, velvet gown, she looked down the table at her children.

On one side, the eldest, sickly eleven-year-old Robert, sat next to her confident darling, Adeliza, now nine. On the other side, their strange boy, redheaded Rufus, seven, sat fidgeting beside little Harry, aged five. She observed with satisfaction that they had all unrolled their napkins and were following her example.

At the opposite end of the table, Duke William lifted the lid of a silver tureen and exclaimed with delight, 'Ah, lamb's hearts. Lovely!' He ladled some of the thick, lumpy sauce onto his plate and forked in a mouthful, chewing the bits like rubber, moving them about and chomping on them with his strong jaws. He licked his lips and dabbed at them with his napkin.

'Mm. Eat up, Robert!' he called down the table.

'I...I'm afraid it's off, sir,' Robert moaned in reply, his teaspoon hovering apprehensively over his boiled egg.

'Off?' the Duke blasted. 'What poppycock! That's good food you're wasting. Eat it!'

Robert hesitantly spooned in a mouthful and forced himself to swallow. 'Ugh! Mummy, do I have to? It's horrid!'

'Don't be angry with him, William, he's only a boy,' Matilda said soothingly.

'No, he's not. He's a young man and it's high time he started behaving like one! Look at his sister and brothers, they're eating theirs.'

Adeliza smiled at him. 'It's delicious, Daddy!'

Meanwhile, Rufus, grinning mischievously at Robert, put his face down close to his egg, and began tapping manically on its shell with the back of his spoon.

'Of course it is,' Duke William nodded. 'You're too sentimental about the children, Matilda. They have to toughen up. It'll be a good job when Robert goes back to boarding school. I'll speak to his headmaster. Maybe a sound thrashing or two'll teach him the value of hard-earned money. I detest waste! It's an insult to the brain.'

Robert began to cry. 'But it's gone rotten, sir!'

'Stop snivelling, boy!' ordered the Duke, but Robert continued to weep. 'Oh, bloody hell!' He pressed a button on the intercom next to him. 'Nanny? Get in here, will you!'

Moments later, the door opened and Nanny, a crabby-looking woman with grey hair pulled back in a tight bun, shuffled in.

'Nanny, take Robert to his room,' Duke William commanded. 'He's not to go out today.'

She bowed her head. 'Yes, Master.' Taking Robert firmly by the hand, she led the dejected boy away.

'May I leave the table, too, please, Mummy?' Adeliza asked in a sugar-sweet voice.

'Yes, run along, darling,' Matilda smiled at her. 'And take Rufus and little Harry along with you, there's a good girl.'

Adeliza and the two boys looked at their father, who waved his consent, and they all skipped from the room.

The Duke let out an irritable sigh. 'Children!'

'You shouldn't be so hard on him, William,' Matilda chided him.

'I know,' he answered, picking some meat from between his teeth. 'But I've got a lot on my plate right now. Anyway, *I* suffered plenty of beatings when I was at school and it never did *me* any harm!' The buzzer on the intercom sounded. He wiped his mouth with his napkin and stabbed at a button. 'Well? What is it?'

'Mr Lanfranc is here to see you, Sir,' came a female voice. 'He says that it's urgent.'

'Excellent! Send him straight in.'

A moment later, the door opened, and Lanfranc entered carrying a briefcase. Duke William jumped to his feet. 'Lanfranc! Welcome! Come and have some breakfast.'

Lanfranc approached with a smile. He bowed to them both. 'My Lord. Lady Matilda. Just a cup of tea would be very nice, thank you.'

The Duke poured a cup from a silver teapot and held it out to him. 'Well, how did it go? What was it like up there?'

Lanfranc laid his briefcase on the table. 'It was incredible, my Lord!' he answered, accepting the fine bone china cup and saucer with a nod. '*Merci*. It was amazing. The sheer feeling of power in the place!'

'And did you see the Emissary?'

'*Oui*, my Lord. Just a quick look through some curtains. He was stupendous!'

'Wonderful! You can tell me all about it later. Now, what have you got there?'

Lanfranc set down his teacup and clicked open the briefcase. 'Here, my Lord, are the symbols of authority you have been waiting for. Your credentials as Xzyatan's holy champion!' He pulled out the folded flag and the ring and passed them over, one by one. 'The Banner of Power...The Sacred Ring...And lastly,' he smiled, holding out the cheque, 'The Immaculate Investment!'

The Duke took it from him and stared at the amount written on it. His face lit up in ecstasy. 'Oh yes! Oh yes!' he laughed. 'Oh, this is absolutely superb. Jolly well done, Lanfranc! Jolly well done. Now we can *really* get started!'

*

Iko and Sushi were sitting together on a wooden bench, between rose bush flowerbeds near the wall of an inner courtyard in the palace complex. He turned towards her and took her slender hands in his.

'Sushi, listen...'

'You said you would take me home, Iko,' Sushi protested tearfully, staring down at her lap.

'I will, my love! I will! And with the money from this I can buy you a big house by the sea, with gardens and servants. You would like that, wouldn't you?'

'I don't want a big house. I want to go back to our village, with you.'

'I know you do, and we will. I promise you! Only wait for me, Sushi, until I come back.'

'I love you so much, Iko.' She fought down a sob. 'You could be killed!'

'Not me! Iko laughed. 'I've got you to live for!' He smiled at her and brushed a tear from her cheek. 'I love you, too, Sushi, but I must do this.' He squeezed her hands and grinned with excitement. 'Just think of the honour and comfort it will bring to our new life.'

*

In drizzling rain, an endless stream of wagons, riders, and men on foot poured through the muddy gateway of the camp. Near the entrance, beside a sodden Norman flag hanging limply on a pole, a line of volunteers queued in front of a table, where a soldier sat beneath a canopy, writing down their names.

Behind him stood a bull-chested sergeant major with a bristling moustache, calling out in a powerful voice: 'Roll up! Roll up! Step forward and sign yer name. Riches and land for all those who'll join Duke William!'

Interspersed among the tents lining the main thoroughfare of the camp were various booths and stalls. A hairdresser's shop had signs up saying, *Get yer 'air cut! Short back and sides!,* while a tailor's booth offered *Smart Suits for the Superior Man.*

Nearby, decorated with flashing fairy lights, a stall run by Charles, the factory owner, sold neckties, bow ties, and cravats. As two soldiers approached and began to inspect his wares—watched from behind the counter by Walter, his assistant, a thin, pasty-faced lad in his late teens—Charles stepped out to greet them.

'Right this way, gentlemen!' he beamed, holding out an array of colourful ties draped over his arm. 'Ties for all occasions. No well-dressed Norman should be seen without one. Oh, excuse me for a moment, would you?' he said suddenly. 'Walter, look after these gentlemen's needs, if you please.'

With that, he laid down the ties and hurried out of the booth. Across the street, Iko was trudging along the muddy lane in his high boots and mailed coat, beneath an umbrella.

'Iko, old boy! Hello!' Charles called out with delight.

Iko smiled in surprise and walked over to him. 'Hello! Charles!' They shook hands. 'So, you came after all?'

'Of course I did, old boy! Wouldn't miss it for the world. But come on in out of this rain.'

Iko pointed at the stall. 'And you have brought your ties with you, I see.'

'Absolutely!' Charles laughed. 'Essential items for the war effort, don't y'know. Can't have our chaps going over there stark naked, can we, what?'

As the two soldiers wandered off, they moved in under the shelter of the awning.

'No, I suppose not,' Iko replied, shaking the water from his umbrella. 'The Duke would be proud of your contribution, Charles.'

'Do I detect a trace of cynicism there, old boy?'

'I do not know,' Iko sighed, fingering the ties. 'Does it not seem a bit ludicrous to you, all this formality?'

'Of course it does, old man,' Charles chortled. 'But how else can you tell the classes apart? A well-knotted tie's the sign of good breeding, and that's what counts. There's nothing closer to perfection than a well-groomed Norman!'

Iko ran his fingertips along one of the racks. 'Yet, anyone can buy that perfection?'

'No, dear boy, anyone can buy a tie. True quality costs more than money. Still, dress a commoner like a gentleman and there's half a chance he'll start acting like one,' Charles laughed, realigning the ties. 'Though he'll never actually be one, of course!'

'Then what you offer is nothing but an illusion?'

'What else do you expect?' Charles frowned with amusement. 'One can't buy class, old boy, one's either born with it or one isn't. All I do is provide the appearance of respectability for those who've got it and for those who haven't. Trouble is, these days people tend to mistake appearance for the real thing.' He gave a shrug. 'Either way, though, thank Xzyatan, I sell lots of lovely ties!'

'I did not know you were such a devoted follower of Bishop Odo, Charles,' Iko smiled.

'Sssh, Iko!' Charles looked around quickly. 'Ears and tongues have their price too, y'know...You really are in a strange mood, aren't you?'

'I am sorry,' Iko sighed again. 'It must be the weather.'

'Listen, my friend, Odo's only the Duke's half-brother, don't forget. He and his chums may be the new world order for us all, but in my book they'll never be true Normans.'

'Why do you say that?'

At that moment, two of Bishop Odo's personal armed guards—wearing red bibs and black collars under their dark raincoats, with snake-swords badges stitched on their lapels—passed by, deep in conversation, their thumbs tucked into their sword belts. Both had blonde crew cuts and were chewing gum. Charles and Iko watched them go past.

'Blighters are too damned presumptuous, if you ask me,' Charles scowled. 'Too greedy by half! I mean, it's all very well exploiting the lower classes, after all that's how the whole thing works, but they want to lord it over everyone. Absolutely no sense of propriety whatsoever. All prizes and no pedigree, that's their trouble. Too busy blowing smoke up their own arses! They may act like they're superior, but they'll never be the genuine article. Still,' he laughed cheerfully, 'who are we mere mortals to stand in the way of progress, eh?'

He slapped Iko on the back. 'Come on, old boy, let's you and me go out the back and get ourselves a stiff drink, what? Toast this great adventure of ours...before you get us both into trouble!"

With that, Charles led Iko away behind the counter and, lifting up the flap, entered the back of the booth.

As they disappeared from view, two new recruits came squelching past the front of the stall, heads down against a sudden downpour. Leaning close to each other, they raised their voices above the noise of the slashing rain.

'Just imagine, us, lords of the manor!' one of them laughed with excitement.

'That's what he said we'd be, all right,' the other nodded gleefully. 'Land for the taking!'

'I wouldn't want much...only a few hundred acres!'

'And don't forget the slaves. Think of it, no more work!'

'Servants, you mean?'

'Same thing. Just waiting to be ordered about by us!'

'And slave girls. To do whatever we want with!'

'Yeah!' They both sniggered, making piston motions with their fists. 'Woo-hoo!'

Giggling like overgrown schoolboys, they hurried on together through the mud and rain towards the end of the thoroughfare, where the camp opened out into a clear space being used as a parade ground for the newly enlisted men.

Meanwhile, off to one side, among the surrounding tents, Duke William, Baron Fitzosborne, Taillefer, and the army's two highest-ranking Generals were sheltering under the awning of the Duke's pavilion, sipping champagne and warming themselves around the glowing coals of a brazier.

'A toast, gentlemen,' Duke William grinned, his white teeth flashing with self-assurance as he turned to his companions and raised his glass. 'To the late Harold!'

'To the late Harold!' they all guffawed and threw back their drinks.

Baron Fitzosborne lifted the bottle from a nearby ice bucket, inspected the label, and gave an impressed nod. 'Only a winner could do zis, my Lord,' he said, gesturing around the camp, as he refilled their glasses. 'To promise ze possessions of his enemy in advance.'

'Absolutely!' the Duke laughed. 'One has to plan ahead in this game, Fitz. Behave like a winner and you're halfway home already.'

Taillefer pointed at the squads of drenched soldiers doing marching drill out in the rain. 'Look at those fellows. Every one of them is just itching to get over there and grab his slice of the pie.'

'You've said it, Tai!' Duke William exclaimed. 'Because it's not Harold's pie any longer. It's ours.'

'Well, let's hope none of them realise, my Lord,' chuckled one of the Generals, as a thrill of confidence ran through them all, 'that when one adds up all those slices of pie being handed out, it comes to an area about twice the size of Africa!'

'A mere detail, General,' the Duke nodded. 'Anyway, half of 'em'll be bird food within a week of landing.'

'Oh, I say, sir, that's a bit steep isn't it?' protested the second General.

'Cruel, but fair, General. Cruel, but fair. And the rest'll get what they're bloody well given! But, by then, they'll have done the job for us, and that's what matters.' Duke William's eyes sparkled with jocular menace as he looked round at them all. 'As my old pater used to say, gentlemen, the more you speculate the more you accumulate.'

*

From a heavy, charcoal grey sky the rain came down in torrents. On the shingle beach below, like stallions straining at the starting gate, a line of black dragon-headed prows stretched away into the murky distance along the foreshore.

Standing out in the open, relieving himself, a drenched Norman sentry looked up at the unbroken clouds and shook his head. He spat down onto the pebbles in disgust and readjusted his leggings. Then, casting a last, sour glance at the misty, ironbark sea, he turned and trudged back up the beach to his fellows, huddled around a small fire under the stern of one of the ships.

*

On the other side of the ocean, three Saxon guards squatted under a stunted tree on a cliff top, peering out through the unremitting downpour at the turbulent waves below. However much they tried to cover themselves, every now and then cold trickles of water still managed to run down their helmets and inside the collars of their capes.

'Damn this rain!' one of them snarled, trying to protect his neck.

'Brrr. I'm freezing!' another shivered. 'There's no way he's coming in this bloody weather!'

'Well, I wish he'd damn well get it over and done with if he is!' growled the third. 'I can't take much more of it.'

'Five months and not a sniff,' agreed the first. 'I don't mind a good fight, it's the bloody waiting that's killing me!'

'I'm packing it in, mate,' the third guard announced with finality. 'I'll give it another day and then I'm off home.'

At that moment, a corporal came running down the track towards them. 'Right, you lot!' he called out as he approached. 'On yer feet. We're moving out. Tostig's attacking the north.'

'Oh yeah? We've heard that one before,' the third guard replied with scorn, not budging. 'And by the time we get there, he'll have bloody disappeared again!'

'If he was ever there in the first place,' added the second.

'Just another frigging false alarm,' the first guard finished with a dismissive nod.

'Shows how much you lot know,' the corporal answered with good-natured derision. 'He hasn't come alone this time. He's got Hardrada's Vikings with 'im. And they've already beaten Morcar!'

20

Set in the middle of the triumphant invaders, now combined into a single Viking force under Hardrada's command, a ghetto blaster was blaring out raucous, incoherent heavy-metal punk music to the troops stretched out on the ground around it.

Down the length of the low, sun-scorched, oblong mound, with their horned helmets, round wooden shields, and a lethal armoury of axes, hammers, swords, and spears laid aside, the assorted rednecks, bikies, skinheads, and pirates were frolicking on the bare earth, sprawling over each other—a boisterous mass of hairy, tattooed, muscle-bound bodies garbed in black leather, sheep-skin, and denim sleeveless jackets, ripped oily jeans, bovver boots, iron swastikas, studs, and chains.

To the envious jibes of their fellows, a lucky few rolled in the arms of their raunchily clad warrior girlfriends, while the rest played cards, dice, wrestled with each other, or simply lazed around smoking and drinking. Among them, one huge, flush-faced Viking, a hulk of a man with an enormous beer gut, went down on one knee to show off his bulging biceps to his drugged and adoring girlfriend. Nearby, an older woman with straggly, grey hair and missing front teeth staggered drunkenly to her feet and began to dance a striptease, to lascivious cheers and whistles of encouragement.

Meanwhile, Scalds—acid priests, with long matted hair and black wizard robes—threaded their way among the troops, chanting deliriously to themselves as they handed out amphetamine pills and magic mushrooms.

At the far end of the mound was a small wooden bridge spanning a shallow stream, which zig-zagged away across the parched crust of the surrounding plain.

In a clear space, in the centre of the summit, stood the Viking standard—a ferocious sea dragon surrounded by runic symbols and pictures of horned gods cavorting with naked women, with its name, *The World Ravager*, written across it in silver lettering.

Reclining on the ground beneath it were Tostig and Hardrada, sharing a bottle of rum. They were both wearing chain mail and war paint, with their helmets lying on the ground beside them.

'It's good to see me boys enjoying themselves,' Hardrada grinned, passing over the bottle. 'They deserve a day off.'

'Yeah, it's been a great start.' Tostig took a swig. 'What d'you reckon, Hardo? Go and finish off Morcar tomorrow and then head south, eh?'

'Sounds good to me, boyo!' Hardrada chuckled and stretched out on his back in the sunshine.

'Wait on! Who's this?' Tostig said, staring into the distance at a sudden cloud of dust on top of a high ridge bordering the plain.

Hardrada sat up. 'It can't be Harold. He won't be here for a couple of days.'

'It must be deserters from Morcar.' Tostig shielded his eyes. 'I dunno, though...It looks like...'

'Shit!' Hardrada snarled.

'How the hell...?'

The Viking king leaped to his feet. 'Get up! Get up!' he roared to his men. 'The Saxons are here!'

*

On the crest of the nearby hill, riding ahead of the main force, were Harold and Gurth, followed by Leofwine, Bernard, Haco, and Stavros. Wearing helmets and mailed jerkins, and all fully armed with swords, spears, and axes, they drew to a halt at the edge of the rise and stared down at the plain.

'We've caught them napping!' Bernard exclaimed.

'We've got 'em if we strike now, mate,' Stavros growled beside him.

'Harold, we can't!' Gurth protested quietly.

'I know, Gurth,' Harold sighed. 'If only he wasn't with them, I'd...' He swivelled round in the saddle. 'Who's got the white flag?'

'Here!' answered Haco.

'Give it to Leo.'

Haco quickly opened his saddlebag, pulled out a folded white cloth, and threw it to Leofwine, who tied it to his spear.

Harold started forward. 'Gurth, Leo, with me!'

Holding the white flag up high, the three brothers freewheeled swiftly down the slope and pedalled across the open space towards the Viking army, now forming into lines along the length of the mound. They came to a stop in front of them.

'Is Tostig, son of Godwin, here?' Harold called out.

A few moments later, Tostig came out from the ranks and walked over to them. He lifted up the faceguard of his black helmet. 'I'm here, Harold. What d'you want?'

'Tostig, this is madness! Don't make us fight this battle, please.'

Tostig gave a quick look around to make sure he wasn't being overheard. 'D'you think I want to, for crying out loud!' he exclaimed. 'I love you guys!'

'We love you, too, mate!' said Leofwine.

'Then why do it?' Harold implored him.

'I want to come home, Harold!' Tostig replied, almost in tears. 'But I have to have something, don't you understand? You've already given my earldom to Edwin.'

'Look, if they'll take you back, you can have the North again,' Harold answered. 'Edwin can have my earldom.'

'I dunno...'

'If not, I'll give you Gurth's and he can have mine.'

'For God's sake, Tostig, take it, gladly!' Gurth pleaded.

Tostig began to waver. 'That'd be all right, I suppose...' He stopped and went rigid, suddenly aware of Hardrada approaching behind him. 'And if I accept, what will my friend Lord Hardrada get?'

'Him?' Harold growled. 'Seeing he's so tall, he can have three metres of land...for a grave!'

'Then, go back!' Tostig barked, raising his voice as Hardrada came within earshot. 'Never let it be said I deserted a mate. Win or lose, we stand together.' He snapped down his faceplate. 'Now, goodbye!'

'Tostig...' Harold began to argue but gave up in despair. 'Goodbye!' With that, he wheeled round and rode away, followed by Gurth and Leofwine.

'Who were those fellas, Tostig?' Hardrada frowned, watching them go.

'My brothers,' Tostig murmured, staring after them.

Hardrada let out a whistle. 'By the god of destruction, me boyo, if I'd known that they'd have never left here alive!'

Tostig turned towards him, with a fierce grin. 'That's why I didn't tell you, mate. We wouldn't want to spoil a good fight, would we?'

A flash of anger crossed Hardrada's face. Then, with a booming laugh, he clapped Tostig on the back. 'Fine sentiments, me boyo! But a good chance missed, nevertheless.'

*

Amid clouds of dust, shuffling feet, and shouted commands, the Saxon troops prepared for battle. With mounting tension, alignments were changed and reference points set as a giant, triangular wedge of armed foot soldiers began to take shape. Harold and Bernard moved around them, directing proceedings.

On either flank, cavalry on bicycles wheeled about, grouping themselves into two squadrons, one led by Gurth and the other by Leofwine. At the same time, behind the wedge, Stavros and Haco arranged spearmen and archers into three lines.

Eventually, everyone was in position. The hubbub died down and the dust settled. With a final look about him, Harold entered the ranks and took his place in the centre of the formation. Raising his arm, he gave a nod to the young bugler beside him, and the signal was blown to advance. With a great judder, like a trireme pulling away from a dock, the wedge lurched forward.

*

Out on the plain, in front of the Viking army, Tostig and Hardrada stood together, watching the Saxon army approach. They gripped hands and, eye to eye, gave each other a solemn nod. Then, while Tostig returned to his position up on the mound, Hardrada walked away along the front of the lines.

There was a great shout of delight as he borrowed a shield from one of his men and began to thump on it, beating out a rhythm with the hilt of his sword. The Vikings soon took up the beat, banging on their shields with their weapons.

Then, to a roaring cheer, Hardrada broke into a rousing punk song, singing loudly in a sneering, gutsy voice. His men already knew the words, yelling back each chorus in demented, raucous unison.

I hate Saxons 'cos they think they're special
So, to prove 'em wrong I've come sailing in me vessel
I usually come on holidays
This time I've come to settle
And they're going to get a bloody nose!

With their whingeing accents
They like to say I'm nothing
Well it's got me gander up
I'm here to do some stuffing!
So, tell me boys where are you going?

We're going where Hardrada goes!
Hey! Hey! Hey!

I like force more than acquiescence
Every day's like Christmas if you steal the presents
A bit of blood and screaming
Makes it much more pleasant
And to frighten girls gives me a buzz!

The beaches here are jam-packed
With fruit just ripe for plunder
On them I'll whet me appetite
Then tear this land asunder!
So, tell me boys what are you doing?

We're doing what Hardrada does!
Hey! Hey! Hey!

There's so much gold here waiting for the taking
Businessmen and bankers fat with profits they've been making

Towns to sack and mobile homes
No need to even break in
Oh, it's great to be a Viking king!

Returning the shield to its owner, Hardrada re-entered the Viking lines and made his way up to the top of the mound, singing as he went.

And once I've quenched my bloodlust
The stores get my attention
All the things you'd ever want
Riches beyond mention!
So, tell me boys what are you winning?

We're winning what Hardrada wins!
Hey! Hey! Hey!

Hardrada's voice rang out from the summit.

And tell me boys how are you going to win?

By now, the Saxon wedge had advanced right up to the mound. Harold moved quickly through from the centre to the front. Meanwhile, the Vikings' answering chant rose to a crescendo.

With rape, pillage, slaughter, terror, fire, blood, destruction
Death, death, death, death, death, death, death!

With the last screaming cry of *Death!* on their lips, the invaders broke ranks and poured down the slope. At the same time, with its massive momentum, the wedge ploughed into them, cutting a deep swathe through their lines, while the squadrons of cavalry swept in on either side.

The undisciplined Vikings, with their haphazard, instinctive way of fighting, were no match for the well-practiced, methodical sword strokes and spear thrusts of the unified Saxon troops—cut, parry, jab, move on...cut, parry, jab, move on—and from the outset were forced to give ground.

As the conflict raged below him, standing on the summit, surrounded by his bodyguards, Hardrada, wearing a spread-winged helmet and leaning on his huge, double-handed sword, watched the progress of the battle from beneath *The World Ravager*. Around him, the Scalds leaped about among the troops, their dreadlocks flying, urging on the Vikings with a constant, frenzied chanting that came and went above the tumult.

Soon, spotting Harold through the mêlée, working his way up the slope in his direction, Hardrada strode down and carved a path towards him, leaving a bloody trail of destruction in his wake. On finally reaching him, he sprang forward with a ferocious roar, bringing his sword down over his head in a great sweeping arc, slicing Harold's shield in two and driving him to his knees.

As the momentum of his swing left the Viking king off-balance, Harold, half-rose and dealt him a backhand blow to the helmet with his long-bladed axe. Dazed and reeling, Hardrada staggered back into the arms of the Scalds, as his bodyguards rushed to come between them, blocking him from view.

While the two armies fought on, Hardrada was dragged back to the summit and administered to by the priests. They removed his helmet and sponged his face with water, incanting over him. After a few moments, spluttering with angry indignation, he pushed them off and struggled to his feet. With his Mohawk crest and his long rats' tails blowing in the wind, he stood like an enraged bear, staring around in fury, searching for Harold.

At last, picking him out near the front of the battle, he grabbed his great sword again and rushed down the slope towards him, unceremoniously dispatching a couple of Saxons who dared to get in his way, the first with a sweep of his studded forearm plate, the second with a sword pommel in the teeth. Ahead of him, Harold was exposed, half-turned away, busy trading blows with a slow-witted, overweight redneck. With a bellowing roar, Hardrada leapt down at him, raising his sword to strike.

As the Viking king's giant shadow fell across him, Harold finished off his opponent and spun round in alarm. In an instant, his initial look of fright was transformed into one of amazement.

With his battle cry metamorphosing into a strangled, gurgling scream, Hardrada stood frozen at the top of his double-handed swing, the flights of an arrow protruding from the side of his neck below one ear and its gory point emerging below the other. His eyes rolled back in their sockets and blood began to pour from his mouth.

For a long moment he remained there, his mountainous body hanging motionless, balanced on his toes. Then, dropping his sword behind him, he crashed forward onto the ground at Harold's feet. An audible groan of dismay came from the Vikings around them.

'Hardrada's down! On to the standard!' Harold shouted. 'The day is ours!'

Giving a huge cheer, the Saxons pushed on up the slope with renewed vigour, forcing the Vikings to give ground, slowly pressing them back towards the top.

At the front of the fighting, Tostig, wearing his distinctive black armour and wielding a short, double-headed axe, his faceplate and small round shield streaked with blood, chopped his way madly through the throng. Suddenly, he came face to face with Harold. Harold instinctively raised his axe to strike, but on realising who it was, stopped his blade and threw up his arms.

'Hold!' he shouted.

Nearby, Leofwine immediately repeated the command, and others quickly took up the cry. Almost at once, the fighting around them ceased. Harold and Tostig exchanged a lingering look. Harold shook his head and lowered his weapon. Without a word, he turned and strode away down the slope. Leofwine watched him go.

Tostig lifted off his helmet and wiped his brow. 'Phew! Let's take a breather, eh, Leo?'

Panting hard, Leofwine nodded and gave an ironic laugh. 'You bastard, Tostig!' He raised his arms and shouted loudly, 'Break off!'

Tostig swung round and yelled out to his men. 'Pull back!'

With that, the armies disengaged and separated. Taking their wounded with them, the Viking remnant amassed along the summit, while the Saxons stood poised for the final assault.

By now it was late afternoon. At the foot of the slope, Harold came down through the rear ranks and stepped out onto the plain. He took off his helmet. He was trembling. Immediately, four attendants rushed up carrying a director's chair, a fold-up table, a fringed beach umbrella, a towel, and a tray with a jug and metal tumblers on it. They set it all up, poured some water for him, then bowed and retired. Harold sat down heavily in the shade of the umbrella and gulped down a drink.

Moments later, Gurth approached, panting hard. He leant on the table, filled a tumbler and drained it. He refilled the cup and tipped it over his head. 'Aah!... You all right, Harold?'

Harold nodded, wiping his face with the towel. 'Go to him, Gurth. For God's sake, make him give up!' he pleaded.

'I'll try. I'm not sure he'll listen, though.'

'He has to! Hardrada's dead. There's no reason to go on. We can't kill our own brother.'

With a grim nod, Gurth turned and walked back towards the mound. Harold stared after him. Then he hung his head and closed his eyes, thinking about Tostig, remembering better times, golden moments of affection when it felt like their lives were in tune.

With excited yells and writhing tackles, the brothers had all been playing soccer in the backyard, when Leofwine suddenly took a fall. Tostig ran over to him and anxiously helped him to his feet. Leofwine grinned at him, unhurt. Tostig laughed with relief and ruffled his hair, giving him a playful shove.

Then, one Christmas night when they had stayed up late, drinking and reminiscing with their father. There were cards on the lounge mantelpiece and decorations around the walls. Dressed in glittering tinsel and gleaming baubles, the tree was aglow with coloured lights. Sitting next to each other on the couch, Tostig had leant over and whispered something witty in his ear, at which they both started laughing. Tostig's happy face was filled with unguarded warmth.

The whole family were gathered together around the dinner table to celebrate Tostig's thirtieth birthday. Towards the end of the meal, Tostig rose to his feet and told a joke. At the punch line, they all burst out laughing, especially Githa. For a long moment, Tostig had gazed at his mother with a child's unconditional love.

But it was small measure for a lifetime as brothers.

All of a sudden, the laughter changed, becoming angry and cold. There were scornful shouts and piercing whistles.

Harold opened his eyes. Gurth was coming towards him. In the distance, up on the summit, the remaining Vikings were calling out taunting obscenities, shaking their weapons in the air, whistling, hooting, and yelling.

Harold rose to his feet and went to meet him. 'Well?'

Gurth shook his head in desperate frustration. 'He wouldn't have a bar of it! He wouldn't even hear me out. He's like a mad dog. He's crazy!' Harold moved to go past him. 'What're you going to do, Harold?'

Harold heaved a sigh of resignation. Without looking at his brother, and with his face hard as stone, he strode on towards the mound. 'What you do with any mad dog,' he replied over his shoulder. He raised his arm and shouted, 'Ch-a-arge!'

*

With a roar of imminent triumph, the Saxons surged up the slope for the kill. Panic quickly spread among the fragmented Vikings. As their last line of resistance was smashed and broken, the remaining Scalds and warriors scrambled backwards onto the summit, where they gathered beneath *The World Ravager*.

Along the length of the mound, isolated pockets of defiance were soon overwhelmed and extinguished. Among them, Tostig, bloody and dripping with sweat, fought in frenzied desperation for his life against a knot of Saxons. Having downed three of them with his axe, as he spun round to the next, a spear was rammed under his breastplate, tearing into his stomach.

With a scream of bitter rage, still railing against his fate, his legs buckled beneath him. He sank to his knees in the dust and slumped over, soon forgotten among the trampling feet.

At the far end of the hill, a solitary, defiant bikie stood in the middle of the wooden bridge behind a wall of corpses, swinging his long-handled axe and thwarting every attempt by the Saxons to dislodge him from his position. Snarling and jeering, he slashed out at anyone who dared to come close, at the same time blocking any arrows fired at him with his shield.

Meanwhile, hidden in the shadows under the bridge, Haco picked his way along the rocky edge of the stream, peering up through the gaps in the wooden planks to get his bearings. Moving across until he was directly below the man, he inserted the point of his spear into the space between the boards, took aim, and then thrust upwards, hard, stabbing him between the legs.

The Viking's face convulsed as the shock hit his brain, a split-second before the pain. Squealing in agony, he flung down his weapon and staggered back along the bridge, leaking a trail of blood and clutching at his groin, before collapsing to the boards, curled up in a moaning ball.

With a final push, the summit was taken. In silhouette against the reddening sky, the Vikings were wiped out, *The World Ravager* fell, and the cheering Saxons threw up their arms in victory.

*

Through deepening hues of lilac and blue, the evening settled into night. Threading their way among the tangled bodies on top of the mound, Harold, Gurth, Leofwine, and Bernard surveyed the carnage, their faces numb with shock. Around them, in the fading light, Saxon medical teams searched with lanterns for their surviving comrades and carried the wounded away on stretchers.

Now and then, amid the moans and groans and shouts for assistance, strangled, gurgling cries rang out, suddenly cut off sharply into silence as, with no time to take prisoners, soldiers moved among the fallen, putting any still living Vikings out of their misery with the blades of their knives.

Bernard stared at the dreadful scene and shook his head. 'Suddenly, I feel very old,' he murmured.

Leofwine wrapped his arms around himself and shivered.

Just then, Haco approached out of the rising mist. 'Harold,' he called gently. 'I'm sorry. They've found Tostig's body.'

*

In a corner of the town banquet hall, barely audible above the noise of the feast, a group of minstrels were playing a light-hearted jig. The air was filled with raucous laughter and loud, jovial shouts as the Saxon officers, seated at trestle tables forming three sides of an open rectangle, all talked at once.

Dishes were being served and plates cleared away by attendants, while jugs of beer and wine were carried about the room. The warm glow from numerous oil lamps around the walls lit up the celebration.

In the middle of the top table, Harold sat slumped in a high-backed chair, staring into space. Gurth was seated beside him. Less able to show his emotions but understanding his brother's distracted mood and sharing his sorrow, he looked at him and sighed.

'Come on, Harold,' he urged in a quiet voice, leaning towards him. 'Put it on the back burner, mate. The men need you to celebrate with them.'

'I can't, Gurth!' Harold moaned.

'I know. But at least try and put a face on it. They all know how we feel.'

Gurth gestured around the room. In the centre of the floor, a burly, ruddy-faced veteran was juggling half a dozen oranges, tossing them high up in the air, at the same time balancing a burning candle on his forehead. As he strained to the side to catch a wayward piece of fruit, wobbling on one leg, the man lost his footing.

Flailing his arms towards it, he toppled over and crumpled in an ungainly heap, to uproarious laughter and applause, brought to even higher delight by the final orange bouncing on his head.

'This is like their gift to us, Harold,' Gurth continued. 'To cheer us up. And it should be ours to them, too. They were part of it, don't forget. They need to know that you forgive them.'

'Forgive them? For what? I was the one who gave the order.'

'All I'm saying is they love you, mate. Don't knock 'em back.'

Harold sighed and gave a small laugh. 'You're right, Gurth,' he nodded. Pushing himself up in his seat, he called across the room with a smile. 'Come on, Stavros. Give us a toast!'

'No worries, mate, my Lord,' Stavros answered tipsily. To cheers and ribald shouts, he took a quick gulp of beer and climbed to his feet. The minstrels stopped playing.

'Mates,' Stavros began, amid continuing laughter. 'Fellow heroes!'

There was more cheering. Then, nodding and smiling, some in self-congratulation, others in self-deprecation, the listeners quietened. Stavros paused for a moment, holding their attention, looking around at them. His eyes twinkled and a wide grin spread like jam on bread across his face.

'We've smashed the mighty Hardrada!' he shouted. At that, the room erupted with an ear-splitting roar. 'Who, as it turned out, was nothing more than a pain in the neck!' he yelled. To catcalls and deep groans of laughter, he rolled his head, miming getting an arrow through the throat.

'But now, mates,' Stavros continued, 'the word is that, in the not too distant future, a certain Norman plans on trying his luck against us.' There was loud booing. 'Well, if he does,' he went on, as the noise subsided, 'I say we give him a warm welcome and offer him some land.' There was an expectant hush. 'In fact, to coin a now famous saying, he can have three metres of it...for a grave!'

Raising his voice above their ecstatic response, their fists banging on tables and stamping their feet, Stavros held up his beer glass. 'I give you the toast, mates,' he smiled. 'To Duke William...Up 'is bum!'

The jubilant Saxons lifted their drinks and yelled back with one confident voice, resonating around the room: 'To Duke William...Up 'is bum!'

Suddenly, amid the ensuing hubbub of laughter and shouting, just as the minstrels struck up again, the double doors at the end of the hall burst open and a dust-covered messenger rushed in. In an instant the room fell quiet. He strode forward between the tables and went down on one knee in front of Harold.

'My Lord King,' he gasped in a hoarse voice. 'Duke William has landed...with a huge army!'

*

Morcar and Edwin stood outside the saloon bar of the pub, watching Harold as he prepared to leave. Behind him, out in the street, cheered on by a crowd of thankful townspeople, the troops were filing past, heading out of town.

Harold mounted his bicycle. 'So,' he sighed wearily, 'I'll expect you in three or four days, five at the outside.'

'We'll be there, mate,' Morcar assured him. 'As soon as we've regrouped, we'll be hot on your heels.'

'Good. Don't be late. I'm counting on you.' Harold adjusted the chin strap of his helmet and gave them a grim smile. 'Well, here we go again!'

'Good luck, Harold,' said Edwin.

'Thanks. Don't forget, though, I can only wait a few days for you.'

'No worries, Harold.' Morcar nodded. 'We'll be as quick as we can.'

Harold raised his eyebrows to them in farewell. 'See y'later, then.'

As he wheeled away to join the column, Morcar stared after him, deep in thought.

'What d'you want me to do first, Morc?' Edwin asked eagerly. 'Round up the men? Check on the wounded?'

'What?' Morcar answered distractedly. He shook his head and smiled. 'Oh, go and get another drink, I reckon.'

'But what about Harold? Shouldn't we regroup?'

'There's plenty of time for that.' Morcar put an arm around his brother's shoulders. 'Listen, Edwin, I've been thinking, this is our chance.'

'What d'you mean?'

'Harold's not going to beat William, we know that,' he said. 'He's force-marched his men all the way up here, fought a pitched battle, and now, without a break, he's force-marching them all the way back down again. They're going to be stuffed! There's no way he can win.'

'But, with our army...?'

'Our army stays here! We regroup, like we said, and then we wait. Let them fight it out. Whoever wins won't be in any condition to put up much resistance, will they?'

'Resistance? Against what?'

'Against a large, fresh army like ours.'

'Ah!' Edwin exclaimed.

'Now do you get the drift?'

'Yeah!' Edwin grinned. 'Whoever's left, we finish them off!'

'Exactly! Meanwhile, I've been looking around for support.'

'From who?

'The far right mainly. "FUN" for one.'

"FUN"? Those fanatics? They're a bunch of bloody loonies!'

'Maybe so, but we can still use their numbers. Don't worry, mate, we'll give them the flick further down the track, once they've helped us get what we want. And then you and I, little brother, will be co-rulers of the whole country!'

'I like it!' Edwin smiled. 'But what about Aldyth? She'll be a widow, without a crown?'

'Oh, she'll get over it. As long as she's got a man between her legs, she's right. We'll find someone else for her. Anyway, it's not like they're in love or anything.'

'That's true.'

'In fact, if you ask me, Harold's made a bit of a monkey out of our sister. Remember what Dad told us. He's still got that woman and their kids tucked away somewhere.'

'The bastard! He's just been screwing her.'

'So, what d'you reckon on my plan, mate?'

'That Algar'd be proud of you, Morc!'

'Now do you know what we do first?'

Their eyes met and they both shrugged at once. 'Go and get another drink!' they laughed in unison.

With their arms around each other's shoulders, they turned and entered the pub. A wave of boisterous cheering greeted them as they went in.

21

In the centre of the palace quadrangle, a group of athletic young officers wearing white plimsolls, tracksuit pants, and singlets, were exercising on a springboard and a vaulting horse, while others did press-ups and sit-ups nearby. At the far end of the courtyard, a small crowd of palace staff were gathered behind a rope barrier, watching and applauding the display.

A squad of soldiers came jogging past them, double marching around the perimeter, singing as they went. Trotting alongside them was a drill sergeant, calling out the timing, while the squad chanted the verses back to him with gusto.

One...Two...Who are you?

We're the Saxon army
We're bold and brave and strong
When enemies bring harm we
Rush to take them on

Three...Four...Tell me more

We're the greatest fighters
That you will ever see
We're off to beat those blighters
Who've come from Normandy

Five...Six...Seven...Eight...One...Two...Who are you?

Repeating the song, over and over, they continued on around the courtyard.

Meanwhile, on the grassy area in the middle, a dashing young captain sporting a trim blonde moustache completed a long vault with a forward roll and stood up sharply to attention. He looked about him, puffing out his chest with pride. Noticing a pretty chambermaid among the crowd of onlookers, gazing at him in admiration, he grinned at her and winked. She squirmed with embarrassment, then, fluttering her eyelashes, gave him an answering smile.

*

Upstairs in the palace, in his musty, wood-panelled second-floor office, Harold was leaning over in his swivel-chair, rummaging through the drawers of his desk, pulling out papers, maps, and folders and stuffing them into a battered briefcase.

Bernard was sitting in an armchair nearby, watching him. Behind him, over by the full bookshelves lining one wall, Leofwine was inspecting the titles. Only half-concentrating on what he was doing, he selected a volume and flipped through its pages.

Beyond them, at the back of the room, Haco stood by the window, gazing down at the troops performing in the quadrangle below, listening to the faint sound of their chanting.

Harold snapped shut the lock of his briefcase and sat up. 'So, what do you think, Gurth?' he said.

In front of him, Gurth stopped pacing the worn, varnished floorboards. 'I hate to say it, Harold, but we've got to wait. It just doesn't feel right. We'd be playing straight into his hands.'

'How d'you mean?'

'By letting him rush us. We're just not ready. The men are asleep on their feet and so am I. We have to wait for Morcar.'

'How much longer d'you reckon he'll be, Harold?' Leofwine called across the room.

'Who knows?' Harold answered. 'He may not even have left yet. But we can't wait forever.'

'And what if he doesn't come at all?' interjected Bernard. 'There's something fishy about that bastard. I don't trust him. He reminds me too much of his dad.'

'Well, if we hold off for a bit, we won't have to rely on Morcar at all,' Gurth said. 'We can gather our own reinforcements.'

'And what about the Normans?' Harold asked.

'In the meantime, we'd send a few companies down to ambush them. Attack them at night. Set traps for them. Pick 'em off one by one. They'll soon get demoralised. They won't risk going anywhere in a hurry. Then, when Morcar arrives...'

'*If* he arrives,' Bernard argued.

'All right, Bern, maybe he won't show up. Either way, though, we'd still have time to put together a big enough army to be sure of winning.'

'With all our nagging at them, they'd still be able to go out and plunder the land at will, Gurth,' Bernard persisted. 'And our lack of action'd look like cowardice. People would think Harold was scared, then we'd get no reinforcements. I vote we attack straight away.'

'Mm...' Harold murmured. 'Leo?'

Leofwine looked up from his book. 'The men deserve a rest, Harold,' he said with a tired smile. 'We all do. Anyway, there's this girl I'd like to see...Just joking! No, I go along with Gurth, there's too much at stake to risk everything on a single battle. I say wait.'

'What about you, Haco? You're very quiet?'

Haco turned away from the window. 'Yeah, sorry, Harold. I was watching the men going through their paces down there.

They're full of themselves. And why not? They've beaten the invincible Hardrada! I think we should strike while the iron's hot. If we don't, their tiredness'll catch up with them. They'll lose confidence, and...'

'Go on,' Harold said, seeing him hesitate.

'Well, I know the Duke pretty well, Harold. He won't wait around. He'll march straight up here. He'll say he's only come to punish you personally and that he's willing to let the Council decide. It'd be too late to argue. He'd already be here.'

'Our trusty councillors would be off to their holiday homes before we could even blink!' Bernard scoffed.

'That's right,' Haco nodded. 'The people wouldn't know who to follow or what to think. He'd have split the country. We've got no choice, we have to fight.'

'You've got an old head on your young shoulders, Haco,' Harold smiled.

'I'm sorry. I didn't mean to be so outspoken.'

'You can tell he's Sweyn's son, all right!' chuckled Gurth.

'Yeah, just like him. A pushy bugger!' Leofwine grinned.

'Well, it looks like it's all down to me, then,' said Harold. 'Since I got us into this mess, I suppose it's only right that I get us out of it.'

'You can't blame yourself for any of this, Harold,' Gurth protested.

'I was the one who swore the oath.'

'The Duke's got his own agenda. He was always going to come.'

'Maybe so,' Harold sighed. 'Anyway, now's our chance to deal with him, once and for all. If we don't take it, people'll say I rushed to attack my own brother but that I'm afraid to face the Normans. And as far as risking the country on a single battle goes, I don't think that's true. If we do fail, at least we'll have set an example for every patriot to follow and thinned out their ranks in the process. Others would soon rise up to finish the job.'

'They'd be selling tickets to get at the bastard!' Leofwine growled.

'But, let's hope that won't be necessary,' Harold smiled. 'As Haco said, we've already beaten Hardrada. Therefore, my decision is we go.'

They all straightened up.

'When?' asked Gurth.

'Now!'

*

Aldyth sat on the sofa, stroking the Persian cat purring on her lap and puffing nervously on a menthol cigarette, every now and then flicking it against the full glass ashtray on the low coffee table in front of her. Her face was pale and drawn, streaked with recent tears. She looked round and her unpainted lips compressed into a thin, combative smile as Harold entered the apartment.

'What've you decided, Harold?' she asked, 'Are you going to fight the Duke?'

'Yes. We leave in an hour.'

Aldyth stubbed out her cigarette in anger. 'You realise that you're mad, don't you?'

'Thanks very much.'

She threw down the cat and jumped to her feet. 'And what d'you expect me to do? Wait here to be raped?'

'Don't worry, Aldyth, I doubt that's going to happen,' Harold sighed. 'You'll have plenty of time to get to safety if you have to.'

'Then, I'd better start packing now!'

'Maybe that's a good idea,' he said with weary tolerance. 'Only, do me one favour before you leave, would you? When your brothers arrive, tell them to get a move on.'

'You don't actually believe they're coming, do you?' she laughed, her voice edged with hysteria. 'Don't be so naïve, Harold! They're waiting for you and the Normans to tear each other to shreds, then they plan to seize the throne!'

'Those bastards!'

'Oh, God. You'll be dead! I'll lose my crown! All that I've worked for!'

'Schemed for, more like. You and your whole bloody family.'

'What're you talking about?' Aldyth snapped, plucking another cigarette from the sandalwood box on the table and clicking the heavy silver lighter, again and again, until it ignited. 'I wasn't party to their plans,' she said, blowing out a cloud of smoke. 'We've both been had, my Lord. And either way, I lose!'

'Selfish to the last, eh?' Harold scowled. 'If what you say is true, Aldyth, your future's still secure. Why should a trivial thing like my death disturb you?'

'Because I love you, you fool!' she cried. 'Don't you know that? I've always loved you!' Shaking with emotion, she ground out her half-smoked cigarette in the ashtray. 'You've used me, all of you!'

'What about your threats to turn your brothers against me? Do you call that love?'

'I had to hold onto you any way I could. I knew that you didn't love me, but I thought that in time...Oh, you're all so cruel!' she sobbed.

Harold paused and took a deep breath. With a sad smile, he put his hands on her shoulders. 'I'm sorry, Aldyth, none of this was ever meant to be.' He held her at arm's length. 'You know, though, that whatever happens I'm not coming back to you, don't you?' he said, as if explaining things to a small girl.

'Yes,' she nodded through her tears.

Harold smiled, pitying them both, and stroked the damp strands of hair away from her face. 'But you'll be all right. You're young and beautiful, and you've got money. You'll have no trouble making a new life for yourself.' His face grew stern. 'As for your brothers, you can tell them from me that they'll never get the throne! Now, I have to go.' He kissed her on the cheek. 'Goodbye, Aldyth.'

'Harold?' she called after him as he strode to the door. 'Regardless of Morcar and Edwin, I still hope you win.'

He opened it and turned. 'Thanks,' he smiled distantly. 'So do I.'

*

Within the close, airless atmosphere of the tunnel of trees, the long column of troops came up the knoll road. Riding at its head were Harold, Gurth, and Leofwine. No one spoke. The only sounds were the wagon wheels and army boots crunching on the dry red earth, the creak of leather, and the rattle of armour.

Gurth caught Leofwine's eye and nodded towards Harold. They watched him with concern. He was lost in thought, reliving his goodbyes in the entrance hall of the family home.

'Oh, Harold,' the Queen's voice had trembled with emotion, as she embraced and kissed him. *'Once, you were just my little brother and now you're my King!'*

'That doesn't matter,' he grinned. *'To me, you'll always be my big beautiful sister!'*

'It does matter, though, doesn't it?' she smiled, her eyes watering.

'Did I say beautiful? I meant serious!'

'Don't joke, Harold! It's an incredible responsibility. The hopes and dreams of a whole nation rest on your shoulders. I used to be married to one, don't forget.'

'Ah, Didi,' he sighed with tender sadness.

'And I also know what a terrible sacrifice you've made,' she went on.

His voice hardened. 'Do you?'

'Yes. Gurth told me everything. You must feel so alone.' She took hold of his hands. 'You're not, you know.'

'Thanks. I guess we've both given up a lot in the name of duty.'

'You more than me. Was it all really worth it, do you think? Doesn't personal happiness count for anything?'

'You tell me. Was it worth it for you?'

'Yes, I suppose so,' she murmured. 'It's just that what you're doing now is so frightening. I'm sorry, Harold, I'm not helping, am I?'

'Don't worry, Didi,' he smiled. 'It'll all come out in the wash!'

'Oh, I hope so!' They hugged each other again. 'My dear brother, be careful. Your country wants you now, but we'll always need you!'

He turned to his mother. 'Well, this is it, Mum.'

'Goodbye, my darling!' Githa sobbed, holding him tight, pressing her head against his chest. 'I love you so much!' She pulled back and looked up at him. 'I want you to know, Harold, I've never blamed you for what happened to Tostig. Your father predicted it and he was right. It wasn't your fault.'

He nodded, his eyes flooding, unable to speak.

'But don't let me lose you, Gurth, and Leofwine, too. I couldn't bear it!' Unconstrained tears rolled down her cheeks. 'You're the only ones I have left. I'll never see my Wolnoth again!'

'Oh, Mum!'

'I won't! He's lost in the clutches of that dreadful man and his evil system.' She gripped his shirtfront. 'For God's sake, Harold, in the name of every mother in the land, destroy him!'

'Harold, we're here!' Gurth's voice cut into his memories, jolting him back to the present.

Harold shook his head to clear it. 'Right...Thanks, Gurth,' he said. He raised his arm and the column halted. 'Leo, take the men on down the road. We'll meet you on the other side of the knoll. We shouldn't be more than an hour. Sorry, mate,' he smiled gently. 'Someone has to stay with 'em.'

'No worries, Harold,' Leofwine nodded sadly. 'Say goodbye to Edith and the kids for me, will you?'

*

The unexpected heatwave following the battle had coalesced into an overcast, pressure cooker of a day that now seemed on the verge of bursting into another violent storm. Out in the backyard, a hot wind was blowing up. Like a panting beast preparing to unleash its power, every now and then a searing gust of air whipped through the outbuildings, sending up spirals of dust before dying away.

Oblivious to the emotional tension of the people around them, the chickens were clustered together in their pen, pressing up against each other. Agitated by the weather, their trembling watchfulness was broken by an occasional flurry of feathers and a short-tempered squawk.

Hilda and Gladys had brought the children out to say their goodbyes to Harold, Gurth, and Bernard. Edith wasn't among them. Time was short and the chatting had been kept to a minimum. After circling each other, avoiding any direct contact except through three and four-way conversations, as the moment for leaving arrived Harold walked over to face Vera, out of earshot of the others.

'I'd better get going now, Vera,' he said with an awkward smile. 'Goodbye.'

'Good luck, Harold,' she answered. Her body remained stiff as he kissed her cheek. 'Be careful.'

'I will. Take care of them.'

'I always have. I'm sorry to have to say this, Harold, but you've been a bastard to them all!'

'I know it must seem like that,' he sighed.

'But, if it's any consolation to you, Edith still loves you.' She shook her head. 'Why, I can't imagine.'

'I had to do what I had to do.'

'Boys will be boys, I suppose.'

'Forgive me, Vera. I do love her.'

'I know you do. Like most men, you just don't know how to live it.'

With a weary nod, Harold turned away and crossed the yard to Edmund. 'I have to go now, mate,' he said with a sad grin, holding out his arms.

'Hang on, Dad, I'll fetch my bag!'

'What d'you mean?'

'It's all packed. I'm coming with you.'

'Not this again! No way, Ed. I'm sorry, you can't.'

Edmund's face fell. 'Why not?' he protested. 'Your dad was even younger than me when he went to war.'

'That was in my dad's day. Things have changed since then, thank God! Now you have to be at least eighteen.'

'But that's only the regular army. Mum said you're so short of men you're bound to take all the local help you can get.'

'Oh, did she?'

'And you won't be able to check all their ages, will you?'

'Maybe not, but my officers will.'

'Your dad lied about his age, why can't I? I'm only a year younger. No one would ever know.'

'I'd know! Now, that's enough, Edmund,' Harold said firmly. 'I forbid you to come! Anyway, I need you here to look after the family.' He put his hands on Edmund's shoulders. 'Come on, cheer up, mate. I'll be back soon. Then we can really start doing things together.'

'Famous last words!' Edmund retorted. 'Like what?'

'Like fixing up this place for a start. Then, when you finish school, we could even go into some kind of business together. Have a think about it while I'm gone. See what you can come up with. All right?'

'Yeah, sure.'

'Good on you, Ed. I'm proud of you, mate.'

Harold hugged and kissed his son, not wanting to let him go, his face twisting in pain as if his heart were being crushed in a vice—torn by the closeness he yearned for with his precious child, the pleasure he took in him yet somehow couldn't express, and the distance between them he hadn't been able to bridge; by the rushing of time, the chances lost, and his failure as a parent in not noticing his needs; by his desperate desire to undo his mistakes, and the impossibility of going back, of making things right; and, now, having to push him away again.

'I love you so much, Edmund!' was all he could gasp, as his throat constricted.

'I love you too, Dad,' Edmund said in almost automatic response, the depth of his own feelings walled off once more by the brickwork of rejection.

With a final hug, Harold let him go. Wiping away the tears stinging his eyes, he strode over to Magnus, who was talking to Gurth. As he approached, Gurth sent him a sympathetic smile and moved away.

'Are you going now, Dad?' Magnus asked.

"'Fraid so, old son!' Harold's face cracked askew in a heartbroken grin, as two large teardrops rolled down his cheeks into his greying beard. He was saying goodbye to his boy! His innocent, scatter-brained, happy-go-lucky Magnus!

'I wish you wouldn't go, Dad. I miss you.'

'I know you do, mate. And I miss you, too. But don't worry, Mag, it won't be for long,' he smiled, struggling to sound cheerful. 'Then we'll all be together again. Meanwhile, I'm counting on you to look after the others for me, mate. Will you do that?'

"Course I will,' Magnus nodded, then all his news came out in a rush. 'Did you know I'm almost as tall as Edmund? I got an A-plus in Maths at school. I'm in the junior cricket team and Mum bought me a new bat!'

'Wow! That's wonderful.' Harold laughed with delight, blinking back the tears, wanting to howl. 'Well done! Soon you'll be taller than me.' He pulled his son to him, kissing the side of his head. Fighting for air, his throat dry, he was barely able to swallow. 'I'm afraid I've got to go now, darling,' he said in a rasping voice. 'I'll see you later, all right? I love you!'

'Love you, Dad. Good luck!'

Harold released him and spun round, clenching his eyelids together to shut out the anguish, then throwing them wide, straining at the sky, like gleaming dolphins draining off the sea. He filled his lungs to capacity and exhaled. Then, bracing himself for the next round of sorrow, he staggered towards Gunhilds, who was standing nearby, her face dejected, stabbing her toe at the ground.

'And you, my little sweet. What's the matter?' he smiled, coming up to her.

'I'm really annoyed with you, Daddy.'

'Why, darling?' he asked, his eyes swimming. 'Why are you annoyed with me?'

'Because you left us,' Gunhilds answered, kicking up the dust to loosen a pebble. 'And because you don't love us anymore.'

Harold knelt down in front of her and pulled her towards him. 'Oh, my baby! I do love you! I love you all so much. I haven't left you!'

'You married someone else,' she stammered in a hurt voice over his shoulder.

'No, I didn't, darling,' he sighed. 'Not really. Not in my heart. Not like I'm married to Mummy.' He held her away from him. 'It was just a piece of paper. A business arrangement, to make the country safe.'

Gunhilds's face brightened. 'Like a bank loan, you mean?'

'Yes, I suppose so!' Harold laughed through his tears. 'Just like a bank loan. Where on earth did you get that from?'

'Mummy and Nanna went to see the bank man. He said they could have lots of money.'

'That's great. And did Mummy say what she wanted the money for, Gunhi?'

'Yes. To dig up the garden so we can grow things. And to build a proper hospital part at the back, so she can help more sick people. I'm going to be the nurse!'

'That's lovely, darling! You'll make a wonderful nurse.' he sobbed, kissing her cheek. 'Where is Mummy now, do you know?'

Gunhilds pointed to the top of the knoll. 'She's up there.'

'Right. I have to get going now, sweetheart.'

'Will you come back, Daddy?'

'Oh, yes!' he cried, holding her tight. 'I'll come back. In just a few days!'

She threw her arms around his neck. 'I love you, Daddy!'

'Goodbye, my darling! I love you, Gunhi. I love you all!' Harold kissed her once more, then tore himself away, his eyes burning.

In tears, he turned to Gurth. 'I'm just going up the knoll, Gurth,' he croaked. 'I'll join you with the men.'

'No worries, Harold,' Gurth replied, watching in sadness as his brother headed off down the yard. 'Bern?' he called over his shoulder. 'Ready to go, mate?'

'Right-o,' Bernard nodded, standing a short way behind him, next to Gladys. He lifted her hand to his lips and planted a kiss. 'Time to go, Glad.'

'I know,' she answered. 'Go on then, if you must.'

'You know I don't want to leave you.'

'Sure you don't. You're just like all the rest, you want to have your cake and eat it, too!'

'That's not true!' Bernard spluttered.

Gladys laughed. 'I'm joking, you silly man!'

'Oh.'

'I think! Get along, Bernie. You've got a job to do.'

'All right, I know when I'm not wanted!'

They gazed at each other for a long moment, then came together, like a grey-bristled walrus and a big-bosomed sea lion, in a passionate kiss.

'You take care of yourself,' she laughed, eventually pushing him off.

'I will. Goodbye, my girl!' he grinned.

'Bah!' she chuckled, with a pleased smile. 'And leave the fighting to the younger men,' she called after him as he walked away. 'You just tell 'em all what to do, you hear? You don't have to prove your manhood to me. I already know how big and firm you can be!'

Bernard looked round at her. 'Well, don't you forget it, either,' he laughed. 'Or I might just have to come back and remind you!'

'I reckon you'd better,' Gladys nodded, her eyes filled with fear and pride, shining like fractured glass.

22

The threat of the storm had abated. Edith was standing at the far end of the summit, watching the trailing edge of the storm approaching in an unbroken line, followed by an endless expanse of blue sky. The shifting wind blew through her hair as it pushed the clouds on by overhead.

All of a sudden, she felt the earth vibrate and heard the sound of footfalls on the grass behind her. A painful smile crossed her face. She turned. Harold was walking towards her across the top of the knoll.

'Harold!' She took an instinctive step to greet him, then stopped herself.

He flashed her an uncertain grin. 'Hello, Edith.'

'How are you?' she answered without emotion.

'I'm fine. You look tired,' he said with gentle concern, coming closer.

'Yeah, well...' she shrugged and gave a hollow laugh. 'So, how's married life treating you?'

Harold shook his head, offering her a rueful, abject smile, 'Darling, I'm so sorry! Can you ever forgive me?'

With a gasp of pent-up anger, she took a pace forward, letting fly at him. 'For what? For going off to live with another woman? For breaking the hearts of your children? You left them without a word, Harold.'

'You wouldn't let me see them!' he protested.

'Only that once. You never came again.'

'I just didn't have time! I tried to explain it to them in my letters. I never got a reply.'

'They didn't know what to say. They cried themselves to sleep for nights!' Edith stopped and gave a weary sigh. 'Anyway, it doesn't matter now, does it?'

'It does! Oh, it does! I want you back, Edith. I love you.'

'Harold, don't.'

'The children need me.'

'You bastard!' she snapped. 'Don't bring them into it. That's not fair.'

'I miss them so much!'

'Well, you should've thought of that before you went and screwed what's her name!'

'Now who's not being fair? I didn't have any choice. It was either that or civil war.'

'And that makes it all right, does it?'

'No,' he said, shaking his head in remorse. 'But if it makes any difference, I was blind drunk each time it happened.'

Edith grit her teeth, shutting her eyes in pain. 'Spare me the details, please! It's too late, Harold.'

'No, it's not, darling. You have to give me a chance!' he pleaded, walking up to her. 'I've never stopped loving you!'

'Oh, God!' she cried in torment, balling her fists.

Harold reached out and pulled her to him, holding her, kissing her hair. 'Oh, my darling, please forgive me!'

She remained rigid in his arms. 'I don't know if I can,' she murmured.

'You can! You must!'

'You've hurt us all so much.'

'I know.'

Edith pulled away. 'I should be screaming at you, Harold. I can't even get angry any more. I'm empty. There are times when I wish I'd never met you.'

'Oh, don't think that! Don't give up on me, darling. I know I've hurt you...'

'You've put us all through hell!'

'I'm so sorry.'

She smiled, the tears welling in her eyes. 'And look at you. You're a wreck!'

'Tell me about it!' Harold laughed without humour. 'Sometimes I think I'm going insane. It's like I've been falling from one nightmare into another. But you're the light at the end of the tunnel, Edith. You and the kids. Without you here, I'd be lost.'

Edith took a deep breath and looked him in the eyes. 'Well, we are here, Harold. All you have to do is wake up. It's still not too late to stop. You want a chance? Don't go. Stay here with us.'

'Edith, I can't!' he cried in frustration. 'What d'you expect me to do, go and tell them that I've changed my mind, that I'm not coming? I have to go.'

'All right, then go, damn you!'

He put his hands to his temples, gripping his hair. 'This is crazy! We're going round in circles.'

'No, you are!'

'We've been invaded, for God's sake!'

'Oh, what a surprise! That's what happens when you put up barriers. Someone comes to knock them down. First Hardrada. Now William. Beat back one, rebuild the barriers, and get ready for the next, and the next. You're the one going round in circles, Harold.'

'The only barriers we put up are in self-defence.'

'You're joking, aren't you? Our whole system's built on them. They're what wars are all about. Kingdoms and empires, countries and territories. All man-made constructs designed to partition the world, which can only exist by keeping us under control.'

'Oh, not this again,' he moaned.

'It's been going on so long we don't even realise it's happening,' she continued, ignoring his protest. 'It's brilliant! Give the middle-class enough comfort and security, then they won't risk losing what they've got and they'll remain silent. And keep the poor so busy just trying to survive that they're powerless to resist. Divide and rule! The haves and have-nots. Who cares if half the world's forced to live in squalor and slavery, without any hope of a future? Competition's good for business!'

'You make it sound like it's all bad, Edith. It's not. There are so many good things that our system allows us to do. That are worth fighting for.'

'Of course there are. We do incredible things. And they would still get done without the barriers. We do virtually everything we need to do already, but it's restricted and selective. It only benefits some and comes at a terrible human cost. We can do better than that, Harold.

'Given half a chance, mankind is basically caring. Without our fear of each other and this mad invention, this money system, to constrain us, we could do them for *everyone*...But, hey, wealth is power. And if you want to have winners, you've got to have losers!'

'That's too simplistic. It's just conspiracy theory.'

'Well the horrors are allowed to continue, aren't they? It must suit somebody's interests. Why else wouldn't we stop it? Either our leaders don't care, or it's beyond their control, or it's deliberate. Which is it?'

'There's more to it than that.'

'Yeah? That's what we tell ourselves, so we can sleep at night! How many tales of hunger and deprivation must we block our ears to in the name of national security and what's good for the economy? We've become callous and numb, Harold. Too frightened to face the truth. Instead of buying and selling we should be giving and sharing. It's as simple as that. A world based on need not greed. We can't have both.'

Harold shook his head sadly. 'It's a utopian dream, darling. It's never going to happen.'

'Maybe it won't!' Edith retorted, her voice trembling with emotion. 'Maybe it never will happen. But whether it does or it doesn't, it *should!* And that means we have to keep *striving* for it! It's called doing the right thing. And I'll never stop thinking it or saying it just because somebody tells me it won't! We have to make a move towards it, Harold. Anything else only perpetuates the suffering.'

'And how do you propose we do that?'

'By setting an example, showing that we *can* live in peace! By making laws that stop the hoarding of profits and power by a few and compels them to be used for the common good. By pooling our wealth and resources, especially the fortune squandered on war, to provide free basic needs for everyone.

'By reorganising ourselves into networks of communities, all helping each other, with enough jobs to go round for everybody to contribute and be of value. By working together, not in isolation, sharing our skills and ingenuity to create a world fit for children to live in. It's easy! If we invested in *that*, who knows where it would lead? Eventually, money would become obsolete. We just have to spend it to end it!'

'And in the meantime, we'd be slaughtered!'

'Don't worry, Harold, the baddies can't kill us all!' she laughed, mocking his negativity, refusing to be discouraged. 'Many people have given their lives for non-violence in the past, and in the process of disarming maybe many more will have to again. But not as many as are dying already in this endless, senseless war. Because, once it started, the movement would spread. The people would rise up! Especially the young. It'd be unstoppable! Like a tidal wave. Those against it would soon run out of weapons, the weapons *we* supply them with. In the face of the free world we'd offer, they'd start turning on each other. They'd give up and join in.'

'It's impossible.'

'No, it's *not!* All we have to do is *try!* We're inventive, aren't we? It's one of our greatest talents. We'd find a *way* to make it work. If only a *few* of those in power, the presidents and the mega-rich, had the courage to join together and set it in motion it would sweep the world. The voice of sanity! It'd be the only political game in town worth playing. Who in their right mind wouldn't follow? Only someone with too much to lose!' she laughed with contempt. 'But all that goes in the too hard basket, doesn't it?'

'You're being naïve, Edith. Greed is the problem, not money.'

'Money's just a tool, Harold. If it was used fairly and in moderation, fine. But it's not and it never will be. It's a drug. People become addicted to it, to the power it brings. Money *creates* greed! You've got about as much chance of stopping greed by using money as you have of curing alcoholism by giving people whisky. Now who's being naïve?'

'We can't just live without money! It's how the world works.'

'No. It's how the world *doesn't* work!' Edith shouted in despair. 'Not if it brings us to *this!* Hell bent on destruction. With you going! And then, of course, there are all those other barriers...'

'No more, darling, *please!*'

'Gender, race, education, occupation. The list is endless. Where we live, what we wear, how we look. As if we don't all have the same human needs or live on the same damn planet!'

'Edith, stop!'

'Oh, I'm sorry! Is the truth too boring for you?'

'There just isn't time!' Harold pleaded.

Her tears began to flow. 'When will there ever be, Harold? When will I ever be able to reach you again? I'm fighting for my world, too, you know.'

'Oh, darling...'

'And let's not forget the ultimate hypocrisy,' Edith laughed with derision, digging at her blurred vision with her knuckles. 'Religious barriers. Hello! If there is a God, there can only ever *be* one!'

'It's a sick world, all right,' Harold sighed.

'Yes, and it's sick of *war!* Oh, why can't you fight to break down those barriers, Harold, instead of defending them? *They* are what's come between us!'

'It's too late, Edith. The only thing coming between us is the Normans and they're *here!* They'll tear our world apart if we don't stop them.'

'It's already torn apart!' she cried in torment. 'Can't you *see* that?'

'Well, I'm trying to put it back together again.'

'How? By more and more killing?'

He shook his head. 'I'm sorry,' he said firmly. 'Some people are just so evil they have to be destroyed.'

'I refuse to believe that, Harold. Good or bad, everything we do has a cause. We're all the product of our own past. Mum says people are like sausages...'

'What?' he blinked in surprise.

'Squeeze them at one end and they'll bulge out of all proportion at the other. Humanity's so tied up in knots by its history of conquest and revenge, it's facing the future twisted round backwards! Someone has to try and undo them before we strangle ourselves to death. By breaking this cycle of violence!'

'It can't be done, my love. It's too far gone.' As a bugle trilled in the distance, Harold started and looked towards the sound. 'Edith, I have to go. They're waiting for me.'

'For what? To wallow with you in another bloodbath? Isn't the death of one brother enough for you, Your Royal Highness?'

Harold rounded on her in fury. 'Don't you dare blame me for Tostig's death! He brought it on himself.'

'You still don't get it, do you?' Edith groaned, shaking her head in pity. 'Your own brother! Your own children! Your own precious family! You're willing to sacrifice us all! Your heart's grown so cold, Harold, I don't even know you any more.'

'Oh, thanks a lot! Listen, Edith, I love you. I'm not a heartless man and I've been as hurt by what's happened as anyone. I'm just trying to do my best, that's all. If you can't see that...' A second bugle call rang out. 'Look, I have to know...when this battle with the Normans is over, can I...please...will you let me come home?'

With a heartbroken sob, Edith threw herself into his arms. 'Oh, Harold! Harold!'

'My love!' he murmured into her hair. 'I know I'm not perfect...'

'I don't want somebody perfect, I want you!'

She lifted her face to his and their mouths locked and fused in a desperate kiss. At length, he leant back from her. 'Can I take that as a yes?' he grinned.

'Yes...No!..I don't know...Maybe...You can take it as a maybe.'

'Then, at least there's still hope?'

'That's for you to decide, Harold. Is there?'

'Oh, yes, there is!' he vowed, hugging her to him. 'Things'll be better, you'll see! When I come back, we can make a new start.'

'How many times has history recorded *those* famous words!'

'I mean it. I'm the king, don't forget.'

'Oh, Harold!' Edith moaned against his chest. As a third bugle sounded, she felt him stiffen. 'Go on. I won't hold you. As if I ever could,' she sighed. They kissed again. 'For all our sakes, be careful!'

'I will.' Their fingertips touching to the last, he pulled apart. 'Goodbye, my love!'

As he broke away from her and started down the slope, she called after him. 'We all need you, Harold!'

'I'll see you soon!' he laughed back to her.

Edith stood motionless, watching Harold bound down the knoll towards the waiting column. At that moment, Gunhilds ran up to her side. 'Mummy, where is he?' she panted. 'Where's Daddy?'

With a sorrowful smile, Edith put an arm around her shoulders. 'Daddy's gone, darling,' she said gently.

'No!' Gunhilds wrenched herself free. Rushing to the edge of the summit, she screamed down after him. 'Don't go, Daddy!... Daddy, don't go!'

As Harold skidded down the slope, her frantic plea was drowned out by the harsh bugle blast announcing his arrival. On reaching the road, he mounted his bicycle. Turning in the saddle, he waved up at them with a cheerful smile.

Edith gazed down at him, numb and confused, holding her sobbing daughter against her. She started to raise her arm, but then let it fall to her side.

Harold looked round at Gurth. 'All right? Let's go!'

As the troops moved off, Edith took Gunhilds by the hand and led her away from the edge.

*

Clucking in histrionic complaint, a pair of red roosters scuttled out of the way as Gladys walked across the empty backyard, carrying a rake and a pair of gardening gloves. Going over to one of the low outbuildings, she pulled back the rusty bolt and turned the handle.

The wooden door creaked open and she entered the dark interior. Apart from the doorway, the only light inside came through the murky glass of a small window at one end and a few chinks in the bluestone walls. Beneath its cobwebbed beams and tin roof, the shed was filled with orderly stacks of gardening tools, flowerpots, boxes, sacks, and building materials.

Picking her way across the rammed earth floor, Gladys placed her gloves on a rickety table and propped the rake up against the wall. She turned to leave. Without warning, the arm of a donkey jacket snaked out from the shadows, hooking around her throat, as Scarf appeared out of the shadows behind her.

'Don't make a sound, Norman-lover!' he growled in her ear with a lopsided, malevolent sneer, his hot breath caressing the back of her neck.

'What do you want?' Gladys gasped in a strangled, frightened whisper.

'Oh, we'll think of something, won't we, ducky?' he leered, stroking her cheek with a grubby hand.

As Scarf's thick, dirty fingers ran over her lips, Gladys yanked open her mouth and clamped down on them with her teeth. He let out a cry of pain, partially loosening his grip on her throat. She tore herself free and dashed for the door. Scarf leaped after her and, in two bounds, caught hold of her dress and spun her around. Gladys punched him in the face.

Gripping her by the front of her blouse, he paused for a moment to lick at his moustache, wet and sticky with the blood trickling from his nose. Then his eyes blazed in anger. Snatching up a wooden mallet from a nearby workbench, and giving a furious cry, he smashed her round the head with it, sending her sprawling among the garden implements and rolling onto the floor.

*

Edith and Gunhilds came down off the knoll and entered the backyard through the gap in the wall. Ahead of them, three locals had a large, bearded man she faintly recognised pinned up against one of the outbuildings. Vera and Mr Jenkins stood nearby, grimly watching them. A short way off, Magnus, his face ashen with shock, was staring at a body lying on the ground, covered by a blanket.

As Edith and Gunhilds broke into a run, Vera called Magnus over to her and went to meet them.

'What's happening, Mum?' Edith asked in alarm.

'Gladys has been killed!'

'What?' Aghast, Edith held Gunhilds against her.

Vera pointed. 'By that monster over there!'

'Why?' Edith exclaimed in horror, staring at the man. She put a protective arm around Magnus.

'He said she was helping the Normans,' Vera said with disgust. She took Gunhilds's hand in hers. 'Come along, darling. You stay with Nanna. I'll take them indoors, Edith.'

'Thanks,' Edith nodded, starting forward.

As Vera led the tearful children away towards the house, Edith turned and called after her. 'Mum, have you seen Edmund?'

'No, not for a while. He's probably inside. I'll have a look.'

While they continued on towards the back door, Edith walked over to Gladys' body. She bent down and slowly lifted back the blanket, gazing at her friend's battered face.

'Oh, Gladys!' she moaned softly, shaking her head in sorrow. Gently replacing the cover, she turned towards the prisoner. 'Why? Why did you do this?' she gasped, her voice filled with desolate rage.

'It should've been you, you Norman bitch!' Scarf answered with a drunken snarl.

One of the locals holding him shoved him back against the wall. 'That's enough of that, you bastard!'

'I'm sorry, Miss Swanneck,' said Mr Jenkins. 'We tried to stop him. We heard him mouthing off at you at the pub. About you being a Norman, an' all. So we followed him. But we were too late. We never thought he'd do something like this!'

Edith walked up close to Scarf and stared into his bloodshot eyes. 'Have you done anything to my son?' she demanded.

'Nah!' he sneered. 'But if I'd seen him, he'd've got the same bloody treatment!'

Fighting back the desire to gouge the smirk off his face with her nails, she peered at him, looking for the slightest flicker of deceit. At length, satisfied that he was telling the truth, she turned away.

'Somebody had better call the police,' she sighed.

'We've already sent for 'em, Miss,' replied Mr Jenkins. 'What we need now is somewhere to put him?'

Edith pointed to one of the sheds. 'You can lock him in there, if you like.'

'Right, lads, you heard the lady, stick 'im in there.'

As the three locals loosened their hold on him to change their grip, Scarf suddenly lashed out, punching the nearest one in the face and kicking another in the crotch. Breaking free from their grasp, he dashed away down the yard.

'After 'im!' shouted Mr Jenkins. One of them hobbling, and another holding his face, the three men gave chase. 'Don't worry, Miss, we'll catch him!' he promised and ran off after them.

At that moment, Vera came out from the back of the house, holding a piece of paper. 'Edith!' she called, waving it in the air.

'Mum, have you found him yet?'

'No, he's not inside. But he's left a note.'

'What does it say?'

'He's gone to follow Harold!'

*

Leaving the knoll behind them, the Saxon army marched away down the road. At the tail-end of the column of regular soldiers came a motley collection of local volunteers carrying wooden staves and farm tools, laughing and chatting among themselves and singing ribald songs.

From his hiding place behind a bush at the side of the road, Edmund watched them go past. He reached down and picked up a handful of earth, rubbing it lightly over his chin to make it look like stubble. Then, with a small bag and a blanket roll over his shoulder, and a long screwdriver stuck in his belt, he stepped out, head down, from behind the bush and joined in, unnoticed, at the end of the column.

⁘

It was as if I were Harold, watching, disembodied, hovering unseen overhead. My whole tortured being strained in frantic desperation to reach him, willing him to turn around, but it was no use. I was invisible, powerless to save a son from being led to certain death!

In soundless, impotent terror, I cried out his name—*Edmund! Edmund!*—but he couldn't hear. The fear of losing him overwhelmed me. Edith would never forgive me! Already crushed by the agonising straitjacket of our own estrangement, my heart was about to break. Thrashing about until I could stand it no longer, I wrenched myself free, out of that sucking sinkhole of guilt, and flew upwards into the dark.

Like detritus left by the ebbing tide sweeping back from a stony beach, I re-emerged once more as myself, spread-eagled on the shingle of my bed, with the skim of reality washing over me, shivering in the shallows of consciousness, rubbing at the sore beside my eye.

PART FOUR

23

As my anguish receded, I lay there, barely breathing, slowly making contact with the here and now. After a while, I could hear the stirring anthems of opposing soccer fans singing at the top of their voices coming from the television, their massed choirs ebbing and surging on the tide of play, rising and falling amid an unrelenting cacophony of ferocious shouting and booing.

Summoning a burst of energy and opening my eyes, I pushed myself up and stretched out towards the end of the bed to grab hold of the covers, which I'd thrown off at some point during the night. For a moment, I paused, struggling to take in the match on the screen. Bombarding each other with cynical fouls and bone-crunching tackles, the two teams were straining in desperation for a breakthrough.

All around the ground, rival supporters were yelling and screaming their war cries, their passions soaring to the heights of hope, only to come crashing down again in anger and despair. There was still no score.

All the strength drained out of me, and with a desolate moan I threw myself back on the pillow. Pulling the covers up around my ears, I huddled over into a foetal position and sank one last time into the maelstrom.

⁝⊹

Out in the mid-morning sunlight, the various sections of the Norman army were rehearsing their tactics in preparation for the coming battle.

Squadrons of cavalry roared about the wide grassy paddock on their motorbikes, while lines of infantrymen formed up, broke apart, and then reformed, co-ordinating their movements. Troops were deploying this way and that, some doing marching drill, others engaging in swordplay, and still others, both mounted and on foot, practising their spear work against straw-filled dummies.

Off to one side, companies of archers were bundling up their arrows and firing at targets, while around the old fence line now demolished by the invaders, in front of a sea of tents stretching away across the plain in three directions, the smoke of numerous cooking fires wafted up, where armour was being polished and weapons sharpened.

Under the watchful eye of a bull-necked sergeant major, two infantry companies were holding a mock battle, with one side, wearing red sashes, attacking another wearing blue. All of a sudden, he blew a shrill blast on his whistle. 'Red company break off!' he roared. 'Fall back. Run!'

At his command, the red side gave up their attack and, turning away as one, rushed back past him, many laughing and chatting as they went.

'Wipe those smiles off your faces, you 'orrible ignoramuses!' the sergeant major called out loudly. 'You're meant to be frightened! You 'ear me? And that goes for you, too, Kingston!' he added, as a lithe, handsome black Jamaican went sauntering past. 'Move it!'

Kingston flashed him a wary smile. 'Yeah, right, Sergeant Major.'

The sergeant major snapped his attention back to the blue company. 'Right, you lot, start chasing 'em!' he bellowed. With a grunt of satisfaction, he watched the group charge off in pursuit of the reds. After a few moments, he cupped his hands and yelled after the fleeing men. 'Red company...wait for it... now turn!'

With that, the red company spun round and headed back towards the blues. As they did so, the sergeant major shouted across to a waiting squadron of mounted knights. 'Now the cavalry...cha-a-arge!'

There was an answering roar of engines as the knights surged across the paddock on their motorbikes to attack the blue company from behind, catching them in a pincer movement.

Meanwhile, gathered together on a low rise at the edge of the field, Duke William stood with Bishop Odo, Baron Fitzosborne, Taillefer, and the two Generals, observing the manoeuvres. Behind them, rising from a thorny bush, an old wooden signpost pointed the way to *Hastings, eight miles*.

'I like the look of that one,' the Duke said, indicating the mock battle between the reds and blues. 'What's the password for it, Odo? The last round-up?' he chuckled.

'Very funny, Billy, very funny! No, since this is a holy war we're engaged in, we're using mostly religious titles.' The Bishop consulted a small notebook. 'And that one's called "Bishop's Crook", I believe.'

'"Bishop's Crook"? How apt! Named after yourself, I presume?'

The voice of Taillefer interrupted their laughter. 'There's a rider coming, boss.'

They all turned to see a helmeted figure approaching fast on a motorbike from the opposite direction. It was Iko. He rode up to them and stopped, leaving his engine running.

'King Harold has arrived, my Lord,' he called out, with an eager smile.

'Ah, at last!' Duke William answered. 'Come along, gentlemen. Let's go and take a look at him.' He gave Iko an angry look. 'This *pretender* to my crown!'

They all mounted up and, following Iko, powered away across open country. Soon, after climbing a ridge, they entered a long, dark stretch of pine forest. Making their way through the trees as quietly as they could, on the Duke's signal they dismounted and proceeded on foot towards the perimeter.

Halting in a line at the edge of the trees, their presence well concealed by the foliage, they stared up at the low hill lying before them. Bordered along each side by an unbroken thicket of trees and scrub, its gently rising slope led up to a wide, flat summit in three, deep, undulating, natural steps. Saxon troops could be seen milling about at the top.

'He is stopping zere,' growled Baron Fitzosborne.

'A wise move,' Duke William nodded. 'I'll have his guts for garters if he tries to come down.'

'They're digging in,' said Taillefer.

The Duke looked around, pondering the terrain. 'Hm. So this is where it's going to be.'

Bishop Odo let out a whistle. 'That's gonna be one helluva nut to crack, Billy!'

'Damn!' Duke William growled. 'Anyone know the name of this place?'

As they all shook their heads, Taillefer pulled an ordinance survey map from his shoulder bag, spread it out on the ground, and knelt down beside it. 'It's called Senlac Hill, boss,' he said, locating the spot and pointing to it with his finger.

'Senlac?' the Duke mused. 'It's got a familiar ring to it.'

'Sen...lac. San...lac. Sounds kinda French to me,' the Bishop drawled.

'You're dead right, it does!' Duke William exclaimed. 'Sang...lac,' it means "a lake of blood!"'

'Holy shit!' Bishop Odo said, crossing himself with the sign of Xzyatan.

The Duke turned and studied the hill, his eyes fixed on the summit, searching for his adversary but unable to find him. 'And that,' he murmured to himself, 'is exactly what it will be.'

*

The top of the slope was a hive of activity, the thin morning air resounding to the chunk of pick-axes and the thump of sledgehammers as the Saxon army erected barricades along the front of each level, with portable gates inserted and lashed into place to allow troops to move in and out.

Among the soldiers constructing the outer barrier of sharpened wooden stakes, many of them stripped to the waist and sweating profusely, Edmund paused from digging a hole to wipe the perspiration from his face. He stared back up the hill, past the middle defence line of roped-together logs and branches, hoping to catch a glimpse of anyone he knew. Seeing no one, he hurried back to work.

Meanwhile, on the flat summit, within the enclosure formed by the final barricade of chain-linked logs, branches, baggage wagons, and bicycles, officers' tents were being set up and food prepared, while armourers sat at their grindstones sharpening a pile of axes and swords.

In the centre of the space, unfurling in the gentle breeze, was the royal standard—a large, green boxing kangaroo on a yellow background bordered by a yellow and green fringe, with long, hanging tassels.

At the rear of the enclosure, Harold, Gurth, and Leofwine stood together inspecting the back of the hill, which was cut away in a sheer, unassailable, bramble-covered escarpment with a single precarious track leading down to the ravine below.

'They won't be climbing that in a hurry,' Gurth whistled.

'No, the only way's straight up the front,' Harold agreed.

At that moment, Haco entered through one of the gates and called out to them. 'Harold, the Duke's sent a messenger.'

'Right-o. Thanks, Haco.'

'Maybe he's come to say goodbye?' suggested Leofwine, as they followed after Haco.

While work continued along the top of the slope, they made their way down from the summit to join Bernard and Stavros among the crowd of men gathered at the outer palisade. Further down the hill, mounted on motorbikes with their engines ticking over, were the envoy, who had delivered the Duke's declaration of war, and Iko.

'You again!' Harold called out. 'All right, what d'you want now?'

'Lord Harold,' the envoy replied, 'for the last time, Duke William demands that you keep your promise and give him his rightful crown.'

'You know the answer to that one already, mate,' Harold replied, amid a chorus of derisive laughter from the defenders. 'The crown's not mine to give.'

'We want Harold, not the Duke!' a soldier cried out, accompanied by a brief spate of chanting Harold's name.

Harold smiled and gave a helpless shrug. 'You see?' he shouted above an ensuing burst of cheering. 'What else?'

'Next, Duke William offers to withdraw his forces if you agree to let our most holy father, the Grand Pontiff, judge between you?'

There was loud booing from the Saxon troops.

'From what I hear, the Grand Pontiff has already given you his blessing,' Harold answered scornfully. 'I reject both his biased judgement and his right to decide. Is that all?'

The envoy gestured towards Iko. 'This knight has one more offer to make. But first, hear the words of the Grand Pontiff!'

As the noise of the crowd abated, he unrolled a small scroll and began to read out loud in a harsh, ringing voice.

'Harold, O pitiful shadow of Godwin, you are cursed! You have broken your most solemn oath and stolen the rightful inheritance of our true son, William. Henceforth, upon you and all who help you, shall fall the divine and dreadful retribution of the Great God, Xzyatan! Your wealth and your loved ones shall be possessed and enjoyed by others, your manhood shall wither, your bones shall melt in their pockets, your bodies shall disintegrate into brief flurries of powder, and your souls shall evaporate! Your names shall become a byword for hatred and scorn! You are henceforth excommunicated from the ranks of the living and are now nothing more than the walking husks of men, to be cut down, eradicated, and forgotten! Repent now or face eternal damnation!'

By then, all work had stopped on the barricades as the soldiers gathered to listen. The Saxons were stunned. For a long moment there was complete silence.

Eventually, with an incredulous grin, Leofwine broke the spell. 'Our bones shall melt in their pockets?' he reflected with audible distaste. 'Yuck!'

'And my manhood'll wither, mate!' Stavros chuckled across to him.

With that, those nearby began to laugh as well. Then, like a rippling wave, it spread throughout the army until, along with mounting boos and whistles, it rose into a tumult. The envoy's face grew livid.

'On yer bike!' Bernard shouted at him with derision.

Iko slowly rode forward.

'Sir Iko,' Harold called out to him, 'you keep strange company!'

'Lord Harold...' Iko replied, his words barely audible above the din.

Harold raised his arm. 'Quiet!' he commanded.

'Lord Harold,' Iko began again, as the noise died down. 'Fully anticipating your reply, Duke William has commanded me to make you one last offer. In order to avoid unnecessary bloodshed, and to demonstrate his humanity, he is prepared to meet you in single combat for the Saxon throne. Will you accept?'

'No way!' yelled Gurth. 'Two men can't decide the fate of millions!'

'This is a war between worlds!' Bernard roared.

'You've taken on the whole ants' nest here, mate!' bellowed Stavros.

'I'm sorry, Sir Iko,' Harold replied. 'Much as I'd like to, I have to refuse. You can tell your Duke to do his worst. We stand here, ready to defend our freedom and halt your invasion!'

*

The night was cold and still. Somewhere, out in the misty darkness, an owl hooted. Making as little noise as possible, leaving the hazy lights and muffled sounds of the Saxon camp behind them in the distance, Harold, Gurth, Leofwine, Haco, and Bernard freewheeled their bicycles down the edge of the hill.

As they went by, two sentries appeared like wraiths out of the bushes at their side. On seeing who it was, they saluted, while the party glided on past into the undergrowth at the foot of the slope.

Riding in single file, the five headed away through the forest, the sound of their passage deadened by the blanket of fog. Soon, up ahead, they saw a flickering red glow shining through the pines, growing stronger and brighter as they approached. At length, they reached the end of the trees and dismounted.

Crouch-running forward, then crawling the last few metres, they threw themselves flat on the ground at the edge of the ridge. Pulling out small pairs of binoculars, they peered down at the Norman camp.

Below them, stretching out across the plain in all directions, lay a vast tent city, divided into sections by bright, torch-lit aisles. Walking along these were priests in white surplices, dispensing blessings to the bareheaded knights kneeling in front of their tents on either side of them and to the crush of ordinary soldiers filling the lanes between.

All of a sudden, to a fanfare of conch shell blasts, the tall figure of Bishop Odo, wearing a gold mitre and flowing white robes, appeared from a large pavilion at the far end of the central avenue. Followed by a retinue of priests with their hands clasped in prayer, he stepped forward onto the long, red carpet laid out between the ranks of kneeling men.

With the glittering gold symbol of the snake-entwined swords held high up behind him on a pole, and with two priests swinging golden incense burners ahead of him, he proceeded down the line. Keeping pace beside him was an altar boy, carrying an open chest full of gold coins.

As the Bishop came to each upturned, rapturous face, he reached into the casket, took out a coin, and, mouthing a blessing, slipped it onto the knight's outstretched, waiting tongue.

Up on the ridge, Harold gave the signal to depart. Putting away their binoculars, the group slipped back into the forest. After retracing their route, a short time later they rode out from the trees at the bottom of the hill and started back up towards the Saxon camp. Soon, as the way became steeper, they dismounted and continued to climb on foot, pushing their bicycles.

'That was freaky!' Haco whispered, with a shiver.

'Fanatics always are, mate,' Gurth's grim reply came out of the darkness beside him.

They all trudged on up the slope in silence, pondering what they had just witnessed and what kind of mindset they were up against. At last, in the distance, the welcoming gleam of numerous campfires sparkled like diamonds through the mist.

'Ah, look!' Leofwine said fondly. 'Our little home on the hill!'

A short time later, to called greetings, the scouting party reached the top and re-entered the lines through one of the portable gates in the outer barricade.

Getting up from his seat on a log beside a nearby fire, Stavros approached them, clutching a bottle of whiskey. 'You men, take the bikes!' he barked to some soldiers standing watching.

'Stavros, me old mate, what's that you've got there?' Leofwine asked brightly, as he handed over his mount.

'Just something to keep the cold out, mate.' Stavros passed the bottle to him. 'Go easy, Leo, it's all we've got.'

Leofwine took a swig and shuddered with euphoria. 'Aah!'

'Don't let the men get too drunk, Stavros,' Gurth said, with a grin. 'We'll need cool brains and steady hands tomorrow.'

'That's right,' added Bernard. 'Believe me, mate, the Normans are going to be stone-cold deadly sober in the morning.'

'No worries, Admiral, I'll keep an eye on 'em,' Stavros nodded, taking back the bottle. 'I've got the wisdom of the bull, mate. I know when to lock horns and I know when to stamp my hoof!'

'You can count on us, Harold!' a soldier called out of the darkness, echoed by shouts of support from those around him.

'Good on ya, lads!' Harold answered. 'But off to bed soon, you hear? Stavros needs his beauty sleep!'

With a laugh, the men settled back around their campfires. Unnoticed among them, at the edge of the light, Edmund watched in silent yearning as his father and the others walked away up the hill and onto the summit.

Following in a line after Harold, they crossed the inner enclosure. Nodding to the groups of officers seated around their glowing braziers as they went past, they approached the royal tent. The two sentries guarding it stood aside. Returning their salutes, Harold stepped in under the awning and pulled open the flap. They all entered.

Removing his travel bag from one of the two camp beds along the walls of the tent and putting it on the floor, Harold reached over to turn up the small oil lamp standing on the low table between them, then knelt down and undid the straps.

'Well, if they can, so can we!' he grinned, pulling out a bottle of whisky and some paper cups.

As Gurth, Bernard, and Haco sat down on one of the beds and Leofwine positioned himself at the far end of the other, he passed them the cups and the bottle, and then sat down himself. When they had all poured themselves a shot, he raised his cup.

'Cheers! Here's to us!'

'Good health!' Gurth toasted back.

'I'll drink to that!' Bernard smiled.

'Right, well we're obviously up against a load of nutters, then,' Leofwine said with a caustic chuckle, sipping his drink.

'They may be nutters, Leo, but they'll come at us with one mind tomorrow,' cautioned Gurth.

Leofwine nodded. 'I thought Odo was in good form, though.'

'I'd like to charge down at that bastard right now!' Bernard growled.

'I know what you mean,' Haco agreed.

Harold looked at them and shook his head. 'If we feel that way now, imagine what it'll be like after they've been at us all day tomorrow? It's exactly that urge to attack that we have to guard against during the battle. We must keep to our ranks. Remember Hardrada. The moment the Vikings left the high ground, they threw it away. All we have to do is hold these positions and we can't lose.'

'It's still not too late for you to leave, Harold,' offered Gurth. 'We can stay and deal with William while you get a second army together?'

'Gurth's right, Harold,' said Leofwine. 'We only have to outlast him tomorrow and then time's on our side.'

'The spies say he's scuttled his ships and set them alight,' Haco put in. 'So, it's all or nothing for him. He's got nowhere to run.'

'One throw of the dice and he's ours to pick off at will!' Leofwine grinned.

'What d'you reckon?' urged Gurth. 'Leave him to us.'

'Come on, Gurth, we've been through all this before,' Harold answered. 'If I leave, people'll say I'm a coward. Then there won't be any second army. Anyway, why stretch it out when we can finish the job in one day?'

'You're as stubborn as Dad ever was.'

'You don't think he'd have left, do you?'

'No,' Gurth smiled and gave a sigh. 'He wouldn't have missed this for quids.'

At that moment, somewhere out among the troops, a melancholy guitar began to play.

Harold took the bottle and, leaning across, topped up their drinks. 'I give you a toast…To victory and home!'

They raised their cups. 'To victory and home!'

A gentle quiet fell on them all as they sat back, listening to the soft, sad music.

Outside, among a group of volunteers seated around a campfire near the inner barricade, a young farm labourer playing the guitar began to sing, his voice filled with wistful longing. Around him, his comrades stared into the flames, passing a bottle between them.

I'm just sitting here waiting
I wait for the morning to come
They say then I must start hating
But I don't hate anyone

Further down the slope on the second tier, a volunteer lay in his sleeping bag, huddled up against the cold, trying to sleep. He rolled over and pulled the bag up around his ears.

Dear Mother, please stop your grieving
Your baby's soon coming home
One more night and I'll be leaving
Then we won't feel so alone

On the edge of the camp, hard up against the outer palisade, a veteran lay on his back under a blanket, smoking a cigarette and gazing up at the vast, starlit, moonless sky.

The campfires round me are burning
The stars in the heavens are bright
Oh, how for my sweetheart I'm yearning
I wish I were home tonight
Home tonight

Inside the tent, as the song ended and the final chords floated away into the night, there was a long, reflective silence. At length, Harold coughed, bringing them all back to reality.

With a tired laugh, Bernard pushed himself up from the camp bed. 'That's it for me, then. I'm away to my bed. Thanks for the drink, Your Majesty.'

'You're welcome, mate,' Harold smiled as they shook hands.

Bernard nodded to the others. 'And I'll see you all bright and early in the morning.'

'Going off to dream about Gladys, eh?' Gurth chuckled.

'Yeah, I reckon!' Bernard grinned. "Night.'

'Sleep well, Bern,' said Haco.

'And don't keep the men awake with your snoring!' Leofwine called after him as he left the tent.

As their laughter died down, Haco followed suit. 'Well, I think I'll just take a stroll around the lines. Thanks, Harold, it's been an interesting evening.'

'That it has. Goodnight, Haco,' Harold said warmly, reaching up and gripping his hand. 'Make sure I'm woken at dawn, will you?'

'Yep. No worries. 'Night.'

'See ya, mate,' said Leofwine. With a wave, Haco went out.

A few moments later, Gurth rose to his feet, stretching and yawning. 'Well, I may as well turn in, too, I suppose.'

'Good idea,' Harold yawned in response and stood up. 'We've got a long day ahead of us.'

'Do you realise, brother,' Gurth said as they hugged each other, 'that after tomorrow, for virtually the first time in our whole lives there'll be peace? Real peace! No more Algar. No more Hardrada. And no more Normans. I wonder what it'll be like?'

'It'll be great,' Harold laughed. 'But don't stay up half the night thinking about it. We've got to get there first, don't forget.'

'I know. Still, it's something to look forward to, isn't it? Coming, Leo?'

'Oh, right.' Leofwine drained the last few drops from his cup and stood up. 'If you insist.' He looked longingly at the bottle of whisky and sighed. 'Ah, well! 'night, Harold.'

Harold smiled and embraced him. 'Goodnight, Leo. I'm counting on you to keep the men's spirits up tomorrow, mate.'

'That's a relief!'

'Seriously, I'm so glad I've got you both with me,' Harold said, opening the tent flap for them. 'To see us through this.'

Gurth looked at Leofwine. 'Oh, great! And we were counting on him!'

'I dunno, some king, eh?' Leofwine tutted and shook his head, as he stepped through.

With further mutterings and their arms around each other, the pair wandered off into the night. Harold smiled after them for a few moments, then closed the flap.

*

It was the middle of the night. All was quiet. The tent was in darkness. Harold lay asleep, partially dressed, under a blanket on one of the camp beds. There was a rustling at the entrance and the sound of the flap being pulled back. Voices whispered, followed by the shuffling of feet. A hand reached out and shook him by the shoulder. Harold opened his eyes in alarm.

'No!...What?...Who is it?'

'Harold!' Edith called softly, leaning over him.

'Edith! What the...? How did you get in?'

'Gurth let me through.'

The bed creaked as Harold sat up. There was the scratch of a match as he lit the oil lamp, then turned it down low. He rubbed the sleep from his eyes. 'What time is it?'

'About half-past two.'

'Darling, what are you doing here? You could've been killed!'

'I had to see you, Harold!'

'You're not going to try and change my mind again, are you?' Harold yawned. 'It's too late.' Seeing the exhaustion on her face, he was suddenly concerned. 'Edith, what is it?'

'You travel so fast...' she said in a faltering voice.

'Here, sit on the bed.' He helped her onto the other camp bed and sat down next to her, putting his arm around her shoulders. 'What's the matter, darling? What's happened?'

Edith leant against him, her eyes watering. 'Oh God, Harold! Gladys has been murdered!'

'What?' he gasped. 'How?'

She shook her head in anger. 'Some thug. Because she helped me. Because I'm a Norman!'

Harold held her against him and kissed the side of her head. 'Oh, my love, I'm so sorry!'

Edith pulled away, fighting back the tears. 'But that's not why I came. It's Edmund! He's run off!'

'What do you mean? Where to?'

'Here! With you!' she cried. 'Out there with your bloody army, sharpening his sword for the kill!'

'Oh, no!' Harold groaned. 'He said he wanted to, but...'

'He's just a boy! He'll be killed! Well, don't just sit there, Harold, we've got to go and find him!'

Harold jumped to his feet. 'Edith, it's the middle of the night! What d'you want me to do, wake everybody up?'

'If you have to, *yes!*'

'I can't do that! I can't. The men have to sleep. Otherwise we'll lose!'

'Oh, this is horrible!' she moaned, burying her face in her hands.

He knelt down by her side. 'Darling, don't worry. I'll find him. We'll all start looking for him at dawn. Gurth, Leo, Bernard, everyone.'

Edith lowered her hands and stared at him. 'Everyone?' she laughed bitterly. 'What're you going to do, pass around his description? Tell them all that he's your son? The king's bastard! While you're still married to Aldyth?'

'No. You're right,' Harold nodded. 'Anyone with any sympathies for her and her family would desert. Anyway, there isn't time. We'll just have to comb the hill from end to end during the battle.'

'Oh, Harold!' she sobbed in despair.

'Don't worry, my love. We'll keep on searching all day if we have to. The veterans'll protect him. They won't let anything happen to a boy that young. He'll be doing the running and carrying behind the lines.' He took hold of her hand. 'I'll know where to find him, darling.'

He watched as the pitch of her emotions relented and her body unwound in resignation. 'And when I do,' he smiled, 'where do you want me to send him?'

'There's a farm up on the next hill...'

'I know it. Then, that's where he'll go. Now, come on, lie down. You must get some rest.'

With reluctance, Edith allowed Harold to help her back on the bed. He pulled off his own blanket and, laying it over her, sat down on the edge. As he stroked the hair from her forehead, she reached up and grabbed his hand. 'It will be all right, won't it, Harold?' she pleaded, her eyes shining in desperation. 'Tell me it will!'

'It will, darling' he said, with a confidence they both needed to believe. 'Don't worry, we'll find him.'

She gripped his hand more tightly. 'And with us?'

'We'll be fine!' Harold grinned, masking his uncertainty, gazing down at her with tender longing. She reached up and touched his cheek. He bent forward and they kissed. Hovering in doubt, on the surface of her lips, neither of them sure what it meant or where to take it, and only willing to go as far as Edith allowed, but yearning to hold her, to be her love again, for things to be as they had been before, the instant he felt her hold back he pulled away.

'I love you,' he smiled, with an understanding sigh. 'Now sleep,' he whispered, and placed a gentle kiss on her forehead. As she closed her eyes, he stood up and went over to the opposite bed. He sat down on it, then leaned across and blew out the lamp.

*

After what seemed like only a moment, Harold woke up with a start. He rolled over and looked at the other bed. In the faint, grey light permeating the tent he could see the crumpled blanket lying on it, but Edith was gone. He sat up, staring around in consternation.

Just then, there was a knock at the entrance and the flap was pulled back. Haco entered, holding a mug of tea.

'Harold,' he called quietly. 'It's time.'

24

As soon as the sun was up, Leofwine and Haco set off to search among the troops for Edmund. Looking this way and that, they made their way along the top of the hill, peering at the faces of the soldiers sitting eating their breakfast around the cooking fires.

Some nodded and smiled up at them, biting happily into hot jam donuts from brown paper bags. Leaving the enclosure through one of the gates in the inner barricade, they climbed down onto the next level.

Further across the slope, Bernard squeezed his body through the crowd of men preparing their positions on the middle step. Every now and then, he stretched up on his toes, staring over their heads in search of Edmund.

Unseen among them, Edmund spotted him coming. He bent down and pretended to lace up his boots as Bernard drew level, looking around in all directions, then pushed on past. Edmund rose to his feet again and stared after him.

Meanwhile, milling about in the early morning light, out on the slope in front of the first barricade, the main body of experienced troops were forming themselves into a giant wedge. Stavros was standing apart from them, yelling commands.

'You blokes in the middle at the back, move forward!' he shouted. 'No! Not you, mate. Them!...No! *Them!*...No-o-o!' He shook his curly black mane in exasperation. 'Ghaargh! You've got to do everything yer bloody self around here!' With an angry growl, he strode in amongst them.

Walking along together outside the front of the palisade, Harold and Gurth paused to watch the preparations, at the same time scanning the ranks above them for Edmund.

'Are you going to tell Bernard?' Gurth asked.

'What? About Gladys? How can I?' Harold sighed.

'No, I guess not.'

Harold halted, once again searching the faces of the soldiers closest to him behind the bank of wooden stakes, and of the sea of men rising up the slope beyond.

'Damn it! I can't see him anywhere.'

'Don't worry, mate, he'll turn up.' Gurth stared at the sky. 'Come on, Harold, we've got to get ready.'

'Yeah,' Harold nodded, giving one last look around. 'Yeah, you're right.'

*

Under the spacious awning of Duke William's tent, Baron Fitzosborne, Taillefer, and the two Generals, all dressed in long coats of mail with their helmets tucked under their arms, stood at attention, watching their leader finish his breakfast.

'Mmm!' the Duke growled with content, gnawing at a small bone. He smacked his greasy lips together. 'Quail! A breakfast fit for a king!'

They all smiled as he bit off the last morsel of meat and tossed the bone away over his shoulder. He sucked the juice from his fingers and waved them in the air. Instantly, a servant stepped forward with a towel and a copper bowl, half-filled with rose water. Rinsing his hands and drying them, then throwing the used towel over the bowl, he turned to the group standing around him.

'Very well, gentlemen, let us commence. Oh, and Fitz...' he called over his shoulder as they all followed him outside, 'I want you to make sure that everyone's properly dressed. Ties to be worn throughout the day.'

Baron Fitzosborne studied the sheer blue sky. 'It is going to get very hot, my Lord.'

'Hm. All right, then, they may be undone, but not removed.'

Duke William strode over to his motorbike, held respectfully for him by an attendant. Taking hold of the handlebar and lifting the helmet from the saddle, he swung his leg across and sat down.

'Remember, gentlemen,' he smiled at them, putting it on and doing up the chin strap, 'the eyes of history are upon us. When future generations of schoolboys look back on this battle, I want it plainly seen just which side the riff-raff were on!'

They all mounted up. With the Norman battle flag—a huge, silver, clenched fist emerging from a giant metallic cog, on a royal blue field—floating in the breeze above the pavilion behind them, they rode away along the waiting avenue of cheering mounted knights. Accepting their accolade with a laugh, the Duke stood up on the footrests and stretched out his arm in salute.

At the end of the line, they came to a low, rectangular grassy mound overlooking the open space in the middle of the camp. Duke William dismounted and, followed by his officers, climbed up the slope to the top. Waiting in the centre was Bishop Odo, standing beneath the Grand Pontiff's 'Banner of Power'—a gleaming gold, cruciform emblem of Xzyatan, studded with gemstones, on a pink background. As the Duke strode across and embraced him, a great cheer went up from the troops assembled below.

Turning towards them, Duke William stepped forward to the front of the mound, where a microphone stand had been set up. He gripped it with both hands and, with an imperious smile, looked down at the lines of cheering infantrymen arrayed before him. While the cavalry took up their positions along either side, he tapped the microphone and raised his hand for quiet.

'Normans!' he called out to them. 'This is your day!'

A surging tide of acclaim rolled back at him from the troops.

'The land is yours for the taking!'

Another huge cheer soared up over the parade ground. As it abated, there was a buzz of anticipation.

'But understand this,' he went on, 'even while you take possession of it, you have come here for one reason and one reason only...' Behind him, Bishop Odo gave a wink to Baron Fitzosborne, who flashed him a knowing smile in return. 'To cleanse the world of this final bastion of lawlessness and arrogance!'

The soldiers gazed up at him in rapt attention.

'The Saxons believe they can resist the universal tide of discipline and competition. They cannot!' he shouted. 'They think they can defy the might of Xzyatan!' He clenched his teeth. 'We shall not let them!'

A deep hum of agreement came from the ranks.

'Even as I speak, they are up there mocking us, calling us invaders and pirates, saying that we've got no right to be here. But I tell you this, there is only one world, and one world only... and it belongs to us!'

With manic enthusiasm, their ferocious, self-assured cries filled the air. The Duke gave a smile of approval and looked around at them, staring into their eyes, nodding with satisfaction as the noise subsided.

'The Norman way is the only way,' he continued. 'By taking what's ours by right of strength, we are true to our animal nature. In seeking the supreme nobility of mankind, through conquest we spread the light of civilization. You are the champions of the highest power!'

There was a pregnant silence. He looked down at their spellbound faces.

'The resistance of Harold, who dares to call himself king,' he sneered, 'is nothing more than the impudent stand of a sea snail against the pounding might of the ocean. He is doomed to failure!'

A tirade of scornful shouts and confident laughter rang out.

As it died away, Duke William grinned at them like a conspirator. 'But you, my trusty warriors, are due for your reward!' There was an expectant hush. 'Destroy Harold and, I promise you, you shall inherit the kingdom with me.' He leant forward, narrowing his eyes, tempting and conniving, sharing the moment with them.

'And what a kingdom it is! Wealth and an easy way of life for you and your descendants forever!' He pointed into the distance, beyond the forest of pine trees. 'All you have to do is climb to the top of that hill with me...and take it!'

Yelling with ear-splitting adulation and ecstatic fervour, the Normans pumped their fists into the air, chanting, 'William! William! William!'

'Now, form up!' the Duke barked at them, his iron voice commanding their instant obedience. 'We have work to do!' He thrust out his arm once more towards the summit, his face beaming with demonic possession. 'In the name of unstoppable progress...*go to it!*'

*

The tent flap was pulled open from inside and Harold appeared in the doorway. Ducking under the low awning, he stepped out onto the sunlit summit. Beneath a cream, mailed flak jacket, he was wearing full cricket whites, boots, and pads, and carrying his long-bladed double-headed axe, padded gloves, and green visored helmet in his hands.

On seeing him, the Saxon troops, gathered in a deep line outside the inner barricade, gave a rapturous cheer. With a broad grin, he raised his axe to them in salute.

Waiting in front of the tent, dressed in similar white battle gear, were Gurth, Leofwine, Haco, Bernard, and Stavros. To continuous cheering, they followed him across the enclosure and stationed themselves below him as he set down his load and climbed up onto one of the wagons to face his men. Standing erect, Harold smiled and lifted his arms, while the soldiers pressed in closer, eager to hear his words, gazing up at him in admiration.

'My friends!' he called out. 'Mates! Old hands and new recruits! Welcome to the greatest day of your lives!' With a laugh, his powerful voice rose above the ensuing wave of excited cheering. 'Win or lose, live or die, today you become heroes!'

A roar of approval went up. As it finally settled, he pointed towards the bottom of the hill. 'Down there, Duke William and his gang of murdering thieves are preparing to attack us. And you and I are all that stands between them and the destruction of our land!'

There were furious growls and a broadside of defiant shouts.

'Make no mistake about it, their one intention is to rob us of everything we hold dear. Our easy-going way of life, our spirit of community, and our freedom to speak out against injustice.'

'Just let 'em try!' a soldier shouted, amid a general rumbling of anger.

Harold lifted his hand for quiet. 'If they can, they'll take away our most precious possessions, the time to dream and the room to move. They'll choke them off and cut them up to serve their private interests. They'll make every man compete against his neighbour to survive. They'll turn our homes into battlegrounds and our children into slaves!'

He looked around at their upturned faces. Every eye was intent upon him.

'I won't deceive you, the Normans are strong. But not as strong as us! We have each other and we have this hill. We have the hopes and prayers of our families and loved ones, and of the whole country, behind us. Meanwhile, help is on its way. Earl Morcar is following fast with another army. But we won't need them. By the time they get here, we'll already have finished the job!'

The soldiers all shouted at once, yelling out boastful assertions of future prowess with raucous bravado.

'Don't forget, you're the ones who did the impossible,' Harold called above the hubbub. 'You beat the unbeatable Hardrada!'

A thundering cheer erupted like a volcano. Harold smiled at them, pausing until he could be heard. 'And, down there, I reckon they'll be shitting themselves about that right now!'

There was an answering wave of loud, scathing laughter.

'Only, remember this,' he went on, his tone becoming more serious. 'The Norman way is to divide and rule. And that's what they'll try to do in the battle today. So, stay together. Hold your places. Stick with your mates. No matter what the provocation, no matter how much you're itching to charge at them, don't break your ranks. As long as we keep to the top of this hill and don't let them split us up, there's no way they can win!'

Amid emphatic shouts of agreement, the men looked at each other and nodded. Then they waited, hanging on his every word.

'Just hold on for one day, one day of unshakeable defence, one day of unparalleled courage, one day of untold glory, and then we can go home again, to live in freedom and peace...and be rid of these Normans forever!'

As a tumultuous cheer surged to the sky, he raised his arm once more. 'Let the older ones among you look after the young,' he shouted. 'Let the strong protect the weak. May God bless you all, and good luck...Now, take your positions!'

With a unaminous roar of assent, the troops turned away and spread out along the hill.

*

The Saxon army divided itself into two separate sections. The first, made up of half of the regulars plus the lightly armed local volunteers led by Leofwine and Bernard, took up their positions behind the barricades. Hiding among them was Edmund.

As they had rehearsed, the second, vanguard section, comprised of heavily armed veterans and regulars, gathered themselves into their wedge formation a short way out in front of the defences. Harold, Gurth, Haco, and Stavros marshalled them, shouting instructions. Finally, when all were in position, Harold took his place at the apex. Staring down the slope, he lifted his gloved hand and pulled down the visor of his helmet.

Moments later, with glinting metal and flashes of colour, the Norman army appeared out of the trees at the bottom of the hill in three block battalions. Trumpet blasts sounded in the distance as they formed up and began to advance.

Meanwhile, perched high up on a tree branch at the edge of the battlefield, Eric Braithwaite watched their approach. He spoke quietly into the microphone attached to the cassette recorder strapped across his chest.

'And here come the Normans! Two divisions of cavalry and... no, three divisions of mixed cavalry and infantry. They're coming up the slope! The Saxons have taken up their positions behind the barricades, with the famous wedge formation out in front, protecting them.

'As one might expect, King Harold is standing right at the point! Meanwhile, Duke William is...yes, I can just make him out, there, with his élite cavalry, at the head of the centre division. They seem to be heading straight for the wedge, while the outer two divisions are making beelines for the ends of the barricades. The one on this side should come right past me.'

He leaned over and called down to the ground. 'Lenny? Are you out of sight?'

Lying in the grass near the foot of the tree, Lenny, his long-time assistant—now a freckle-faced young man, still wearing his back-to-front baseball cap—was chewing on a blade of grass and reading a comic. In the undergrowth behind him was his bicycle. He looked up and quickly scanned the surrounding area. 'You bet, Mister Braithwaite,' he called back, and returned to his picture book.

'Good. Well, keep your head down!' Braithwaite lifted the microphone and started to record once more. 'But, wait on, what's this? One of the Normans is riding out ahead of their lines. He's coming this way...It's Taillefer, the Duke's minstrel! And, would you believe it, he's actually singing!'

Out on the slope, Taillefer was steering his motorbike up the side of the hill towards the Saxon lines, waving a golden sword in the air and singing in a jaunty voice, conducting himself as he came.

Po-pom...po-pom...po-pom
Po-pom...po-pom...po-pom

We're Normans and to serve us is your fate
We'll overcome your ignorance and hate

Our mighty iron fist
Makes it futile to resist
This vision of the future we dictate

We're the way you need
The truth to heed
The life to lead
Our noble breed
Is greater than the great!

We are the Normans!
We are the Normans!
We're the chosen ones
You'd better run
Before it's too late!

We are the Normans!

Shouting out the last line of the song, he increased speed and began weaving about provocatively in front of the barricade, at the same time juggling his gleaming sword, spinning it up in the air and catching it by the hilt.

'Come on, you chicken livers!' he taunted. 'Cluck! Cluck!... Cluck! Cluck! Come to Taillefer! Come to Taillefer!'

Almost immediately, one of the gates in the palisade opened and the dashing young captain from the gymnastic display rode out on his bicycle to a great cheer from the Saxon ranks. With spear pointed, he charged down the hill. Taillefer's eyes narrowed in a sardonic smile as he watched him approach.

At the final moment, before they engaged, with almost magical dexterity, he veered out of the way, double-spun his golden sword and, catching it deftly in his fist, slashed him with a backhand across the throat. The captain rolled out of the saddle and crashed to the earth on his back. There was a gasp of amazement and a groan from the barricades, while an ecstatic cheer rose up from the Norman ranks below.

'Is that the best you can do, to send a boy against me?' Taillefer jeered, circling around, still juggling his sword. 'Come to Taillefer! Come to Taillefer! Saxons are yellow! Saxons are yellow!'

With that, another cavalry officer rushed out through the gate on his bicycle and, yelling in fury, bore down on him. Leaving it to the very last second, when the Saxon was almost upon him, all of a sudden Taillefer swung off to the side, his wheels spinning in the dirt. Swiftly twirling his sword once more, he reached out and stabbed the man in the back as he went past, sending him tumbling in a backward somersault. His neck cracked as he hit the turf, and he lay still.

Taillefer turned away and, with an exaggerated, contemptuous shrug, headed off down the hill, his loud guffaws floating back over his shoulder.

'Hey, Norman!' a voice suddenly shouted behind him. 'Don't run away! Come to Leofwine! Come to Leofwine!'

Taillefer wheeled round and stared. Leofwine sat mounted in the gateway, bare-headed and holding a spear. With a sneer and a booming, incredulous laugh, the Norman started back up the slope, juggling his sword, while Leofwine lowered his spear and charged.

With gathering momentum, they hurtled towards each other, drawing closer and closer. Once again, an instant before impact, Taillefer swerved out of the way and stopped dead. Spinning his sword in the air and catching it, he slashed out sideways.

Leofwine was prepared. Ducking down and flattening himself along the crossbar, at the same time changing his grip on his spear, as the blade passed harmlessly over his head he slammed on his brakes and skidded to a halt. He lunged out and sunk the spear into Taillefer's side.

Face to face, motionless, Taillefer looked down in stunned disbelief at the spear shaft embedded in his waist and the blood seeping out between the links of his mailed coat.

'Try and juggle that one, Norman!' Leofwine snarled.

There was a ripping sound as he rammed the blade in deeper and then yanked it out. Taillefer stared at him in surprise. His eyes rolled back and, with a gurgling moan, he slowly keeled over and fell to the ground.

A great cheer erupted from the defenders as Leofwine wheeled in a circle, gazing down at Taillefer's lifeless body. He stopped beside it and leant down to pick up the golden sword. Then, waving it above his head, he rode out across the slope.

Beyond the reach of Norman bowshot, he dismounted. Laying his bicycle on the ground, he drew back his arm and, with a scornful yell, hurled the bloodstained weapon towards the approaching army. With a lazy *whomp...whomp...whomp*, it looped through the air in a high arc, before soaring down and landing with a *thud* in the unprotected chest of a knight in the front rank, who collapsed with a clatter of metal from his motorcycle.

'There's payment for the entertainment!' Leofwine shouted, shaking his fist.

Climbing back into the saddle, he turned and rode back up the hill towards the jubilant Saxon lines.

*

On the neighbouring hilltop, Saxon women, children, and old men were gathered in the sloping front yard of a ramshackle, weatherboard farmhouse. A gaggle of young boys wearing cardboard and tin foil armour zig-zagged around their legs, fighting a running battle with wooden swords. Off to one side, the farmer and an old priest stood talking together, nodding their heads in sage agreement as they reflected on the situation.

Standing nearby, a young boy and his mother watched a vendor coming up the track towards them. He was pushing a handcart, decorated with lettering and a mouthwatering picture advertising *Hot Jam Donuts*.

The vendor drew to a halt beside the front gate. Puffing from his exertion, he pulled out a large spotted handkerchief and dabbed at his chubby, perspiring face.

'Oh, Mummy, can I have a donut?' the young boy begged with excitement.

The vendor smiled and shook his head. 'Sorry, son, they're all gone. The King's army bought the lot!'

The farmer scowled in amazement and took an angry pace forward. 'You mean you sold them to our own men?'

'That's right, mate. Can't fight on empty stomachs, can they?' the vendor answered with a cheerful grin.

'You bastard! You're worse than the bloody Normans! You should've given 'em to them!'

'Fair crack of the whip, mate! A bloke's got to earn a crust, hasn't he? I've got a family to feed!'

The farmer spat on the ground in disgust, then turned and walked away, shaking his head.

'What was happening when you left?' the priest called out with concern. 'Has the battle started yet?'

'Reckon it must have by now,' the vendor nodded. 'They were just squaring up to each other as I was leaving.'

'Anyway, why aren't you out there fighting with them?' demanded the boy's mother.

The vendor shook his head and patted his thigh. 'It's me gammy leg, missus...It's got a bone in it!'

Leaving the woman open-mouthed and speechless, he winked at the young boy and pushed on with his cart.

Further along the low picket fence, standing apart from the others, was Edith. 'What about the King?' she asked anxiously, as he went past. 'Where was he?'

'Down the front at the head of his men,' the vendor answered. 'If I was him, I'd stay right up the back, that's for sure!'

Edith stared across the valley towards the rear escarpment of Senlac Hill. All of a sudden, there was a distant, blood-curdling roar as the two armies engaged, out of sight, over on the front slope. Her heart jolted in fear.

'Oh, Lord!' she gasped. 'Please keep them safe!'

25

Rising above the tumult of screaming and yelling, the clash of weapons, the revving of motorbike engines, and the constant roar from a sea of voices, came the war cries of the two sides: *'Out! Out! Normans Out!'* and *'Normans rule! Up school! Up school!'*

At both ends of the defence line, Saxon regulars and volunteers were fighting in desperation to hold the outer barricade of sharpened stakes against the unrelenting waves of cavalry and infantry. Further down the hill, the front of the wedge was under attack from the mixed division led by Duke William and his squadron of élite cavalry, their brightly painted farings emblazoned with each knight's personal insignia, freshly enameled with confident splendour for the occasion.

There, the axe blades of Harold's battle-scarred veterans flashed and crashed against the long pearl-drop shields and nose-guarded helmets of the Norman infantrymen, while their own smaller shields took the cuts and thrusts of the foot soldiers' swords in return, and at the same time deflected the incessant jabbing lances of the mounted knights.

The struggle was long and intense as the two sides pressed against each other with equal blood-seeking, deadly fury. Eventually, feeling the battle going against him, the Duke backed his machine out of the fray and surveyed the field. His troops were being held on all fronts. Up at the palisade closest to him, Baron Fitzosborne was making no headway against the well-protected defenders.

Quickly beckoning two young runners waiting nearby on the edge of the battle, he gave them instructions and they both ran off, one down the hill and the other around to the far side of the wedge. Then, looking about him, he spied Iko circling the fighting on his motorbike.

'Sir Iko!' he shouted, pointing up the hill. 'Come with me! Help Fitzosborne!' He raised his sword up high and waved it in a circle. 'My squadron! To the top!'

Led by Duke William and Iko, the élite cavalry group broke away from the wedge and charged up the slope towards the end of the barricade.

A few moments later, behind them, on the shrill blast of a whistle, the mixed division engaged at the front of the wedge split into two and concentrated their attack along the sides. At the same time, a large company of Norman archers advanced up the middle of the slope to take their place and levelled their short bows at the point.

Now standing together in a clear space in the centre, Harold and Gurth spotted this new threat.

'Shields up!' Harold shouted, raising his own.

'Brace yourselves!' yelled Gurth.

In practiced response, the soldiers in the front rank at the apex squatted down behind their shields, while the middle rank leaned forward to make a wall above them with theirs. Completing the structure, the third rank held up their shields to form a flat roof, just as the Norman archers unleashed a torrent of arrows, which rattled harmlessly against the Saxon tortoise.

On the sharp blare of a trumpet, in a pre-arranged tactic, the archers then moved aside to allow a phalanx of grim-faced, heavily armed infantrymen to rush past them against the wedge.

As they approached, Harold and Gurth pushed their way through the packed formation to meet the onslaught head on.

*

Further up the hill at the back of the second step, protected by the volunteers and regulars manning the middle barricade, Edmund was clambering about, collecting and distributing spent Norman arrows for future use by the small number of Saxon archers.

All of a sudden, he heard a flurry of sound from above as, an instant later, another flight of incoming arrows struck home among the defenders. Letting out a cry of pain, he looked down in shock at a patch of blood on his sleeve where one had sliced his forearm, before burying itself in the leg of the bowman standing behind him.

*

For two, long, hard hours of bloody hand-to-hand combat, the assault continued at the end of the outer barricade. The air was as hot as an oven, thick with the hideous sights and sounds of human conflict.

Resembling a scene from some infernal *opera seria*—with a ghoulish orchestra following a score composed in the pit of hell, performed to a libretto written and choreographed by the Devil himself—a brass section, made up of both high-pitched and low-throbbing engines, shrill whistles, and blaring trumpets, accompanied a rasping string section of tearing cloth, sawing muscle, and scraping arrowheads, backed by a percussion of clanging metal, shattering bone, and hacked flesh.

To a male chorus of inhuman vitriol, murderous yells, driving battle cries, and screams of agony, on a grassy stage wet with gushing blood, dead and dying Normans lay heaped on the ground, many being trampled underfoot by their fellows. Some hung contorted on the palisade, cut down as they attempted to climb, while others, pushed from behind, were pressed hard up against the sharpened wooden stakes.

Above them, the Saxon defenders, too, were being killed, in lesser numbers, by jabbing sword blades, piercing arrows, and upward spear thrusts; their throats ripped open, their chests punctured, and their stomachs split, with their entrails bursting out like ruptured figs.

In the midst of the carnage, mounted on his motorbike at the rear and taking a rest from the fighting, Duke William turned and looked back down the hill at the battle going on around the wedge. There, bit by bit, the Saxons were pushing forward, and his infantry were starting to break. His face grew livid.

'By the Holy Profit Motive! We're fighting like women!' he yelled in fury. 'Back down, with me!'

Leaving Baron Fitzosborne to continue the attack on the barricade, he powered away down the slope at the head of his cavalry. Opening their throttles to the full, with their spears and sword points levelled, their teeth bared, and their eyes gleaming with the thrill of destruction, they plunged like meteors into the side of the vanguard, churning through to the third rank.

On feeling the shockwaves from the impact coursing through the packed formation, Harold left Gurth to continue holding the infantry at bay at the front and quickly forced his way between his men, over to the side.

Before long, as the effects of the attack were absorbed, the Saxons recovered and began to push back. Soon, as the fighting closed in around them, to avoid becoming entangled and trapped, the élite knights started pulling their machines out of the fray. Among them was Iko. As he turned to see what was behind him, he was struck from the saddle by a lunging spear and sent rolling beyond the wedge.

Meanwhile, Harold cut a path towards the Duke, coming upon him as he was struggling to wheel his damaged motorcycle to safety. Barely taking time to meet Harold's eyes as he appeared before him out of the mêlée, Duke William gave a wild laugh and swiveled round, swinging his mace at his head. At the same time, Harold ducked and delivered a crushing blow with his axe, smashing the Duke's shield into his face. As he staggered back out of the wedge and collapsed on the ground, straight away a cluster of knights gathered around him, hiding him from sight.

'The Duke's down!' a nearby infantryman cried in dismay and ran off down the slope, yelling in panic. 'The Duke's dead! Run for your lives! We've lost!'

As the cry was taken up and the news spread, the rest of the Normans broke off their attack and fled down the hill.

'Hold your positions!' Harold called out, seeing his men about to give chase. 'Keep to your ranks!'

'Nobody move!' Stavros shouted.

Away from the wedge, with his senses dazed and his ears ringing, but otherwise unhurt thanks to his nose guard, Duke William was assisted to his feet. Angrily throwing off his knights' helping hands, he accepted the offer of a mount to replace his own and, with his cavalry following, roared off in pursuit of his demoralised troops. On seeing this, Baron Fitzosborne called off his assault at the barricade and retreated down the side of the hill, soon copied by the force engaged at the other end of the defence line.

All fighting stopped and the noise subsided. Lying face down out on the slope, Iko groaned and opened his eyes. Spitting out a mouthful of foul-tasting grass, he cast aside his dented shield and pushed himself up off the ground, groggy and bruised, minus his helmet. He stared across at the wedge, some distance away. They were regrouping.

In the front rank, Harold was watching him. Iko bowed his head to him in sad respect, receiving an almost imperceptible nod in return. Then, stumbling over the bodies around him, and helping along one of the few injured knights who had survived, Iko turned and hobbled away towards the Norman lines.

Behind him, all across the hill, the defenders looked at each other in amazed relief and broke into joyful cheering.

Meanwhile, further down the slope, Duke William and his squadron swept through the rabble of fleeing infantrymen, knocking some of them to the ground.

'Stop, you idiots! I'm alive!' he screamed, waving his helmet above his head as he rode. 'Don't fear the Saxons, you fools! Fear *me!*'

*

Below the ridge, Edmund moved among the breathless volunteers reassembling on the middle step, offering them water from a canteen slung over his shoulder. Among them was Reggie, the upper-class Saxon, now in his forties and prematurely balding, his florid face, ginger moustache, and eyebrows wet with perspiration. As he accepted the bottle and took a drink, he noticed the blood-stained handkerchief knotted around Edmund's arm.

'Are you all right, old bean?' he asked with concern. 'You're bleeding.'

'Yeah, no worries, thanks,' Edmund grinned. 'Got nicked by an arrow, that's all. How are you doing?'

'Oh, you know, still going strong!' Reggie answered, handing back the water bottle. 'Thanks. Reggie's the name.'

They shook hands. 'Pleased to meet you, Reggie. Edmund.'

'Smashing show, what!' Reggie grinned.

'Yeah, smashing,' Edmund nodded, with a doubtful smile.

Reggie gave an understanding laugh. 'I know. It's the accent, isn't it?'

'No offence, Reggie, but you do sound a bit like one of them down there,' Edmund blurted in embarrassment.

Reggie gave a knowing chuckle. 'And between you and me, Edmund, I think my family would prefer it if I was. Still, couldn't let the bastards just walk in and take over, could I, what? Which just goes to prove the old saying, "the habit doesn't make the monk".'

'Definitely!' Edmund smiled.

'Anyway, at this rate I'll be home before dear Mama even notices I've gone. Sooner still when Morcar arrives.'

'Don't hold your breath waiting for Morcar, mate,' a nearby regular grunted and spat on the ground. 'We won't see him today. He's miles behind us. If he's coming at all.'

Just then, a grizzled veteran, who was struggling to drag a dead body out of the ranks, called across to Edmund. 'Here, kid, give us a hand with this bloke, will ya?'

Edmund stared at the corpse in horror. With a gulp, he passed the water bottle to Reggie and hurried over to help.

*

With the rout halted, the Norman divisions began to regroup, forming up in front of the trees at the bottom of the slope. Sitting astride his motorcycle, watching them, Charles spotted Iko among the injured knights coming down off the hill. Giving a laugh of delight, he rode over to him.

'Iko, old boy! I thought we'd lost you!'

'It was close, Charles,' Iko replied, with a tired smile. 'Very close.'

As a squire approached with a fresh motorbike and a new helmet for him, Iko released the wounded knight he was assisting into the care of a medical orderly. He straddled the machine and sat down heavily on the saddle.

'Well, Charles, how has it been for you?' he asked, doing up his helmet.

'Exhilarating, old man! Absolutely exhilarating! Haven't killed any of 'em yet, of course, but I've come pretty damn close to it a couple of times! And look,' Charles grinned, holding out his arms, 'not a scratch on me!'

'You are a miracle, Charles,' Iko laughed without humour. 'Nothing seems to dampen your enthusiasm.'

'Why should it, old boy? We're winning, aren't we?'

'Perhaps.' Iko sighed. 'If that is what you call it. Excuse me, Charles, I must go and get a drink.'

Without waiting for a reply, he kicked his engine into life and rode away. Charles stared after him. He tutted and shook his head. 'Poor boy's gone mad!' he muttered.

Meanwhile, further across the base of the hill, Duke William was in conference with Baron Fitzosborne and the two Generals. As they gazed up at the battlefield, assessing the situation, the Duke saw that, in repelling their assault, the Saxon wedge had inadvertently pushed diagonally forward down the slope, leaving a wide gap between itself and the barricades behind.

'By Xzyatan, the fool's over-reached himself!' he exclaimed, pointing. 'He's left his defences exposed!'

'Now we can just go around zem!' the Baron laughed.

'What do you plan to do, my Lord?' asked one of the Generals.

Duke William pondered for a moment. 'Right,' he said at last. 'I want the cavalry to go up both flanks and attack the barricade, General, with your infantry in support. Meanwhile, Fitz, you and your chaps charge the wedge. Then, at the right moment, I want you to give the signal for "Bishop's Crook". Got it?'

'I understand, my Lord,' Baron Fitzosborne nodded. 'Charge the wedge and try "Bishop's Crook".'

'Good.' The Duke's eyes glinted with cunning. 'You never know, that just might do the trick.'

*

A short time later, standing outside the front of the wedge, Harold, Gurth, Haco, and Stavros watched with concern as a dense pack of Norman cavalry roared up the far right-hand side of the slope ahead of a large contingent of infantrymen. Following the direction of their attack, Harold turned and stared at the palisade, some distance away.

'Damn it! We've come too far!' he said anxiously.

'And here comes the Duke!' said Gurth.

Harold spun round. Riding out in front of another force, Duke William and his élite cavalry were starting up the near side of the hill.

'They're going for this end! I have to get there!'

'You won't make it, Harold,' Gurth objected, looking back at the defences. 'The gates are shut. They'll never get 'em open in time!'

'The Normans'll cut you off, mate,' Stavros warned.

Harold peered across at the trees running along the edge of the battlefield. 'Quick! Get me a bike! I'll go 'round the back!'

Gurth turned and barked into the wedge. 'Bring a bike! Now!'

'I'm coming with you, Harold,' Haco insisted.

When Harold didn't object, Gurth shouted again. 'Make that two! Hurry!'

Moments later, two bicycles were run out from the centre. Harold and Haco mounted up.

'Keep the wedge together, Gurth,' Harold commanded. 'Whatever you do, don't let them break formation.'

'She'll be right,' Gurth nodded. 'Off you go!'

'Good luck!'

'You too!'

'See y'Gurth!' Haco smiled.

Giving his nephew an affectionate slap on the back as he set off, Gurth stared after them as they sped away across the slope ahead of the Duke's approaching cavalry. With a sigh of relief, he saw them finally disappear into the undergrowth.

He turned and looked back down the hill. While the squadrons of cavalry raced up the sides, followed by battalions of infantrymen, a massed division of Norman footsoldiers was heading up the centre towards the wedge.

'Come on, Stavros, let's sort this lot out,' Gurth said. 'Get ready!' he yelled, as they re-entered the ranks. 'Keep to your places!'

'Anybody moves, they'll answer to me!' Stavros shouted.

*

Coming out of the trees at the back of the hill, Harold and Haco threaded their way in single file along the narrow track that skirted the base of the escarpment. As they rode, they looked up to the top of the neighbouring hill where clusters of tiny figures could be seen gathered in front of the farmhouse.

'Families of some of the men, I reckon,' Haco called ahead. 'It's tempting to go up and join them!'

'What? And miss all the fun?' Harold laughed back.

At that moment, with a roar of engines and blood-curdling shouts, two Norman knights on motorbikes suddenly surged out from a thicket thirty metres behind them and charged along the path. As they drew closer, one behind the other, with their lances pointed, at the last minute Haco leaped from his bicycle, up onto the grassy bank.

He scrambled to his feet and, as the Normans swept past, swung his sword, chopping the second knight across the back of the head. Still astride his machine, the rider fell over onto his side and slewed off the track, smashing headfirst into a rock.

Meanwhile, with his shield on his back, as the front rider bore down on him, Harold vaulted from the saddle and hurled his bike into the path of the oncoming motorcycle. Unable to stop in time, the knight crashed into it and went flying. In an instant, Harold leapt upon him and killed him with a blow from his axe.

'You all right?' he asked, as Haco approached, wheeling his bicycle.

Haco nodded. 'That was close!'

'Come on. Let's go. Leave the bikes.'

They started off along the track on foot. 'Look over there,' Haco pointed, moments later, as a woman came into view a short distance away. 'She's a bit close, don't you reckon?'

Harold stopped. 'I know her,' he said. 'You go on ahead, Haco. I'll catch you up.'

With a nod, Haco continued on round the bottom of the hill. Meanwhile, Harold ran off down a side path and came to a halt at the edge of a fast-flowing creek. Standing under a tree on the opposite bank was Edith.

'Harold!' she cried out, as he appeared.

He waved his arms in desperation. 'Edith, get away! The Normans are coming!'

'Have you found Edmund yet?' she called out.

'No. But I will. Don't worry!'

'What's happening?'

'We're still all right. I'll send him to you,' he shouted.

She pointed behind her. 'I'll be up at that farm.'

'All right, but get back, Edith. Please! You're in danger! I have to go. I love you!'

Sending her a last yearning look, he turned and ran back up the track. Edith stared after him. Then, with a heavy, aching sigh, she turned away.

Behind her, unseen among the bushes, there was a glint of foil as the leaves parted. From beneath homemade cardboard helmets, two pairs of young eyes gazed up at the hill with excitement.

*

In single file, Harold and Haco climbed up the zigzagging, overgrown path to the top of the incline. Scrambling over the lip onto the summit, they stopped to take in the tumultuous scene.

The noise was deafening. Under a relentless sea of voices, roaring like soccer crowds, the hot afternoon air was rent by the torturous powering of motors, the clash of weapons, and the deathly screams and incoherent shouts of the combatants.

Men were running everywhere: fetching water, carrying messages, and collecting fresh weapons from two blacksmiths busy sharpening bloodied blades on their grindstones. At the same time, a team of overworked doctors were tending to the wounded, while still more injured men were brought into the narrow enclosure, some on stretchers, others being assisted or simply dragged in by their mates.

Below them, the battle was raging. Duke William and his élite knights, with cavalry and infantry support, had penetrated the outer palisade and were attacking the second barricade. Leofwine and Bernard were down at the front, trying desperately to beat them back. Without a word, they rushed across the summit and out through an open gate to join in the fight.

'It's the King! King Harold's with us!' a soldier shouted with joy, quickly followed by others repeating the cry across the hill. Hearing it, the defenders surged forward with renewed confidence.

Further along the congested middle tier, trembling with fear and excitement and bracing himself for action, Edmund caught a quick glimpse of his father through the crowd before he was lost from view. He craned on tiptoe to see over the backs of the men in front of him, straining to follow the course of the battle. Spotting the familiar ginger-haired figure of Reggie ahead of him, leaning against the barricade, he pushed his way through to stand behind him.

'Reggie!' he called out above the din. 'What's happening?'

Reggie grunted and swiveled round to face him. The feathered flights of an arrow were protruding from his chest. Edmund stared in horror as his newfound friend's knees buckled and he slipped to the ground.

'Reggie?' he cried, dropping to his side. 'Reggie?'

Reggie opened his eyes. A faint smile flickered across his lips as blood bubbled out between them. 'Cheerio...old...boy!' he whispered. He gave a shudder and died.

Around them, with the added impetus of Harold's arrival, the Saxons pushed forward, hacking the Normans away from the barricade and forcing them out through the gates, pressing them back to the outer rampart. At last, after a gruelling, blood-drenched struggle, the palisade was retaken and the invaders driven off.

As the defence line was restored against him, Duke William began waving his arms in the air, shouting and signalling to his knights. Moments later, leaving others to continue the assault, his cavalry broke off their attack and roared away with him down the hill.

Stepping aside from the fighting, Harold leant his axe against a wooden stake and stared down at the wedge, vastly outnumbered but holding its own out on the slope.

'Come on, Gurth!' he yelled in encouragement through his cupped hands. 'Pull 'em back!'

*

Halfway down the hill, amid a cacophony of human vitriol, Baron Fitzosborne's infantrymen continued their relentless attack against the wedge.

Like prehistoric ants swarming around a beleaguered thousand-legged isopod, all risen up from some primeval swamp—their snapping pincers probing and piercing each other's armour plating, gouging flesh and severing limbs in a gargantuan struggle for supremacy over the Earth—the two sides blended into one, a heaving scrum of mailed bodies locked together in deadly combat.

Among the Norman troops straining at close quarters against the Saxon front rank, a group of three infantrymen picked out one particularly nervy, bellicose, bulging-eyed Saxon regular and began taunting him with additional vehemence, jutting their chins at him, jeering in his face with contempt and loathing, their upper-class voices throaty and sluggish, dripping with arrogant venom.

'I'm going to have your mother!' one informed him with a lecherous grin, waggling his tongue in anticipation.

'I'm going to destroy your home!' another snarled with glee, baring his teeth.

'I'm going to hurt your children!' the third gloated, widening his eyes with sadistic menace.

At the same time, crouching down on one knee behind the attack, Baron Fitzosborne put a whistle to his mouth and blew three short blasts, the signal for 'Bishop's Crook'.

Hearing their cue, the three infantrymen suddenly pretended to be frightened. 'It's no use, we're beaten!' they cried out. 'Run for it. They've won!' In a charade of demoralised panic, they turned and pushed away from the wedge, taking those Normans nearby along with them.

'Hold your positions!' Stavros bellowed at his men.

Oblivious to his cry, on seeing the enemy at last turning tail and running away down the slope, the Saxon regular in the front row, his face twisted with hatred and rage, finally saw red. 'You bastards!' he screamed, unleashing all his pent-up fury as he lurched forward.

Watching him rush off in pursuit, those next to him in the front rank of the wedge looked at each other with uncertainty. An instant later, having been on the receiving end for so long, a second soldier broke after him, followed by another and another.

Standing among them, Stavros tried with all his strength to hold them back, but soon the whole front rank, followed by a large section of the inner ranks, left their places and gave chase. Fighting in frantic resistance to hold his ground, he too was finally swept away along with them by the surging avalanche of men.

As the yelling Saxons hurtled down the slope after the fleeing infantrymen, all of a sudden, with furious cries and a machine gun rattle of exhausts, a large squadron of mounted knights poured out from the trees at the edge of the hill and raced towards them. At the same time, on another whistle-blown signal, the apparently defeated infantrymen stopped their headlong flight and, turning all together, charged back up the slope towards their pursuers.

To complete the encirclement, Duke William and his knights came sweeping down the hill to attack the breakaways from behind. As he roared past the remnants of the wedge, the Duke laughed out triumphantly and gave them a taunting wave.

Gurth watched in helpless impotence from the front. Raising his arm, he spun round to his troops. 'Close up!' he shouted. 'Form lines! Come on. Rebuild the wedge!'

Meanwhile, with the invaders closing in on them from all sides, the fragmented Saxons skidded to a halt, staring about in terror for a way to escape. Seconds later, like a horde of Valkyries, the combined forces fell upon them with a demonic roar, scything down the stragglers on the outer edge with ease and then closing in.

'Regroup!' Stavros yelled. 'Form into wedges!'

The killing was fast and brutal. A few groups of Saxons managed to lock themselves together and put up some resistance, while all about them their scattered compatriots, in twos and threes, were cut to pieces by the Norman onslaught.

In the meantime, Gurth, having rebuilt the shattered wedge, advanced down the hill to their rescue. As many of the smaller groups as possible, fighting as they ran, hastened across the open ground to join him before being cut off.

Further down the slope, Stavros and a dozen veterans had formed themselves into a triangle and, struggling to defend themselves against the overwhelming odds, tried to force their way out of the trap, back to the safety of the wedge.

'C'mon, mates!' Stavros yelled, slashing out to deadly effect with his sword. 'Up to the wedge!'

Only a stone's throw away from them, the main wedge was forced to a standstill by the sheer weight of numbers attacking it. As the space between them became more and more congested with cavalry and infantrymen, Gurth shouted across to him, frantically waving his arms. 'Stavros! Hurry!'

Stavros turned and looked at him. He gave a sad smile and slowly raised the hilt of his sword to his forehead in a gesture of farewell. Then, with a final burst of defiance, he returned to the fray. Barely a heartbeat later, their swords and axes flashing to the last, he and his little group of Saxons disappeared from view behind a solid wall of screaming Normans.

Across the slope, Iko looked on in horror. 'Stavros!' he cried to himself. 'No!'

His face wracked with sorrow, Gurth turned away. 'Fall back!' he shouted, pointing to the summit. 'Up to the barricades!'

To wild cheering and strenuous yells of encouragement from the defenders, and with agonising slowness, the wedge ground its way back up the slope towards the Saxon lines. Finally, surrounded and pressured on all sides by the continuing onslaught, it was once again brought to a halt. Fighting hand-to-hand and toe-to-toe like caged beasts, the remnant lashed out in rage, desperate to maintain their formation.

Suddenly, two of the gates in the wall of stakes were thrust aside as Harold and Leofwine charged out at the head of contingents of troops. With furious shouts, standing up on their pedals, they powered down the slope to attack the nearest Normans from behind, scattering them to right and left and carving a path through to the wedge.

Then, all together, still battling as they went, the whole body of Saxons surged back up the slope to the sanctuary of the barricades. As they poured in through the gateways, with a flourish of blaring bugles, the Normans broke off their attack and retreated down the hill.

Harold waited at one of the gates to greet the exhausted survivors as they filed through. 'Well done, lads!' he said as they trudged past in shock, giving them a smile and a pat on the back.

Last of all, Gurth, bruised and bleeding, re-entered the lines, and the gate was pulled shut.

Harold put his hand on his brother's shoulder. 'Good on you, mate,' he said.

'Gurth, you beauty! Well done!' Bernard called out, as he and Leofwine hurried over to them.

'We lost Stavros,' Gurth told them in a flat voice.

'Oh, no!' Harold moaned.

'And it looks like half the veterans, too, Harold,' Leofwine said.

Harold heaved a resolute sigh. 'Right. I want everyone inside the barricade. Spread the regulars out along the hill.'

'It'll be a bloody thin line,' Leofwine grumbled.

'Well it'll bloody well have to do, won't it!' Gurth snapped at him.

'Come on guys,' Harold intervened gently. 'Go and grab a drink. We'll be right,' he smiled encouragingly. 'It's only a couple more hours till dark.'

Gurth lifted his head. With a tired laugh, he gave Leofwine an affectionate shove. 'Yeah. No worries!'

26

In the soft, warm haze of late afternoon, weary and dispirited, the Norman army came down off the hill. Tossing aside their helmets and dropping their weapons, they threw themselves on the uneven ground among the trees at the foot of the slope.

As the wounded were carried away on stretchers, some of the troops lined up at water tanks to fill their bottles from the taps, while queues formed in front of small kiosks dispensing food. In a clearing in the centre, beneath the Norman flag, Duke William and his cavalry officers sat down to wine and light refreshments under the awning of his tent.

Further back, in a hollow among the tree roots, three soldiers stretched out on the soft bed of pine needles in exhaustion. One of them, Nobby, a small Cockney with an eager, ratty face, was panting hard.

'Crikey, I'm all done in! I don't fink we're ever goin' a take this bleedin' 'ill!' he gasped.

'We have to, man,' Kingston, the Jamaican, replied, lighting a cigarette with a match. 'We don't have any choice. Not unless you know how to walk on water, Nobby!'

'Gor blimey, yeah! Whose brilliant idea was that then, to burn the boats?'

The third soldier, Ranjit, a smooth-shaven Indian with a meringue of black, oily hair atop his cheerful face, waggled his index finger in the air. 'Duke Villiam is indeed a very fine general, Nobby. Burning the boats vas a stroke of genius. It has given us impetus!'

Kingston gazed at him in wry amusement. 'Yeah, right.'

Nobby shook his head at Ranjit in mild disbelief. 'Anyway, 'ow come you're 'ere in the first place, Kingston?' he said, turning back to his self-contained friend. 'I fought you 'ated bein' bossed abaht?'

Kingston shrugged. 'If taking orders gets me some land and buys me my freedom, man, then that's what I'll do.'

They all looked round as a barrel-chested, moustachioed sergeant major appeared, striding among the troops nearby, clearing the men on the ground out of his path with an occasional swish of his cane, his voice echoing through the forest. 'All right, you lazy good-for-nothings, let's be 'aving you! You're going up again!'

'Oh, bloody hell!' Ranjit grinned, massaging his calf muscles. 'Duty calls!'

Kingston groaned in cynical resignation. 'Yeah, right.'

Nobby shrugged. 'Still, the Duke must know what 'e's doin', mustn't 'e? Ranjit's right. We got 'a follow orders, ain't we, an' at's that?'

Ranjit climbed to his feet. 'Come on, chums. There's no peace for the vicked!'

Shortly after, out in front of the trees, the weary but still optimistic troops reassembled into battalions at the foot of the hill. Behind their formations, dispatch riders dashed backwards and forwards on their motorcycles. While the soldiers shuffled about in the balmy air, officers strode among them bellowing orders. Helmeted heads turned as Baron Fitzosborne walked past, deep in conversation with the two Generals.

As their platoon lined up at the edge of the trees under the auspices of their sergeant, Nobby, Ranjit, and Kingston, with a cigarette held tightly between his lips, slipped in at the rear. Trying to be as inconspicuous as possible, they hurriedly buttoned up their shirts, adjusted their neck ties, and tightened their helmet straps. They stopped what they were doing and watched as the Baron went by.

'That Baron Fitzosborne is a very fine general, indeed!' Ranjit pronounced, rolling his head from side to side.

'You fink everyone's a fine bleedin' general, Ranjit!' Nobby laughed.

'It'll take more than generals to win this battle, man,' said Kingston. 'What we need now is reinforcements. Lots o' reinforcements!'

'You three, get into line!' the sergeant shouted. 'Put that fag out, Kingston. You're in the army now!'

'Yeah, right, Sergeant,' Kingston replied, taking a last drag and treading out the butt.

''Ere, Sarge?' Nobby called out. ''Ow come we ain't seen the reserves yet?'

'You will, lad, you will. They'll be 'ere soon enough, don't you worry!'

At that exact moment, there was a sudden crashing of branches, a fanfare of horn blasts, and the sound of tramping feet, followed by jubilant shouts. The whole assembly swung round to see Bishop Odo riding out from the pine trees at the head of a wide column of perfectly synchronised marching men.

Sitting tall in the saddle, his eyes hidden by maroon-tinted sunglasses, the Bishop was wearing an open sleeveless silk robe over a fine-meshed, gold chain-mail bodysuit, with a scarlet and black collar. A gleaming snake-swords medallion hung around his neck.

In his hand he gripped a gold-plated crosier, with a long-pointed spike at the end. Behind him, his reserve force, dressed in silver suits and carrying upright spears and leaf-shaped shields, were all chewing gum, their faces intense and confident under their shining nose-guarded helmets.

The Bishop raised his hand and halted the column. Meeting the soldiers' acclaim, he lifted off his white Stetson and waved it above his head, smiling benignly at them as they gathered excitedly around him.

'Howdy, pardners!' he called out loudly, with a cheerful drawl. 'Guess you been waitin' for me!' At their cheers and shouts of relief, he gave an understanding laugh. 'I hear you! You're tired, ain't you?' He pointed towards the top of the hill. 'Well, look up there at them Saxons,' he grinned. 'Now that's what I call *really* tired!'

The troops' answering laughter rang out, much of it in scornful sympathy for the enemy.

'Seems to me like you folks already done cracked this nut for me,' Bishop Odo nodded in praise. 'So, from here on in, it's gonna be easy pickings! All we gotta do now is capitalise on the situation. And, believe me, that's what me an' my boys do best!'

Gesturing with his hat, he pointed to where Duke William stood outside his tent, his arm raised in greeting, and waved back to him.

'Just as soon as my brother the Duke, over there, gives us the signal,' he told them, 'we're gonna have ourselves a time! Now stand aside, pardners...the mighty men of Xzyatan are comin' through!'

*

Positioned at the back of the line of defenders manning the second barricade, Edmund listened to the distant cheering and watched with apprehension as the whole Norman army began to advance up the slope, led by the distinctive figures of Duke William and Bishop Odo. Suddenly, a hand fell on his shoulder.

'Edmund!'

He turned in surprise. Harold was standing behind him.

'Dad!' Edmund grinned with relief. 'You scared the life out of me!'

'Follow me,' Harold ordered. He led the way through a gate, up onto the quiet summit. Once there, he stopped and turned towards him. 'You shouldn't have come here, Ed.'

'I had to, Dad. I wanted to be with you.'

'Well, now you have to go.'

'No! I want to stay.' Edmund said defiantly. 'I'm fighting for my country!'

'You're too young.'

Edmund pointed to the wound on his arm. 'I've already given my blood. That qualifies me, doesn't it? I want my revenge!'

'Have you killed anyone yet?'

'No...'

'Thank God for that!' Harold sighed. 'Now, as your father and your king, Edmund, you'll obey my command. You see that farm up there?' He pointed past the back of the enclosure to the neighbouring hill. 'Well, that's where your mother's waiting for you. I want you to take a message to her. Tell her that I love her with all my heart. And tell her...that I hope she's right. She'll understand.'

'But what'll happen to you, Dad?' Edmund asked in a trembling voice.

Harold laid his hands on his son's shoulders. 'I'll be okay, mate,' he said, with a tender smile. 'Don't worry, I'm in good company. Now, off you go. And whatever Mum says, you listen to her, right?'

'I will,' Edmund nodded, smiling with uncertainty through his tears.

Harold's voice began to break. 'And give your brother and sister a big kiss and a hug from me.'

Edmund suddenly lurched forward into Harold's arms and hugged him. 'I love you, Dad!'

Harold held onto him tightly, pressing his lips to his cheek. 'I love you, too, Ed!' he croaked. 'I'm so proud of you, darling!' Then, with gentle firmness, he pushed him away. 'Now, go quickly. Down the other side. Go on!'

Through misty eyes, he watched his son run across the summit and, with a final wave, disappear over the edge of the escarpment. 'See ya, Ed!' he cried softly after him, choking back the tears.

*

As, wave after wave, in long, deep lines, the Norman army advanced up the hill, still perched astride his tree branch on the edge of the slope, Eric Braithwaite spoke into the microphone of his cassette recorder, his voice filled with mounting excitement.

'So, with the light fading, King Harold and his band of battered heroes prepare themselves for the final onslaught! They came here without any reserves, already exhausted from beating the Vikings and then the long journey down, to take on the superior numbers and better equipment of a well-oiled Norman fighting machine. It should have been a walkover! Yet, here we are at the end of the third quarter and they're still in there battling. You little beauties! And now their depleted team, half made up of part-timers and local ring-ins, only have to hold on until nightfall to gain the draw they so richly deserve.'

He paused for a moment to watch the Normans coming closer.

'Throughout the day, Duke William's thrown everything he's got at them, including the kitchen sink! Lightning raids up the wings, a barrage of long shots and massed charges up the centre. But nothing could break the Saxon defence. Until tragedy struck! In one terrible moment of lost concentration, the mighty Saxon wedge fell for the oldest trick in the book. The dummy retreat. And, oh, what a price they paid! Cut to ribbons in a three-way pincer movement. Stavros, the magnificent, is gone. What a dreadful blunder! But Gurth has survived to fight on.'

He stopped again to observe the lines of troops moving up the slope. By now, their snarling faces were clearly visible, and he could hear the vicious threats and graphic taunts being hurled at the Saxon defenders.

'But it's not over yet,' he continued. 'The barricades are still manned and time is fast running out for the Normans. Now the Duke's brought on Odo and his reserves in a last-ditch attempt to break the deadlock. But will it be enough? For the sake of the whole free world, I hope not! If Harold's men can manage to hang on, with Morcar's fresh troops on the way, they must be better than odds-on favourites to win the rematch. Whatever happens, it's been a great and glorious day!...With the Normans in front by a nose but all still to play for, this is Eric Braithwaite for the *Anglo-Saxon Chonicle*, Senlac Hill.'

With a sigh of satisfaction, he reached down and pressed the 'stop' button on the recorder. He pondered for a moment, then his forehead creased in a worried frown. 'I'd better get out of here!' he thought anxiously.

At one and the same moment, he felt a sudden stinging blow in his side, followed by a shooting pain across his chest to his heart. He gasped in agony and his eyes went wide in shock as he turned and stared down at the arrow lodged under his ribs. Like air escaping from a tyre, the strength poured out of him and a heavy curtain of darkness descended over his eyes. Dropping the microphone, with a grotesque look of horrified amusement on his face, he swiveled round and tumbled from the branch.

In a flurry of leaves, Braithwaite's body crashed through the branches to the ground, landing at the feet of a company of Norman archers stealing through the undergrowth. Ignoring him, they swarmed on up the side of the hill, past the freckle-faced figure of Lenny lying propped up against the trunk of a tree.

With his baseball cap knocked askew, he had a fixed smile on his freckled face, his eyes crossed and staring, and an arrow through his head. His comic and his smashed bicycle lay in the grass nearby.

*

This was it. Win or lose. Live or die. The final assault. With a nod and a handshake, a wink and a smile, the defenders lined the barricades. Nearly all bearing wounds, grim-faced, exhausted, and heroic, they waited with teeth-gritted confidence, gulping trepidation, ice-cold anger, and total commitment, watching with grudging admiration as the Norman steamroller came up the hill towards them.

Advancing ahead of the main body of troops were small companies of archers. As soon as they were within range, on a whistle blast they halted and, a moment later, let fly a torrent of arrows at the Saxon ranks, who easily blocked the missiles with their shields. Then, on a second signal, with an ear-shattering roar of engines and dry-throated, ferocious battle cries, the galvanised mass of foot soldiers and mounted knights rushed past the archers and hurled themselves against the outer palisade.

Some tried to scramble up between the sharpened wooden stakes and were quickly cut down by the defenders, but soon, by sheer force of numbers and continuous pressure, they managed to force their way over. At the same time, the gateways in the outer defences were breached and the Normans poured in through the gaps, up onto the first step, where, like butchers chopping meat, they laid into their opponents.

Giving way, inch by inch, stepping over the dropped weapons, severed limbs, and crumpled forms of their slain comrades, their feet slipping on the slicks of viscera and pools of crimson soaking the turf, the depleted Saxons fell back to take up new positions behind the middle barricade.

'Press on, Normans! Onwards and upwards!' Duke William shouted out in the midst of the action, swinging his studded mace at the heads of the Saxons as he urged on his troops.

Further across the slope, level with him, Bishop Odo reached out from his motorbike with his golden crozier and pulled a defender from the rampart. He dragged the man to the ground and stabbed down at him with its spike.

'Keep right on pushin', boys!' he yelled, waving the blood-dripping crook in the air. 'Move in, spread out, and take over!'

Like a surging tide, the Normans swarmed forward, up, and over the roped logs and branches forming the second line of defence. For a long time, the battle raged, poised on the precipice of destruction, the pendulum of thrashing violence swinging both ways. At last, with the whiff of success fuelling the invaders' voracious appetite, the exponential weight of hatred and greed proved too much.

Having gained precious time, but seeing that further resistance was futile, the outnumbered Saxons, with their faces still to the enemy, fought their way back to the safety of the inner enclosure.

The cost had been great. There was a lull in the battle as both sides stopped to get their breath. Waiting for a signal, the Normans pulled back to the second barricade and stared up the hill, gulping at the prospect of scaling the final barrier of wagons, bicycles, and logs protecting the summit. Before they had time to lose heart, on another whistle, the companies of archers formed up again in front of the ranks. They took aim and unleashed a storm of arrows up the hill but again inflicted little damage. Then, on a third whistle blast, with a great shout, the whole force attacked once more.

As his men stormed the barricade and the archers continued firing whenever a clear shot presented itself, Duke William rode through the debris behind the fighting, watching intently. On seeing how ineffectual his bowmen were being, he raced in fury across the slope to where some of them were regrouping. His face contorting in anger, he called their captain over to him.

'What are you? Stupid?' he yelled at the man. 'Can't you see your arrows are being wasted? They're just bouncing off their shields! Shoot up in the air, damn it!' He pointed up at the sky. 'Fire over the top! Make 'em come down on the bastards' heads! You hear me?'

Red-faced, in fear, the captain saluted. 'Yes, sir! Sorry, sir!'

'Now pass it on!'

The captain scurried off to his company. A few moments later, they commenced firing a steady stream of arrows up over the defences, down into the enclosure beyond. Almost immediately, above the general tumult, a new wave of screaming and groaning came from the summit.

Meanwhile, the Duke wheeled away to the middle of the first step. He stopped and sat studying the assault. After a short while, as he observed the results of his directive with mounting satisfaction, Bishop Odo rode over and halted beside him, his engine purring quietly. He pulled a hip flask from under his blood-spattered robe, unscrewed the cap, and passed it across. In turn, they both took a swig and stared up at the crest together, following the arrows' descent.

'That's more like it,' Duke William grunted with pleasure.

The Bishop flicked the brim of his stetson. 'I tip my hat to you, Billy. That was a damn fine move!'

'Should give 'em something to think about, what!'

'Not to mention one helluva headache!'

'Now we'll see,' the Duke mused, taking another sip.

'Poetic justice, I reckon,' Bishop Odo nodded. He took a last drink and put the flask away. 'Divine retribution raining down from the sky.'

'That's right. Still, they do have a choice.'

'And what the hell's that?'

'Well, they can either shield their heads and get a spear in the chest or guard their fronts and get an arrow in the brain!'

'Some choice!'

With mirthless chuckles, they gazed up at the summit, savouring the warmth of possible success.

*

Protecting themselves as best they could from the arrows shafting down into the enclosure, slicing into their heads, necks and chests, the thin line of Saxons stood shoulder to shoulder, continuing to repel each Norman attempt to get past the barricade.

At the forefront, his shield splashed with blood and his axe soaked to the grip in gore, Harold paused for a moment and looked off to his right, where the sun was sinking beyond the distant hills, casting a surreal, amber glow over the conflict.

'Come on, Saxons!' he shouted, waving his axe in the air. 'Hold your ground! Half an hour and we've won!'

Back down the hill, Duke William rode across the slope at the rear of his troops. Bumping over ground made uneven by dead bodies, smashed motorcycles, discarded weapons, and broken barricades, he stood up in the saddle, sternly observing the progress of the battle. Suddenly, his face lit up.

Veering across to Baron Fitzosborne, who was standing, legs astride, urging on those lagging behind with the flat of his sword, the Duke leant down and spoke to him, at the same time pointing towards the far end of the summit, where a small number of Saxons were holding back a company of Norman infantry supported by a few archers.

Baron Fitzosborne grinned and nodded, then turned and shouted an order. On his command, a squad of soldiers broke away from the main body and, after listening to his orders, ran off with him towards the end of the barricade.

While they did so, Duke William beckoned to his cavalry group, who were hovering close by, waiting for orders. As his knights clustered around him, he gesticulated fiercely towards the edge of the hill, giving them precise instructions.

A short time later, Baron Fitzosborne and his men arrived at the end of the defence line and joined in the fight. Shoving aside those Normans already there, they pushed their way through to the front and laid into the Saxon defenders.

In the meantime, Duke William led his body of knights out through one of the smashed gates in the palisade and down onto the slope. They raced across the hill, passing behind the company of archers still busy firing arrows up at the summit, and rode on into the trees.

As the vicious do-or-die struggle continued at the inner barricade, once again Baron Fitzosborne eased himself out of the fray to the rear of the attack and blew the signal for 'Bishop's Crook'. With that, his squad of infantrymen pretended to give up. Eyes rolling in despair and defeat, and shouting with dismay, they pulled back from the fight. Followed by the rest of the Normans around them, they ran off down the hill past the archers, who continued firing.

On seeing the bowmen, their constant tormentors, suddenly alone and exposed in front of them, the Saxon defenders were unable to resist the temptation to charge any longer. Clambering in anger over the top of the barrier, while others cut through the ropes that tied it together, pushing aside all obstacles to their revenge, they poured down the slope, leaving a wide gap in the barricade behind them.

As the breakaway Saxons approached in a headlong rush, the Norman archers lowered their bows and let fly at them. At the same time, on another whistle, the fleeing infantrymen stopped and spun round, then started back up the hill with swords bared. A moment later, with screaming engines and triumphant shouts, half of the Duke's concealed squadron surged out from their hiding place in the underbrush and swept across the slope with lances pointed.

Caught in the trap, the hapless Saxons were soon cut to pieces. At the same time, Duke William and the rest of his cavalry wing poured out of the trees at the top of the hill and raced across the short stretch of open grass towards the breach.

*

Standing beneath the standard in the centre of the summit, Harold watched the events at the far end with mounting concern. Closer in, Haco was sprinting along the enclosure towards him.

'Harold!' Haco called out as he approached and stopped in front of him, gasping for breath. 'The Normans have...'

'I know!' Harold cut in. 'I saw it. Come on!' He turned and shouted across to Gurth, who had his back to them, directing the fighting at the inner barricade. 'Gurth!' As his brother looked round, he pointed into the distance. 'They've broken through at the other end! Bring some men!'

'Right-o. I'll catch you up,' Gurth called after them, as they ran off.

In the meantime, riding at full throttle, Duke William and his élite cavalry had reached the broken barrier to be met by ferocious resistance from the defenders. Only a few of his knights managed to make it through into the enclosure before more Saxons arrived to fill the space and hold them back.

Roaring onto the summit, two of those who had made it in caught sight of Harold and Haco, in their distinctive officer's white battle gear, running towards them. With guttural, predatory shouts, and waving their lances in the air, they charged.

As the riders bore down on them, Haco suddenly darted ahead of Harold and dropped onto one knee in their path, thrusting his shield towards them with both hands. Seconds later, as the leading knight swerved out of the way, the one behind, braking madly, smashed into it and went flying from his motorbike. Haco was sent reeling by the collision.

The first knight wheeled round in a tight circle, levelling his spear at Harold, and charged again. Harold quickly sprang aside and delivered a backhand blow with his axe, chopping him from the saddle, then strode across and dispatched his fellow with an off-drive as he struggled to his feet. He paused and looked beyond them to the far end of the enclosure, where, having finally overcome the thinly stretched defenders, the rest of the

Duke's squadron were pouring in through the breach and onto the summit.

Further down the hill, the archers unleashed another deadly salvo up into the air.

Lying on the ground, his face gushing with blood, Haco heard a rushing sound from above. He looked up and stared in horror at the dense cloud of arrows dropping out of the sky like a swarm of hornets. Frantic with fear, he turned towards Harold and yelled at the top of his voice, pointing upwards. 'Harold! Look out!'

Harold turned at the call and lifted his head. That very instant, an arrow struck home, slicing between the bars of his visor with a sickening crunch of metal into gristle and bone, sinking deep into his right eye. He cried out loudly, as his body spasmed and the axe fell from his grasp. The excruciating, white-hot bar of pain burning in his face was almost unbearable. He gripped the rim of his shield with both hands and leant on it heavily, hanging his head, gasping for breath, puffing and blowing against the debilitating dizziness and the heart-stopping shock, fighting to keep from blacking out. A moment later, he heard the roar of an engine in his ears and glimpsed a flash of metal out of the corner of his eye, before his left thigh exploded in agony as it was hacked through to the bone. A stream of crimson gushed up into the air, all hope pumping out with his lifeblood from the wound. Letting go of the shield, he tried to take a step, but his strength was gone. Arched up in silhouette against the distant setting sun, clutching the wooden shaft embedded in his face, as his legs gave way, he stumbled back and crashed on his side at the foot of the standard.

Seconds later, Gurth rushed over to him and knelt next to him, covering them both with his shield as more arrows rained down. 'Harold!...Oh, God!' he cried.

Harold was white as a sheet, groaning in pain, almost incoherent. 'Aaghh!...Don't let...see...Gurth...Oh, Edith!' With a last choking sob, he slumped over on his face in the dirt, the arrow snapped, and he lay still.

'Harold! No!' Gurth shouted in disbelief.

Meanwhile, the arrows had stopped falling. Numb with grief, Gurth rose like an automaton to his feet. Haco staggered towards him, wounded and aghast. In shock, unable to voice a warning, Gurth pointed past him at the riders roaring down the enclosure towards them. Haco turned in alarm and, picking up his sword, advanced unsteadily to meet them. He raised his arm to strike, but in an instant was skewered by a lance in the chest.

Seeing Haco killed jolted Gurth into action. With a dry-throated, snarling cry, he threw himself back into the fight.

*

As darkness began to fall, along the length of the hill the last defenders fought in vain to hold the line. With numb fingers locked around the handles of weapons they could barely feel, let alone lift, their legs and arms knotted with cramp, every sinew screaming, all their strength failing, adrenalin reduced to a drip, the background pain of their sliced limbs and pierced bodies rising to the fore, almost unbearable, their minds giving way and wandering home, snapping back to reality too late, all their resistance was overcome.

With their overwhelming numbers bursting in hateful triumph through the last of the gateways, more and more Normans swarmed up onto the summit. Some trapped against the defences, and the rest forced out into the open, the remaining Saxons were soon engulfed by the flood of invading troops and their slaughter complete.

Only Gurth, on one side, and Leofwine and Bernard on the other, managed to fight their way free of the mêlée and gather together around the royal standard, waiting in their blood-soaked whites, bleeding from numerous wounds, panting with exhaustion, weapons at the ready, watching as the Normans slowly closed in.

His body rolling to and fro as if on the deck of a ship, and his face spattered with flecks of gristle and clotted blood, Bernard turned and called across to Leofwine. 'How y'doin', Leo?'

Leofwine was bent over, gasping for breath, his sword stuck in the ground in front of him and his hands resting on the pommel. 'No worries, Bernie,' he answered. With a dry hawk, like the rasp of an empty soda syphon, he spat a gobbet of something red onto the ground. He stared at it and gave a sad chuckle. 'This is it, then?'

'Looks like it.'

'I gotta tell ya...they killed Gladys!'

'What? Who?'

'Them!' Leofwine swung a limp, bloodied thumb towards the Normans. 'Those bastards...They're responsible...Sorry, mate... Couldn't tell you before... She'll be there waiting for you.'

Bernard's face, at first wracked with sorrow, went in quick succession through a gamut of emotions, his initial shock and horror finally giving way to seething rage and withering hatred. 'Right, then!' he growled, grinding his teeth. 'You ready, Leo?'

'Reckon so...See you on the other side, eh?'

'I'll be there, mate.'

Like sprinters flying out of the starting blocks at the crack of a pistol, with heart-stopping screams of fury, they leapt as one towards the enemy. At the same time, the Normans rushed forward. Striking out in all directions with his axe, Bernard scythed his way into the pack, until, forced to a stop by the press of bodies both living and dead, with a cry of pain he was stabbed in the stomach and cut down from behind.

Nearby, with the ferocity of his attack taking the Normans by surprise, Leofwine easily sliced through their ranks, parrying blows and dealing out death with his flashing blade, before, by a miracle, forcing his way out of the throng and retreating, badly wounded, back to the flag.

On the opposite side, with concentrated rage and incredible strength, blocking blows with his shield and swinging his axe, over and over again like a machine, Gurth hewed down the battle-weary infantrymen. At last, momentarily beating off his attackers, he stumbled back to the standard.

While the Normans paused for a moment's respite, the two brothers stood on either side of the 'Boxing Kangaroo', breathless and dripping blood. For a lingering, poignant moment they looked round at each other and gave a nod and a loving smile.

As the invaders came forward again over the corpse-strewn ground, moving in warily for the kill, Leofwine let out a weary, self-mocking laugh. With a final sad shake of his head, he launched himself at the nearest soldier, slashing him across the throat with his sword, and then lunged at another. A split second later, he was speared, stabbed, and clubbed round the head, collapsing among the dead under a continuing blood-crazed rain of blows.

With ecstatic shouts, the Normans started towards the flag. There was a clash of weapons, cries of agony, and a confusion of falling figures. At the height of it, there was an audible gasp. Then, as if by common consent, they stopped and drew back, their faces filled with awe and disbelief.

Gurth was still standing, unbeaten, up to his knees in bodies, blood gushing from numerous wounds, his axe dangling from his hand. Unsure what to do, they formed a deep circle around him.

There was silence, broken only by the moans of the wounded and dying, the laboured breathing of the combatants, the ticking over of motorcycle engines, and the gentle flapping of the flag.

'Halt!' Baron Fitzosborne's voice shouted from the rear, shattering the moment. 'Wait for ze Duke!' he commanded, forcing his way through to the front.

Moments later, Duke William and Bishop Odo rode into the circle. The Duke braked to a stop and looked sternly about him, taking in the situation. All eyes were on him. Quickly making up his mind, he called across to Charles, who was seated on his motorbike next to Iko, on the far side of the ring.

'I say, Charles, you're the tie man, aren't you?' he laughed with supercilious charm. 'Well, do me a favour would you, old boy, and untie that flag!'

Charles bowed his head. 'It will be a pleasure, my Lord.'

With that, the factory owner gave a quick wink to Iko, adjusted his grip on his spear, revved up his engine and, overcoming a moment's trepidation, slowly eased forward towards Gurth.

'The man's dead on his feet!' a knight called out. 'I'll give a hundred to one on Charles!'

'Done!' Iko answered without thinking, his eyes fixed on Gurth.

Standing with his back to Charles, Gurth was bent double, his knees about to give way. Swaying gently, his head was hanging and his eyes were shut, one hand gripping the flagpole. As the Norman picked up speed and bore down on him from behind, his eyelids suddenly sprang open. With a massive surge of will, he straightened up, swiveled round, and raised his axe.

Anxiously over-revving his engine, Charles roared up to him and hurled his spear from close range. At the last moment, forcing himself to focus, Gurth leant out of the way. Charles stared in horror as his missile sailed harmlessly wide of its mark.

Transfixed and mesmerised, he could only watch in helpless terror as Gurth's axe swept round in a wide arc towards him and chopped him from his machine.

'By Xzyatan, the man's superhuman!' the Bishop gasped in amazement.

'Spare him, my Lord!' Iko pleaded. 'Let him live!'

There were calls of agreement from the knights. Duke William stared round at them all in fury. Then, without answering, giving a ferocious laugh, he let out his clutch and ploughed forward over the piles of bodies, sending up jets of blood with his wheels.

As if in slow motion, Gurth turned towards him and tried to lift his axe. With the strength finally draining out of him, his arm dropped. He let go of the weapon and clung to the standard with both hands. Dying on his feet, his body teetering, he rubbed his eyes against the back of his thumb, angrily trying to wipe away the blood, fighting to keep them open.

Barely discernible, a dark, shapeless mass moving against the final glimmer of fading daylight, the Duke surged out of the gloom towards him and swung his studded mace.

27

The black, moonless sky was a sea of shimmering stars, its limitless depths sprinkled with innumerable pinpricks of light, studded throughout by bright firestones of greater and lesser reknown, like the sorrowing eyes of the fallen staring down from their deathbed and demanding the truth.

Breaking their concentration, one of the stars began to move, gliding silently across the heavens in a straight line from east to west. Seconds later, abruptly turning back on itself at an impossible angle, it shot straight upwards, becoming fainter and fainter until it disappeared completely. With his mission accomplished, the Emissary of Xzyatan had made his final, unobserved departure. Stillness returned and the stars resumed their spectral vigil.

Beneath their unremitting gaze, the wreckage of battle covered the slope. Pitiful wailing and heartbroken shrieks came out of the night. Here and there, in the darkness, the abstract shapes and surreal configurations of the carnage were lit up by lanterns and torches, as Saxon families searched among the dead for their loved ones, their arms spread backwards on finding them, like figures by Giotto, beseeching, howling in anguish.

As they went about their gruesome task, turning over the corpses and peering closely at the faces, teams of looters scrambled about them, busily ripping off and collecting anything of value—necklaces, rings, boots, weapons, or armour—then stuffing it into their sacks.

On top of the hill, in the middle of the summit, after removing the bodies of the Normans who had died there, the remains of the Saxon defenders had been heaped aside to make room for a large pavilion, all aglow with multi-coloured fairy lights, with sentries posted all around it.

Standing under its entrance awning, listening to the muffled laughter and conversation coming from within, was a sergeant of the guard. The sound of a knifeblade tapping on glass brought quiet, followed by the sonorous voice of Baron Fitzosborne.

'My Lord, Your Holiness, officers and gentlemen, we are gazered here togezer not only to celebrate our great and glorious victory, but also to honour ze spirits of our dear departed fellows.'

'Hear, hear!' other voices called out in solemn agreement.

'Zerefore, kindly be upstanding and raise your glasses.' There was a scraping of chairs being pushed back. 'I give you ze toast... To our fallen heroes!'

'To our fallen heroes!' a chorus of voices echoed back in unison.

Two monks appeared out of the surrounding darkness and approached the tent. Hanging back behind them, on the fringe of the light, was Edith.

*

Inside the pavilion, the victory banquet was in progress. Placed in the corners and at intervals around the walls, tripod braziers sent up spirals of sweet incense smoke to cover the smell of the dead. Servants moved about the interior, waiting on the two dozen officers feasting at a single long, bare wood table.

At its head sat Duke William, sipping a glass of champagne and smoking a cigar, laughing and swapping stories with Bishop Odo and Baron Fitzosborne. Pinned to the tent wall behind them, hanging between the Norman flag and the Grand Pontiff's 'Banner of Power', was the torn, bloodstained 'Boxing Kangaroo'.

Halfway down the table, four officers were in mid-conversation.

'You should've seen the look on his face!' one of them said, with a twisted, drunken smile. 'Absolutely hysterical. Crumpled like a sack of potatoes at m'feet! One little jab and "pop", down he went!'

'Ha, ha! Well done, Roger!' a second officer guffawed.

'Well done, be blowed! Blighter put blood all over m'boots!' Roger replied with a look of indignation, then threw back his head and bellowed with laughter along with his fellows.

'I say, Pongo!' a third officer called across the table to a fourth. 'Fetch us another bottle, would you, there's a good chap?'

'Let the servants do it, old bean,' Pongo called back. 'No point keeping a dog and barking yourself, what!' He leant round in his seat and clicked his fingers. 'You, there!'

In immediate response, an attendant approached and bowed. 'Sir?'

'We need more champagne here!'

'Certainly, sir.'

'And while you're at it, put some more incense on the burners, why don't you. The stench of those Saxons is intolerable!'

At that moment, the sergeant of the guard entered the tent and made his way down to the head of the table. The Duke turned in his seat and looked up at him as he approached. 'Well?'

'My Lord, there are two Saxon monks outside asking to see you.'

'Monks, you say? Well bring them in! Bring them in! We're all holy men here, what! Eh, Odo?'

'Indeed we are, Billy boy, indeed we are!' the Bishop chuckled. 'Pure as the driven snow!'

The sergeant saluted and left the tent.

'What about you, Fitz? You a holy man?' Duke William asked with a grin.

'Definitely, my Lord,' The Baron laughed fruitily. 'Ze more holes ze better!'

Moments later, the sergeant reappeared, escorting the two monks. Dressed in brown habits and sandals, they were both middle aged, one stocky with a beard, the other portly and balding. They stood there, nervous and uncertain, as the Duke tapped his glass with his knife for silence and the tent went quiet.

'Welcome!' he greeted them with an expansive smile. 'Have no fear, you're amongst friends.' There was a ripple of laughter around the table. 'Now, what can I do for you?'

The bearded monk exchanged a quick look with his partner, who nodded for him to go ahead. Taking courage, the monk proceeded. 'Lord Duke,' he began, in a melodic Italian accent, 'we have come to beg for the body of King Harold.'

'We bring all of the money we possess,' added his companion.

'He'll be unrecognisable by now!' Baron Fitzosborne scoffed loudly. 'Zere are probably pieces of him scattered all over zis hill, knowing ze way my boys do zeir job!'

'I told you I didn't want that sort of behaviour from the men, Fitz,' Duke William chided him with an affable frown. 'It's too gross!'

'With your permission, Lord Duke, we would still like to try,' the bearded monk persisted. 'If one of your knights could just show us where he was when he fell, there is a woman with us, outside, who knew him intimately. She will be able to recognise him.'

'Oh really? Intimately, you say? And who might that be, pray tell? I take it you don't mean his wife?' Under the Duke's penetrating stare, the monks looked away, embarrassed. 'Ah! So, if it isn't her...' He looked round at his men with a smirk. 'Then it must be his bit of stuff on the side!'

'She is the mother of his children!' the bearded monk objected, amid the ribald laughter of the knights.

Duke William sat forward with keen interest. 'So, Harold had children, did he? How many?'

'I do not know,' the monk gave a shrug and shook his head. 'Two or three, I think.'

'How old are they?'

'We 'ave never seen them. Teenage, perhaps?'

'You! What is ze woman's name?' the Baron barked at the second monk.

'Edith...Edith Swanneck,' the man blurted, paling with fear.

'Swanneck? Swan...neck. A funny-sounding name.' Baron Fitzosborne gave an ominous growl. 'When you cut it in two!'

The monks shuddered.

'Hm,' the Duke murmured. He balanced his cigar on the ashtray and sat back, his elbows on the arms of the chair, pressing his fingertips together, pondering. 'So, Harold was an adulterer, was he?' He turned to Bishop Odo. 'That news should stop these Saxons pining for him, wouldn't you say?'

'They'll be glad he's gone, Billy,' the Bishop agreed.

'Good...Good,' Duke William nodded thoughtfully. He took a sip of his champagne and held the glass up to his eyes, watching the bubbles rising and falling as he reflected on the news.

After a while, when no more was said, the bearded monk cleared his throat and spoke. 'Lord Duke?'

'Oh, go away!' the Duke snapped, flicking his hand at him in irritation. 'Wherever Harold's corpse is, the crows can have it for breakfast!' The monks shrank back and turned to leave. 'Tell the silly bitch we've done her a favour,' he threw after them, as they scurried away with the sergeant of the guard. 'She should be glad he's got his comeuppance!'

At the far end of the table, Iko pushed back his chair and stood up.

'My Lord...' he called out, then paused. Everyone looked at him, as the tent fell silent. 'My Lord, I will gladly forfeit any reward coming to me if you will let me help them. Lord Harold was a friend to me in the past. I wish to give him an honourable burial.'

Duke William stared at him in wonderment, while the knights held their collective breath. His lip slowly curled in disdain. 'All right, then, Sir Iko, take him,' he said dismissively. 'It's your loss.'

'Thank you, my Lord.' Iko bowed.

'His ghost can rule the cliffs,' the Duke sneered. He turned to his officers and grinned with derision. 'He can command the seagulls!'

With their answering roar of laughter ringing in his ears, Iko left the table and followed the monks out of the tent.

*

Holding cloths up to their faces and shining their torches about them, Iko and the two monks slowly navigated their way through the dark mounds of twisted bodies, torn armour, and broken machines, taking care to avoid the jagged blades and sharp bits of metal hidden among the rigid, blood-caked debris. A cool breeze had sprung up, blowing the monks' cowls around them.

'Edith!...Edith!' the bearded monk called out into the night.

Iko stared at the tangled remains around him. 'His face may be mutilated,' he said. 'We could be right on top of him and not know it.'

'That's why we need Edith. If only she had waited for us.'

As Iko stepped over an indistinct mass at his feet, out of the corner of his eye he caught the gleam of something moving below, to his right. He looked down and shone his torch.

Lying among the dead, their broken bodies turned towards each other, with their arms outstretched, their fingers almost touching, were the two boys from the farmhouse. Their wooden swords lay snapped into pieces beside them, their cardboard armour all in tatters and covered with blood, their little corpses sparkling like fallen angels beneath a fluttering blanket of ripped silver foil.

Iko swallowed hard. Moved by the harrowing tableau, a feeling of abject sorrow came over him and his eyes pricked with unexpected tears.

'Can you remember where the King fell, Sir Iko?' the bearded monk called across to him.

Hiding his sorrow and adopting his habitual impassive visage, Iko surveyed the murky extent of the hilltop, trying to get his bearings.

'There was so much going on,' he answered. 'Without the flag, it is difficult to tell. He was standing close to it.' He pointed into the near distance. 'I think it was further over there. Where that person with the light is.'

Ahead of them in the darkness, lit by a lantern on the ground, a kneeling figure was dragging at a pile of bodies. Stepping and stumbling, they made their way forward.

'It's Edith!' the chubby monk exclaimed as they approached.

They clambered over to her as fast as they could and stopped in a group behind her, training the beams of their torches to give her light. In fevered desperation, Edith was pushing and pulling at the layers of dead. Suddenly, the ghastly, upturned face of Haco was exposed.

'It is his nephew!' Iko gasped. 'They were near each other at the end.'

'King Harold must be around here someplace,' said the bearded monk, peering about him.

Edith ignored them. Mumbling incoherently to herself, she picked up her lantern and rushed over to another heap of bodies. In a frenzy, she began heaving them aside, digging down until, eventually, she dragged one up and, on her knees, began tearing at its clothes. With a wild, despairing sob, she collapsed over it.

They ran to her and shone their torches. Edith lay across the corpse, weeping and moaning. The bearded monk put his hand on her shoulder. 'Edith,' he said with gentle insistence.

As she sat up, Harold's badly gashed torso came into view. His shirtfront was ripped open, showing the birthmark 'E' on his chest. His head hung back outside the circle of light, the dark silhouette of the broken arrow shaft jutting from his visor.

She turned and looked up at them in desolation, her face streaked with blood and tears. Then, all emotion draining away, a veil of detachment fell over her grief.

'This is the body you want,' she informed them in a frozen, lifeless voice.

*

At daybreak, out of the sheer, ultramarine sky, a burning north wind coursed through the Norman camp, its powerful gusts whipping up the cloaks of the knights, billowing the canvas tents, ripping pegs from the ground, sending loosely-tied bundles and boxes rolling and tumbling, snapping the heavy brocade banners in their fastenings and tearing at the smaller flags on their bending poles.

Above the turbulence, orders were shouted and bugles trilled as the army dismantled their tents and loaded up the wagons.

While infantrymen checked their equipment, some forming into companies for grave-digging duty at the hill and others assembling into foraging parties, squadrons of cavalry roared off on reconnaissance missions.

Hardly noticed amid the confusion, with his bare head lowered, hunched against the wind, Iko slowly rode down the camp's main thoroughfare on his motorcycle. Behind him walked the two monks, followed by four soldiers pulling a handcart bearing Harold's body, wrapped in a grey tarpaulin.

A number of soldiers, including Kingston, Nobby, and Ranjit, stopped what they were doing and watched in silence as the small retinue went by.

'I fought I'd feel better 'an 'is,' Nobby said, removing his helmet in respect. 'Seein' 'im there like that, it just don't seem right.' He shivered. 'I don't fink I'll ever get over it.'

'It vas a very terrible thing,' Ranjit nodded sadly. 'But ve had no choice in the matter, isn't it?'

Kingston gave a deep sigh and shook his head. 'Maybe so, man,' he said. 'All I know is that for my whole life now I'll never be free from what I've seen and done here.'

Standing off to one side under the awning of his tent, sipping a mug of steaming coffee, Duke William observed the funeral procession going by.

'Sir Iko!' he called out, waving for him to come over.

Iko dismounted and approached. 'You called, my Lord?' he asked in a tired voice, with a slight bow of his head.

'You do realise you're being a damned fool about all this, don't you, Iko?'

'My Lord?'

'Are you actually prepared to give up everything you fought for, for this...gesture?'

'I must, my Lord.'

'Your one chance to get rich quick and you'd chuck it all away? I can't believe it. You know this means you'll probably have to work for a living, for the rest of your life?'

'I know, my Lord,' Iko nodded.

The Duke sighed. 'Very well, then,' he shrugged. 'Be it on your own head. But don't bury him on land, you hear me? He couldn't defend it and now it's mine. Stick him on a beach somewhere, where the sand crabs can get him!'

Iko bowed again. 'As you wish, my Lord.'

Duke William watched as Iko walked away, mounted his motorbike, and rejoined the group. 'You're a bloody idiot, Harold!' he murmured to himself, as the cart bumped off on its journey. 'You should've stayed at home.' He half turned his head and called over his shoulder. 'Sergeant Patch!'

Immediately, a powerfully built trooper in a calf-length, black leather overcoat, with a long sword and scabbard strapped to his belt, emerged from the tent. His meaty, moustachioed head was stuffed tightly into a helmet and he wore a black patch over one eye. 'My Lord?' he enquired, in a deep, gravelly voice, marching forward and coming stiffly to attention behind him.

'Follow Sir Iko,' the Duke commanded. 'He'll lead you to the woman. If she has any children with her, wait until he's gone and then kill them.'

'And if she's on her own, sir?'

Duke William emptied his mug on the ground and turned to face him. 'I'll leave that up to you, Sergeant,' he said with a cold stare and strode on past him towards the tent.

With a malicious grin, Sergeant Patch threw back his shoulders and snapped his boot heels together. 'Very good, my Lord!'

As the burial party made its way out of the camp, Iko turned in the saddle and looked back towards the pavilion. He frowned. For some intangible reason, he had an unsettling feeling as his eyes were drawn to the dark figure of the sergeant strolling away. The Duke had already gone.

*

The tide was coming in like a conveyor belt, the lines of rippling waves bursting into spume on the rocks and sweeping into the shallows, running up the flat, damp sand at the entrance to the secluded cove in creamy ribbons of dissipating froth.

Further up the beach where the water never reached, where the dazzling white sand was softer, whipped up around them by the hot wind, the four soldiers hurried to complete their work. Iko watched sadly as they let out their ropes, hand over hand, lowering Harold's body into the grave. The monks stood close by, their fingers clasped in prayer, their mouths moving in silent benediction. As the ropes were pulled clear and recoiled, they both picked up a handful of sand and sprinkled it down onto the shrouded form of his friend. Leaving them to their ministrations, while the soldiers took their shovels and began to fill in the hole, Iko nodded in approval and, with a heavy sigh, walked away.

On reaching the end of the beach, he stopped and looked back, drinking in the scene, fixing the place in his memory. With a world-weary shiver, he gazed out across the glassy sea to the piercing orb of the sun radiating on the horizon. All of a sudden, he was startled by a clacking of pebbles behind him. He turned in alarm, but there was nobody there.

Then, lifting his eyes to the top of the nearby cliff, he saw Edith and Edmund standing at the edge, staring down at him. Edith's pale face remained impassive as she nodded to him in recognition. Iko came to attention and gave a low bow in return. When he straightened up, they had gone.

Hearing what sounded like the scraping of a boot on rock, he looked towards the base of the cliff. A few small pebbles were trickling down at the foot of a flute in the chalky slope. Catching a glimpse of movement out of the corner of his eye, he spun round and stared at a bush further away, waving in the wind beside a stony path leading up the face of the cliff. For a fleeting moment, he saw behind it what could have been a shadow, then it disappeared.

With his nerves on edge, and hearing approaching, faint voices on the wind, Iko turned and looked back down the beach. In the distance, the two monks were trudging up the bright sand towards him. Raising his hand to shield his eyes from the glare, he watched them approach. Hunched over against the wind, they were deep in conversation, the musical intonation of their voices growing louder as they came closer.

'What a waste,' the chubby monk moaned. 'King Harold's grave would have made our monastery famous.'

'Don't worry, brother,' replied his bearded companion. 'In a couple of days, once they've all gone, we'll come back and dig him up. Then we'll put him on show.'

'But that would be desecration!'

'Of what? A temporary hiding place, that's all.'

'I don't know about that...What would the Abbot say?'

'Nothing!' the bearded monk laughed. 'He's a realist. Listen, my friend, there's a new world order now, one in which it pays to be inventive. From here on in, even the Church will have to sell itself to survive. The Abbot knows that. Why else do you think he sent us?'

'I had no idea.'

'Opportunism, that's the name of the game now, brother. As long as it's for power or profit, anything goes. Mark my words, from now on morals'll be even harder to find than money. And only those who kiss the right arses or offer a big enough return will get the official stamp of approval!'

The chubby monk shook his head. 'That's not new. Governments have always been corrupt.'

'Yes, but not like this. Now the thieves are in power everywhere. Exploitation has become the universal creed.'

'This is terrible! It'll turn our community upside down.'

'You can forget our community, brother, it won't exist any more. Not unless we keep one step ahead of the times. There are only winners and losers now.'

'My God! Can't they be stopped?'

'Not on the battlefield, that's for sure. No, the Normans are here to stay and we'd better get used to it.'

'What are you saying? That we go into business?'

'Exactly!' the bearded monk grinned.

After a few moments pondering this, his portly companion sighed. 'Well, if we've got no other choice...I suppose we could have some kind of exhibition. Personal memorabilia, that sort of thing. We could charge school groups and tourists to come and see it.'

The bearded monk patted him on the back. 'Now you're getting the drift! We could even put his body on display in a glass coffin. Tastefully done, of course. Nice music, soft lighting.'

As they drew level with Iko, they both gave him a perfunctory wave of thanks and walked on. He stared after them with quizzical amusement as they plodded away along the beach, their voices gradually fading on the wind.

'We'd have to give the exhibition a title,' the chubby monk said with growing interest.

'That's right,' the bearded monk nodded. 'Nothing too inflammatory. Something strong yet simple, easy to remember.'

His friend thought for a moment, then his eyebrows went up. 'What about, 'Harold, king of the resistant Saxons?' he suggested, with an eager smile.

'I like it!' the bearded monk laughed. 'It's catchy. And it puts him in historical context without criticising the new regime.' He put his arm around the chubby monk's shoulders. 'Brother, you're a man of the future!'

*

The wind had died down, settling into a warm, steady breeze as Edith wheeled her bicycle along the narrow, grassy path close to the edge of the cliff. Edmund was walking beside her, dried blood on his sleeve, his body aching and stiff, using a branch as a walking stick. They were both lost in thought, deep in shock, trying to come to terms with what had happened.

Unable, until then, to go near the dreadful reality and the monstrous images of the battle walled up inside his brain—of the haunting faces of the dead, of his own feeling of terror, and the unbearable loss of his father and uncles—a minor incident that had been playing on Edmund's mind led him, like the start of Ariadne's thread, down into the labyrinth of his pain, prompting him to break the silence.

'Mum, do you think the stars can predict the future?' he asked.

'Why? Who told you that?'

'Some of the men were talking about it. They said that the comet was a bad omen and that the stars were against us. Was that why we lost?'

A wave of maternal sorrow at what her child must have been through brought fresh tears to Edith's eyes.

'Oh, Edmund,' she sighed sadly, putting her arm round his shoulders. 'Hatred's not in the stars, darling, it's in people's hearts. You saw the destruction out there. One side killed more than the other, that's all, but nobody *won*. They were all once some poor mother's son and now they've all left a trail of unspeakable grief behind them. Everyone lost.'

'How can you say that?' Edmund demanded angrily, breaking away from her, his voice fraught with emotion, close to tears. '*We* lost!'

'No, the whole *world* lost. Because, once again, what it means to be human has been reduced to legalised barbarism, telling future generations that their only hope is war!'

'What else is there? We have to defend ourselves!'

Worn out with grief, still reeling from the horrors she'd witnessed and aghast at the violence of men; so weary from arguing for peace when everybody else said war was right—though they *had* to know full well in their hearts that the dreadful outcome was wrong—Edith had begun to question her own sanity, to the point where her words sounded hollow to her even as she spoke them. She felt so hurt and alone, it was almost beyond her strength to keep hold of her battered, fragile conviction.

'I don't know,' she murmured tiredly, shaking her head. 'With love, I suppose.'

'No way!' Edmund snarled. 'Not after what they did yesterday. I'm going to turn the heat up on those bastards!'

'What are you talking about?'

'As soon as I can, I'm getting an army together. Then I'll come back and avenge Dad!'

'Don't be ridiculous, Edmund. We'll all stay together.'

'Magnus'll be in it, I know he will.'

'Stop it! This is madness!'

'Stay right where you are!' a harsh voice suddenly ordered them from behind.

They both spun round in shock, as Sergeant Patch stepped out from the cover of a gnarled tea tree and drew his sword. In immediate response, Edmund raised his stick.

'What do you want?' Edith demanded.

'You're Harold's bastard, aren't you?' the sergeant jeered, ignoring her, pointing his blade at Edmund.

Edmund took a pace forward. 'I'm the son of the bravest man who ever lived!' he sneered, lifting his chin with contempt. 'What's it to you, Norman?'

'Oh, I'm going to enjoy this!' Sergeant Patch chuckled, his deep voice rumbling thickly in his throat. He began to advance, swinging his sword like a scythe in front of him, lopping off the heads of the small white daisies sprouting up along the path.

'No!' Edith cried.

At that moment, as if out of nowhere, Iko emerged from the bushes beside him. 'What is the trouble, Sergeant?' he asked, with a relaxed, amiable smile.

'Stay out of this, Sir Knight!' The sergeant flashed him a warning look, remaining on his guard. 'I'm under orders from the Duke.'

'Do not get me wrong, I am on your side!' Iko laughed, spreading his hands in innocence.

Sergeant Patch gave him a quick sideways glance. 'What's your business here, then?'

'What do you think?' Iko leered. 'Do what you like with the boy, Sergeant, but I want the woman for myself.'

'Well, you can have her,' the sergeant growled. 'After I'm finished with her!'

Iko pondered this for a moment, then nodded in agreement. 'That seems fair,' he shrugged. 'After all, you will be doing all the work.' As Sergeant Patch grunted and started forward, Iko reached out and touched him on the shoulder. 'But wait! What is that on your face?'

The sergeant stopped in surprise. 'Where?' he said uncertainly.

Iko leant towards him, pointing his finger, peering closely at his cheek. In a sudden blur of movement, he grabbed hold of the elasticated eye patch, pulled it back to full stretch, and then let it go. As it snapped against his fat face, Sergeant Patch yelped in pain.

At the same time, Iko shoved him hard with both hands, sending him stumbling away across the track and, with arms flailing, over the edge of the cliff. There was a long, fading scream and then silence, leaving only the soft caress of the sea on the beach below and the sounds of the sea birds squawking on the breeze.

Edmund took an aggressive step towards Iko, but Edith put out her hand. 'Wait! He's a friend!'

'Lady Edith, are you all right?' Iko asked.

'Yes. I suppose I should thank you for that, Sir Iko?'

Iko bowed his head. 'It was my pleasure.'

'I hope you won't get into trouble for it?'

'Accidents happen,' he shrugged. 'Anyway, it is what I owe you.'

'Is that why you did it? To repay a debt?'

'I could not let him kill you, Lady.'

'Ah, yes, chivalry. I'd forgotten.'

'I wanted to help you...'

Edith sighed. 'Then you should've stayed in Normandy, Sir Iko.'

'Lady Edith, I am so sorry for what has happened.'

'You'll get over it, mate!' Edmund interjected with scorn. He put his arm round Edith's shoulders. 'Come on, Mum, let's go.'

'Wait!' Iko called out, as they turned to leave. 'Lady Edith, Duke William knows who you are. He knows your name. He will send men to look for you and your children.'

'Oh, my God!' she cried.

'You must hurry. Take your family and escape!'

'I will. Thank you, Sir Iko...But what about you? Where will you go?'

'I do not know, Lady,' he smiled. 'There is a girl still waiting for me at home, I think. Perhaps, I can find a place with her...where it is safe to wear Lord Harold's hat!'

Tears welled up in Edith's eyes. 'It used to be here,' she said brokenly. 'Goodbye, Sir Iko.'

'Goodbye, Lady.'

Iko gave a long, low bow from the waist. Then, straightening up, he gazed sadly after them as they hurried away along the cliff top.

Up ahead of them, Captain Guitaro was standing alone beside the path. As Edith and Edmund went past him, he raised his wide-brimmed plumed hat to them, receiving a slight nod of thanks from her in return.

With a sad smile, he watched them walk off into the distance, Edith pushing her bicycle, and Edmund every so often slashing out in anger with his stick at the tall grass growing beside the track. Then, lifting up his guitar, he stroked the strings into a gentle, familiar rhythm and began to sing.

Now fare thee well friends
For my story is over
But in time like the tide rolling in
Your turn may come
To play hero or lover
And you must decide who'll win
Just like Harold
Harold
Harold
Harold
Last of the Saxon Kings

*

Vera's house lay sleeping in the afternoon sun. Insects droned on the warm, drowsy air and birds chirped in safety among the trees, while the green leaves on the branches swayed to the wafting currents of the faint, balmy breeze.

All of a sudden, the peace and tranquility were torn apart by the sound of approaching motorbikes. Seconds later, a detachment of Norman cavalry roared up to the house. They stopped and dismounted. An officer, followed by three knights, flung open the gate and strode down the garden path to the front porch, while the rest of them peered in at the windows and rushed around the sides. An unseen bird began whistling a strident alarm.

Pounding with arrogant force on the door, the officer stood waiting, but the house remained silent. He stared at his companions for a moment, listening hard, then his leather-gloved fist thumped against the wooden panel once more.

There was the sound of a window breaking at the back of the house.

28

With the noise of shattering glass ringing in my ears, I woke up with a jolt, my eyes flying open and my nerves jangling. I quickly raised my head and stared at the window, listening hard. The curtains were still drawn, undisturbed. After a few seconds, I let out my breath and slumped back on the bed, my chest rising and falling with relief.

I was exhausted. My pillow was saturated. My face was still damp, but the fever had broken. Taking in deep gasps of air, while gently fingering the abrasion beside my eye, I searched back, going over the nightmare in my mind, trying to keep hold of its elusive, evaporating images and the fast-fading sequence of events. For a final, fleeting moment, I saw Harold's face as he clutched at the arrow in his visor. I shut my eyes and groaned.

At last, as my heart rate settled and the last sights and sounds flickered away, disappearing like miners' lamps down a tunnel, I pushed myself up onto my elbows and stared about the room. The bed was a wreck, and the lamp and the television were still on.

I peered at the screen in disbelief! In a surreal overlapping of dream and reality, Eric Braithwaite was there again! Wearing a camouflaged helmet and flak jacket this time, he was standing high up on a hotel balcony overlooking an Asian city, glancing with uncertainty to right and left, waiting for his cue. While he stood there, heralded by a sudden series of flashes, loud explosions erupted among the congested buildings in the middle-distance behind him, followed by billowing plumes of black smoke.

I scowled in anger and turned away.

Taking it slowly, trying to absorb the strain and not give myself a headache, I swung my legs out of bed and sat up on the edge. My throat was parched and my breath stank of alcohol. Looking up, I saw the framed photograph of Mary and the kids above me on the shelf. I reached out a trembling hand to take it down, and for a few moments gazed at it, smiling warmly, remembering my life with them.

As I replaced it next to the one of my brothers in uniform, my smile turned bittersweet. I looked at them all standing there, the paragon of bravery, and sighed with regret, my pleasure melting away. Lying on the shelf below was my book. I pondered it for a moment and, shaking my head, gave a bone-weary, cynical laugh.

Suddenly, the crash of more breaking glass came from outside in the street, followed by shouting and laughter. I heaved myself up off the bed. As I staggered along its side, on TV, at a particularly loud bang behind him, Eric Braithwaite ducked in reflex and looked round in alarm. He spun back to the camera, checked to the side once more for the go-ahead, nodded to someone off-screen, and then spoke rapidly into his handheld microphone.

'The invasion has begun!' he exclaimed. 'As the bombs start to fall on this ancient city and the rockets land with pin-point precision on the enemy's defences, hidden as they are among the civilian population, we are perhaps seeing history in the making and witnessing the first step on the long road to freedom and victory!'

With a growl, I scooped up the remote from the floor, where I'd dropped it the night before, and stabbed at the 'off' button.

'This is Eric Braithwaite, for the...'

The screen went black.

Carrying on to the window without breaking stride, I drew back one of the net curtains and peered out through the grimy pane. Down in the narrow, deserted side street, a gang of youths had smashed in the front of the neighbourhood electronics store and were busy looting its contents. At the brazen effrontery of it, my blood boiled. The fog lifted and it all came back to me, why I was there.

'Shit!' I swore out loud and swung around. Lurching away, I hurried past the end of the bed and along the far side to the alarm clock on the bedside table. I stared at it. It was almost midday. 'Oh, no!' I gasped. I was already three hours late! I sat down on the mattress and put my head in my hands.

In my line of sight, I spied the call-up letter lying on the carpet. I reached out to pick it up and re-read it with dread. Letting out a long, fateful sigh, I gazed off into the distance, trying to make up my mind.

So here it was. The balancing of opposites. Did I give them up or refuse the call? This was it. I couldn't hedge my bets forever. Had the dream been a real warning or just a phantasm of my own fear? The fear of not conforming. Or the fear *of* conforming? The old adage that those who don't learn from history are doomed to repeat it sprang into my mind.

But I wasn't Harold, I told myself, and Harold wasn't me. Was I just trying to escape the inevitable? I'd always sought individuality, but what was individuality worth if not part of the common cause? There again, *whose* common cause? The cause of the weak? Or the system that was trying to protect them but in the process caused them such irreparable harm? Did the ends justify the means or did the means have to end? In the space of a moment I had to decide. It was time to choose!

I scanned the letter once more, folded it up, and slipped it into my top pocket. Breathing in a deep, resolute draught of air through my nose, expanding my chest with resolve and determination, then blowing it out like a jet stream through my mouth, like Joshua's trumpet dispelling the walls of doubt, I launched myself into action.

*

Two Berrocas later, washed but unshaven, and still wearing the same crumpled clothes that I'd slept in, I was beginning to feel at least halfway human. I pulled aside the long calico drapes and opened the bottom of the window. As the lounge filled up with bright morning sunlight, I noticed with distaste that, although the smoke had dissipated, the room still reeked with the sour odour of tobacco.

I turned and went over to the computer. Ignoring the debris above it from the night before, I lifted the phone from its cradle on the upper shelf. I paused for a moment to collect my thoughts. I had to do it! I punched in the numbers and waited. A few moments later, my face spasmed into an uncertain grin as Mary came on the line at the other end, and the words just poured out of me.

It was funny. Afterwards, when I went back over the conversation in my mind, all I could remember was what I had said, not how Mary had answered.

'Darling! It's me!' I had stammered. 'No, I'm still at the flat... Yeah, I know, I'm very late. But I just wanted to tell you how much I love you, before I leave...No...No, I'm not...No...That's right...I can't!...I know...Me, too!...Look, I'd better get going.'

I gave a caustic laugh. 'Yeah, before they come and get me!... No, I'm all right. I had a raging fever last night, though...No, it's gone now...And I had the most incredible dream! We were all in it...All of us! You, me, the kids, my whole family. World leaders.

Everyone. Even your mother!...I know! It *was* a nightmare! But it suddenly made everything clear to me, about why I'm here and what I have to do!'

*

As it was described to me later, Mary took the call standing by the wall phone in the back hallway, the receiver pressed to her ear, listening intently. Matt, Ben, and Naomi stared at her from the opposite wall, their faces filled with a mixture of wide-eyed hope and expectant fear as they hung on her every word.

'And it took a dream for you to see that?' she laughed in tearful, mild rebuke. 'I know you were, darling...Yes, we all have to do what we think is right...That's right, it *would* be taking the easy way out...Of course it would...No...*And* not dealing with the problem...That's right...Yes, you'd *definitely* better go!...I will... Don't worry, darling...Oh, it's so sad it has to come to this!...I know...I love you so much, Jack!'

Her eyes swam with tears. 'Please be careful!...Yes, I'll tell them.' She looked over at the children, then turned away again, holding the phone even closer. 'Just come back safely, you hear?...I know...We will...All right...I love you! I love you!'

Mary hung up the receiver and pressed her forehead against the wall, her shoulders heaving in a shuddering sob. At last, she twisted round to them, her eyes shining, glistening with tears. Then, like the sun coming out from behind the clouds, her face lit up with radiant excitement.

'Daddy's coming home!' she cried.

The boys laughed out loud with astonished relief, while Naomi shouted, 'Yippeee!', throwing up her arms and jumping for joy, her pigtails flying.

As they danced around and hugged each other, Mary spoke to them with gentle seriousness, preparing them.

'And we're all going on a long journey,' she said.

*

In the faint light of dawn, with the moon just a sliver above the trees, I stepped out onto the road in front of the house. Naomi was in my arms, still half asleep and wrapped in a blanket. Behind me, with patient care, Matt and Ben helped their grandmother with her sticks through the garden gate.

Finally, Mary backed out onto the porch. She reached inside to switch off the light and, for the last time, closed the front door. With a heavy sigh, she turned away, leaving the house in darkness.

I walked over to the bus, already loaded up with our belongings, and dragged open the side door with one hand. I set our daughter down and kissed her on the head. Sucking her small piece of sheet, she climbed in, soon followed by the others. As soundlessly as I could, I slid the door shut.

As Mary approached, I opened the front passenger door for her. She stopped for a moment and gazed wistfully back at the house. I touched her cheek and gave her an encouraging kiss. She smiled with sad fortitude and nodded. I hurried around the front of the bus and we both got in. I started the engine and put it into gear. Without turning on the lights, we slowly pulled away.

Coincidentally, at that very moment Captain Guitaro and The Landing Party were passing by, heading out early for another itinerant day's busking in the nearby town. Standing in a line up on the grassy bank at the edge of the next-door paddock, they serenaded us off on our journey. As we travelled on down the road, before entering the trees at the bottom I could see them in the rear-view mirror, slowly sauntering along after us, still playing.

Suddenly, there was a flash of headlights behind them and the sound of vehicles approaching. I slipped into second and stretched up closer to the mirror to see. With a screech of tyres, a military jeep and two motorbikes appeared, skidding to a halt and training their lights on the house. Four MPs leapt out of the jeep, opened the gate, and rushed up the path towards the front door. With the window open, I could hear them thumping on it with their fists. I imagined them staring in at the front windows, then standing there, waiting in silence.

Meanwhile, turning on the lights and switching to full-beam, I put my foot down and headed up the winding road towards the top of the neighbouring hill. Nearing the summit, I looked back at the house in my wing mirror. I could picture the front door, imagining the crack of splintering wood as it was kicked in.

With the rim of the sun rising like molten gold over the ridge ahead, the red brake lights flared behind us as we stopped—just long enough for one last look back—then we continued on, over the crest and out of sight.

EPILOGUE

But all that was long ago. It seemed like another lifetime. Now we, and thousands like us, were trying to escape.

The old bus had finally given up the ghost. We'd driven it hard and far. When the sump split on a rock and then a tyre burst, we were finally forced to leave it, camouflaged as best we could with branches and tufts of grass. Taking what essentials we could carry, we continued across the plain and up the valley on foot. The climb had almost killed Mary's mother, but somehow she'd managed to make it. With any luck, the bus wouldn't be found until daybreak.

I could see torches moving around where I reckoned we'd hidden it, though, which wasn't a good sign. Maybe they were just regrouping, still preoccupied by the battle? No! There were car headlights now, skidding around in wide, silent arcs, sweeping the ground for tracks. Surely they wouldn't risk the same precipitous climb we'd made up this bluff in the dark?

I was concentrating on them so hard it made my eyes ache. The seven or eight vehicles finally converged, as if planning their next move. I got ready to run if they came this way. All of a sudden, the cluster of lights broke apart, turning in separate circles, then rejoined in a convoy and sped back across the plain.

Cautiously, I let out my breath. For now, we were safe.

I thought about our next move. A few years before, we'd bought a twenty-acre block down in the Otway Ranges to use for camping holidays and to keep in our back pocket for a rainy day, and that's where we were making for. In the beginning, we'd heard that roadblocks were being set up all along the Great Ocean Road and that the inland routes to the coast were being closely monitored. So, to start with, we'd gone north, up past Bacchus Marsh and over towards Ballarat, travelling only at night and laying low during the day.

But, after six weeks, we'd decided there was a good enough chance we could get through. We came back down behind Birregurra and then headed over into the misty blue hills to the southwest. En route, we'd come across a few other families displaced by the war. We told them about the place and how to reach it. If they could get there, it would be big enough for us all. It had running water, the pod house we'd built had solar-powered batteries, and we could grow our own food. If we managed to stay hidden from the drones, there was a strong possibility we wouldn't be discovered.

Just then, I heard a twig crack behind me, followed by the muffled sound of somebody approaching. Habitually on guard those days, I spun round. With relief, I saw Mary coming towards me.

'Jack!' she called out softly. 'Come on! We're all ready.'

'Coming,' I whispered back. Then, stepping with noiseless precision over the clumps of tussock and dry bracken in my path, I crossed the open space between us.

'How's it looking?' she asked with concern as I reached her.

I gave her a reassuring smile. 'It was touch and go there for a while,' I said. 'But I think we're all right.'

As chance would have it, at that very moment the moon elected to break through the clouds, catching the silver threads in her hair with its beams. She was still so beautiful! Overcome by a sudden wave of passion, I pulled her towards me and kissed her on the lips.

Mary easily responded to my unexpected ardour, but soon took control and broke free, pushing me off with a laugh. Her eyes shone as they looked into mine. She took me by the arm and hugged me to her.

'Come on, big boy!' she said quietly. 'Let's go.'

In single file, without a backward glance, we melted away among the trees.

ABOUT THE AUTHOR

Born in London, at various times in his life Andy Butcher has been a labourer, a storeman, a hippy, a clerk, a cartoonist, a stagehand, a cleaner, a film extra, a painter, and an art teacher.

He lives near the beach with his family, in Australia.

www.ingramcontent.com/pod-product-compliance
Lightning Source LLC
Chambersburg PA
CBHW030745030726
47497CB00001B/138